WILD RIDE

A ROOKIE REBELS NOVEL

KATE MEADER

Copyright © 2024 by Kate Meader

Cover design by Qamber Designs

Editing: Kristi Yanta

Proofreading: Julia Griffis

ISBN: 978-1-954107-46-5

Please see my website for content warnings pertinent to this book.

1

"Here we are, O'Malley. Again."

Dex O'Malley raised his eyes to the stony gaze behind the big, oak table. He'd become accustomed to this setup. Unwieldy furniture, disapproving glares, crushing disappointment. Not Dex's disappointment. God, no, that wasn't an emotion he regularly indulged in. Instead, he let others carry the load and tell him he'd been a naughty boy.

"This isn't like the other times, Fitz." The outcome might be inevitable, but it was expected that Dex make a token effort to defend himself.

"I can see that." With a world-weary sigh, Hale Fitzpatrick put down the coffee cup labeled "Hottest General Manager Ever," a gift from his wife. "The other times were more of an embarrassment for the franchise because you seem to be incapable of shame. It's not every day I have to organize and manage a fake relationship for one of my players because he's been recorded getting a blow job at a nightclub."

More than the usual irritation had crept into Fitz's voice. The boss evidently still held a grudge because that fake rela-

tionship had led to Dex's five-minute engagement to Tara
Becker, now Mrs. Fitz. Never mind that the man had scored
the gorgeous wife and cute baby. Still a sore winner about
it all.

"That was different," Dex said, returning to explaining
away his latest screw-up. "I can't help it if people follow me
around, looking to catch me out."

"But you seem to be caught out more than the average
player." Fitz started a count on his fingers. "The two ladies at
the nightclub—"

"Which we were able to fix with the help of your wife."

A death-wish glare was Dex's reward for that interruption with a bonus burn-in-hell gaze for the "your wife"
addition.

Dex was starting to enjoy himself.

"The multiple speeding tickets—"

"But I wasn't drag racing like they said. That guy thought
he could trick me into it with the red light rev."

"Your comments about your teammates on Jordan
Hunt's podcast."

Okay, not his finest hour.

"All I said was they're kind of boring. So loved up, never
wanting to hang and have fun."

"Most of your colleagues are family men, O'Malley.
You're a bit of an outlier, so I can understand why it's tough
for you to settle."

So he hadn't exactly gelled with anyone on the team.
They were all good guys, but none of them were down for
raucous nights at the club or a good session at the bar post-
game. Everyone had to race home or to their hotel rooms to
call the little woman (or man, in the case of Grey and
Burnett). Team gatherings tended to be family-focused
affairs with kids running around and everyone talking about

the latest Disney shit or little Timmy's science project. Don't get him wrong: Dex liked kids, but he was a bit young to be calling it quits and hanging up his condoms.

A couple of new, younger players were on the roster this year, but they were still so green. Dex felt bad about leading them astray, or about as bad as a shameless troublemaker like him was capable. Like his eighteen months on the team and twenty-five years on this green earth had accorded him the status of pseudo-elder statesman. Instead he was stuck in this limbo.

Too old for this shit, not old enough to know better.

"I've no problem settling," he said, hating the defensiveness in his voice. So his history hopscotching around care homes and foster family situations meant "settling" wasn't really his thing. But once he'd found hockey, he'd found his place. "I'm just not so good at staying still."

Fitz looked almost sympathetic at that admission, and as Dex hated pity more than he hated censure, he was glad that the GM's next words didn't match that *poor-little-orphan-Dexter* expression.

"Or at keeping out of bar brawls with fellow hockey players."

"Hardly a brawl. Plus he was the opposition."

"Kyle Hughes was already penalized for wrist slashing during the game and now he'll sit through the player safety hearing in a few days and get fined. That's the process, O'Malley. But that's not enough for you. Instead, you take your beef with him off the ice and turn it into a new problem. For us."

"He had it coming."

"Well, now *you* have it coming. Because unlike your other escapades, this has put you in legal jeopardy. Which puts your position on this team in danger."

Dex sat up straighter. "But it'll be a fine or something, right?" The court date was two months out, just before the playoffs. Plenty of time for the team lawyers to craft a good ole stay-out-of-jail strategy. What was the point in having millions if it couldn't be put to use keeping the wealthy out of trouble?

"General counsel isn't so sure. You broke Hughes's nose."

"After he assaulted a woman. I was defending her."

Fitz narrowed his eyes. "And for once, given how cameras are usually magnetized to your ass, your good deed was not recorded. Rather, the only part that went viral was you playing fisticuffs with an opposing player."

Fisticuffs. Dex almost laughed at the old-fashioned language, but the look on Fitz's face dampened the bubbling threat of humor.

"But the girl? She'll testify for me." Damn, she had to.

The boss made a face. "Have you forgotten that Hughes is her boyfriend? I wouldn't rely on that for your defense. No, we need something else. In the months before your court date, we need to rehab your reputation. Again."

"Another fake it till we make it vanish sitch?"

Fitz's hand white-knuckled around his coffee cup. He *really* did not like being reminded of that.

"No going back to that well. This time, we'll have to make you look purer than the driven snow. Sophie has some ideas."

He pressed a button on his office phone and murmured a summons for Sophie, head of PR at the Rebels. Poor Soph was unfortunately well used to coming up with strategies to make Dex look like a choirboy, or maybe not so unfortunately. Job security for her, right?

"What if it doesn't work?"

"You'd better hope it does. Because a conviction will put

you on waivers, boot you off this team, and then it's bye bye hockey."

In a daze, Dex stepped out of Fitz's office and tried to catch his breath.

Bye bye hockey?

That couldn't happen. Hockey was the only thing in the world that mattered to him, the one thing he could rely on. If he couldn't play hockey, he was nothing.

"Hey, Dexter! How did it go?"

He met the green-gold gaze of Tara Fitzpatrick, former fiancée, current hair stylist, and his closest friend in Chicago. Like a lost mutt, he'd been wandering the halls of the Rebels compound and arrived at her "salon," where she cut the hair of the players and staff. She was currently brushing away some stray strands, which looked like the lustrous locks of chatty D-man Theo Kershaw. The guy spent more time on his hair than on his sticks.

A happy gurgle called his attention to the other person in the room. One-year-old Esme, Tara and Fitz's daughter, was clamoring for attention from her stroller.

Sorry, Esme, the Big Bad Boss of Attention Hogging is here for your throne.

"You busy, T?" he asked Tara.

"I've got twenty minutes until my next appointment. Have a seat."

With an unceremonious plop into the comfortable leather chair, he took a good look at himself in the mirror, then swiveled to face his friend because he was sick to his back teeth of that loser.

"I might be going down."

Tara raised an eyebrow. "Going... down?"

"Prison or the AHL." It was debatable which was worse. "Your husband thinks I've really screwed the pooch on this one."

She winced.

"Shit, he told you already?" Which meant Fitz wasn't trying to mess with Dex out of some twisted desire to exact revenge for dating Tara—which the man had set up, mind you—but instead was a thousand percent worried Dex might be in major trouble here.

"He mentioned that the lawyers were concerned," Tara said. "Some of your other shenanigans were more acceptable in a 'boys will be boys' kind of way. No one got hurt except the prudes and their sensibilities. But a physical injury against another player off the ice was always going to be trouble."

Dex put his head in his hands. This was not good.

Tara squeezed his shoulder. "But we can fix this! Here, hold Esme, that'll cheer you up."

Within a few mind-numbing seconds he had the infant in his arms. Those gorgeous green eyes, a carbon-copy of her mom's, with her dad's wavy black hair was a dynamite combination. Tara was right. He did feel slightly cheered, even if the kid was named after one of those *Twilight* vampire chicks. *A little forethought, people.*

"Your daddy doesn't like me, Esme. He's still mad because I got there first. In another universe, *I* would be your pop."

Tara rolled her eyes. "Dexter, we both know our relationship never got out of the blocks, so to speak."

True. Of course, he'd thought she was hot—still did—and had fantasized about her because he did that with most every woman he met, but they'd never made it to the bedroom or anywhere else sexually interesting, and neither of them had caught feelings, leaving them as good friends.

Tara dropped the swept-up hair into a trash can. "So what did Sophie say?"

"Something about volunteer work, but because of my past indiscretions they don't think I should be allowed to teach kids hockey, which would have been my first choice. Apparently, I'm off to the Riverbrook Animal Shelter because I'm barely qualified to work with puppies and kittens."

"That's a great gig! Kennedy used to volunteer there, so she can tell you all about it."

All he needed to know was how it would extract him from this fix.

"Not getting how it's going to make me look that good. 'He's kind to animals, your honor, so don't be too hard on him.' Is that really going to fly?"

Tara's smile was pinned on. Hell, she could usually fake it better than this so he must be in deep doo-doo.

"Tara?"

"Of course it will! Sure, you could donate some money to various causes but that looks like you're trying to buy your way out of it. This way, you'll be putting in the work. Helping poor little animals. And I'm sure Sophie will do some filming and add it to the socials, which will make you look like a saint."

She took Esme back from him and settled her against her chest. Who would've thought Tara would make such a great mom? He was really happy for her, if not a touch envious of how she'd found her place. After all, the Rebels were supposed to be his hood, but he hadn't settled in the way Tara had.

"Will it be enough?"

Tara looked serious. "Okay, real talk, Dexter. To use a well-worn cliché, you are skating on thin ice. Sure you have been for a while, but there's only so long you can keep treading that same territory and not expect to fall through to a frigid, watery death."

"Uh, kind of morbid."

"I know!" She grinned. "It's a metaphor for your life and career. I want you to succeed. I always have. So what do the guys think?"

The guys? Other than his captain, Vadim Petrov, pulling him off Hughes in the bar and waiting with him while the cops questioned, then arrested, him, not much. He didn't expect them to drop everything to be his buddy.

"They've got their own lives going on."

"Well, I'm sure they'll have plenty of advice at Hunt's poker game."

"Hunt's what now?"

Another wince, then she twisted away to put Esme back in her stroller. "Never mind. I'm spouting my usual nonsense! Now, maybe we could give you a trim." Turning, she reached for his hair, but he scooted back on the chair like a crab on wheels.

"Hold up! There's a poker game at Hunt's place?" And he was only hearing about it now?

"I probably misheard, but ..." She sighed and folded her arms beneath her stellar rack. Married mom or not, he could still appreciate *that*. "Dex, I thought you were going to make more of an effort. Sure, most of the guys have families and commitments, but that doesn't mean you can't be more involved. More present. The guys want to stand up for you, but you have to show you're interested in being a Rebel. And not just on the ice."

He shifted uncomfortably in the leather seat. Dex had

always been a pretty easygoing guy and traded on that as good teammate currency. But he also kept most of his connections to a surface level. Evidently the guys had picked up on that. *Everyone* had picked up on that.

Now there was a chance he was going to be booted before he could make amends.

"I'm going to fix this, Tara. All of it."

Tara brightened. "Excellent. But just so you know, part of fixing it means no clubs, drag racing, or post-game benders. Keep your energy for the puppies."

Keep your energy for the puppies. Hopefully it would be enough.

2

Coco

Domestic short-haired cat
Likes: Climbing into cupboards
Dislikes: That Al Pacino won an Oscar for Scent of a Woman
and not any of his earlier movies.

"YOU'RE SUCH A DIRTY BOY."

For Ashley Adams's efforts, she got a saucy wink in return.

"Oh, yeah, absolutely filthy."

She squeezed the soapy sponge and applied it to the hairy body at eye level. With a vigorous scrub, she lathered up and went to work on the dirtiest parts.

"Oh, you like that, don't you?"

"You really need a boyfriend," she heard behind her.

Over her shoulder, Ashley grinned at the new arrival. Cora Ramsey ran Riverbrook Animal Shelter and never failed to have opinions on Ashley's lack of love life since her divorce was finalized six months ago. (Though the opinion dispensing had started long before that, around the time

Greg announced he was leaving and bonus, he'd knocked up the babysitter.)

"Why would I need a boyfriend when I have all the male company I can ask for here?"

She squeezed the wet sponge over her current boyfriend, Bandit, a terrier mix with a patchy coat and a whole lot of attitude. He didn't like baths, but Ashley encountered that with a lot of the pups in her care. Definitely more of an issue with the male of the species.

"That's your problem," Cora said as she checked the volunteer schedule hanging on the back of the door. "You think this job is an adequate substitute for your love life. It is not."

Ashley covered Bandit's ears. "Don't listen to her. I'll never leave you."

If anything, Bandit would leave her first. He wasn't in bad shape. Whoever had cared for him over the last year had kept him fed and his patchy coat could easily be remedied with some TLC. At some point, his previous owner had decided they didn't want him and dropped him off with a note saying he was aggressive. Other than an aversion to baths and a tendency to growl when near the other dogs, Ashley didn't see it.

Bandit would probably get a new home soon enough, and maybe even a new name because people liked to do that. Put their own stamp on things.

"So who's in today?"

Cora flicked a glance over the clipboard. "Toby and Gillian. Though I don't know why Toby bothers. All he wants to do is share on Instacart."

Cora meant Instagram, but Ashley enjoyed her slips of the tongue too much to correct her.

"It gets good coverage for the shelter. Every time he features one of our strays, we get people asking to see them."

"Asking to see Toby more like. He's such a little ho. But you're right, we did get at least ten applications to adopt Coco." She put the clipboard back on the hook. "Speaking of men only too willing to dispense their favors, I need to run something by you. About a volunteer."

Ashley raised the showerhead to finish Bandit's rinse. "Sounds great. We need all the help we can get."

Cora cleared her throat and looked a touch shifty. "Not sure this is the kind of help that will be all that useful. It's some idiot hockey player."

"Like a professional idiot hockey player?"

Cora passed off a towel. "Professional idiot is right. The Chicago Rebels have donated a lot to the shelter over the years."

That statement might have sounded like a non sequitur, but Ashley could read between the lines. An organization like theirs existed on the goodwill of donations. Sure they had adoption and foster fees, but none of that covered the expenses. They depended on the kindness of strangers.

The city's pro hockey franchise practically paid Ashley's salary, which made for a certain degree of uncertainty. As a single mom with no particular skillset, she needed a decent-paying job. Luckily, she was able to muddle through with the help of her family, and her ex's job paid for their daughter's insurance.

Cora waved her clipboard. "Ever hear of Dex O'Malley?"

"The club whore guy?"

"That's the one. Up on his latest stunt?"

"Something about a bar fight ... wait, is that who wants to volunteer?"

That made Cora chuckle. "More like voluntold. They're

trying to shine up his rep ahead of his court case. He'll come in for a few shifts, take some pics feeding the kittens, and then be on his way."

Ashley lifted Bandit out of the tub, though the little trickster squirmed enough to guarantee a spoonful of sudsy water landed in her eye. She started drying his paws. "Sounds like it's a done deal."

"Well, yeah, but here's where it's tricky ... you'll have to watch him. I'll be out of town and that means it's more work for you. On top of the work you're already doing getting ready for the Empty the Shelters event." She grimaced. "I should tell them no. It's not a good time."

And have the Rebels be a little less generous with their donation next time? No way. Ashley was fully aware of the stakes here.

"I can handle this guy. Like you said, just a few photo ops, shares to the Rebels social media, and then we're clear." Besides, Willa was going to flip out when she heard an actual Rebels player was volunteering. Ashley's daughter was a die-hard fan of the team, and while Cal Foreman was her favorite, she would be very impressed to hear that Dex O'Malley was in the house.

Cora winced. "I hate to do this to you—"

"It's fine!"

Bandit gave a little yelp now that he was clean and free to go, or free to enter his cage. Ashley hated that they had to cage them, but they couldn't risk the dogs fighting and hurting each other. Far too much doggie testosterone.

Which reminded her of what she had agreed to take on.

"When's he starting? The club whore?"

"He'll come by for an orientation tomorrow at noon, after his skating practice. I can be here ..."

"No, you will not! You'll be packing for your trip." Cora

was about to embark on a month-long cruise with her son, daughter-in-law, and two grandkids, followed by another fortnight at their home in Fort Meyers, Florida. She hadn't spent much time with them over the last couple of years and she'd been looking forward to this trip so much.

"If you're sure?"

"Absolutely. Am I not your most reliable employee?"

"You're my only employee. But I couldn't do this without you."

Cora wasn't usually one for sentiment, so it was nice to hear her get all touchy-feely.

"We've got this. Just leave me the details."

"HAVE YOU DONE YOUR HOMEWORK?"

Ashley lifted her hands from the soapy dishwater—seemed she was destined to be forever wrist-deep in the stuff—and checked over her shoulder. Through large glasses, Willa, the nine-year-old light of her life, returned her gaze with the eyes of her father. A lovely, deep blue, a reminder of good times and not so good.

Her lips quirked. Ashley remembered that, too.

"I got most of it done on the bus."

"Most of it?"

Willa tilted her head, likely trying to decide how much she should reveal. "I just have some math to finish."

Well, don't ask me.

A new voice rang through the kitchen. "If you finish your homework, sweetie, then you can have all the ice cream you want."

Ashley's sister, Maeve, was a big fan of bribery.

"That would be resplendent!" Today's word of the day. "And then I can work on my butterflies."

Willa jumped up and headed to her bedroom to finish what she was supposed to be doing anyway.

"Good word!" Maeve called after her as she grabbed a wine glass from the rack. "Damn, she's so smart."

"She is. And she's probably been looking for a chance to use 'resplendent' in a sentence, so thanks, I guess. But could we do less bribery?" Ashley dried her hands and turned to her sister. Older than Ashley by five years, she'd been a life-saver, offering her a place to stay after she and Greg, Willa's dad, fell apart. Of course, Maeve had predicted it would happen: *he's going to break your heart, Ash. Mark my words!*

And he had. So congrats on being right.

Maeve loved to be right. After all, she had predicted the demise of her own marriage ten years ago and had held onto the bitterness like a dog with a chew toy. Every now and then she squeaked about how she was destined to be alone. That it was the lot of women, even the ones who claimed to be happy. (No one is truly happy in a relationship, per Sister Maeve.)

But Ashley was grateful for the place to live. Greg had other commitments: the new baby with his new-ish girl-friend, Lottie. Maintaining two households was impossible right now.

Maeve opened the fridge and took out the cheese plate she'd prepared earlier for her book club.

"Everyone needs an incentive, especially kids."

"She needs to know that homework isn't transactional. It's required and I'm not paying her—in ice cream or anything else—to do it."

Maeve squinted. "What's up?"

"Nothing."

"No, seriously, you seem kind of stressed."

Ashley threw up her sudsy hands. "I'm living with my sisters, my ex is stiffing me on support, I have no social life, and I constantly smell of wet dog."

"So what else is new? I thought you were going to try that dating app—Skin Deep. Though it sounds kind of desperate."

"From the person who gave up on dating nine years ago."

Her sister shrugged, just as Vera, Ashley's other sister, walked in. "Anyone read this book? I like the hitman character best."

"Ashley's having one of her crises."

Vera grabbed the wine from the fridge and a glass from the rack. "Worried you're going to die alone?"

"No!" *Well, yes.*

"She's thinking of bailing on the dating app you recommended."

"Bailing" was such a defeatist word. Anxious to not sound like she was giving up on life, Ashley chimed in with a compromise, one she often fell back on in times of stress. "Maybe when Willa's older ..."

"That's the spirit," Vera said with a knowing grin. "Best to put it off as long as possible. See how your elders handle it."

Both her sisters were divorced, though Vera the middle child wasn't quite as miserable about it as Maeve. Vera saw it as a chance to bang anything that moved and spent more time out of the house than in. Where Maeve thought of men as the enemy, Vera saw them as compatriots in decadence. Neither of them were looking for new relationships; they'd been hurt too much before.

And now Ashley was here, a year out from her separation, and she felt herself slipping into a deep, dark hole. One constructed by Maeve, where the sides were doused in grease by Vera. *Stay in your lane. Misery loves company.*

She loved her sisters, but their attitudes toward relationships gave her pause. Though they were careful not to dwell on man-bashing negativity and extracurriculars in front of their niece, it was impossible to avoid some bad-mouthing of her ex to creep in. Ashley didn't want her daughter to grow up thinking all men were losers, even if that was an appropriate label for the most prominent one in her life.

"It's all very casual anyway. I only downloaded it because I was app-curious." It was far too soon to be worried about being left on the shelf at the ripe old age of thirty.

Maeve frowned. "But why one with no photos?"

"Because looks aren't important."

Vera gave a dirty grin. "Yeah, I had this super ugly dude who really knew how to float my boat. It was like he made the extra effort. Grateful."

"That's not what I'm interested in." Good grief, she hoped she'd be attracted to anyone she met, but she was conscious of her daughter's impressionable age, and how she had recently come home from school crying because someone called her Four Eyes.

Ashley worried that she gave off the wrong vibe to her daughter, one that implied looks were overly important. So her father had traded her mother in for a newer, younger model, and Lottie was barely twenty-two and absolutely gorgeous with a firm, stick-thin body, even after the baby's birth, but that didn't mean those who were left behind were suddenly less valuable.

Removing the focus on how people looked seemed like one way to help her daughter see that what was inside mattered. A small blow for abandoned women everywhere.

"Looks aren't everything and neither is sexual attraction. Compatibility is more important."

"In bed," Vera said, while Maeve rolled her eyes.

The doorbell rang, announcing it was time for Book Club, which meant Ashley could put her problems aside and instead muse on why someone thought a hired assassin made a viable love interest.

NUMBER ONE RULE for Book Club: don't talk about book club.

Or the books.

Or anything remotely related to literature.

As usual, there was a lot of chatter about who had read the book, whether it was worth the price (or best-selling status or as good as the author's previous), and who wanted to start the discussion.

Then it quickly devolved to a romance book club. Or hockey romance club.

Okay, they just talked about Dex O'Malley.

Pure coincidence, because Ashley didn't bring him up. Lainey (recently separated, two kids under five, husband now with his personal trainer) had just finished commenting on how hardcovers were too, uh, hard when Mallory (three years divorced, no kids, ex about to remarry) cut in with the following:

"You see Dex O'Malley is up to his old tricks?"

Ashley remained silent. She might have looked up the video of him punching that other hockey player in that bar, purely so she knew what she was dealing with tomorrow, but she didn't really have an opinion.

Okay, she did. A mom *always* had an opinion.

The man was an idiot. A brawling idiot, with too much

money and too little sense. God knew what she was going to do with him when he showed his far-too-handsome face at the shelter. Hopefully she could palm him off on one of the other volunteers while she worked on the Empty the Shelters event they had planned for next month.

"Good left hook," Vera commented after she'd viewed the video.

(The mention of Dex's "old tricks" prompted everyone to review his sordid online history, which included that *other* video from last year, the one where he received a very enthusiastic blow job from two women in a nightclub. Two! Ashley tried to puzzle together the notion of "sharing" a guy like that, but she was too skeeved out to let her imagination complete the picture.)

"Pity you can't see the peen," Mallory offered. "It's hidden by the blonde's head."

"I'd have thought the team would have scrubbed the internet of it." Maeve took a sip of her wine and winced because Vera had bought Chardonnay and Maeve hated Chard. "Don't they have social media people to do that?"

Vera spoke around a cracker and a slice of Gouda. "Even if they got it taken down, it's whack-a-dick. Anyone can put it up again any time they want. He'll always be known for it, poor guy."

Don't get into sexy situations on camera, then, Ashley's inner prude responded. She hated that bitch. But as a mom who hadn't seen action in a very long time, the prude often had her way.

"I'm sure he'd rather be known for his hockey," Eva added (divorce still fresh, still reeling from the affair). "Maybe he hit that guy so people would talk about him in a different way."

Vera scoffed. "It just reminds everyone of how much trouble he's caused."

Cora might be making a big mistake in letting Dex O'Malley use the shelter to rehab his image. But they were so reliant on that Rebels moolah ...

The way people were talking about him, though? Ashley didn't enjoy it, so while this would be the perfect opportunity to mention that "hey, guess who's coming to volunteer at the shelter tomorrow?," it seemed prurient. Now that she'd heard about him more, and how the world reacted to him, she might not tell her hockey-mad daughter, or anyone else in the family, about their new volunteer. With a bit of luck, he would be in and out of the shelter—and her hair—quicker than Bandit would squirrel his way out of her sudsy hands.

Tired of the book-free conversation, which had moved onto the Sins of the Exes portion of the evening, Ashley headed upstairs to see how Willa was doing. She found her on her iPad, drawing butterflies. No surprise there. Her daughter was obsessed with butterflies.

"Finished your math homework?"

An absent nod, then a dreamy smile. "We'll see the butterflies feeding, Mom."

"We will? Oh, right, we will."

Greg had signed Willa up for Bunking with Butterflies, an overnight event at Chicago's Nature Museum. The idea of spending a whole night learning about butterflies and their habits was the most exciting thing to ever happen to her.

"I hope Lottie doesn't mind," her daughter mused.

"Doesn't mind what?"

"That Dad will be with me and the butterflies. Babies need a lot of attention."

Ashley sat down on the bed and raised her arm to invite Willa in to snuggle close. Her room was an ode to winged creatures, mostly butterflies, but also dragons, fairies, and one that looked like Mothra. Since moving in with her sisters, the last six months had been spent trying to make this room as close to the one in their old house. Smaller than before, it was still her daughter's haven.

"Your dad's a little busy with the new baby, but he's still your dad."

"I know." She touched her iPad and brought up a photo array, pictures of her new sister, born four months ago. "Emily's going to be beautiful when she grows up."

"I'm sure she will be."

"I mean, really beautiful. Because Lottie looks like a model."

Okay. "She's got your dad's genes, which means you're beautiful, too."

"She probably won't need glasses, though." Willa peered at the screen through her glasses, the ones she'd worn since she was seven. "She'll have perfect eyesight."

"We don't know yet. Anything could happen. But if she needs glasses, then you'll be able to tell her how it works."

"They're just glasses, Mom. You put them on and they work."

Lately, Willa had gotten it into her head that her father thought the new baby was more beautiful than his oldest daughter. That this time he'd got it right.

"You know you're perfect the way you are."

"You have to say that." Willa sighed. "But I appreciate that you think so."

"So wise. Okay, I've got to get back to Book Club, though I doubt anyone missed me."

Willa smiled, but she was already in her drawing app, coloring a wing.

On her way back to the living room, Ashley passed a full-length mirror in the hall and for the first time in a while, stopped to take a look. She used to consider her reflection more often, the mess of caramel-blonde hair, the silver-green eyes, the curves and dips that made up her body. Lately she'd stopped looking beyond a superficial check that she was free of boogers and spinach in her teeth. It brought up too many memories, but mostly the most devastating one.

I'm just not attracted to you anymore.

Later Greg had said other things: about Lottie, getting her pregnant, how they'd co-parent Willa like they should have from the start instead of taking that one-night stand and trying to turn it into a marriage. A life.

But it was the comment about his attraction to her that stuck long after the others had faded into her rearview. He didn't have to say that. He could have let the obvious fact they'd drifted apart—or had never really gelled—do the heavy lifting.

For some reason he'd needed her to know that the body that produced his daughter just didn't do it for him, which made her think that it never had. That they'd let Ashley's pregnancy override all else—attraction, compatibility, even love. He might have added "anymore" to that parting shot, but all she heard was "have never been."

Now all she could see were the flaws. A surplus of pounds, too much junk in the trunk, a non-existent thigh gap. And don't get her started on how her eyes were too close together, or cheeks too round, or her chin came to a point.

Now, whenever she rushed by this mirror, the ghost of her previous self flashed in the corner of her eye. Good enough for a one-and-done, but what had she been thinking trying to stretch that goodwill to ten years?

That no-photo dating app wasn't just to set an example for her daughter. If she could make an impact with her personality first, looks wouldn't matter.

Probably not true, but a newly-single woman could hope.

3

Pittsburgh defenseman Kyle Hughes will attend an NHL player safety hearing this Sunday. Hughes is facing discipline for slashing against Chicago Rebels forward Dex O'Malley. The incident occurred at 19:50 of the third period near the Rebels bench in Chicago's 3-1 home win against Pittsburgh last week. Hughes received a major penalty for slashing on the play. O'Malley was able to finish the game. The hearing was delayed because of an after-game incident between O'Malley and Hughes, which resulted in injury to Hughes and O'Malley's arrest and charge with assault.
— NHL Player Safety

DEX TRIED NOT to roll his eyes on seeing the name on his caller ID. Kit Mallinson was a great agent and all-around good guy, but Dex had given him a lot more trouble than the average client and Kit was taking the tough love thing to the max.

"What's up?" He stifled a yawn. His next-door neighbor Georgia had one of her epic parties last night, and while he hadn't attended—*trying to be good, trying to be good*—the *thump thump* of the party's bass had kept him up.

"Just checking in on my man! Ready for a little rep renovation?"

"Sure, I can spend a few hours petting puppies."

"A few hours for a few days for a few weeks. Just enough to impress on any judge that you're not the bad boy everyone thinks you are."

Dex jerked to full awareness at this update. "A few weeks? Where am I going to find time for that? I have practice, away games, a very full schedule. I can't fit in that much time with a bunch of animals."

"Yes, you can. And you will." Kit's voice had turned serious. "Do you have any idea of the strings I had to pull to get this for you? The Rebels didn't have to go along with it. They could have benched you and let you ride out your contract. Which may I remind you is up at the end of the season. As it stands they're probably going to trade you as soon as it's expedient."

Dex slumped on the sofa. What did he care about being traded? He was used to moving around, being the team's new guy. No big deal.

"So I go to another team."

"And who wants a troublemaker who makes headlines for anything but how well he plays? Because you might think your play will supersede all that, but it won't. Orgs want guys who are 100% devoted to their game, solid, team and family-oriented guys, not people who are a distraction. If the Rebels put you on waivers, then good luck trying to find a team to pick you up. You'll be lucky if you get a spot on the Bumfuck Titans or whatever AHL team cares to have you. Your brand is cheapened, Dex. Sex tapes, the Tara business, and now punching a colleague—"

"He wasn't a colleague," Dex said morosely, desperate to get a word in and end the lecture. "Just someone I don't get along with."

"Right. Meanwhile you're losing fans by the truckload. That's why we need you to be spending all your spare time with cute fucking animals. Jesus, Tara couldn't rein you in, so these kittens better do the trick. I want you to head down to that shelter today, do your duty, and stay in the good graces of the people who run the place until Sophie, Fitz, and I decide you're done. Got it?"

"Got it," Dex mumbled. Damn, everyone was so serious.

Kit hung up before Dex could get the jump on him. Usually, he was able to laugh off the disapproval of his elders, but he wasn't quite feeling it this time. What Kit had said rankled.

He had a good relationship with the press and his fans. The sports media enjoyed his antics because it yielded plenty of clicks and the fans got a kick out of his class clownery. It didn't stop him from playing lights-out hockey. The team should recognize that and anything else shouldn't matter.

Into his second year as a Rebel, he was playing well. Still second- or third-line, so it could be better, but every team needed second, third, and fourth-line players. It wasn't that he was unambitious, but he preferred to stay in his lane. No one expected more from him, and he'd rather be of use wherever he went. If that was to another team, then so be it.

Except he liked Chicago. He hadn't expected to, given that this was where he'd been born and raised. His early memories of it were fuzzy and fractured. After all that shit went down, he'd hoped his aunt in Dallas would pick up the slack. But she had too many kids of her own to worry about him, and so began the Dexter Roadshow to all points in Chicagoland.

Most families found it hard to deal with his energy. He chewed up the goodwill of six of them over the course of sixteen months before landing back in the group home. And there he would've stayed except for a curious stroke of luck.

He was discovered.

A chance encounter with a hockey Hall of Famer, a placement with a family of hockey nerds, and eventually the career of his dreams. A career that could be cut short at any moment.

Which reminded him he really needed to answer that text from Anton. His old coach had checked in this morning (and yesterday morning). Dex opened the thread and reviewed the last message.

ANTON

You good?

DEX

Never better.

The phone rang because Dex had just sent proof of life. "Hey."

"Don't 'hey' me. Why haven't you been answering my calls?"

Because I'm embarrassed. "Didn't want to bother you."

"Bother me?" Anton spluttered, which sent Dex's mind back to those days when the guy would have a conniption every ten minutes over some antic his hockey protégé engaged in. "Why would hearing from you ever be a bother? Tell me what's happening."

Dex filled him in. "Don't know why they want to go to all this effort if they're just going to dump me anyway."

"Maybe they see your potential. It's happened before."

When Dex was twelve. The first time he held a hockey stick, years later than most of the hockey-playing kids his age, something magical had happened. He'd gone from some down on his luck street kid to someone with a future. On a day out from the group home, a man had called him over after seeing Dex gliding around on a crappy rink with a bunch of other charity cases.

"Where'd you learn to play hockey?"

Dex had snorted, deep into his little punk phase. "Never played before."

"You're telling me this is the first time you've hit a puck?"

Fuck-you shrug. "Why, is it hard?"

The guy had looked like he'd wanted to clip him one. Of course, at the time Dex had no clue this man was a big deal in hockey. In sports. In life.

"Where are your parents?"

"Dead." Half-true, or he assumed it was. He had no idea who his father was, and his mom may as well have been six feet under for all the use she was to him.

"Poor little orphan, huh?" The sneer was mixed with a grudging respect. "And you've never played hockey?"

Dex's friend Scottie had wanted to meet his favorite player on the Chicago Rebels, Bren St. James, and Dex would never say no to any opp to get out of the home for a day. He'd skated once before when he stayed with the Mulligans, his second to last foster family. He'd liked how free he felt, gliding along the surface. How natural the motion had come to him. But today was the first time he'd picked up a stick and hit a puck. He'd skimmed by a couple of guys easily, hit the rubber disc as hard as he could, and sent it like a rocket into the back of the net.

Then he did it again.

Each time it hit its target like it couldn't possibly go anywhere else. Like that was Dex's purpose. All this rage inside him seemed to find an outlet at last.

"You need to join a league, kid. Who's in charge of you?"

Dex looked around for Frank, the group leader, who, with his pot belly and general lack of coordination, should really not be on skates. "That guy."

When Dex had skated back to Scottie, he'd received the funniest look. "I can't believe you talked to him!"

"Who?"

"Clifford Chase! He owns the Chicago Rebels!"

As if Dex cared. Just some big shot who liked bossing people around.

Not expecting anything to come of it, he was surprised when two weeks later, Anton Ballard showed up at the home with instructions from the great Clifford Chase to train him up. From that moment on, Dex knew this was his ticket out.

So whenever Anton called after one of Dex's fuck-ups, he had a hard time justifying the why of his fuck-uppery. That he might be broken was something he'd considered but in typical "avoid self-reflection at all costs" fashion, he'd dismissed it.

"They've got a lot of good players here. Hard to rise above."

"Bullshit. So you're gonna bail on them before they bail on you?"

"I'm sorry if you're disappointed."

"Are you?" He could feel Anton's disgust all the way from the east coast. "Because it sounds like you're just enjoying that pity party for one."

"Maybe it's time to move on."

"Thought you liked Chicago."

He and Kit must be in cahoots.

"It's no better or worse than anywhere else. Nashville was a better party town."

"Now you're just trying to piss me off." *Correct, sir!* "Quit making excuses and start knuckling down, or you're going to find yourself out of a job and a place to call home. If I wasn't in Vermont, I'd come over there and tell you in person exactly what I think."

Anton used to live in Chicago but got a coaching gig out of state a couple of years ago just before Dex had been acquired by the Rebels. Maybe, if he was around, Dex wouldn't be so off the rails, if only because Anton was the one guy Dex hated to disappoint.

And why did the mention of losing "a place to call home" upset him more than the thought of finding himself out of a job?

When he didn't say anything, Anton continued, more conciliatory this time. More like the man who was as close to a father as Dex had ever had. "The Rebels are a good org, son. I think you can make an impact there, but you have to want to do that."

"I do. It was going well for a while and then ... I don't know." He could barely articulate why he couldn't get his act together.

Anton coughed slightly. "I know the thing with Tara didn't work out, but I'm not even sure you cared all that much."

His ego cared. His heart? *Nah.* For a while he'd thought that Tara was one of the success signifiers he craved. The trophy wife, the sign of a winner. Breaking off their engagement had left him feeling somewhat hollow, like he couldn't even get the pro-athlete-meets-hot-WAG equation right. (The most basic of the sports world equations.) But he also preferred where he and Tara had landed, as friends.

"She's happy as Larry with Fitz. They're a super couple, kid and everything." He tried not to sound bitter. He didn't want kids, but that feeling of belonging ... maybe. When he'd found out he was going to be traded to the Rebels eighteen months ago, he'd been so excited. There was something destined about it, Clifford Chase's team, the place where it all started.

But Dex was still Dex, and not even a change of location could change the person you've always been.

"I've got to go. I'm having breakfast with the guys before practice."

"That's the ticket!" Anton sounded more animated at the mention of food, or maybe the notion Dex was making friends. "I'll check in with you later."

Of course he would.

TWENTY MINUTES LATER, Dex walked into the Sunny Side Up Diner in downtown Riverbrook and looked around. Bast Durand waved him over, and Dex took a seat beside never-shuts-up D-man Theo Kershaw, opposite quiet-spoken forward Hudson Grey and center Dylan Bankowski, a recent trade from Nashville, Dex's old team.

"Gentlemen, how goes it?"

Kershaw grinned. "We should be asking you, Oh-Em-Gee! Heard you're going to be knee deep in dog shit for a while."

"That's the plan. Not sure people won't see how transparent *that* is, though."

"People love puppies, man," Bast said. "And people love

athletes covered in puppies and kittens. A few photos, a nice character reference from whoever's in charge, and you'll be golden."

It sounded as easy as the amazing cherry pie they served up at the diner.

"Tara said Kennedy works there." Kennedy was married to Reid Durand, Bast's brother, also a Rebel.

Bast stirred his coffee. "She used to volunteer, but her concierge business has taken off and with the baby on the way, she doesn't have much time. Trying to get an in before you go?"

Right, another Rebel pregnancy. This team was constantly pumping them out.

"Just curious if I'd see a friendly face."

"Other than the puppies?" Banks gruffed out. "I think you're going to be fine."

"Yep," Dex agreed because he wanted to move on. "I'll head over after practice and turn on the charm."

"You'll have them eating out of your hand," Kershaw said while perusing the menu. "Literally."

The conversation shifted to the home game tomorrow against their old rivals, the Detroit Motors. After they put their menu orders in—the French toast here was out of this world—Dex considered that now was as good a time as any to get something off his chest.

"So, I wanted to run something by you guys."

His teammates looked up, curious.

"Are you guys pissed at me?"

Rolling his shoulders, Kershaw settled back in the booth. "What makes you think that?"

"A little bird told me there's a poker game at Hunt's place once a week, and I'm guessing my invite got lost in the mail."

"And you think we're pissed at you? Nah, we kind of assumed it was too boring for you."

Shit. They *were* pissed at him.

"No, not at all." He raised his gaze to Banks, who was checking his phone. It looked like he was reading the *Chicago Tattler* website, which was strange, but then Banks was an odd duck. There was no good reason why he should already be deep in the Rebels' fleshy bosom, yet Dex had a weird feeling the guy had managed to weasel his way in. "Are *you* on this invite list?"

"Yep. But I might be off it since I took a grand off everyone last week."

Kershaw snorted. "Beginner's luck, Psycho."

"Psycho?" Banks squinted at his teammate.

"From the movie. Norman Banks. Mommy issues. Fun times in the shower. That's one of my best."

"It's Norman Bates, asshole, not Banks."

Kershaw screwed up his mouth. "You sure?"

"Yes, I'm sure."

"Because Psycho is a really good nickname and I'd hate to have to re-think it."

Banks got even squintier. "Well, I'm feeling like a psycho right now."

That cheered Kershaw. "Nailed it. I'm the king of the nicknames."

Even that misattributed one was better than Dex's. He didn't mind Sexy Dexy but Kershaw usually bandied about "Oh-Em-Gee" because of his caught-on-camera sexual escapade. Most of the videos had an OMG sticker over his crotch, completely unnecessary because his dick was hidden by a big puff of blonde hair. Forever click bait.

He turned the conversation back to poker night. "I'm up for a card game. Anytime."

Bast looked skeptical. "But you did say that we're all boring as shit because we've settled down to make babies. Though I'm not up for breeding yet, at least not while Pepper is finishing up school. As for Grey here—what's your deal, Hud? You and Jude gonna get into the child rearing business soon?"

Hudson blushed, which was par for the course with him. Per Tara, he and his firefighter boyfriend were cuter than all the puppies and kittens Dex expected to be puddled in later.

Now that he thought of it, he got all his team gossip from Tara instead of the guys themselves.

"It's been mentioned but I want to be sure I'm not traded soon." Hudson gave a quick shrug, affable as ever. Like anyone would trade him after this past killer season, not to mention everyone adored him. He was practically the team's mascot. "Our dog Crosby is all the baby we need for now."

Appearing satisfied with that answer, Bast turned back to Dex. "So yeah, us boring homebodies are okay with pizza and beer and poker. Guessing clubs are more your bag."

Sure, but he liked hanging with the guys as well.

"So I have a big mouth. I'm full of shit most of the time. You know that."

Healthy suspicion greeted that until finally Theo chuckled and spoke for the group. "Oh, we do, Oh-Em-Gee. We do. And now we know you're interested, then we'll get you on the text chain."

"There's a text chain?" Fuck, how much had he been missing?

They razzed him a bit more, and by the time the food had arrived, he was feeling on a surer footing with them. Anton and Tara were right: he needed to make more effort. These were his ice-brothers, and he had to put in what he expected to get out.

4

———

Rory
Part Golden Retriever
Likes: Most humans
Dislikes: Vague booking

"SHE'S BACK."

Ashley looked up from the adoption forms she was reviewing at Toby, who had put his head around the door to Cora's office. She didn't need to ask who.

"Did you tell her she can't come in here?"

Toby nodded. "She said it's her constitutional right to be able to pet the puppies."

Ashley growled, a half-decent impression of one of the animals in her charge. The day was going from bad to worse.

First, they'd had a roof leak after heavy rain, and they were making do with a bucket in the middle of the floor of the cattery.

Next, Donna, one of her volunteers, had been involved in a fender bender—no injuries, thank God—but it was traumatic enough for her to need to take a mental health day.

But what really got her goat was the hockey player no-show.

Dex O'Malley was supposed to be here at noon.

It was now 4 p.m. and not a word from anyone at the Rebels org.

Ashley had called Cora to verify she'd had the time and date correct (she had). She called the Rebels contact, Sophie, and left a message (no response). And while this shouldn't have bothered her because she wasn't relying on this Dex character to make any significant input, it niggled all the same because this was just typical of entitled men-children who dropped a load on the carpet and expected everyone to clean up after them. Take her ex, for example. He had no problem impregnating her—in fact, he'd had a great time dropping his sperm off—but when it came to the real work of raising a kid, he bailed when the going got tough.

She had enough of that with the puppies!

Now another problem was manifesting in the form of Bronte Finn, today's visitor. Twice now, she had let three of the dogs out of their cages because she thought they looked "so sad." Maybe they did, but they were enclosed for a reason.

Unfortunately, Bronte's father, Councilman Finn, was a big wig in local politics, owner of several businesses and a major donor to the shelter. After the last disastrous visit, he'd come in to thank them all in person for not making a fuss and assured them that he wouldn't be halting his dona-tion. Not too hard to read between the lines there. Ashley was so tired of these big shots who viewed the shelter as their personal playground.

Sighing, she stood and practiced adjusting her expression as she headed outside.

"Bronte! So good to see you!"

Bronte smiled abstractly. "Oh, thank God you're here. This guy won't let me in to see the puppies."

"Well, we have reasons, y'know. Last time you opened the cages—"

"Because they need the fresh air."

"We take them out on a regular basis, but we can't give anyone who doesn't work here unregulated access."

Bronte screwed up her mouth. "I applied to be a volunteer, but I didn't hear back."

"We're actually at capacity with volunteers right now." Ashley stepped in closer and lowered her voice. "Hey, I know you love the animals but there are liability issues if you're here. We let you in before and you let them out. Some of them are damaged and we can't risk them biting people. You understand, don't you?"

"Aw, let her pet the puppies."

A new voice had entered the conversation. A new, deeper, rumbly voice.

Ashley turned to face the source of that voice and met the eyes of ... okay, not the eyes because he was wearing sunglasses. More like she met The Hair. Gelled and teased to within an inch of its life.

She'd seen him online. Everyone had. Dex O'Malley wasn't shy about sharing himself and his body with the world.

Neither was he shy about sharing his opinions, apparently.

She turned back to Bronte. "Hey, thanks for coming in." She had a feeling she was going to regret this, but Ashley had always been a sucker for a begging face. "You can say hi to the animals as long as Toby is there. For five minutes. But no opening of the cages, okay?"

Bronte's eyes brightened. "Okay!"

Ashley turned to Toby. "Five minutes, okay?"

Toby looked up from his phone. "Got it! Come on, B! Let's go pet some puppies."

Which left Ashley alone with Dex O'Malley. She waited for him to speak.

"I'm Dex." Said like he was Cher or Zendaya. "I'm looking for Ashley?"

"Well, you've found her. And you're late."

"I am?" He checked his watch.

"By four hours."

"Didn't someone call?"

"No."

She couldn't see past his sunglasses, but the smirk said it all.

"This is a volunteer gig, right? Thought the timing was flexible."

"Your time might be but mine isn't. This volunteer gig to you is a business to me."

She sounded prissy—she hated hearing it in her tone—but what was she supposed to do? It wasn't her job to wrangle naughty jocks with time-keeping issues.

He pushed his sunglasses on top of his head. Maybe he thought his eyes would do the heavy lifting of an apology. They were a deep, drown-in-me blue, but had no impact on her. Handsome men-boys had long ago stopped making her feel anything but a mild contempt.

"Hey, I'm sorry." Said with the least sincerity ever.

That's when she saw the dark circles under those eyes, the troubled gaze, the tiredness.

Those baby blues might be gorgeous, but they were also

weary. The mouth might be pretty, but the smirk was half-hearted at best. And his hair, which was rakeable—was that a word?—looked like he'd been tearing through it with his fingers.

"I'm sorry, too. Unfortunately, I don't have time to wrangle you when I'm this busy."

"Wrangle me? Hey, I'm not one of your puppies." He stepped in, and she was abruptly conscious of his size. The man could give a Sequoia a run for its bark. "I said sorry."

He added a grin, which was supposed to make that lazy-ass apology more palatable, she supposed. *Not today, buster.*

"I bet that usually works on everyone you meet."

"Not everyone." He sounded genuinely perplexed. "Some people prefer to be hard asses for no good reason."

Had he forgotten they were doing him a solid? So, there was a quid pro quo in the favors department, but he was the one who'd arrived hours late. In some recess of her brain, she knew she should let this slide and forget about it. But the words to smooth it over refused to come.

"Is this how you think the world works? You don't get your way, so you act like I'm the problem?"

He ran his fingers through his hair again. At this rate, they risked exiting their follicles and drifting to the tiled floor. His chest rose on a deep inhale, the Rebels R on his gray long-sleeved tee stretching taut as his lungs filled and his pecs firmed. She felt her gaze drift on a dreamy cloud downward to his trim waist, narrow hips, and thick thighs wrapped in dark sweats. The perfect pro-athlete body.

Unable to stop the catalog, she took note of the angel's face with its iron jaw, slashed cheekbones, Roman nose, and sensual lips. With a package like that, no wonder he was used to getting what he wanted.

Having observed her interest, he reactivated the smirk,

and all the goodwill engendered by his face and body left the building.

"No."

He looked taken aback. "No?"

"No," she repeated, liking how it sounded on her lips. She was usually a "yes" girl and it probably was in her interest to be a "yes" girl right now, but this guy was rubbing her all wrong and was fully deserving of her rejection.

When would she ever get a chance to say "no" to a man this hot?

Bafflement creased his brow, and even that looked attractive on him. Poor dumb jock, who didn't understand why she wasn't bowing down to serve him.

He opened his pretty-boy lips, and she steeled her spine for whatever charming absurdity might come next. She expected to be highly entertained by it.

"Okay, Ashley, maybe we should—"

She didn't hear the rest because in two seconds it had turned to shit.

The door behind her flew open and a couple of her charges came bounding out. Peanut was a rambunctious terrier who loved to hump anyone and anything (kind of like her sister in that respect). He jumped on Dex, who held up his hands—to protect The Face, no doubt—then stumbled back. Peanut was clearly overstimulated, but he was largely harmless.

The same couldn't be said for Bandit.

Who did not like seeing his buddy, Peanut, getting up close and personal with the hockey player. Bandit lunged and, despite not being a big dog, still managed to knock Peanut out of the way—to presumed safety, at least in Bandit's eyes. Then he stood and growled at Dex.

Leaving the apparent stalemate, Ashley pushed through

the door to find a mess in the cages, or rather, out of the cages.

Toby was frantically trying to undo the damage wrought by Bronte who was sitting in the middle of the room with Rory, a Golden Retriever mix in her lap.

"Toby, you were supposed to keep an eye on her!"

"Yeah, I know. I'm sorry. I was feeding Benji and he squirreled his way past me and—hey, c'mere, fella!" He grabbed a Basset hound called Gaston and one of their three Jack Russells, Belle, and popped them into their respective cages. Ashley got busy corralling the remaining dogs.

"In you go, Joey! You've had your fun for today." Joey the Pitbull gave her the sad eyes, but waddled his way in.

"What should I do with this little guy?"

Ashley turned to find Dex with Peanut, cradled in his arms, who looked like he was really enjoying the ride.

"Hey, you're Dex O'Malley," Bronte said. "I saw your dick online."

"Bronte, you need to leave." Ashley scooped up a York-shire terrier they'd yet to name and put him in his cage. "You promised you'd be good and now I can't trust you."

She turned back to Dex, wondering how he managed to pick up Peanut without incurring the wrath of Bandit. "Mr. O'Malley, I can take Peanut—uh, where's the other dog?"

"He was getting a bit unruly, so I left him out there for now. I locked the door as well, just in case someone else comes in."

"Oh, okay. Thanks for that." A decent level of foresight, but she supposed Dex O'Malley was more adept than most at cleaning up messes. She took Peanut from him and placed him in his cage. "In you go, little guy."

When she turned, Dex had vanished, and then she

heard it: the worst combination of sounds possible in a shelter.

An animal growl and a human yelp.

She rushed out. Dex was holding his hand—his bloodied hand—and glaring at Bandit.

"The fucker bit me!"

"Yeah, he's a bit of a wild card. Oh—" Ashley moved closer. That was quite a lot of blood. "We should get that fixed up."

"Has that mutt had his shots?"

Ashley didn't enjoy the implication that they didn't run a clean shelter around here. "Have you had yours?"

He blinked at her. "My hands are pretty valuable, y'know."

She had a million possible comebacks for that. Instead, she went with, "I can only imagine. Toby!"

Toby emerged carrying Lilith, a bulldog mix. "Yep?"

"Could you take care of Bandit? I have to manage this."

Toby took a look at Dex, then back to Ashley. "Got it, boss. Here, fella." Bandit growled but Toby knew how to handle him—gently.

She turned back to the injured hockey player. "If you come through, we can wash it and—"

Dex O'Malley was on the phone. "Yeah, not sure of the damage. Might be best if I come in." Dramatic pause. Quick flicker of disgust in her direction. Blood still dripping all over the floor. "Yeah, later."

He hung up. "I need to see the team doc."

"Oh, right. Did you want to wrap it first? To stop the mess?"

He looked torn, but not quite as torn as his hand which was still leaking fluids of the bloodier variety all over the kennel floor.

Nice donation. Shelter stays open. Keep your job.

The Yes Girl was back.

She made an executive decision because that's what Cora paid her for. Cupping his elbow, she gentled him forward through to the clinic.

"Come on through and let's take care of it."

5

"DOES IT HURT?"

"It stings more than hurts. I can't believe that dog went nuts on me."

"Oh, can't you?"

Sarcasm noted.

"I was trying to help."

"If you'd been on time, this probably wouldn't have happened." She grabbed some alcohol—the medical kind, unfortunately—and bandages from a cupboard. She'd taken him to what looked like an urgent care center at the animal shelter.

"How does me being late explain a dog you lost control of?"

Her eyes flashed. "I didn't lose control. That was Bronte's fault."

Bronte? Sounded like some tree-hugger type. "So you can't control your employees."

"Bronte's not an employee. She's a visitor, like you. And I'm a soft-hearted sap."

She didn't sound soft-hearted. She sounded like a humorless drone.

Right now, she was focused on cleaning his wound which gave him a chance to study her. Caramel blonde hair in a pile on her head with a cat whiskers clip. Apple-green eyes ringed by a streak of silver. An upturned nose, ruby-red lips, and color in her cheeks, probably because she was angry about having to fix him up.

She applied some ointment from a tube and he bit back the gasp at the sting.

"Wait, is that stuff for dogs?" He took another look around. This clinic must be for animals of the four-legged variety.

"Works just as well on cats."

He pulled his hand away. "I don't want cat medicine!"

"Cool your jets, hotshot. It's antibacterial ointment, for humans. The people who work here get a lot of scratches and minor injuries."

"Okay. But this is a vet's clinic, right?"

"It is. We have a part-time vet in here most mornings. Sorry, you're stuck with me."

Funnily enough, he didn't mind, especially as her actions were so gentle. Despite the humor deficit and clear-as-day annoyance with him, she had great hands, soft and supple as she applied the ointment to the wound with care and patched a gauze pad over it.

"Do the dogs usually go off the hook like that?"

"No, they don't." She raised her eyes to Dex, peeking at him from under the veil of her lashes. Those eyes were something else. "And the fewer people who know what happened here, the better."

"Right. You wouldn't want it getting out that you let killer dogs roam the facility, ready to bite unsuspecting visitors."

She stopped what she was doing and took a step back. The bandage remained in a loose drape over his hand.

"Wait, what's going on?"

"Nothing. Toby can drive you to wherever you need to go. Rebels HQ, you said?"

"You're not going to finish wrapping me up?" Blood was starting to seep through the gauze.

She glared at him, the silver in her green eyes flashing like diamonds. "I don't need to stand here while you make jabs about the dogs in my care. Bandit is very highly-strung—"

"Hell yeah, he is."

"And he's had a hard life. Strangers make him nervous and he's also very protective of Peanut." When he looked blank, she said, "The other dog. The terrier."

"But I was just trying to help get them back in their homes. Cages. Whatever."

She picked up the bloodied supplies and threw them in the trash, then started to tidy up. He used the moment as an excuse to check out the rest of her. Even turned away from him, he could tell she had an amazing rack, which filled out her purple V-necked tee like a dream. She wore jeans, rolled a couple of inches above her ankle, and damn, that was one fine ass cupped by the denim.

Still obviously annoyed, she responded with, "I get that. I'm sorry you were hurt. I'm trying to help. But I was a little overwhelmed at the situation, and your tardiness—by several hours, mind you—didn't help."

"I guess it didn't." He didn't really see the connection, but he figured agreeing with her was better so they could move on. "Listen, I thought I was helping, but I guess not. Only now I need your help to patch this up because it might get infected and I'll be out of a job before you can say, 'Gordie Howe Hat trick'."

God, he was tired. He'd headed home for a quick lunch after practice and fell asleep on the sofa. Hockey players were used to afternoon naps. He'd figured showing up late to the shelter gig was better than not showing up at all, but now it had descended to the usual Dex O'Malley shit-show.

Ashley stood before him, hands on hips, contemplating whether he was worthy of her medical attention. He really needed to get going, to head to Rebels HQ where they could do a proper job of stitching him up. But something held him locked in place, something strangely powerful. She had a strength of character about her that drew him in.

She was talking and he'd missed it.

"Right," he said because it looked like she was waiting for a response.

"You'd do that? Apologize?"

He shrugged, not sure why she was asking. Hadn't he just said sorry? "Like on camera or something?"

"Well, he's a bit fussy. Not sure we'd want too many people around him."

Him. Were they talking about the dog?

"Would he even understand?"

Wrong response. She turned her attention to the bandage, looking to wrap it up—heh—as quickly as possible. "I'm not sure this is going to work out."

"What?"

"You. Here."

"You're turning down a volunteer at the shelter?" Christ on a Zamboni, how bad did you have to be to lose the volunteer gig at the animal shelter?

Dex O'Malley-bad, it seemed.

Sophie and Fitz and just about every other responsible

adult in his life was going to freak the fuck out if they heard he'd been canned by the Shelter Lady. He needed to fix this.

But before he could apologize more fulsomely, her phone pinged.

"Your Uber's here."

"My Uber?"

"I called one to take you to the Rebels HQ. Again, I'm sorry about Bandit. Take care of yourself, Mr. O'Malley."

For a moment, he thought she might say something else, but she merely shook her head slightly and headed out the clinic door.

"Well, it could be worse." Dr. Morgan, the Rebels doc, patted the wound with some gauze and squinted. "It's not too deep, but it'll keep you out for a couple of weeks."

"You're kidding." It felt sore, with the five stitches and the antiseptic, but he could flex it, which he did.

"Don't do that just yet. You'll re-open the wound." The doc started to wrap it. "We'll do daily redressing, and you need to keep it dry for a while. About a week."

Sophie burst into the exam room. "What the hell happened?"

"Just a minor accident with a dog at the shelter."

"The dogs are dangerous?"

He didn't like Sophie's tone, which implied that there was blame to be assigned here. Human blame. "It was completely my fault, Soph. I got a little too friendly with the dog and he wasn't ready for it."

"No one said anything about dogs that bite."

He locked eyes with her. "This was your idea."

Her body language changed in a flash. "I just talked to

Ashley, the woman in charge of the shelter. Guess what she told me?"

Here it is ...

"You were supposed to show up at noon. She assumed we'd changed our minds."

"I fell asleep." He tried to make it sound cute.

"Asleep? Dex, you can sleep as much as you want when you're out of a job. If you don't follow this plan—"

"I did follow it. Just ... a few hours later. But then ..." He waved his newly-bandaged hand.

"Am I supposed to be sympathetic? Do you realize that I'm the head of PR for the Chicago Rebels hockey franchise?"

"Well, yeah—"

"The franchise, Dex. The entire team. Yet, for the last year and a half, I've spent a good fifty percent of my time as your personal publicist. Cleaning up after *your* problems. Do you think that's fair?"

"No, I suppose not."

Sad head shake. Her phone rang and she grimaced. "I have to take this. Excuse me a second." Out she went.

Dex turned to the doc, who was tidying up his triage station. "Tell me this is just a couple of days. I can't be out for long." Not when he needed to prove himself. One more black mark against him and he'd be out on his ear.

Or maybe it was already a foregone conclusion.

A part of him wondered if it was for the best. If this was a sign he wasn't meant to be here with the Rebels.

Dr. Morgan smiled thinly and gripped his shoulder. "I'll take a look at it tomorrow before morning skate and we'll assess." He headed out, leaving Dex to review the current state of play.

Injured hand.

Legal jeopardy.

Shelter volunteer reject.

No sex for a week.

Still no invite to Hunt's poker game or the team group text.

So, not great. There was only so long a man could skate by on his natural-born talent, and the people Dex needed to help make this right might have finally run out of fucks to give.

LEAVING REBELS HQ, a sneaky feat Dex managed to engineer by keeping his head down to avoid a bout of real-talk with Sophie, Fitz, or, God forbid, Tara, Dex ran into Banks with his gym bag, also headed for the exit.

"What the hell happened to you?"

Dex filled him in as they walked out.

"Only you, O'Malley. Why do you make it so difficult for yourself?"

"Some people aren't as boring as you, Banks."

The man snorted. He and Dex were the same height—six-two—but Banks was a husky guy who took up a lot of space.

"Better boring than the shit you seem to spend your life dipped in."

Dex sighed. Maybe he was right. Boring seemed to have its perks, such as stable careers and teammates who invited you to card games and what Dex imagined was a lack of anxiety about what came next.

"So my car is back at the shelter. Could you give me a ride?"

Banks squinted at him, and Dex was feeling low enough

that he actually expected the guy to tell him it wasn't happening.

"Alright. And I'll throw in dinner at the Sunny Side Up."

An unexpected offer, but Dex wasn't going to pass up the opportunity to get some man-to-man time with one of his teammates. At the diner, they took seats at the counter. Dex ordered the meatloaf while Banks asked for two turkey burgers because, in his view, they were tiny.

"So what do you think I should do?"

"About?"

"Everything. My legal issues. My fast-fading hockey career. The fact I haven't gotten laid in a week."

His teammate sniffed. "You expect me to fix your getting laid problem?"

"No. But it's piling on, man. It's like everything is going wrong at once. And I don't feel like I'm in control." He'd never felt that. Being shunted from place to place as a kid kept him in a perpetual state of insecurity. Hockey was the constant.

Hockey was still the constant.

"The Shelter Chick thinks I'm a loser."

Banks stared for a long beat. "And you care because?"

He didn't. But no one could possibly enjoy being judged with those shamrock-melted eyes, even while her gentle hands soothed and fixed him up. He shouldn't care a jot about some rando's opinion, but Ashley Adams seemed like the kind of person whose opinion carried weight.

"She pretty much said I wasn't suitable for the job. Like I can't figure out how to look after a few puppies."

Banks dropped his gaze to Dex's bandaged hand but remained silent.

"Well, yeah, there was this, but that couldn't be helped. Okay, so it could be helped. But I can figure this out. I don't need some crappy volunteer shelter gig. I just need to charm some stone-faced judge, make sure I'm back on the ice soon so no one forgets me, and get some action for my neglected dick." The server put down a couple of Diet Cokes and gave Dex a grin. Yeah, the dick part of this problem wouldn't be an issue for long.

But the rest of it seemed like a slog.

Banks's phone buzzed and he checked what looked like a group text thread.

"The guys?" Jesus, why did it feel like someone had jammed a puck down his throat?

"My sisters. They're coming to visit in a couple of months. It's a ... thing."

"Must be nice."

"Nope. Just annoying."

People always took their families for granted, like you could have too many texts from someone you loved. Dex couldn't even begin to imagine what that was like, the sheer privilege behind it.

Their food arrived, so all talk was suspended during chow time (not that Banks had said more than a couple of words). Dex had only ever had breakfast food here, so it was good to know the place also knocked it out of the park at dinnertime.

With the last bite of Banks's second turkey burger put away, he turned to Dex.

"O'Malley, you need to figure out what you want."

"Hockey. This spot, this team." There was other stuff. Soppy, soapy, ridiculous trash thinking, that existed in some deep, inaccessible-for-now recess. But right this minute, his career had to be the focus.

"You've fucked up. But you can fix it." Banks wiped his mouth with a napkin. "You don't want to go through life regretting your decisions. What might have been." He seemed to think about that for a second before shaking it off. "You're here and you need to work your ass off to stay here. No one gets a free pass, no matter how talented they are."

Dex knew all this but it was good to hear it from someone so seasoned. Maybe Banks might have his back at his court date because Dex was starting to realize just how isolated he felt despite being part of a team. This is what he needed to do. Fix things with the boys, play his cup off, and make nice with his PR team. So he'd screwed up with the animal shelter and that Ashley chick thought he was no better than the doggy doo-doo she probably spent her days cleaning up, but he'd find another way. He always did.

"I appreciate it. Listen, I need to hit the head. I'll get the check when I come back."

Banks grunted at that.

In the corridor heading towards the john, Dex spotted a woman in a server uniform, coming out of the women's restroom as she tied her apron. His skin prickled with awareness, some preternatural inkling of imminent change. Their gazes clashed and Dex's tread and heart stuttered to a stop.

She said his name, and any doubt he had as to her identity vanished in the wake of hearing that smoke-scarred voice.

He tried to take in the details—the uniform, the severe hair pulled back from a worn face scrubbed clean, the fact she was standing before him after all this time. They say bad luck comes in threes but lately, this crap seemed to be raining in multiples of it.

"What are you doing here?"

"I-I'm working here. Have been for the last month."

But I've eaten here in the last month.

The last Dex had heard, she had finished up a prison stint at Decatur Prison, about two and a half hours south of Chicago. That would have been a year ago, maybe more.

Ruby O'Malley hadn't tried to get in touch with her only son, at least not recently. The last time she'd reached out was when Dex signed his first contract with Philly six years ago. He'd received a letter from her, return address the slammer, and he'd thrown it unopened in the trash. She'd already been inside for eight years at that point, and apparently she'd thought it was the right time to reach out.

It wasn't. It never would be.

Now she was here in Dex's neighborhood.

"I wanted to call but—"

"No, you didn't," Dex gritted out.

She looked confused. Years of abusing a body and brain will do that.

"No, I did." She sounded uncertain.

"And I'm saying you didn't. Because I'm not going to talk to you. So calling would be a waste of yours and my time. I'm not doing this. We're not doing this."

"Dex—"

Dex raised a hand, wishing the gesture could stop time, praying it was enough to stop any speech coming from this woman's lips. And in case it wasn't he barreled past her, past the restroom to the end of the corridor where his blurred vision could just about make out an exit sign. He hit the crash bar and accepted that the alarm he set off was the perfect soundtrack to that clusterfuck mother-son reunion.

He didn't stop there. He kept going, as fast as a third period breakaway. Because he couldn't risk another meeting with the woman who had left him as a sniveling ten-year-old kid. The woman who had preferred alcohol and drugs to motherhood. The woman whose shitty decisions had condemned Dex to a childhood of uncertainty and misery.

His life might not be perfect, but he was determined to get back on track—the guys, his game, the fucking puppies because yes, that was apparently part of the solution—and he would not allow his life to be derailed by her.

6

Mowgli

Tabby cat

Likes: Sleeping (napping is for amateurs!)

Dislikes: Guys who start sentences with "No offense"

"SOMEONE WANTS to adopt the black kitten with the white paw. TinTin."

Ashley put her tote bag down on the chair behind the reception counter. "That's amazing news! Did they fill out the paperwork?"

Toby grinned. "Yeah, made a deposit and everything. I said I had to run it by you being the boss lady and all."

She didn't feel like the boss lady. She felt positively un-boss-like, to be honest. She'd considered reaching out to Cora, needing assurance that in refusing to babysit Dex O'Malley, she'd made the right call. But she was already on her cruise and Ashley had promised her she'd take care of it. Only, she might have taken care of her way out of a job.

She picked up the clipboard with the application for the kitten. All looked to be in order, so that was good, wasn't it?

Another $300 for the coffers. But yesterday's events niggled at her.

"Any sign of Bronte?"

"God, no. She has to know better." Toby quirked an apologetic smile. "I know I screwed up, not keeping an eye on her. I forgot how slippery Benji can get when I open the cage and as soon as he got by me, Bronte took her shot." He pushed a cup toward her. "I got you an English breakfast tea."

"Suck up."

"Yep. Sometimes we have to go to great lengths to seek forgiveness."

She picked up the cup and took a sip. Lukewarm but comforting all the same.

"It's my fault. I shouldn't have let her in here at all after the last time. And I shouldn't have let myself be distracted by Dex O'Malley."

Toby grinned. "Well, he's one of those 'sucks focus everywhere he goes' kind of people."

"Too right. I do feel bad that Bandit was such a pill to him, but at least I don't have to worry about it anymore."

"You mean Bandit? Because he's not going to stop being the worst."

She chuckled. Picking up her tea, she put the clipboard under her arm and headed toward the office. Pushing the door ajar, she continued talking to Toby over her shoulder.

"No, Bandit can't help it. But at least I don't have to deal with famous hockey players who need to have their dicks sucked in public because they're little attention whores."

She blinked at the sight in Cora's office.

Dex O'Malley was sitting in the chair.

Behind the desk.

Holding a kitten.

What fresh hell ...?

"You were saying?" he asked with an *aren't-I-adorable* grin.

"What are you doing here? We established that this was not the right fit for you."

"Right. Well, *you* said that, but I'm hoping you might be open to persuasion."

Mittens dug his claws into Dex's shoulder but was too weak to get any traction. Ashley wished he was a tiger.

She threw a dark look over her shoulder at Toby. "You let him in here?"

"Well, yeah. He said he needed to talk to you and—oh, what's that?" He cocked his ear dramatically. "Pretty sure I heard the door. Back in a sec."

She turned back to O'Malley, who with the kitten, somehow managed to look like a sexy James Bond villain.

"That's my chair." It was actually Cora's, but the principle was the same.

"Right." He stood, still carrying Mittens, who was snuggled into his neck, the traitor. Walking over to the windowsill, he planted his ass there instead of in the seat in front of the desk like a normal person. "So I was hoping we could start over."

Ashley approached and curled a hand around the kitten. His warm little body was so soft that for a moment she forgot that she was angry, possibly because her fingers brushed against the hardest block of muscles she'd ever encountered.

Then she looked into the gorgeous blue eyes of Mr. Entitled and recalled that he was a jerk. For a few minutes—okay, more than a few minutes, perhaps an hour last night—she'd thought she might have made a mistake in telling Dex O'Malley he was a bad fit for this organization. Now he was here taking up all the oxygen, she realized her instincts were correct.

People like that didn't deserve kittens.

"I'll take him. You really can't help yourself to the animals."

"He looked lonely."

"Cats are never lonely. They're independent." She took a seat behind the desk with Mittens against her breast. "What can I do for you, Mr. O'Malley?"

"I think we got off on the wrong foot. With this injury—" He raised his hand and paused as if waiting for something. An apology perhaps? Not in this lifetime. "I'm out of action for a few days so that gives me more time to help out here."

"I thought you had to do it, injury or not."

"Yeah, well, I wasn't sure I'd have the time and I might not have taken it as seriously as I should have before. Which was wrong of me, not cool at all. I realize that my attitude wasn't terribly respectful. In fact, you don't have to help me out at all, but I'm hoping you'll reconsider."

That was the last thing she wanted, but he did get bitten on her watch. No one had called her out on it officially, though that Rebels PR woman had sounded very concerned yesterday when she called to check up on her player's behavior. As well she should. Dex O'Malley's appendages— all of them—were probably worth millions.

"How's your hand?"

"I'll live. How's my nemesis?"

She repressed a smile, strangely pleased that he was taking it so well. After all, he was unable to play and that had to be difficult for someone so driven.

"Bandit's bloodlust has been sated for now. Might be best to stay away from him."

"You think I'm afraid of that little punk?"

That made her laugh, though she hated herself for it. "He is a little punk, that's for sure. I'd never question your bravery, but Bandit has been through a lot. He doesn't trust easily."

"So what can I do to help?"

Ashley blinked, not so much at the words but the sincerity behind them. That couldn't be real. All part of his act to weasel his way back into her good graces.

"I'm still not sure this is a good idea."

"So you've said. But the thing is, I need this."

"This?" She looked around as if he was referring to Cora's pokey office.

"I've been steadily burning bridges for the last year, and this might be the only intact one left. Even if it's more like one of those rickety across-a-gorge ones from *Indiana Jones*."

"Hmm. Worried I've taken a—what are those curved knives the bad guys were always using to fray the edges of the ropes?"

His lips twitched. "A scimitar dagger?"

"Yeah, one of those. Worried I've cut that bridge away from one side of the gorge?"

He tilted his head, clearly enjoying how she was going with the analogy here. She was strangely enjoying it herself.

"Right now, you're my only hope."

It sounded a touch dramatic. But then she recalled his words a few moments ago: *I need this.*

Running a shelter that managed all sorts of waifs and strays, especially ones no one wanted, gave Ashley a unique perspective on the concept of second chances. She didn't know what had led Dex to the conclusion that this bridge might be his last one, but he had clearly pissed off a lot of people. His injury, his legal troubles ... maybe the risk of losing what was so important to him had him reaching for a lifeline.

"Are you sure you can do this with your hand the way it is?" She couldn't bear to be responsible for an exacerbation of his injury, yet neither did she want to turn him away when he was clearly in a bad place.

"I can't get it wet for now, so bathing puppies is probably out."

"Darn, that's what I had in mind for you." She felt a grin tugging at her lips. What was wrong with her? This guy was the worst. "Maybe you could organize the stock room? Not very glamorous but important work."

"And if I do, you'll report to the relevant authorities what a good boy I am?"

He said it with such cheek that she wondered how anyone ever said no to him about anything. She'd tried, and here they were.

"Let's see how well you do first. How long can you stay?"

"As long as you need me."

7

Forward Dex O'Malley has been placed on injury reserve
following a right hand injury sustained during practice. All other
players are expected to be present. — @RebelsInsider

BEGGING WAS NOT Dex's style, but somehow he'd managed to frame it as a poor-adorable-me situation and Ashley had bought it. After that run-in with Ruby, he'd realized that things needed to change. This town might not be big enough for both of them but he sure as hell would not be the one to blink first. He was staying, he was going to get a contract, he was going to play for the Rebels and win the damn Cup! And the best—easiest— way to make that happen was to follow the rules for a while.

Which meant charming Ashley into submission. Yesterday she'd listened as he laid out his sad story, about how he needed this to work. She'd considered it and hadn't rejected his plea out of hand.

She'd taken him seriously. Or felt sorry for him.

Either way, he was here now and he would be the best volunteer she'd ever had.

"Finished watching the video?"

Dex looked up from his phone, which had just popped out a message from Roxy, the gorgeous blonde he'd last popped, over a week ago. A long time for him, but he'd promised to be a good boy.

Such promises apparently included homework.

He wasn't allowed to interact with animals, people, or the shit that came out of either, until he'd watched a ten-minute video about the shelter—its history (82 years), its mission (save every four-legged unfortunate that crossed its path), and its rules (don't put your fingers in the cages unless you're not particularly attached to said fingers). It all seemed easy enough, but Ashley had left him alone for twenty minutes. Maybe he was supposed to play it twice?

He pocketed his phone. "Yep, seems clear enough."

"Great! Let's do a quick quiz." She grabbed a clipboard, then sat down in the chair opposite him. He took a moment to admire her form, all those curves in rolled-up jeans and a cute floral top that a woman he once dated had described as a peasant blouse. It had strings at the front, tied in a bow, and he let his mind consider the possibilities. Pulling on that bow and separating the sides to reveal pale, creamy skin

...

"So where do the animals come from?"

"The animals here?"

She nodded slowly. "Yes."

He knew this. The voice on the video—Ashley's voice, smooth and mellifluous—had just said something about ... "Mostly from other shelters where the animals are in danger of being euthanized. Which is so fucking wrong, I don't even know where to start."

Ashley's eyes widened. Maybe she didn't approve of

cursing. There was something a little prim and proper about this chick.

He liked it, even if she didn't like him.

She hadn't warmed up to him yet, but that didn't worry him. He'd have her eating out of his hand soon enough.

"That's right. We're a no-kill shelter so we collect animals that have been dropped off at others in the area and process them here. We also get some animals brought in because they're strays. We check for—"

"Microchips."

"Correct." She looked pleased, and there it was: a zing of pleasure because she approved of something he said. He couldn't believe she was quizzing him like Mrs. Gilligan used to do in tenth grade English *and* that he was strangely enjoying it. "We have a wand that allows us to scan and find out. Unfortunately not enough people chip their pets."

"Probably want the option to dump them later. Leave no trace."

Cue Ashley *not* looking pleased, which didn't seem to make a difference as far as his dick was concerned. He was digging everything about this woman, which was strange because she was not his usual type. She was too earnest, too judgmental, and curvier than he typically went for.

"I wouldn't take such a pessimistic view. Chipping is expensive for some pet owners. They might not be able to afford it."

Confirmed: she was a glass half-full type. You'd have to be, working here.

"We also get some owners who drop off their animals. They say they don't fit the family anymore or their landlords don't allow them, that kind of thing. It's rare when people are up front about it. Most people don't want to admit they've made a mistake." She sounded disturbed by this behavior, so he waited while she sorted that out in her head and took a breath. "Okay, next. What is the recommended attire for our volunteers?"

He must have glazed over at that part while watching the video. For the volunteer manager in front of him, he'd say a pale blue bra with lace trim and—*focus, man.*

"Hazmat suit." He threw it out confidently, so she'd assume he was joking while he stalled for time.

"If only they were provided," she said with a laugh. "Some of the messes we have to deal with."

He liked her laugh. It had a dirty tone to it.

She waited patiently for his answer.

"Casual clothes?" he offered, less sure now, but taking his cue from her outfit.

"Yes, but more specifically ..."

"Sweats?" He gestured to his shorts, which dropped her gaze to his thighs. Despite it being early March and the temps outside being in the forties, he tended to run hot. Lucky for her, that meant he was showcasing thick, muscular thighs, the gold standard for a hockey player. Would she take the opportunity to ogle now that he'd given her permission?

She did look, but more of a quick assessment with no heat in it. Interesting.

"Actually, it would be better if you wore longer pants. Sweats are fine but you want to be covered up in case the dogs scratch or the cats get clingy. They'll be climbing you like a tree before you know it." She added a few extra words under her breath.

"What's that?" Though he'd heard. *"Like everyone else."* That's what she'd said, the cheeky minx.

"Nothing." A shockingly pretty blush suffused her cheeks.

"Something about people climbing me like a tree?"

She looked up through the curtain of her caramel-brown lashes, a little embarrassed. *Now we're getting somewhere ...*

"Sorry, that was rude."

"Just sayin' how it is, right? I'm a popular guy."

"Yes, you are."

"Do we need to discuss the elephant in the room?"

She smiled thinly. "No elephants here, Mr. O'Malley. There are other facilities for the exotics."

"It's Dex. And it's okay if you've seen that video. A lot of people have."

Her expression was pained. "I don't typically follow celebrity gossip, but yes, I've seen it. I needed to research you if you're going to be volunteering here. You have a good left hook."

Cute, but they both knew that wasn't the video he meant.

"I was thinking of the other video. The one from last year. My sex tape." He finger-quoted the phrase, though it wasn't clear which part needed that. Maybe *tape* because that was old tech. Or *sex* because it wasn't some full penetration deal, just a blow job. No big deal.

The mention of sex had the desired effect: the air was suddenly charged with ions of electricity. *Zing.* Oxygen was in short supply. *Zing.* The chair creaked with a squirming body. *Double zing.*

Ashley smiled, again with the patience of a saint because, as it turned out, *she* was completely unaffected.

In fact, Dex was the one feeling a bit hotter than usual. *What the ...*

"I'd have thought you'd be sick of people discussing it." She leaned in and patted his arm lightly. There was that zing again, though less enjoyable now. "Don't worry. This is a safe space, a gossip-free zone, miles from the paparazzi. No one will be asking for selfies or making glib references to your sex life or pumping you for free tickets. No muckraking here, except for the dog kennels. I'll make sure of it."

"Oh, okay." That was good, right? He wouldn't have to suffer pointed looks or jibes about his dick. He could fly under the radar, and just be ... himself.

Anonymous. Regular. Ordinary.

Except he wasn't sure he wanted to be that guy, or even who that guy was. If anything, *that* Dex was one boring fucker. Hell, why was he getting up to all sorts, if not to make life more interesting?

Another quick, almost pitying smile from Ashley. "Back to the orientation, okay?"

~

ASHLEY CLOSED HER OFFICE DOOR, took a seat behind the desk, and opened the Skin Deep app.

Three hits since she'd looked at it last.

All of them were older, as in at least fifteen years older. Definitely on the upper range of her profile wants, but then maybe she was on the upper range for theirs. Maybe they all wanted twenty-two-year-old Pilates instructors with side-lines in babysitting and she was the best they could manage.

She wished now she'd gone with a regular dating app, one with photos. But she was trying to set an example for Willa, one that said looks were unimportant. It was what was inside that mattered.

At least that's what she'd told herself. Deep down she knew there was more to it, that glimmer of hope that she could make an impression with her conversation before anyone saw she had a few extra pounds of baggage, both literal and metaphorical.

First up was a forty-eight-year-old mortgage advisor named Steve.

Likes: sailing, Italian food, and Survivor.

Dislikes: people who can't take a joke.

Next.

Rob was forty-six, divorced, and a father to twin toddlers. He was looking for someone with a "nurturing personality." Sounded like he was looking for a stepmom for the twins, and while Ashley couldn't fault him for laying it out there, she wasn't sure that was the dynamic she needed from the start.

Which left Jerome, a forty-five-year-old realtor who seemed to have a sense of humor. "Looking to make a connection—but that's what they all say, right?"

Right, Jerome. That is what they all say.

This was so much work. Why couldn't she just meet someone and go straight to the "comfortable with each other" part of the 'ship? Romance for Ashley, these days, was little more than a fuzzy concept, something gleaned from books or Hallmark movies. There had been none of that with Greg. Everything had happened so fast. Too much alcohol, too few inhibitions, one night of drunken passion. His reaction when she told him she was pregnant: *You're not going to keep it, are you?*

And when she said she would, whether he could help or not, he stepped up.

If stepping up was inviting her (reluctantly) to move into his one-bedroom apartment and making about 25% of her OB appointments. He loved Willa, but he had never fallen for Ashley. The romance didn't have time to bloom, not when reality crashed the party so soon.

While Ashley might miss having a co-parent on the spot, she didn't miss the sniping or the bitterness that enveloped them because they'd tried to be a full-fledged family. Too many wasted years, and now, at the grand old age of thirty, Ashley felt like she was behind the eight ball, playing catch-up with her best years already in the past. Was it too soon to be dipping her feet back into the dating pool? Willa wanted her to date—along with Vera, the two of them should open their own life coaching business—but surely this feeling of ambivalence signified she wasn't ready.

What would forty-five-year-old Jerome expect of her? A connection? But then he undercut it with a joke about how clichéd that sounded. Did that make him funny or jaded?

This was her problem. She had started to second-guess everything during this journey back into the dating scene. Even the most seemingly innocuous interaction made her anxious.

Like this morning with Dex O'Malley. She'd made that crack about how everyone wanted to climb him, which was so inappropriate. There he was with his thick thighs and hairy calves and broad shoulders. Not to mention his sparkling blue eyes and easy smile. He hadn't taken offense, just used it as an opening to talk about his sexual history.

There was no shame attached to his attitude. Not that she felt ashamed about sex, but it had been so long. She could barely remember what it was like to be attracted to someone in an all-encompassing, pulse-spiking, loins-throbbing way. That part of her had gone dormant years ago, even as she and Greg continued their once-a-week coupling, something she engaged in for his sake rather than hers. A way to keep him invested.

Look how that worked out.

Now she had this very sexual being in her place of work, and it made her think things.

Naughty things.

Such as how good he looked in those shorts that she'd had no choice but to urge him to follow the rules and cover up.

Or how his sinful mouth screwed up in concentration as he tried to recall the answers to her quiz.

Her mind had definitely strayed to that video, the one from the nightclub. Two women servicing him, and Dex O'Malley lying back like the lord of the manor, accepting all that pleasure as his right.

She couldn't imagine being that free, not when she'd lived in a cage of her own design for longer than a decade.

But she needed to start with baby steps, not corrupting thoughts about a volunteer in her charge. Less focus on the transient pull of sexual attraction and more on building a connection. In the Skin Deep app, she hovered a fingertip over the contact button for Jerome.

And tapped it.

8

Tuxedo
Domestic short hair
Likes: Staring out the window
Dislikes: Grandma Jean because she uses all caps in her text
messages

DEX WOULD NEVER HAVE SUSPECTED that working with animals was so hard. Of course, he hadn't done anything with an animal yet other than been bitten by one. Instead, he was stuck with administration and janitorial duties—inventory and cleaning, all behind the scenes, too. Sophie had insisted. *We can't have anyone seeing you there just yet. Any sightings have to be carefully planned.*

He understood that, and it seemed Ashley was in on it as well, acting as if his time here allowed him to take a break from the seedier parts of his existence. Here he could be an ordinary joe, one who wouldn't be "bothered" by fans or reporters or puck bunnies.

Maybe it was good. A chance to catch his breath. He could take a little time to just *be*, which meant that he could spend time with the kittens. Ashley might have insisted he stay away from the animals until he had "proper training," but screw that. A week into his sentence, he waited until she'd gone on her lunch break and snuck into the cattery.

An older woman with purple hair was parsing food from a large plastic jug into small bowls.

"Hey there," she said, looking up.

"Hello. I'm here to see a kitten."

She grinned. "Well, you've come to the right place. Dex, right?"

"Yeah, that's right. I'm helping out for a while."

"Nice. I'm Perry. So, are you a kitten tourist or are you looking for a fur-ever friend?"

"More of a tourist." He moved in closer and walked along the aisle, his gaze arcing over the multiple cardboard boxes. They were deep and filled with small blankets, bowls of water, and food. From each one, big, luminous eyes met his.

"Wow, how many cats do you have here?"

"Right now? About 200, roughly split between adults and kittens. We usually try to place the kittens in foster homes, so they get more supervision, but sometimes we don't have enough applicants."

Dex had never seen so many cats in one place. "I wish I could bring one home, but I travel a lot for work."

He shuffled along, looking for the little gray one who'd taken a shine to him a week ago. "There he is! Hey, little guy, what's your name?"

On the wall behind the box, a polaroid said Mittens, which made sense because he had white paws. Beside the name was a note with Likes and Dislikes.

Likes: Lying in the sun

Dislikes: Orange cats because they're "special."

Someone had a sense of humor.

"Want to go for a walk, Mittens?" He checked in with Perry. "Could I pick him up? I'll stay here."

"Sure. As long as Mittens is up for it."

Mittens seemed amenable, so Dex did a circuit of the cattery, taking the kitten to visit with the other cats. Each of them had a label with entertaining little snippets about their personalities.

Katy, a black kitten with big green eyes, liked catnip and disliked the musical "Cats." (But not the film. The film is A+.) Bongo, a feisty gray, liked scratching posts (but never quality furniture!) and disliked capitalist oppression because it incentivizes imperialist expansion.

"Perry?"

"Yeah?" She placed a bowl of food in one of the boxes.

"Who figured out the cats' likes and dislikes?"

She chuckled. "That would be Ashley. She says it gives her a creative outlet."

Huh. Maybe she wasn't such a humorless drone after all. He wasn't sure what to make of her lack of attraction to him. So she'd made that comment about climbing him like a tree, but she could have been talking objectively about anyone who was reasonably attractive. Dex was unused to being dismissed so readily.

He re-focused on Perry. "How long have you worked here?"

"Well, I'm a volunteer. I try to come in twice a week, and I've been doing that for a couple of years since my husband died."

"Sorry to hear that. About your husband."

"Thanks. Lung cancer. Smoked forty a day from the age

of fifteen." She shook her head. "But some people can't be told, right?"

True. People usually did whatever they wanted, even when it was not in their best interest. Dex was the living embodiment of that philosophy.

Perry didn't seem to know who he was. He supposed not everyone was a hockey fan or followed celebrity gossip, or they did and chose to pretend it was unimportant.

He shouldn't be annoyed about that. So Ashley wanted to treat him like a regular guy. Except he wasn't a regular guy. He was Dex Fucking O'Malley, emphasis on the fuck-ing, and that usually gave him some sort of cachet. Without those labels, he was a very dull boy.

Maybe *with* those labels.

Dex O'Malley
Likes: Hockey, sex, and having a good time
Dislikes: Prudes and party poopers

He was nothing without hockey. That was running a circuit in his brain. If he lost that, he'd lose everything. He needed to make this volunteer thing work because he could not emerge from that courtroom with anything close to a conviction.

Which meant he had to be extra nice to their fearless leader.

"How many volunteers are there?"

"Maybe ten? Cora and Ashley are the only full-time employees, and we have Vet Marty as a part-timer. This place really needs as many hands on deck as possible. Every day, we get new animals, and any money that comes in has to go to food, medical care, and keeping the lights on."

"So how is this place funded?"

"Donations. The biggest one we get is from the hockey team. Without that, we probably couldn't keep afloat."

That made sense. It also explained why Ashley was forced to take him on against her better judgment. This place and likely her job were dependent on donations and the Rebels controlled a major stream of income.

He wasn't sure how to feel about that. It didn't make him feel wanted, that was for sure. But it did mean that he had some leverage.

So they could do with money. Tara said he shouldn't try to buy his way out of it, but an anonymous donation would be a good thing, wouldn't it? At least, he'd know then that he wasn't a one-trick pony. He helped charities!

But what he really needed to do was work his magic on Ashley.

"So what's the deal with the boss lady?"

"Cora?"

He shook his head. "Ashley."

He was taking a chance that Perry might have a touch of the gossip hound about her, not unlike some of his teammates who liked dealing in a bit of dirt.

"Ashley is wonderful. Works harder than anyone here, is amazing with the animals and the humans. Never has an unkind word for anyone."

Dex couldn't agree with that last observation. She'd called him an "attention whore" when she found him in her office. But maybe she was right.

"Is there a Mr. Ashley?"

Perry passed him a couple of small bowls and pointed at the boxes on one side of the room. "There was. She's recently divorced." She lowered her voice. "He cheated."

"Sounds like a jerk."

"But she's dating again. I heard her talking about it with Toby. Using her phone."

Like an app? Apps were filled with weirdos and people looking for casual sex. Not that he'd ever used one, but he'd shared a hotel room with Hudson Grey a few times and that guy had met his firefighter fiancé on a hook-up app.

"Must be tough to get out there, especially for a single mom," Perry continued, clearly enjoying the room to run Dex had offered with his nosy questions. "But a woman like that has so much to offer. She'll be snapped up in no time."

Probably. Though guys had weird ideas about single moms. They came with responsibilities that tended to interfere with most men's need for undiluted attention. Dex didn't like the idea of Ashley getting the runaround from some guy.

He didn't like the idea of her dating at all, which was strange considering he'd only met this woman a week ago.

"Perry, tell me more."

9

"Hey, girl, how's it going?"

Ashley looked up from the order sheet she was working on to see Kennedy Clark with Bucky the Wonderdog. Kennedy used to volunteer at the shelter before her concierge business took off, and every now and then she stopped by to say hi. She also happened to be married to Reid Durand, one of the Rebels centers.

"Hey! It's been ages." Ashley stood to hug her friend, a gesture made slightly awkward because of her baby bump. "When are you due?"

"Beginning of June. Three months and I am so ready."

"I remember that. Enjoy the quiet time now."

"That's what my gran says. But Reid just wants it over with, too. Mostly because he's dying to meet the baby." She thumbed at Bucky, who was waiting patiently like the good one-eyed dog he was. "He thinks his experience with this little guy makes him qualified."

Ashley laughed as she gestured to her friend to take a seat. "Wait until the baby's keeping him up all night—we'll see how qualified he thinks he is then."

Greg had been pretty much useless when it came to the nighttime feeding. Fairly useless overall. But Willa said he got up in the middle of the night the few times she'd stayed over with him since his new baby was born. This time, he seemed determined to get it right.

Not bitter. Not at all.

"You should see him with Bucky." Kennedy was still waxing lyrical about Reid's father-to-be potential. "Plus he's reading all the books. Reid's big on research."

"I'm thrilled for you guys." She meant it even if her lived experience didn't quite make the grade. "I do miss you around here, though."

Kennedy grinned and ran a hand through her blonde hair, which seemed to have a few more pink streaks in it than before. She'd always rocked a punk girl vibe and Ashley was gratified to see that marriage and imminent motherhood hadn't changed her.

"I miss it, too. Oh, I said I'd scope out a puppy for my brother-in-law and his girlfriend. Have you met Bast and Pepper?"

"Uh, no. But I'm sure I will when the Rebels org decides he needs a little reputation rehab. At your service." She gave a mock bow from her seat.

Kennedy's eyes lit up. "Right, Reid said you were babysitting Dex O'Malley. How's that going?"

"Well, he showed up several hours late, was bitten by one of the residents, and seems to think we're all obsessed with his love life. So fairly excellent, I'd say."

"Sounds like Dex. He's got quite the rep. Must be nice to have something pretty to look at, though. Very easy on the eyes."

She couldn't disagree. Only this morning, she'd found her gaze drawn to his tightly-knit back muscles while he hauled a 20lb bag of cat food down from one of the shelves. Then she remembered that she was old enough to be his ... older sister.

"Sure, he's handsome, but I'm done with lookers. I've been trying this dating app that doesn't have photos."

Kennedy made a face. "Why do people think that would ever work? Appearances might be deceptive but think of the disappointment if you connect with someone and then find out they do nothing for you below the waist."

"Better to separate that out. At least, in my experience." If Jerome turned out to be handsome, then bonus points. But she couldn't trust that. Animal attraction was all well and good, but it faded. Sometimes as soon as the test turned positive. "Sex is overrated."

"Hmm, okay."

Ashley laughed. "I'm thinking I might be too old for all that nonsense. I just want to meet someone I can have a conversation with, who isn't so obsessed with that surface stuff. Who'll rub my feet and make me tea when I'm sick." So far, her text exchanges with Jerome were promising. Boring, but then that was probably for the best. No chance she'd be taken unawares. "I know, I sound so ancient. This is what happens when you become a mom—just you wait!"

Kennedy chuckled, more at Ashley than with her. "Speaking of the true love of your life, how is Willa?"

Ashley talked a few minutes about her daughter and her latest obsessions—Taylor Swift, manga, butterflies, weird, inaccessible art—and then clammed up upon realizing she was babbling.

"Sorry, sometimes I forget she's my daughter and no one else is as interested."

"Except her dad." Ashley must have made a face because Kennedy asked, "So what's the latest on that front?"

Back when Kennedy worked here, Ashley had shared about Greg's shortcomings. "He continues to disappoint me and my kid, but nothing new there."

"I'm sorry." Kennedy winced, obviously conscious that she'd landed a good one in Reid and didn't want to brag.

"Yes, yes, Reid adores you."

"He does." She grinned. "But not every guy has the emotional intelligence to make a relationship work. And it did take him a while to get there. Now back to you. You're looking for someone to rub your feet and make you soup—"

"Tea."

"Okay, tea. But you also have other needs. Maybe don't be so quick to give up on your sex life, grandma." She looked thoughtful. "Is this about what Greg said, about not being attracted to you anymore?"

Ashley had forgotten just how much she'd confided in Kennedy. Blame that on one too many Bacardi and Cokes down at the Empty Net.

"It's not exactly a confidence booster. 'I'm leaving you for the gorgeous nubile twenty-two-year-old babysitter. And by the way, you repulse me.'" At Kennedy's grimace, she held up a hand. "So he wasn't that blunt, but he didn't mind sharing his lack of attraction to me. And it makes me wonder if it was always like that. If he had to force himself to have sex with me because I just didn't do it for him after the one night that changed everything?"

Kennedy shook her head. "Nope, not likely. Sure, there are degrees of attraction and levels of chemistry that make it better. But most guys will take whatever's on offer." She made a face. "Not making it better, am I?"

"No. But I appreciate you trying to convince me I'm not a complete troll."

"I thought there was a guy from a few months ago. The one with the Rottweiler?"

Ashley sighed. "He was mean to his dog."

Kennedy looked alarmed. "He hurt him?"

"No. Well, not physically. He would tell him he was ugly, and not in a cute, humorous way." Ashley lay her head down on the table. "Is it so hard to find a guy who takes me dancing, remembers my birthday, and tells me when I have weird goat hairs on my neck?"

"Weird what now?"

"You know, how every now and then you find a long, wispy hair attached to your neck or under your chin and you're wondering, why the hell didn't anyone tell me?"

Kennedy didn't look like this had ever happened to her. Probably attributable to Ashley's old lady hormones.

"So, the list is getting longer," Kennedy said, counting off on her fingers. "Foot rubs, tea-making, dancing, birthdays, goat hairs. What you need is a reset. A good cleaning of the pipes before you settle for the guy who rubs your feet and pinpoints your goat hair."

"Pipe-cleaning. Sexy."

Her friend pointed. "Seriously. You need someone who knows what he's doing and has no expectations. Just a little fun to clear out the cobwebs."

Like Dex O'Malley.

There Ashley went with the inappropriate thoughts again. She had no doubt that he'd be fantastic at a bout of cobweb-clearing and pipe-cleaning, but she really should not be thinking of him that way at all.

Kennedy was on a roll. "You know that's all I wanted from Reid when we first met. Didn't care about anything serious, just wanted to jump his bones."

"But you were living together, right? As roommates."

"Worse. I was the dog nanny and he was on a sex fast. Not for long, though." She brushed her hands together, like she'd taken care of business. "And now I'm carrying the guy's kid."

"Well, if you think it's a win ..."

"I do! I didn't at first. I didn't want to fall for someone when I had a world to still see, but Reid and Bucky made me change my mind." She gazed down at Bucky who was laying quietly at her feet, and whose ears perked up at the mention of his name. "That's what happens when you meet the right person. A complete switch-up of your world view." She touched a finger to her lips. "I have several single and recently-divorced clients who might fit the bill. I'm sure we could find someone to get you back on the horse. The sex horse."

Ashley knew she looked skeptical, but before she could voice it, Dex walked in wearing a T-shirt that said, "Sorry. Can't. Hockey. Bye."

Damn, the door had been ajar ...

"Dexter! How's it going?" Kennedy stood and leaned up on her tiptoes to kiss him on the cheek. "I heard you're having fun with the baby animals."

"That would be a negative. Ashley won't let me near them yet. I'm not qualified."

"I never said that. We just need to ease you in gently, so you don't get bitten and we don't get sued." According to Toby, Dex had tried making friends with Bandit, walking by his cage every now and then to get him used to his presence, which was very forward-thinking for a man who had a limited future with the shelter. He'd also visited the cattery, per Perry. Kind of sneaky, but she couldn't begrudge anyone time with the kittens.

Bucky moved in and sniffed Dex's sweatpants, now

covering all those muscles, which meant Ashley was forced to spend more time imagining all she was missing.

"Okay if I pet him?" he asked, possibly a little gun-shy when it came to strange dogs, though Ashley would have thought Dex had met Bucky before.

"Of course! He's very friendly."

Dex hunkered down and gave Bucky a good old rubdown. The lucky dog was practically purring by the end of it.

"Aw, you've made a new friend," Kennedy said proudly.

Dex and Bucky looked so happy at this prospect that Ashley's heart softened toward the scallywag. The human one.

"Did you need something?"

Dex looked up at Ashley, then at Kennedy, as if contemplating whether to speak freely. He redirected his ocean-blue gaze at her. "Just wanted to apologize."

"For?"

"Bringing up the video the other day. I embarrassed you and that wasn't my intention."

Ashley opened her mouth to respond, then shut it again. Had she been embarrassed? She didn't think so, but she'd obviously given him the impression she was some sort of prude. She wasn't! Not at all.

"I'm sorry if I came off as judgmental."

"That's okay. Kind of used to it." He stood and placed his hands in the pockets of his sweats which drew her attention to his hands.

In his pockets.

Near all that ... action. Did the man have to be so virile and male?

She swallowed and shifted in her seat, as if that could

stop the color rising in her cheeks. It was rather ridiculous the effect he had on her.

"You shouldn't be used to it. People judging you. That's not fair."

Dex looked like he didn't agree. "Anyway, just wanted to let you know. Feel free to ignore me when I start spouting crap again."

She laughed, a little too loudly. "Oh, you're fine. Not to worry."

"Okay, then." His lips curved as he headed out, all teeth and sparkle. Gah, that smile!

Once they were alone again, Kennedy turned to her, a big grin on her face.

"What's that about?"

"Hmm?"

"Come on. You two were all cute around each other."

Ashley shook her head. Was that cute? It had felt nothing but awkward on her side. It was so long that she no longer recognized cute.

"Here I am offering the services of unnamed single and divorced clients, when you have someone a lot closer to hand who'd do the trick."

"Toby's gay." Kennedy was not referring to Toby.

"Ahem. I'm talking about a troubled professional hockey player who you're spending a lot of time with."

It was like the woman could read her mind. "Are you kidding? I'm his boss." And why did her voice sound so squeaky?

Kennedy scoffed. "Hardly. You're his supervisor during this particular short-term venture." She added finger quotes around "supervisor" despite the fact it was not finger quotable. It was reality.

"And I'm supposed to report on whether he's done a good job. To a judge. That's a conflict of interest."

Yet her blood had fizzed at the mention of it. Dex O'Malley interested her, which made no sense. He was not unlike her ex: feckless, charming, a complete ne'er-do-well. Except he obviously did something well enough to get media attention, and she wasn't talking about his game on the ice.

"I'm not interested in someone like that." At Kennedy's frown, she added quickly. "Not that there's anything wrong with him. I'm sure he's a very nice, charming man underneath all that square-jawed handsomeness. It's just—he gets around. And that's a little too similar to my ex."

"Right, but you're not looking for anything serious. Just a little fun. Orgasms."

"That's what *you* said. I said I wanted conversation and foot rubs and tea."

"Well, some of us have all that *and* hot sex in one muscled package."

"So. Smug." Ashley pointed over Kennedy's shoulder. "The door's behind you."

"I'm trying to help you get laid, lady."

"Yeah, but not with someone I'm working with. That's not a good idea?"

Where did that question mark come from? It was as if her voice thought that upward lilt at the end of that sentence was appropriate.

Not appropriate. So not appropriate. None of this was appropriate.

Kennedy shrugged. "It's not *not* a good idea."

"I don't know what that means."

"It means that if you're both interested, you should go for it."

The hockey hunk and the frumpy mom ... sure, that could happen.

"I'm not immune to his charms. But that's all there is to it."

"You sure?"

"Very sure. He's far too attractive."

Kennedy grinned. "No such thing."

10

"LET'S TAKE A LOOK, SHALL WE?" Dr. Morgan unraveled the bandage and studied the stitches. "Not bad. Healing nicely."

"Can I practice?"

"Give it another couple of days. You can work out in the gym, though. Just be careful about anything you have to hold onto. Equipment and the like."

A chuckling Cal Foreman chirped in from his position, flat on his back one exam table over while he got a massage on his adductor. "Yeah, be careful about holding onto your equipment, O'Malley."

"Luckily I'm left-handed, so I'm okay there."

"Ha." Foreman sniffed. "So how's it going at the puppy shelter?"

"Fine. Making friends. Influencing people."

"I heard."

As the doc was still bandaging his hand, Dex squinted in his teammate's direction. "You heard what exactly?"

"That you pissed off Ashley, i.e. the woman you need to impress. Making her watch your sex tape."

"Uh, that did not happen. In fact I apologized in case me bringing it up made her uncomfortable."

"So you made her talk about your dick instead?"

"No. Did not do that." What kind of rumors were being spread about him? "Who told you that?"

"Kennedy might have mentioned that you were super sweet to Ashley."

Exactly. "And?"

"That you were super sweet while saying sorry for being an asshole."

"Who's sorry for being an asshole?" Kershaw had just walked in, unpeeling his T-shirt as he took a seat on one of the benches.

Foreman responded with, "O'Malley. He's been laying the groundwork at the puppy shelter, talking up his sex tape."

"I have not. I was trying to apologize for—"

Kershaw snorted. "Sounds like you're just making trouble for yourself. Ashley's not gonna stand for that."

"You know her?"

"Yep. She was amazing when we adopted our cocker spaniel, Bacon. Let us do playdates with Hatch and the puppy to make sure we were a good fit. She's kind of by the book but cool as well."

So everyone kept telling him. She had a poor opinion of him, that was for sure, and because of that, yesterday he'd done something he would never have dreamed of doing in a million years:

He had listened at a door.

Twice.

As he raised a hand to knock on the office door, he overheard Kennedy and Ashley chatting about her dating. And her ex. And all these things she wanted in a guy, none of which sounded all that unreasonable. Quite enlightening, in fact.

Then because he'd learned so much, he decided to linger outside after he'd visited and delivered his apology. Surely the two friends would chat about the hockey player volunteer who had just stopped by—and yep, Dex was rewarded with a gift for his stealthy eavesdropping.

I'm not interested in someone like that. He gets around.

He didn't usually indulge in shame but hearing that from Ashley had made him feel … something. So he wasn't good enough for her. Fine. He wasn't interested, either.

"She's been pretty by the book with me, too. Won't let me do any fun stuff until I've done all the crappy jobs."

Cal grinned. "And you thought it would just be petting puppies and playing with kittens. Because *that's* how the world works."

He'd thought it would be a suck on his time, and it was. But he'd hoped the perks of being around animals would make up for it. Instead, he was hauling cat food, sweeping floors, and overhearing negatives about him.

The doc finished up his bandage and Dex walked out of the exam room to work off his energy in the gym. It wasn't long before his thoughts returned to Ashley.

Her ex had run off with the babysitter and told her he wasn't attracted to her as his parting shot. Sure, if faced with the choice between a tight-bodied hottie and a—fuck that! Ashley was gorgeous, with all those delectable curves, the great rack, the hair he could imagine tunneling his fingers through while she wrapped that prim little mouth around his cock. The father of her kid had actually told her she didn't do it for him? What a tool.

On the other hand, Dex didn't have the first clue about marriage. The closest he'd come was his fake engagement to

Tara which lasted less than twenty-four hours. Marriage took work, or so he'd heard, and people fell out of love, or were never in love in the first place. Maybe attraction faded in the midst of laundry and child-rearing and all the mundane stuff that made up a life.

All that reality could dampen the spark of anyone's sex life.

But Dex knew this much: Ashley Adams was hot as hell, even if she didn't think Dex was worth giving the time of day.

AFTER PRACTICE for everyone and gym for Dex, Durand Junior—Bast—suggested they go to lunch, and everyone decided on the Sunny Side Up Diner.

Maybe she wouldn't be there.

But he didn't want to risk it. No way in hell was he going to breathe the same air as Ruby O'Malley.

Dex tried suggesting the Italian place on Main but got no takers. It would have looked weird if he said why he couldn't go, so he told them he'd forgotten something and would catch them up later. As that left him both irritable and hungry, he stopped by the players' lounge where he ran into Isobel Chase. One of the Rebels co-owners, Isobel was married to their captain Vadim Petrov and offered skating consultancy with selected players.

"Hey, Dex, how's it going?"

"Good. Just here for a bite to eat."

"Mind if I join you?"

Like he could say no. But he didn't mind, really. He didn't know Isobel all that well, but she'd always struck him as a cool girl. A former hockey player, she knew the game inside out, and because she was married to his cap, there was no chance of him even thinking about her in that way, not if he valued his balls.

He grabbed a prepared sandwich and sat at one of the lounge tables with her.

She pushed her dark hair into a pony-tail. "How's the injury?"

"Okay. Should be back in action soon."

"I heard a dog bit you? For real?"

He relayed the story, which had her laughing. After a moment, she tilted her head and looked at him squarely. "So what do you think about this reputation rehab business? Really?"

Really, he thought it was BS and while he was probably not going to be incarcerated, he would likely be convicted of something and put on waivers before the end of the season.

"I think ... I shouldn't have lost my temper. It had already been addressed in the game. I should have let the penalty process play out."

Two days ago, Kyle Hughes was forced to sit through a phone-in disciplinary hearing and was fined twenty grand, which would be added to the Players' Emergency Assistance Fund. Dex would have given anything to be a fly on the wall.

She shook her head. "I get it. Sometimes it's easier to lead with our gut. Good for the ice, not always off it. At least, that's the advice my father would give."

"You must miss him." Clifford had died seven years ago, leaving his floundering team to his three daughters, who had taken the baton and turned the org's fortunes around, much to the hockey world's surprise.

She blinked. "Yeah, I do. I'm the only one of us that does, to be honest. He was tough on all of us. Well, me and Harper. Violet never met him, but he left his mark."

"I met him a few times. When I was a kid." Should he tell her this? She might think he was trying to make himself sound special. But she looked interested, so he plowed on. "He sort of mentored me from afar."

Isobel's eyebrows lifted. "In what way?"

"He spotted me at a rink when I was twelve. I'd never played hockey and I was dicking around when he called me over and said he thought I should take it seriously. Learn to play. Then he sent Anton."

Her green eyes went wide. They weren't quite the same shade as Ashley's, which were more of a Granny Smith apple green.

"Anton Ballard?"

"Yeah. I'm not sure I'd be here—playing hockey, any of it —without your dad getting involved."

She smiled her approval. "Well, he loved finding a prospect. And I'm thrilled that he had such a positive influence on you. I know you had a rough go of it."

Of course she did. As the team owner, she would have background information on all the players. He wondered how much. Did the details of Ruby O'Malley's case make her file?

A shiver went through his body at the idea she might have heard the sordid details of his childhood. She might even think "like mother, like son," or blood would out. Maybe that was what Ashley sensed in him—a no-good troublemaker who led with his dick and fists.

"Hockey means everything to me. Nothing else matters." It was suddenly important that Isobel know this, especially with all the trouble he was knee-deep in. If he could make an impression, maybe she'd remember when it came time to talk trades or worse, waivers.

She smiled. "I remember feeling that way. Don't get me

wrong, it's still important, but it's good to have some balance, y'know. Friends, family, hobbies."

Friends were few and far between and as for family, forget it. "My hobbies tend to be the X-rated kind."

She laughed, but then she turned serious. "I think you underestimate yourself, Dex."

How could he think of himself any other way? Even St. Ashley of Riverbrook Animal Shelter didn't think he was good enough for a turn in the sheets, which was fine. He didn't need this woman's approval. All he needed was whatever reference she would provide to the judge in his court case.

Well, your honor, professional hockey player Dex O'Malley, despite his inability to be good at anything other than striking a puck—and that's currently debatable—and screwing anything that moves, was a model volunteer at Riverbrook Animal Shelter. Every kitten adored him, every dog wanted to be his friend, and he managed to get through his shifts without drawing any negative publicity or attention to himself or the shelter. Please go easy on him.

"I'm not really anything special," he murmured, in response to Isobel's observation.

"That's where you're wrong." She patted his arm. "Everyone on this team has something to offer. My dad saw something in you, Anton saw it, and the brass in Rebels admin saw it. It's why you're here. Hockey is great—it's our lifeblood—but it can't be the only thing. That's why I think this volunteer gig is good for you, not as a PR move, but because it might make you see yourself in a different light. Not just as a great forward, but also as a cool human being. We have to take these challenges and see them as the opportunities they truly are."

She shrugged. "Or maybe I'm just envious of the guy who gets to play with kittens and puppies as punishment."

DEX HELD the door open for the woman coming out of the coffee shop and got a sexy smirk in return.

See, Ashley? That's how women respond to me.

Fucking hell, it was ridiculous that he was still hung up on this! It had been three whole days since he'd overheard her talking about him to Kennedy. In that time, he'd focused on getting back to form and proving his worth to the powers that be. He'd watched tape, crushed it at the gym, attended morning skate, all the necessary to prove he meant business. And if all that busyness helped him forget about Ruby, all the better. This was his team and his town. He was going nowhere.

As for Ashley ... so he'd met a woman unimpressed by his charm, good looks, and thick thighs. Big deal. No one liked to be dismissed out of hand as if they had zero to offer a top-quality woman like that, but it couldn't be helped.

After ordering his double tall Americano, he was waiting for it on the other side of the bar when this gem tickled his eardrums:

"I don't think men are cut out for monogamy."

Usually that would be a woman's line, but here it was, spoken by a guy in one of those voices where every statement was likely accompanied by a smirk. Dex couldn't see him as he and his companion were seated behind a pillar, but he could make out a shapely leg—female—clad in dark tights with a green chevron design. They tapered to fur-lined ankle boots with cats' whiskers on the zipper. Cute.

The reply when it finally came, because a line like that

clearly prevented speech for a good ten seconds, knocked him back on his heels:

"That's a rather pessimistic statement."

Spoken by ... fuck, Ashley.

She sounded so disappointed, and who could blame her? It *was* pessimistic.

It was also strange that he would hate this guy and his male-centric wisdom when it roughly aligned with Dex's own brand of thinking. It wasn't so much that he thought men incapable of monogamy—he had the evidence of his teammates to put the lie to that—but Dex himself wasn't really a one-woman kind of guy. Not that he'd ever cheat or lie, but he preferred to be up front about his commitment levels.

As in, *this thing we got going on is going nowhere, baby*.

So why was he pissed at another member of the dick-owning brigade for being up front about *his* needs? That was clearly where this conversation with Ashley was going and Dex should not care one iota.

Yet here he was on tenterhooks waiting for the rest.

"But it's evolution," the smirker said with no irony whatsoever. "Men are predisposed by genetics to spread their seed. Kind of hard to go against nature."

"Is it though? That sounds like an excuse to justify bad behavior."

"Oh, Ashley, Ashley, Ashley."

If Dex didn't want to punch the guy before, he certainly did now. His fingers tingled with the desire to ball them into a fist and lash out, just like he had when Kyle Hughes started pushing his girl around in the Empty Net.

The little Dex knew of his supervisor at the shelter was that she was a no-nonsense kind of chick. Surely she wasn't going to put up with this garbage person?

Apparently she was the most patient woman alive because the guy was still talking.

"Women are always so anxious to tame a man's true nature. You work with animals, so you must know how difficult it is to overturn years of genetic programming. The seed needs to be out there."

Okay, enough.

Dex rounded the pillar and placed himself squarely in front of the table. Two sets of eyes looked up—one wide with surprise and possibly anticipation because the possessor of said eyes had just met his favorite hockey player (wishful, but not entirely unlikely), the other narrowed in disdain because that was par for the course for this woman when faced with one Dex O'Malley.

"Ashley." That's all he had.

"Uh, hi." She blinked, looking slightly hopeful that he might have a better reason for interrupting than the need to make his presence known.

"You're ... Dex O'Malley!" The Smirk had finally picked his jaw off the floor.

Dex took another look. Ashley's date—because that must be what this was and fuck if it didn't chap his balls for some reason—was older than her. Far too old, in fact, for this vibrant woman.

And since when had he thought that?

Ignoring The Smirk, he turned back to Ashley. "So I couldn't help overhearing your conversation while I waited for my double tall Americano. Now, I know you're looking for adult conversation, a cup of tea, and a guy who'll rub your feet, but surely you're not going to put up with this bullshit just for a shot at a decent foot massage. Hell, I can give you that. Maybe not the adult conversation, but you shouldn't have to come out of it with bleeding ears."

Ashley bit her lip and fuck if that wasn't a hot-as-Hades move right there. Every time he met her, he was struck by something else. This time it was her lips, which were pink and plump and the perfect shape for his—nope, that was not why he was here.

He fought his way back to reality. "So what do you say?"

Her brow crimped. "About what?"

"Are you going to put up with this bullshit from ..." He waved at her date.

"Jerome," Ashley supplied.

"Jerome." He turned to The Smirk, aka Jerome. "Listen, man, I don't know what your goal is for dating, but let me give you some free advice. No woman or hockey player wants to hear about evolutionary genetics being the reason for your inability to keep your dick in your pants. Now I'm probably not one to talk given that I have spread myself around fairly indiscriminately lately, but I *always* wrap it before I tap it." Back to Ashley. "I wouldn't trust this guy is doing that, not with the love-words he's been spouting about his seed."

Ashley blinked, and her lips kicked up at one corner, and that's when Dex knew he had won. He wasn't sure what yet, or whether there was even a prize up for grabs, but he'd won something. A ray of the woman's sun, which was probably impossible to catch. But he'd let it warm him for a precious moment.

"Okay, I'll be over here if you need me." Dex nodded at Ashley, ignored Jerome, and returned to the bar to pick up his drink.

Then he waited.

11

Jerome
Likes: Coffee, Breaking Bad, U2
Dislikes: People who claim it was better in the old days.

ASHLEY HELD her breath as she watched Dex walk away. Of course she wasn't going to put up with Jerome's bullshit. In fact, she'd been about to say something suitably cutting and incredibly witty when Dex showed up and stole her thunder.

I'll be over here if you need me.

She didn't need him. She had this situation completely under control.

The moment she'd sat down, she could tell Jerome was not going to work out. He'd given her one of those up-down-what-the-fuck-are-you-wearing looks, then added a sneer which made her feel awful.

She thought she looked Spring cute, with her fun tights and corduroy skirt and cat whisker boots. It was a nod to her job and her love of animals, but Jerome obviously did not approve.

Then he'd said she looked like a mom.

Her profile was honest about her mom credentials, yet this guy thought she needed to know she had mom energy. Because that was what ... his out when this didn't go well? (Which he'd clearly already decided because she wasn't sexy enough for a coffee date at two o'clock in the afternoon!)

Politely, they'd exchanged some words about the music playing in the coffee shop (Joni Mitchell, who Ashley loved, but who Jerome proceeded to label as "some whiny folk singer"), coffee prices, and using an app with no photos for dating.

Jerome was definitely regretting that part of his dating strategy.

And so was she because Jerome did absolutely *nothing* for her. Kennedy was right about that. Jerome was conventionally attractive, she supposed, but his eyes weren't as blue as Dex O'Malley's and his shoulders weren't as broad.

None of that should have mattered. It was incredibly unfair of her to compare a forty-five-year-old realtor to a professional athlete in his prime, yet she couldn't help thinking about her volunteer.

And why oh why had Jerome brought up the spreading of his seed? Curiously, it happened right after he asked why she was no longer with her child's father.

Sometimes these things don't work out, Jerome. You're forty-five and unmarried. You do the math.

She hadn't said that, but she'd wanted to. She wanted to quit this date before it sucked from her chest any more of her hope about human beings. Instead she'd listened, worried that this might be the best she could get. That she wasn't attractive enough for a normal guy, so she would have to compromise and date weirdos.

And then Dex was there, looming over them and

looking like he might want to repeat the fist-first actions that had landed him as a volunteer at the animal shelter. He'd seemed so outraged on her behalf, an almost youthful outrage that reminded her of a time when Ashley used to get mad at people and situations and the world in general. A time when she cared more. Dex's outrage was really ... nice.

Better than nice. Wonderful, and completely unexpected.

Now he was sipping his coffee and studying his phone, but every now and then he would raise his gaze and meet hers in a "you okay?" kind of way that made her feel wonderfully supported.

Jerome was staring at her, more interested now than he had been for any of the twenty excruciating minutes before Dex had walked over.

"You know Dex O'Malley?"

He didn't need the specifics. She opened her mouth to say he was a friend and Dex's voice came out.

"Yes, she knows me. I've been trying to bang her but she's not having it."

Ashley blew out a sigh, ostensibly annoyed, but really thrilled that Dex O'Malley didn't mind an entire coffee shop knowing she was bangable.

"He's a friend of a friend," she explained.

Jerome looked confused. Over his shoulder, he spoke out of the corner of his smirking mouth in Dex's direction. "I'm just being up front about my needs. You get it." As if a fellow dick-owner needed the explanation instead of the woman who had to put up with those "needs."

"We all get it, man," Dex said without looking up from his phone. "You're prepping the soil for your seeeeed." He dragged out the word "seed" so much that it sent Ashley into a fit of giggles, which wasn't like her at all.

Jerome stared at her until she stopped. "Have I insulted you with my opinions?"

"No, not insulted. I appreciate the honesty, but we should probably draw a line under it. I'm not looking for a guy who spreads his seed around, whether it's an evolutionary necessity or not."

Her date straightened his shoulders and shifted in his seat.

"Okay, then. If that's what you'd prefer."

"That's definitely what she'd prefer, buddy."

"Not your business," she called out softly.

Dex made a zipping motion across his lips and dipped his head, but she could tell he was smiling when he did it, which made her want to smile as well.

She looked up as Jerome stood. "Sorry about my friend." *But not really.*

"I've seen him online, so I guess I should consider myself lucky to get out of here with my nose intact."

On that prim statement, Jerome upped and left.

She folded one of her paper napkins, a touch prim herself. "Happy?"

"Thrilled," Dex said. "Don't tell me you were having a good time."

"Okay, I won't."

The scape of the chair Dex wasn't using at his table sounded like an invitation. (He had pushed it out a few inches with his foot.)

"Excuse me?"

"I'd rather not sit in the same chair as your date. Come visit."

"Do you promise not to talk about spreading your seed?"

He gave a cheery salute. "Scout's honor."

She picked up her tea, napkins, and purse and headed

over. Once seated, she took a good look at her new coffee shop companion.

Handsome as ever, but a pronounced weariness pulled at his eyes. "You okay?"

"Me? I should be asking you that."

"But I asked first." She smiled at him. "You seem a bit on edge."

He shook his head, then seemed to revise his opinion. "I've just been dwelling on the past, and how it really shouldn't have anything to do with the present or future, but somehow always manages to find a way."

She hadn't expected that, but it was rather in tune with her own thoughts.

"And this is the result."

A negligent shrug of those broad shoulders. "I'm trying to be a good guy, but then I scare off perfect strangers because I don't like what's coming out of their mouths. Should I apologize?"

"To Jerome?"

"To you."

She chewed on her lip. "I had it under control, so I didn't need your input."

"But?"

"Why do you assume there's a but?"

"I'm very attuned to the unspoken 'but' of a sentence. You wouldn't believe how much I hear it."

She shook her head, annoyed he was right. "*But* ... it was nice to have someone confirm I wasn't losing my mind. That was some wild first date conversation."

He leaned in, his expression amused, and she got a whiff of male perfection. Body wash, aftershave, a generally sexy scent that went straight to her most receptive parts.

"Right? Inside thoughts, man. Though even thinking that is past the city limits, destination Crazy Town."

"There are women who would get a kick out of that. The man they can't pin down. The seed-spreading rogue they want to tame. So much work."

He tapped his fingers on the table. "Well, dating is work. Or so I hear, given I don't actually date. But guys like that must make it harder."

"It's been a long time since I've dated. Ten years, in fact."

He gave a non-committal hum of encouragement (or she took it that way).

"My sisters raised me because our parents died when I was young and they kept me on a tight leash. Meeting my ex was my way of rebelling against all that structure. But we didn't date. Not really. It was a one-night stand and then boom, pregnant and hitched."

His eyes went soft. "Did you ever think of *not* getting married?"

"Yep, when we were headed toward divorce. We were never really compatible. He's not a settling down type, or at least I thought so until he got someone else pregnant and did all the things with her and her pregnancy that he passed over with me."

"Ouch."

She smiled ruefully. "We were so young back then and he wasn't ready to be a dad. Now, he's got some experience, so he'll be a better dad to his new little. I hope."

"But that sucks for you and your kid. He, she, they?"

Another smile. "She. My daughter."

"How old?"

"Nine going on ninety. She's amazing. So smart and funny, much more grown-up than me. She's into butterflies and comic books. She loves Skittles and astronomy and anything with wings."

"You're really proud of her."

"I am. She wants me to date. One of my sisters does as well, but ..."

"You just want someone to rub your feet and make you tea when you're sick."

Oh God. "Eavesdrop much?"

He didn't even look guilty, though why should he? She tried to recall her conversation with Kennedy which she was sure included some choice statements about this man's whoring ways.

"I love getting the inside scoop on a woman's deep-down and dirty thoughts, especially on why a woman like you would have given up on sex."

She covered her face with her hands. Oh God, how was this getting worse? She'd mentioned her lack of interest and how unattractive her ex made her feel. But right now, she was more concerned with what she'd said about *him*.

"I said some things about you that I'm not proud of. Please forgive me." That she might have hurt him made her feel awful. So he was a bit of a slut, but she shouldn't ever say that aloud.

She felt the lightest touch of his fingers brushing against hers, then one finger curling around her palm and pulling her hands away.

"Ashley, it's okay. People who listen at doors never hear nice things about themselves. I had it coming."

"That's not fair on you. I'm sorry about what I said." What *had* she said?

Of course, Dex had the receipts. "You were right. I do get around. And I'm definitely not the kind of guy a good girl like yourself would be interested in."

Good girl. She squeezed her thighs together as parts of her unused to clenching liked that phrase. Liked how it sounded on this man's lips.

"I-I'm not a good girl. One-night stand led to pregnancy, remember?"

He was still holding her hand. The warmth of his skin fizzed through her veins, making her blood bubble like Champagne.

"So you had your spotlight in the bad girl camp, but these days ... you're a very good girl."

Gah! Slippery warmth pooled between her legs for the first time in forever. She could feel her cheeks heating, her body flushing with sexual awareness. Did she have some sort of praise kink? Though given how long since she'd had decent sex, who knew what she liked?

This wasn't the time for sexual self-discovery. She had groveling to do.

"I have no right to judge you, Dex. You're young, fit, and hot. You have a lot of money and are incredibly good at your job. So you've made a couple of mistakes that landed you in hot water, but on the whole, you're just enjoying life and all it has to offer. And why not?"

"You think I'm hot?"

Of course that was what he focused on. "Like you have to ask. You know you are."

"But *you* think I am."

Interesting. "Does my opinion suddenly matter?"

"Well, you did say sex was overrated."

She pointed. "Spoken behind closed doors! And I can think that and still think you're objectively attractive. But looks aren't everything."

"No ..." But he sounded unsure, like he didn't have a Plan B. "But it's how things get started, isn't it?"

Things? "It can be, but there are other ways to connect. Looks and money only get you so far."

He made a funny sound in his throat. "What other ways?" His voice sounded weird, like she'd hit a nerve.

"Conversation, understanding, attentive listening. For example, I think you're more than a guy who gets around or a guy who's good at hockey. I think that maybe you're also good at making people feel better, or rescuing damsels from mansplaining coffee dates."

He smiled. "Thought you didn't need rescuing."

"I didn't but it was still nice of you to step in. Everyone appreciates being supported."

They were both quiet for a moment, absorbing that admission. When next he spoke, he seemed to have found his normal tone.

"So what were you doing with that guy anyway?"

"Just making my way through the apps. Looking for that ultimate foot masseur." She added a cheery wave, then felt silly and lowered her hand.

"He was too old for you."

"That's what I matched with. No one my age is interested."

He considered that. "What about the other end of the spectrum?"

"The age spectrum?"

"Right. Someone younger."

Did he mean ...? No, just a general statement about age-appropriate dating.

"Guys my age typically want someone younger than them," she said. "Older guys are usually looking for stability but maybe not with a ready-made family. People like to put their own stamp on things, start afresh."

"Damn kid getting in the way of your sex life."

"Right?" She chuckled. "But I wouldn't trade her for the world."

"Maybe you don't have to."

"What does that mean?"

"Maybe you can have your cake and get eaten out, too."

She laughed nervously. Those were provocative words for the middle of the day in a neighborhood coffee shop.

"Well, good thing I think sex is overrated."

"Ah, but it's not." He leaned in, squeezed her hand. "You just haven't been laid well in a while, I'm guessing."

Another nervous chuckle. "Are you offering?"

"Yes."

Oh. That was supposed to be a joke, practicing a flirty move, something she had little to no experience of in her repertoire. Getting drunk and knocked up at twenty required no flirting skills whatsoever. But now that she was supposedly dating again, she figured she'd need to up her game. And who better a sounding board than the always-erect-and-ready Dex O'Malley?

So yes, a joke. But that response, that clear, succinct, one-syllable response sure didn't sound like a jocular retort. It had weight to it. Sensual weight.

She pulled her hand away, but not her gaze which was locked with Dex's. Like it meant something. Like letting it slip would take them out of this bubble, a place where both of them needed to be.

"Good thing I'm your boss, then."

"Makes it hotter."

She shook her head. "Stop joking."

"Who says I'm joking?"

"Dex, I appreciate what you did earlier and what you're doing now, trying to make me feel attractive. But we need to call a halt to it."

"If that's what you want."

So serious. So not what she wanted.

"I probably should get going. I took an hour from work for this." She stood, smoothing her skirt, which drew attention to her thighs. When she looked up, he was watching her with something like hunger in his eyes.

Not that. It was in her imagination, which she needed to rein in. And he needed to stop this playacting before she let this strange emotion that felt curiously like hope permeate and sink into her marrow.

"See you for your shift tomorrow?"

"Sure, Ashley. Tomorrow."

She felt his eyes on her as she left along with the thudding of her pulse loud in her ears, and she let herself enjoy it for a few seconds before she scattered those thoughts into the cold March air.

12

ASHLEY WAS REFILLING the brochures in the reception area just as the door opened and in walked her daughter. She was supposed to be with her father.

"What happened?"

"Dad had to cut the visit short. Lottie needed him for something."

Ashley checked her phone. No further explanation from Greg.

"How did you get here?"

"He dropped me off. But Aunt Vera said she could pick me up later."

That jerk. (Not her sister, but her ex.) She stepped out from behind the counter and pulled her daughter into a hug. "You okay?"

"I'm fine." Willa drew back, but not before Ashley saw the look of hurt on her face. "The baby's important, so of course she's going to need Dad more."

"Yeah, but it's not really fair on you, is it?"

"Who said life is fair?"

That sounded like Maeve talking. Ashley didn't like when her daughter spoke and the voice of her cynical aunt emerged.

"You want to see the kittens?"

"Sure." Off she trudged, leaving Ashley a mix of angry and sorry. Though *sorry* was on the lowest register of her emotions right now. Anger was winning the day.

She shot off a message to Greg. *Are you kidding me right now?*

Then deleted it.

She tried something else. *Is Lottie okay?* Maybe it was passive-aggressive. Did she really care if Lottie was okay, given that the woman had supplanted Willa in her father's affections?

Supplanted you.

That wasn't what this was about. Ashley had been doing her best not to view the disintegration of her relationship with Greg through a lens of bitterness. Otherwise she'd end up like her sisters.

Otherwise, she'd pass on that acrid taste in her mouth to Willa.

But, for Heaven's sake, Greg made it so hard for Ashley to take the high road. At times like this she wanted to get down in the dirt and fight.

Instead, she kept her cool even when it ate away at her. Even when inside she felt like she was shriveling up, her youth slipping away until she wondered if she was going to bypass middle age and go straight to her senior years.

Because sometimes it felt as though this was it. This was all she had to offer. Reasonable comfort to her daughter, food and shelter to her animals, a sounding board for her sisters. But nothing tangible for herself. Nothing she could hang a hat on and say "this is mine."

Yesterday she had gotten a thrill out of Dex O'Malley's attention at the coffee shop. A notorious fuckboy had smiled and flirted with her and she felt like Cinderella at the ball. So pathetic.

She didn't have time to moon over a playboy hockey player who thought flirting with a soccer mom was amusing (not that Willa played soccer, but "manga mom" didn't have the same ring to it).

She had her daughter's well-being to consider. She took out her phone and started typing a message to her ex.

～

DEX KNELT BEFORE THE CAGE, where Bandit sat, looking like he was having a bad day. Dex understood completely.

"Hey there, grumpy."

Bandit ignored him.

"Yeah, I get it. You've had a bad week. Maybe a bad year. Well, I forgive you."

Again, not impressed.

This little guy wasn't like Loki. His childhood dog, a mutt with more Beagle in him than anything else, had been a friendly fella, who probably ended up in a shelter like this after Dex went into care. He hoped someone had recognized his worth, taken him home.

The sign over Bandit's cage said:

Bandit
Likes: Dinnertime
Dislikes: ~~When nerds argue about the grandfather paradox as it relates to time travel.~~ Gender inequality.

That made Dex chuckle. Ashley, he assumed.

He was tempted to touch the cage even though that was one of the big rules: don't put your fingers through the wires, especially if you're attached to them. But he was a rule-breaker through and through, or so everyone kept telling him.

Yesterday, he'd broken a rule—he'd flirted with Ashley. Not that it was a rule as such, but Sophie had been very clear that he needed to get this right and stay on Ashley's good side, especially after his inauspicious start. So what had he done?

Interrupted her date.

Called her a good girl.

Made her an offer she most definitely could refuse.

Flirting with Ashley should have been harmless, a fun way to pass the time, but something about her reaction chafed.

She didn't take him seriously. There were two possible reasons for this.

One, he wasn't worth taking seriously.

Two, she didn't believe he was sincere.

A little of both, perhaps. She'd laughed his offer off, as if she couldn't quite believe his audacity. She could have eighty-sixed him from this gig—again—but instead she'd chosen to take pity on him. He was obviously joking around, with his naughty words. After all, what else was someone like Dex O'Malley good for?

But he'd meant it.

He wanted to make her feel good. He got the impression that Ashley wasn't used to thinking of herself. Sure she was putting herself out there, but her heart wasn't in it because she didn't believe she deserved a little fun. Even that date with The Smirk seemed like a chore for her.

If she hadn't laughed in his face, if she'd recognized that he was serious in offering to show her a good time, then she wouldn't need to view sex as overrated or a chore or whatever other negatives she associated with it because it had been so long for her.

Now he was wondering how long since someone had touched her.

How long since someone had made her cheeks flush and her body hot and her pussy wet? Because he had a feeling he might have had that effect on her yesterday. She'd looked positively heated when he called her a good girl.

Ashley, the good girl. Damn, he wanted to break every rule in the book finding out how good a girl she really was.

"That would be a very injudicious thing to do."

Dex turned his head to take in the new arrival, a girl of about nine or ten with caramel-blonde hair and a serious demeanor. Her eyes blinked at him from behind big glasses, owl-like and blue and filled with the weight of the world.

"That's a big word."

"It's my word for the day."

"Cool. What does it mean?"

Her face fell and for a moment, he worried he'd asked the wrong thing. Maybe she just spouted big words without any care to their meaning. But now he realized that she wasn't worried about knowing the meaning, but that she was about to insult him.

"It means ... foolish."

"Ah. So you think me trying to make friends with Bandit here is inju—what did you say?"

"Injudicious. And just the fingers thing." Moving in closer, she squinted at him. She wore rolled-up jeans, Hello Kitty sneakers, a purse with "Swifty" on it, and a butterflies-themed sweatshirt. The ribs of the insect's wings had little jewels sewn into them. "You're Dex O'Malley!"

"Guilty. And you are ...?"

"Willa. What are you doing here? Are you going to adopt a dog?"

"I wish I could. But actually I'm volunteering."

She sat down cross-legged on the floor beside him, in that easy way that kids had. "The TV said you were injured. What happened?"

He held up his bandaged hand and thumbed in Bandit's direction. "This guy. An injudicious move on my part."

She was trying not to smile. "You mean he already bit you and you're going back in?"

"I'm kind of a sucker for punishment." Dex took another look at the dog, who was watching this exchange with interest. "I think we both are, right, fella?"

"But you have to be careful. People are depending on you."

Dex whipped his head around. "What people?"

"The team, silly. And the fans. You're a great hockey player but it's not all about you."

Well, she sure told him.

"Okay, noted. So, what's your story?"

Her lips curved. "I don't have a story."

"Sure you do. Everyone does. Let me guess, shall I?"

She nodded, her eyes sparkling with anticipation.

"You like butterflies and Taylor Swift and Hel—hmm, maybe not Hello Kitty." He looked down at her brand-new Hello Kitty sneakers. "Those were a gift but you don't wear them much."

"How did you know?"

"They have barely any scuffs on the soles, but this design was popular a couple of seasons ago." He remembered because Harper and Remy's daughter, Amelie, had received a pair during a birthday party he was invited to.

Willa looked astounded at his Sherlockian insight. "My dad gave them to me because he knows I like manga. He thinks I must like all Japanese stuff."

"So you wore them today because you were seeing your dad?"

Her shrug was more sad than careless. "I was supposed to, but he had to cancel because of the baby. Emily's my half-sister and she needs a lot of attention."

"Babies, the worst."

That made her giggle.

"There's a lot of that going around. All my teammates have babies."

"Are they cute?"

He shrugged. "If you like that sort of thing."

More giggles that were like sunshine in his chest. "And you don't?"

"That's not strictly true. A friend of mine, Tara, has a pretty cute one called Esme."

"Like in *Twilight*?"

He threw up both his hands. "That's what I said! It's kind of tempting fate to name your kid after a vampire, don't you think?"

She squinted at him and said very gravely, "But vampires aren't real."

"True. But it's still kind of weird. All I can think of is her imminent bloodlust and baby fangs. When they grow in, of course."

"You're kind of weird yourself." Her tone was one of unmistakable approval.

"Willa." Ashley stood at the door. "Don't be bothering Mr. O'Malley."

"He said I could call him Dex."

He didn't, but he liked her fudging of the truth. A woman after his own heart.

"Well, don't be bothering Dex. You can help Perry with the kitten feeding."

"I was giving him advice. Good advice."

He nodded. "True. No fingers in the cage and stop thinking of myself all the time."

She stood and brushed off her jeans. "Just be careful, okay?"

"Okay." He shared a quick glance with Ashley, who suddenly looked softer in the presence of her daughter. "Take care of yourself, Sparkle."

"Sparkle?"

"Yeah, like the jewels on your sweatshirt."

Willa's mouth stretched in a smile that lingered as she headed out.

Ashley remained behind. "Sorry, she's kind of bossy."

"That's okay. I'm used to people bossing me around."

She came in and stood before him, looking down. "What was that about fingers in the cage?"

"She told me it would be ... injudicious?"

"Ah. She's on a word of the day kick, trying to improve her vocabulary. And that's something you want to do?"

"Just trying to get him used to me. Maybe I could walk him sometimes?"

She bit her lip. So cute. "There are liability issues. If you were to get bitten again or if he bit someone else ..."

"Not on the street. Just in the play area, when no one else is around. I think he was just scared the last time, but if we spent some quality time together he might adjust better."

She gave that some consideration. "I'm a little worried about letting him go to a home with kids, especially after what he did to you. So anything we can do to socialize him ..."

His heart checked. "He's up for adoption?"

"They all are. We're organizing an Empty the Shelters event next month. Most of these animals will find homes then, but not all. But for some of them, the ones who need a little extra attention, we hold them back to see if we can get them ready for prime time."

Not all of them would find homes. That was a little closer to the bone than he expected. He pulled himself upright.

"Can I help with socializing him? I'll sign something legal absolving you of any liability."

"If you really want to do this, I don't want to stop you."

"Ah, so you're fine with me doing this probably stupid thing."

She chuckled, light and breezy. "I'd never want to stop a man from doing something stupid."

Dex put a hand on his chest. "That's cold, Ashley."

"It is, isn't it? You go ahead and walk Bandit and see if that decision comes back to bite you."

"Fair enough. Can we start now?"

"Give it ten minutes. I'd prefer if Willa wasn't here. She'll want to pet him."

Or talk to me. Dex understood Ashley's concern. He wasn't the best influence.

"I know you said you were young when you had her—"

"Pregnant at twenty, twenty-one when she came screaming into the world. Which makes me thirty, in case you're trying to work it out." Color climbed her throat, flushing her cheeks. "Not that you *would* be trying to work it out. I don't even know why I said that because our ages in relation to each other are not at all relevant. That was—I don't know what that was!"

He'd figured she was older than him, but purely because of the way she carried herself. Five years was nothing but there was a chasm of life experience.

He made her nervous, which he was used to with rabid fan girls but not with real women. That's what Ashley was— a real, authentic woman who would usually not give someone like Dex the time of day but for some reason, was skittish around him.

Christ, that turned him on.

"I was going to say that you look amazing."

Gone was the playful vibe. *Stupid, Dex, so stupid.*

"For the mom of a nine-year-old?"

"It's not like you're a gnarled crone."

"Willa would like that word, both of them. I'll have to tell her Dex O'Malley thinks I'm a gnarled crone."

He shifted closer to her, watching how her chest lifted on a quick inhale. "I specifically said you're not. And if you were, I guess it means I have a thing for gnarled crones."

She narrowed her eyes. "What exactly are we doing here?"

"The charming ritual known as the mating dance?"

She battled her smile. Valiantly won the fight.

"Dex ... I think you might have the wrong idea. If I've given you any reason to assume I'm available ..." She trailed off.

"So I offered you a no-strings fling and you turned me down. Fair enough. That doesn't make you a tease, even if your cute cat whisker boots and peasant blouse game do strange things to me."

Those gorgeous green eyes blew wide. "You think I'm teasing you with my clothing?"

He held up a hand. "I'm not blaming you! This is just me being honest about what I like about you and your outfit choices." He grimaced. "Should probably keep that to myself, huh?"

"Perhaps. It's not really the place for it."

Right. Her place of work. Kid on the premises. The supervisor thing. How he was supposed to be a good boy.

"Got it. No more propositions for torrid affairs or talk about my sordid past or commentary on how your collar-bones are really accented by the cut of your blouse—"

"Dex!"

But she was laughing and he joined in, and the way their laughter blended lit him up because it sounded so fucking good. What he wouldn't do for more of that.

More of this.

Her phone buzzed and she took a quick look at a notif-ication on her screen, maybe that app she was on.

"Someone who wants a date?" It came out like a growl, but she was too distracted to notice.

"Maybe."

"So how does it work these days? On the apps?"

"Well, there are a slew of them out there, but the one I've been using doesn't have photos. It's called Skin Deep, and it's supposed to focus on compatibility without looks getting in the way."

No idea what that meant. "Looks getting in the way?"

"Looks tend to overshadow more important things like values and goals and general personality stuff. A lot of people put up with bad relationships because someone is hot or the sex is amazing. This way, you don't focus on that. It's removed from the equation."

She looked embarrassed, but continued on in a gush.

"I'm trying to set an example for Willa. Let her know

that what's inside is what counts. Appearances are just a smokescreen."

It sounded like there was something else going on here. "Why would she need to know that?"

"She sometimes gets bullied at school. She's a bit self-conscious about her appearance."

The idea that a lovely, amazing girl like Willa would be bullied or feel self-conscious made him furious. But it wasn't his place. Not his family.

He returned to the dating app. "But this system is obviously not foolproof because you end up with people like Jerome. He's clearly not leading with his seed argument on the app, otherwise you would have eliminated him from contention."

She couldn't disagree because of course, he was right. "Everyone talks themselves up in their profiles. But this way, you can cut through some of the surface attraction nonsense and get to the real stuff."

The real stuff? Like it was an either-or game. Attraction or compatibility. It all sounded needlessly complicated. "For fuck's sake, you're gorgeous, Ashley. Why the hell are you selling yourself so short?"

Shock dilated her pupils. "I know you must be bored around here so this is a way to get your kicks—"

He raised a hand and touched her cheek.

"Not bored. Not looking to get my kicks. I am seriously flirting with you. How can you not see that?"

She looked exasperated, but she wasn't pulling away from his touch. If anything, she was leaning into it. Her gaze fell to his lips then away again in confusion.

"But ... why?"

This woman had no clue how attractive she was. Clearly his well-crafted wordplay wasn't enough to convince her.

He needed her to see he meant business. He wasn't just some fly-by-night flake who didn't mean a word he said or wasn't prepared to put in the work, both on the ice and off. That was Dex 1.0.

New Dex had something to prove.

And it seemed the best way to do that was to kiss her.

13

Ashley
Likes: Kissing
Dislikes: How much time do you have?

DEX O'MALLEY WAS KISSING HER.

She had asked why he was flirting with her, not quite believing a word out of his mouth. After all, why would he do that? He was young, fit, hot, rich—all the adjectives she'd thrown at him yesterday at the coffee shop—and she'd seen online the women he dallied with. Club goers. Supermodels. Bright, young things with not a care in the world.

A man like this didn't flirt with a woman like Ashley. A woman with weight on her shoulders. With responsibilities. And if he did, it was merely because he was looking to alleviate his boredom.

Not because he liked her.

But this was still a kiss. A gorgeous, exploratory kiss with the added bonus of a strong, callused hand on her cheek. Now sliding to the back of her neck, curling around and infusing warmth to match his lips.

And those lips! As firm as the kiss was supple. It was as if his mouth knew things about her: which way to slant to get the maximum pleasure, how far to push without losing control. Because she had no doubt that Dex was in supreme control here. It was as if he was trying to prove something.

Ashley had nothing to prove, except maybe she'd like him to remember this kiss in some far-off future. Maybe she'd like to leave an impression.

So she kissed him back.

She clutched at the fabric of his T-shirt, right at the top of the R, hoping she wasn't grabbing chest hair, and let herself fall into pleasure. Some weird sound emerged from her throat, and it yielded a grunt from him. The palm around her neck tightened; his thumb moved into the hair-line at her temple and dug in for sensual purchase.

Then the kiss *really* started.

Evidently, he liked her response—her wild, uninhibited answer to his question—and he was leaning into it. His lips pressed, the kiss deepened, and tongue entered the picture. Glorious, wet, tangling tongue, and that melding had her moaning. Hearing herself awoke something inside her, a long-buried need to be worshipped, kissed, and slammed against a wall—or a cage—and taken hard.

Which is when she realized where she was and what she was doing, with her daughter somewhere close by.

She pulled back, breathless, and met the gaze of a similarly panting Dex. He looked shocked.

Welcome to the club.

He was probably horrified at what had just occurred. Likely, he didn't mean for it to go that far, but then cougar Ashley unveiled her claws and climbed all over him like one of their more rambunctious kittens.

"Sorry," she said quickly.

"Why?"

"For grabbing your shirt and ..." She waved to fill in the rest.

"This old thing?" He looked down at the balled up, creased-ness of his shirt and chuckled. His hand was still curled around her neck, about the only thing keeping her upright. "Unless you're sorry for me kissing you or that you kissed me back?"

"No, but my brain seemed to short-circuit there. I think I made some weirdly embarrassing sounds and—uh, I was a bit too enthusiastic. You can probably tell it's been a while."

He watched her, waiting while she babbled on about her poor performance and enthusiasm being no replacement for skills and how it was probably wetter than he was used to.

Then he held up the hand not fitted like a glove to the back of her neck.

"Ashley, that was a great kiss. I liked everything you did from the shirt grabbing to those throaty moans to the level of tongue involved. In fact, I'd love to do it again, maybe horizontally and with fewer clothes."

Apparently taking her flabbergasted silence for assent, he moved in, possibly to pick up where they'd left off. Now it was her turn to hold up a hand, which she rested on his chest because, why not?

It felt absurdly natural there.

"This is where I work and my kid is—" She looked around. Only the judgmental eyes of the dogs had witnessed that. "—around here somewhere."

She braced herself for his enthusiasm to shift at the mention of Willa. That was usually how it went.

"So only objections of the logistical variety?"

She blinked, trying to parse that statement.

"Meaning you don't object to doing this again, but you'd prefer a more private location?"

Was he serious? He wanted ... *more?*

"I don't believe this is happening."

"Why?"

She stepped back, needing distance to clear the fog of lust. "Look at you. Look at me."

"Still hung up on what your ex said?"

She gasped. "How long were you listening at that door?"

He reached out with his thumb and ran it across her lower lip. So sensual, her knees almost buckled.

"Long enough. So your ex dumped you for some younger chick. I get that it's knocked your confidence, but what I see is a hot, vibrant, sensual woman with a body I want to kiss and lick and do very bad things to. So all I need from you is a yes, a when, and a where."

Stepping back, he bent down and seemed to communicate something non-verbal to Bandit. Then he gifted her that scorching grin and headed out the door.

14

Willa
Likes: Butterflies, Taylor Swift, hockey, Mom's lasagna, too many
other things to mention
Dislikes: Root beer, fart jokes, all the boys at school

"I MET DEX O'MALLEY TODAY."

Maeve looked up from her phone at her niece. "The hockey player?"

"He's volunteering at the shelter."

Her sister stared at Ashley, who was slicing a baguette on the kitchen counter. "Is this true?"

"He started there a couple of weeks ago. We were asked to be discreet. By the team." Of course she hadn't told Willa to keep it a secret, but after what had happened today, she wished she'd mentioned it sooner, if only so she could have prepared for the heated flush that consumed her body on hearing his name. "So, don't gossip about it."

Maeve snorted. "This is about his court case?"

"What court case?" Willa asked.

Ashley made the eyes of 'don't go there' to her sister,

who responded casually with, "He got into a bit of trouble. A fight with someone." She returned her attention to Ashley. "Has he talked about it?"

"No. I've barely spoken to him." *We're too busy flirting and mauling each other.* "He's just there to put in some hours, like a pre-emptive community service."

Though she had wondered today if there might be more to Dex. Seeing him with Bandit had melted her ice-compacted heart a touch. Surrounded by cute, often pathetic animals all day should have made her immune to that kind of display, but apparently not.

That was before the kiss.

She was still reeling from it. She couldn't count the number of times she'd touched her lips in wonder, still questioning whether it was all a dream.

"He's not one for following the rules," she said diplomatically. If he was, he wouldn't be messing around with a woman of her advanced years.

All I see is a hot, vibrant, sensual woman with a body I want to kiss and lick and do very bad things to. Who talked like that?

Willa giggled. "He put his fingers in the cage! I told him that was *not* a good idea. It would be injudicious."

Ashley smiled at her daughter. "He was pretty impressed with you."

"He called me Sparkle. Oh, I need to get my sweatshirt." Willa jumped out of her chair and left the room.

"Not sure that's the most appropriate company for my niece," Maeve said sourly. "What if she starts searching online for him and reads about, y'know?"

Ashley had assumed one casual meeting between a naughty jock and her innocent daughter would be harmless, but Maeve made a good point. Dex was the ultimate bad boy, yet here she was thinking about what might happen between them, because he had definitely implied that kiss wasn't the end of it.

She should not be considering any non-work contact with the likes of Dex O'Malley, or any contact that involved lips, hands, or other body parts. With any luck, he'd forget all about it by tomorrow.

She, on the other hand, would treasure the memory and come back to it when she was feeling low.

"He'll just be there for a few more days. They'll take some photos, release a press statement, and he'll be gone."

Maeve looked unimpressed. "And you have to testify for him?"

"Just provide a statement about what an asset he is at the shelter, that kind of thing."

A flurry shivered through her. Was that why Dex was flirting with her? Did he think it would get him a better reference? Or was he merely sorry for the frump who got dumped?

The doorbell rang, while Ashley preempted Maeve's barrage of questions.

"He's kind of annoying. He showed up late, got bitten by one of the dogs, and had to go on injury reserve. It was a nightmare."

Then he told off my date, offered to eat me out, and said my collarbones do things to him ...

Maeve's expression said it all: *Dex O'Malley is trouble.* Ashley was inclined to agree, especially after that kiss. "Why didn't you mention it?"

"Because ... it's his private life, I suppose? I didn't want to gossip about him. He must get that all the time." When Maeve didn't respond, Ashley went on, feeling more and more flustered. "He's just a transient presence. Dex O'Malley will be done and dusted before you know it."

"I wondered why my ears were burning."

Ashley turned to the sound of a deep, sexy rumble.

Dex O'Malley stood in the kitchen with a bottle of wine, a bouquet of flowers, and that knock-her-dead smile.

"WHAT ARE YOU DOING HERE?"

Dex frowned. "I'm here for dinner."

Dinner? Ashley stared at her daughter, who stood beside Dex, having likely let this man into her house. Though she couldn't blame her daughter for the grip Dex had taken on Ashley's peace of mind. "Willa, what have I told you about answering the door?"

"Not to. Except no one else was taking care of it."

"We weren't expecting anyone. Did you invite Dex to dinner?"

"No."

"So ..." Ashley stared at Dex, completely confused.

"Your sister did," he supplied.

Vera flounced in, grinning like a homewrecker. She grabbed an apple and took a bite, then spoke with her mouth full because manners had never been her thing.

"There I was picking up my niece and outside the shelter, I run into Dex O'Malley. My first thought: 'now why have we not heard about this nice young man's volunteer work?' My second? 'Maybe we should discuss over lasagna.'"

"Sure but—" She met Dex's gaze and saw ... embarrassment. "It's just I wasn't expecting you." And here he was, a potent reminder of her poor decision-making from earlier.

"I'm getting that," he murmured, sounding a touch regretful. "Don't worry, I'll get out of your way."

Vera lunged forward as if Dex needed protecting from

Big Bad No Fun Ashley. "No freaking way! You're our guest. Let me get you a drink. What'll it be? Wine, beer, me?"

"Vera," Ashley warned.

"No, it's fine." Dex resisted Vera's grip and started backing up. "I've obviously intruded."

"Not at all." Ashley felt awful because Dex's initial embarrassment had now graduated to something closer to hurt. "You took me by surprise, that's all."

Vera was pulling at Dex's jacket. "Dex said he doesn't get home-cooked meals very often. So I thought, Italian food's on the menu tonight and why not."

Ashley exchanged a quick glance with Dex who murmured, "If you're sure."

She needed to put this right. Just because she couldn't handle the aftermath of a scorching hot kiss didn't mean she should be rude.

"Not a problem. Dex, meet my sister, Maeve. You already know Vera and Willa."

Vera gave a slinky seductress smile. "Look, Ashley, Dex brought flowers."

Dex spoke again to Ashley, those deep blue eyes graver than she'd have thought possible. "Only if you're sure it's okay." Before Vera could divest him of the bouquet, he deposited it in Ashley's hands. Their fingers brushed and there was that thrill again.

"Of course it's okay. You're very welcome. Hope you like lasagna, meddling, and probing questions about your personal life."

~

So this wasn't awkward at all.

Earlier this afternoon, he'd walked out of the shelter

into the street, dazed as fuck after that kiss. It had scrambled his brain and lowered his defenses. When he ran into Vera, smoking while scrolling on her phone, he assumed she was a fan.

"Dex O'Malley, what are you doing here? Are you getting a puppy?"

He'd planned to be polite—sign an autograph, mumble about his injury, move on his merry way—when she said, "My sister runs this place, y'know."

That was when he saw it, the similar twinkle in those apple-green eyes, though Ashley's were more vibrant, except when they smoked over during a particularly amazing kiss. Christ, just the feel of her in his arms ...

Three minutes later he had an invitation to dinner and instructions to come by at seven. In truth, he wanted to see her again. His next shift was in two days and had suddenly seemed too far away. This opportunity to witness Ashley in her natural habitat combined with an invitation to do so from her sister was too good to pass up.

He'd known it would blindside her.

He wanted to blindside her. Because Ashley looked like the kind of woman who needed a little excitement, and here was Dex O'Malley appointing himself as the bringer of fun to the staid life of a single mom.

Yep, he was a Class A jerk.

And now the jerk was nervous. He never got nervous around women, but Ashley had that effect. Again, he was struck by her authenticity. She had a life, a family, a wealth of experience, and Dex had nothing but a bad reputation and a cheeky smile that seemed to be faltering by the second.

Of course she didn't want him here. She had not looked

pleased to see him, like he was a mistake that had followed her home. Would this feeling ever not suck?

But he was here now, and he needed to make the best of it. Maybe he could show her that he wasn't such a bad bet after all. Vera certainly didn't mind his presence. She had a predatory gleam in her eye and had floated her fingers up his arm when she gripped his wrist, urging him to stay.

The other sister was sour-faced and disapproving. He was used to that reaction, usually from a foster mother, general manager, or police officer.

But then he looked at Willa who gave him a toothy grin, like he was the best person ever, and he felt that maybe this was the place to be.

"Do you like lasagna?" Willa asked, and he got the feeling this was the first of many questions he'd have to field tonight.

"Sure do, Sparkle."

That lit her up like a firework.

"So, Dex," Vera said. "Beer or wine?"

"Water, if you have it."

"Good idea. Keep the defenses in place."

"Vera." Ashley shook her head, as if to say, not in front of the children.

He liked Vera.

Maeve's brow rumpled, so no headway there. Yet.

"Sit, Dex," Vera said. "Tell us how you're enjoying volunteering at the shelter."

He eyed Ashley who stood at the counter with a spatula as she divided up the lasagna into giant slabs. She was still wearing jeans, the ones that did amazing things for her ass, but had changed into a more loose-fitting top than before. It fell off her creamy-skinned shoulder, revealing a blue bra strap. As baggy as the top was, it couldn't quite hide those curves.

"It's great. The people are nice, the dogs are fun, the kittens cute." *The manager is an amazing kisser ...*

"Are you a cat or a dog person?" Willa asked.

"I like both. Probably more of a dog person. You?"

"I prefer cats. Mom won't let us get a pet because she looks after them all day. Do you have a girlfriend?"

"Nope."

"Boyfriend?"

"That'd be a negative."

"Why did you hit that other player?"

Ashley spoke up. "That's none of our business. And you shouldn't know about that."

"It was in the news. The hockey news."

Damn. No one would be voting for Dex on the family values ticket.

Willa peered up at Dex. "Was he being a jerk? There are lots of guys like that in my class."

Dex flicked a look at Ashley, which she met with a shrug that encouraged him to explain himself. He needed to tread carefully.

"He was. But so was I. I shouldn't have handled it that way. It was all wrong and now I have to take my punishment."

Willa's eyes went round. "You mean prison?"

"Nah. I made a mistake and I'm going to own up to it, but I'm confident we can sort it out with an apology."

And a few kind words from your mom.

"This lasagna is amazing," he said a few minutes later.

"It is?" She shook her head, and there was that blush again. "Thanks. Old family recipe. Do you cook?"

"A bit. You kind of need to be able to do it, otherwise you

end up relying too much on takeout, which is never good for my diet."

Vera leaned in. "I'm guessing you work out every day."

"I do. Need to stay in shape, even when I can't play."

"One of the dogs bit him," Willa said. "I told him he needed to be careful. People are relying on him."

"Don't know about that," Dex said. "There are plenty of people who can take my place."

Willa stared at him. "But there's only one you. You're the only person who can do that toe drag and knock the puck through the five hole when you have three defenders trying to pin you down."

Well. Dex rubbed his mouth.

"You saw that game?" It was only two defenders, but he liked the embellishment. One of his better performances back in January, almost two months ago. He hadn't played that well since. Too many distractions.

"Yes. No one else could have done that. Maybe Bastian Durand but he's injured, too. Is *he* talking about how anyone could replace him?"

Jesus. This girl needed to go into sports psychology. "No. Just sees that spot on the team as his right."

"Exactly." Willa went back to her lasagna.

Dex turned to Ashley. "Your daughter's very smart."

"She certainly didn't get it from her father," Maeve murmured.

Ashley frowned. "Hey."

Maeve raised a hand, as if to say "I know best," but Ashley didn't look happy. Maybe she still had feelings for her ex. Maybe this dating losers business was her way of trying to get over him.

Dex could think of a million better ways of doing that, most of them involving Ashley under him.

"So Dex, do you have annoying family you'd like to throttle?" Ashley smiled at him, trying to smooth over the awkward moment. Of course she didn't realize she'd created another.

"No one nearby."

Because she was the intuitive type, she knew she'd said the wrong thing and was clearly prepared to drop it when Vera asked, "Where did you grow up?"

"Chicago for a while, then Minnesota and a short spell in Canada."

"Military family?"

"No, foster care."

There it was, the embarrassed pause. His background rarely came up, so he'd forgotten what it felt like to be pitied.

"Like the kittens?" Willa was trying to work it out.

"I guess. A couple of foster brothers I wouldn't mind throttling, though." He winked at Willa, which made her giggle.

"So where are your parents?"

"Willa! Don't pry."

"But Aunt Vera asked him where he grew up."

Ashley grimaced. "Yes, she did, but she shouldn't have."

Dex took a sip of the wine he'd brought. "They're not around anymore. But I've survived."

Willa put her hand over his. "You have your teammates. And Bandit."

He could have laughed in her face. Fat lot of good they were. But instead he just squeezed her hand and nodded. "You're right. I'm doing okay."

15

"YOU DON'T HAVE to do the dishes."

Vera had disappeared to ready herself for a date (read: banging session) and Maeve was on the phone with one of the book club divorcees. Willa was in her room doing her homework, and now Ashley was looking at the flowers Dex had brought and arguing with him about chores.

"But it's just a matter of putting them in the dishwasher," he insisted. "It's the least I could do after that great meal. Which I'll have to work off with an extra hour on the tread-mill tomorrow."

"Hmm, sorry?" Ashley picked up her wine and took a seat, prepared to savor the sight of a shining god doing household chores.

"No, you're not. And you shouldn't be. That lasagna was a beautiful thing."

He rinsed a plate and placed it on the bottom rack, slightly askew, but she'd worry about it later. Hot guy, washing dishes, serving wine ... she was in heaven.

She took a sip of the Merlot he'd brought.

"This is nice."

He looked at her glass, then raised his gaze to meet hers. "So, you like the wine?"

That wasn't what she meant but she went with it. "It's lovely. Do you know much about wine?"

"Not a clue. But my teammate Burnett does, so he recommended this."

"You asked Cade Burnett for a wine rec?"

He shrugged. "People always know more about that kind of stuff than I do. All the guys on the team are experts at something. Burnett and wine. Kershaw and soap operas. Grey and sneakers, like which ones are collectible."

"Kershaw and soap operas?"

He chuckled. "Theo Kershaw's a huge *Days of Our Lives* fan. Never misses an episode in the player lounge. Hunt and Bond, too."

"What's your specialist subject then? Surely you've got some weird, specific knowledge that sets you apart."

"Sure. How to slip a hundred dollar bill to club security so I'll be left alone or how to get the bartender's attention with the barest rise of an eyebrow."

"These are good skills." She tried to be empathetic, though those situations weren't exactly relatable to a mom in the burbs. "But you'd rather be known for something else. Or your hockey."

"First world pro hockey player problems, right?" After placing the last dish, he turned, folded his arms over that expansive chest, and assessed her.

"I'm sorry for everyone being nosy at dinner and putting you on the spot about your childhood."

"It's okay. It's not a secret or anything. In fact, people don't really ask me much personal stuff." He paused, thinking on that. "Probably because I don't seem like the kind of guy with an interesting interior life."

That was a very self-aware thing to say.

"Is it something you *want* to talk about?"

His mouth quirked in what looked like surprise. "You don't have to do that." In his voice she heard an ache, a longing to share something he usually kept hidden.

"You can tell me anything. But only if you want to."

"Sure, my sad sack childhood makes for great foreplay."

She tilted her head. "Some women love when a guy gets vulnerable."

"You mean, all these years I've been leaving this very useful strategy out of the Dex O'Malley playbook?"

She smiled. "Not sure you've suffered. You're never short of attention."

"True. But maybe I could try it out—this new, vulnerable little-orphan-Dexter?"

So he had to frame the sharing as self-deprecation, a silly joke. She could run with that.

"How long were you in foster care?"

"Eight years, from ten until I aged out. I spent time with a few families, but I was a bit of a terror, always making trouble. Some of the stories ..." He rolled his shoulders back, pushing away something. Maybe a bad memory or three. "Another day, perhaps."

All that uncertainty and rejection had to have messed with his head, wondering if the next foster situation was going to be the one. She saw it with the puppies and kittens they fostered. When the animals came back, they seemed to know deep down that their situation was no longer as stable.

She bent over to get a dishwasher tablet and inserted it in the compartment before closing the door. When she straightened, she found him dragging his gaze away from her ass.

"Do you still keep in touch with any of the families?"

"Anton, mostly. He was my coach and I lived with his family for a while. Without him, I'd probably be digging roads or part of a chain gang. Hockey saved me."

"Being part of a team must be nice. Band of brothers."

His brow creased. "It's okay, but most of the guys are in a different place than me. I've moved around a lot and I'm not so good at making connections."

"I find that hard to believe." She put her empty wine glass on the counter. One was enough or she'd start spouting nonsense.

Such as how cute he looked with that forlorn puppy dog expression.

Or how she'd love nothing more than to wrap him in a hug and tell him it would all work out.

Or maybe how she wished she was brave enough to take him up on his offer.

"Can I ask another personal question?"

"You're on a roll tonight, so go for it."

"What happened in that bar? Was it because of the game?"

He inhaled deeply. "He and I know each other from early days playing hockey and we've never really gotten along. He was being abrasive to this woman he was with. Calling her names. Saying she was no good, and it hit a nerve with me. I can't stand to see anyone being cruel to someone else, especially a guy being rude to a woman. It's not something I'm prepared to put up with so I stepped in and told him to stop being such a jerk. Then it all went south pretty quickly. He threw the first punch, but no one saw that in the video."

"But surely people will come to your defense. The woman you stood up for?"

"Maybe. The lawyers are working on it, gathering witness statements, but the video evidence seems to override everything. Makes me look like the aggressor."

She'd seen it. He was on top of the guy, whaling on him, even when it was clear he'd gotten the upper hand.

"You went all in."

He rubbed a hand over his mouth. "I know. I screwed up."

She squeezed his arm. "Yes, you did, but you're working on making it better. The guy's okay, isn't he?"

"Hughes is fine. His lawyers are looking for a settlement and an apology, so I expect I can pay it off. Listen, Ashley, I'm not proud of myself. I know I messed up and I also know that a guy like me with a past like mine is not what you want in your home. Near your family and your kid."

That was interesting. He knew this, yet he still came over for dinner. Also, those words made it sound like he wanted more than just a quickie behind the cattery. He was conscious of how disruptive his presence was for her and her family.

"Why did you accept Vera's invitation?"

"I wanted to see you again."

She swallowed. "You're on shift the day after tomorrow."

"It's not the same. There's no privacy."

Her breathing had picked up.

"There's none here." Why had she said that?

"Yet here we are. And you have every right to question it, my presence in your home, whether being in your family's orbit is a good idea."

"I just wanted some more context about all this drama in your life."

He tilted his head. "And you want this context because?"

She could lie and say it was sheer curiosity about a

famous person in her immediate orbit, just a random looky-loo into his glamorous, salacious life.

But he deserved the truth.

"Because I think there's more to you than the guy who attracts the attention of gossip sites and paparazzi like honey to a bear."

Surprise lit up his eyes. Had he really gone his whole life without any form of validation?

"Ashley, don't go thinking I've got hidden depths. I'll just disappoint you."

"I know disappointment." She could feel herself drawing closer to him, her hurting heart reaching for his bruised one. "Yet I don't think you could ever make me feel that."

His hand dropped to her hip and cupped it gently. "This would be the moment where I warn you not to put me on a pedestal. Not to have any expectations. All the usual things I tell women I want to fuck." He swallowed quickly. "Sorry, that was crude. I shouldn't—"

She cut off his apology with a kiss. God, she loved how his mouth felt and tasted. Its velvet luxury, supple strength, the way his lips took control without being sloppy or pushy. She would never become accustomed to the care he took with her. As though he thought she might be skittish, when in truth, she was so damn hungry.

She pulled back.

"I know," he said, panting slightly. "Willa's here. Your sisters." He looked as dazed as she felt.

"I can't seem to help myself around you."

"That's me. Temptation incarnate."

Maeve walked into the kitchen and Ashley jumped back. Her sister gave her that look, the one that said she needed to watch out for stormy seas ahead.

"Willa needs help with her math problems and I'm no good at that, so ..."

"Got it." She smiled an apology at Dex. "Might be best if—"

"Sure. It was nice to meet you, Maeve. Thanks for letting me join you for dinner." He took Ashley's hand. "Walk me to the door?"

"O-okay."

He's holding my hand! She was acting like a silly school-girl with a crush, but that's how he made her feel. And Lord knew it had been a lifetime—her daughter's lifetime—since she felt this way. Even with Greg, it hadn't been this swarm of rabid butterflies ...

At the door, he grabbed his jacket hanging on a hook, but didn't put it on, possibly because he'd have to let go of her hand.

"So, I'm back on the ice tomorrow and there's a game. Do you think Willa might like to go?"

"I think she'd love to."

"How about her mom? Any interest there?"

"Well, she'll need a chaperone. She's only nine."

He grinned. "Right. I've forgotten what nine is like."

She doubted that. She suspected Dex carried his child-hood experience around with him like a crushing weight.

"Willa's going to be thrilled."

"You're leaving?" Her daughter appeared, looking woebegone. She never looked like that when Ashley left the house.

"Yeah. I had a great time," Dex said, "but I need to leave you guys to ... whatever you do in the evening."

"We watch hockey games. Boston-Denver is about to start."

Willa looked a little too hopeful that Dex would give up

his evening and stay here to watch it.

Ashley nipped that in the bud. "Dex has to go and you need to do your math homework first. But he did invite you to a live hockey game."

"Really?" Foxy-fast, her daughter hugged the hockey player.

Dex's surprise was evident, maybe even in the region of panic. He didn't seem to know what to do with his hands and held them aloft as if to prove he wasn't doing anything irregular. Ashley watched with interest, wondering about men who had little or no intuition around kids whatsoever.

Which is when he surprised her and let his hands rest on Willa's shoulders, then with a quick squeeze, he set her back gently.

"The next home game is tomorrow. If that's too short notice—"

"It's not!" her daughter yelped. "Mom, we can go, right? I'll get my homework done before, I promise. We can go to the arena early. Maybe get a hot dog?" She turned to Dex, who was watching her in wide-eyed wonder. Nine-year-old girls were *a lot*. "They have hot dogs, don't they?"

"Pretty sure they do. All sorts. You can have whatever you want." He shared a quick look with Ashley. "Or whatever your mom thinks you should have." He mouthed "sorry" at the same time she did.

Then they both started laughing.

Wow, why did *that* feel so good? Probably because it had been a while since she felt a connection of any sort with a man. Best not to read anything more into it, because this man was not unlike most nine-year-olds, meaning he was *a lot*.

"It's okay." Ashley patted her daughter's shoulder. "Time to let Dex get on."

"And can we visit the locker room?" Willa's voice was extra squeaky.

"Let's not push our luck."

"Of course you can," Dex said easily. "I'll make sure your name is on the list. But Willa?"

"What?"

"You have to cheer for me because you're my guest."

Willa nodded enthusiastically. "Yes! I was already a fan, now I'm a superfan. Thanks, Dex!" And off she trotted, secure in the knowledge that life couldn't get any better—at least until tomorrow night.

Dex grinned. "Guess you're coming to the hockey game."

"Guess I am."

"Did you want to bring anyone else? Your sisters, perhaps?"

She thought it over. "I could call Jerome and see if he's interested?"

Storm clouds scudded across his face and a muscle in his jaw bunched. Well.

"Kidding."

"That guy and his seed would *not* be welcome."

Just the mention of Jerome's emissions had Ashley laughing again, and thankfully Dex joined in.

"I'd better head out."

She nodded, feeling a little lost, which was ludicrous. He had to go. She *needed* him to go. Yet a part of her craved what was happening here, this new and easy back-and-forth between them. Only when she spent too long in his presence, ease disappeared and in its place was a heady desire, charged and thick.

She wanted to kiss and be kissed, touch and be touched. She wanted skin on skin and any number of naughty things to be done to her.

So he really needed to leave now.

"Thanks for having me over," he murmured, then leaned in to kiss her on the cheek, just as she turned her head. Their mouths brushed. Groaning, he touched his forehead to hers.

"Fuck, Ashley, you have to quit that."

"What?"

"Making me hard as a puck for you."

A blush crept up her cheeks. "I'm not doing it on purpose. I think, maybe, you're just prone to constant erections. Your youth and all."

"Don't try to fob it off on me. This is a 'you' problem."

The words of a consummate charmer. For Dex, this was merely a run-of-the-mill flirtation with a woman who was clearly desperate for attention.

Still, it wouldn't hurt to luxuriate in the glow, if only for a while. Making a nice play of reluctantly pulling away—the moves were something else—he placed a hand on the door handle. "I'll text about the game, okay?"

"Okay."

Once the door had closed, Vera appeared, her face creased in a dirty grin. "Ashley Adams, look at you!"

Ashley waved to keep her voice down. "It's nothing."

"Nothing? That boy is into you. I invited him, purely so we could have something pretty to look at, but he came through. The way he drooled over you was something else."

"Stop it. He's just keeping me sweet to make sure I give him a good reference."

Vera shrugged. "So what if he is? Doesn't mean you can't enjoy it."

No, it didn't, but she would keep her shields up all the same.

16

Dex put his gym bag in his locker and pulled off his sweatshirt. He'd woken up this morning in a great mood, except for one tricky thing.

The erection that would not quit.

He'd managed to tame it with thoughts of a certain hot mama and how her lips tasted. And that was as far as he got before he exploded all over his sheets.

Apparently a kiss was doing it for him now?

Who the hell are you and what have you done with Dex O'Malley?

He had a whopping big crush on this woman. A woman of substance, so out of his league because she was a real person. Not that any of the women he'd fucked before weren't real, but he hadn't really bothered to find out any more about them beyond their willingness to get down and dirty. They probably had problems like student loans or bad bosses or gluten intolerance and he'd never known because he didn't care to ask.

But with Ashley, he wanted to know things. Her favorite color (though why the hell that was of interest, he had no idea). Or how she liked her tea. Or which of the animals at the shelter was her favorite and why his name was Bandit.

Mostly he wanted to know why she sometimes looked sad and what the hell he could do to fix that.

He'd never wanted to fix anything for another person. People with "issues" like Dex weren't usually any good at fixing other people's problems. They were too self-involved.

But Dex was beginning to think he might have more bandwidth than previously suspected. He might be able to set aside his own selfishness for a while and worry about another person.

Like Ashley. And even Willa, if her mom would let him.

During tonight's game, his guests would be sitting in his seats. Tara hadn't even done that when they were faking things—she always sat in the owners' box, which should have been his first clue that she had a thing for Fitz and wasn't about to give Dex the time of day.

This was better. The first time he'd give his seats to someone would mean something. Real high school stuff.

His seats ... shit, he needed to take care of that.

Kershaw and Burnett walked in, chatting away.

"Hey, who do I call about my comps?"

They stopped talking and stared at him. Finally, Kershaw broke into a grin.

"You're bringing someone to the game?"

"Yeah."

Burnett picked up the conversational baton. "First time?"

"No, I just ..." Now he felt stupid. Here he was getting all gooey about the prospect of giving his seats to Ashley and instead he looked like a loser who had no friends. "I don't usually bother. But I have guests tonight and I need to get it sorted. Quick."

Unfazed by Dex's change of tone and clearly having no intention of being helpful, Kershaw asked, "Who's the guest?"

"Guests, he said. Plural." Burnett dropped his bag on a bench. "Does this have something to do with the wine recommendation I gave you yesterday?"

"Wine recommendation?" Foreman had just walked in with Reid Durand and stopped midway to his locker. "You're buying fancy wine?"

"Perhaps he's serving it with fava beans. And someone's liver." Durand Senior's brilliant contribution.

"So the wine was a success?" Burnett asked after sending a look of disgust Reid's way. "What did you eat?"

"Lasagna. Turkey and fennel."

"That sounds good." He unzipped his jacket. "Not sure the Merlot would go well with that, but when you don't know what they're serving up, you're going in blind. Next time, you should get more information in advance, and I can make a better recommendation."

Kershaw held up both hands. "Who cares what they ate and drank? Who's inviting O'Malley for dinner? And is it the same people he needs tickets for?"

"It's Ashley."

The D-man's mouth dropped like an oxygen-deprived trout. "From Riverbrook Animal Shelter?"

"With her daughter." Dex shifted from one foot to the other. Why was this such a big deal?

"Willa's coming to the game?" Reid asked.

Dex whipped around. "You know Willa?"

"Sure. I used to pick up Ken at the shelter when she volunteered there. Met Willa a couple of times. She's a cool kid. Is she still into butterflies?"

"Yeah, she is." A streak of jealousy chilled Dex's gut. He

didn't like that Reid already had an in with Willa and maybe even Ashley.

Jesus, not even high school. More like middle.

"So that's who's coming tonight?" Kershaw getting everyone back on the gossip track.

"If I can get the tickets organized!" These assholes!

Burnett cracked up. "Go talk to Mindy in Player Relations. She'll see you right."

"Okay. Thanks. And the rest of you? Don't make a big deal out of it, alright? She's just a nice person with a kid who likes hockey, and who's been kind to me, helping me out of this fix. So stop making out like there's something going on. She might be coming to the locker room after and the last thing I need is you jabronis spouting your smart comments and embarrassing her. And me."

Dex's outburst sent the room into an awkward silence. A couple more players had walked in—Petrov and Bond—and the sight of six pairs of judgmental eyes boring into him made Dex feel one inch tall.

Foreman broke the awkward silence. "Sounds like O'Malley has a crush."

"Just shut it." Dex walked out with the sound of laughter echoing in his ears.

Fuckers.

Coach Calhoun called Dex over to the bench after skating drills during morning practice.

"Doc says you're good to go."

Dex agreed, though he was good to go last week as well. Best to keep that to himself. The brass hated when players got chippy.

"Looking forward to tonight. Ready to play."

Coach narrowed his eyes. "We'll see."

Dex's heart dropped and practically burned a hole through the ice. "But I have to play." He'd endured all that bullshit in the locker room and had sorted out the tickets. He sure as hell refused to be riding the pine when he had guests in the house. "Coach, I'm ready, I swear."

"I know you are." Coach grinned, which was not a good look on him. Fucking creepy, to be honest. "Just yanking your chain. I've seen the work you've been putting in since your spot of trouble. Makes a nice change. This last year, I've not been convinced of your commitment to this team, O'Malley."

That his attitude had filtered through to Coach—and the rest of the team—rankled. He didn't want anyone thinking he wasn't a hard worker or might even be a liability.

"I'm sorry for giving you that impression. You should know I'm here to play. Seriously."

"Okay, that's what I want to hear. And if the doc says you're good to go, then we'll be putting you in tonight."

Relief coursed through him. Excitement, too. Someone was coming to see him play.

After practice, he shot off a message to Tara.

You busy?

Always have time for you!

He headed over to the salon and found Tara with a life-sized doll's head, adding streaks of purple to it.

"Okay, what's happening here?"

"Just testing a color combo." She hugged him. "So what's going on? How's the hand?"

"Better. And I have a cool scar to show for it." He showed

her the still red-raw evidence of his injury. "Best of all, I'm playing tonight."

"Awesome! How are things at the shelter?"

He took a seat and swiveled a few times, feeling almost giddy.

"Good. There's this dog that's taken a shine to me. Well, he bit me first but now I think he likes me."

"Not a great start, but I've heard worse. Real enemies to lovers stuff there." She took a strand of his hair in her fingers. "How about a little trim?"

"Not too short." He knew she loved to cut while she dispensed wisdom, so if it opened things up for her, then he'd allow it.

After a moment of weighing a hair-related decision between her fingers, she asked, "How was the Merlot?"

"The Mer—wait a second. How do you know about the Merlot?"

"Oh, Hudson was in here earlier and I guess it was quite the topic of conversation amongst the boys. Bringing wine to dinner and inviting women and their kids to games. It's a big deal."

"No, it's not. It's just … politeness."

She smiled at him in the mirror, all pity. "Start at the beginning. You went to Ashley's for dinner?"

"Went to … how is it that everyone knows my business? You don't know her, do you?" It seemed everyone had some experience with the shelter and with Ashley.

"No, we haven't met, but I had a chat with Kennedy while I was doing her balayage and I heard all about Ashley. Besides, I don't need to have met her to figure out what's happening here. A single encounter with the woman and I will know all!"

"Like you did with Fitz? You sure had him figured out

after one encounter. Or was it two? No, wait, you didn't figure out your shit until I asked you to marry me."

Scissors raised, she stopped and stared at him in the mirror. "Are you still annoyed with me over that? I thought we'd sorted it out."

"We have," he mumbled. "I just wish people didn't think I was such a joke." He held up a hand of apology for his outburst. Giddy fervor had been quickly replaced with irritability. "And before you say it, I know it's my own fault. I've been acting like I don't give a fuck about anyone or anything, so why the hell should anyone give a fuck about me?"

"I wasn't going to say that at all." She looked thoughtful. "You really like this Ashley, don't you?"

"I don't know," he lied. Because it was easier than putting his heart out there where Tara could eviscerate it with her scissors and homespun wisdom.

She smiled sympathetically. "So what's happened between you two? Give me the details."

"We kissed." Twice, but he preferred to keep that to himself.

"Okay. Nice. And then what?"

He shrugged. "That's it. First, I offered to, uh, clean her pipes, and she laughed. Said I can't be serious. But I think she might be coming around." They'd definitely left it on a promising note.

"Okay, first of all—clean her pipes? Did you say that?"

"I overheard her and Kennedy talking about Ashley needing to get laid. So I said I'd be open to that. I was just using her words." Or maybe Kennedy's.

When he put it like that, it sounded less than sexy. What woman could fail to be seduced by those stellar lines?

Tara rolled in her lips, obviously biting back what she

really wanted to say. Instead she snipped some hair from the back of his head. He was starting to think that maybe having his hair cut while Tara was in this mood might not be such a good idea.

She took a breath. "Why would she say you can't be serious?"

"I don't think she believes I'm attracted to her. Or she thinks I'm a total fuckboy. The kind of guy who messes women around."

"Did she say that?"

"She didn't have to. So now I'm just trying to be a good guy, not such a user. Someone a woman could trust."

He hadn't been thinking that at all, but talking to Tara often raised these lightbulb moments.

She squeezed his shoulder. "I think you're being really hard on yourself. You're not a fuckboy or at least, not at the level you think you are. So you've hooked up a lot in the past and it sounds like you want that to change. Which is great. But ..."

"But what?"

"Ashley's a mom, with responsibilities and I'm guessing, a life that isn't going to stand for any nonsense."

"Like mine?"

"Like anyone's. So she might let you in for great sex—which I've no doubt you can give her—but if you're hoping she'll let you in for something more, that might be tough. Not because of you, but because a woman in that situation has probably had her heart broken. Maybe even by inconsiderate men who care only about getting their dicks wet." She held up a hand. "I know that's not you, or at least not anymore, but you're still kind of young to be claiming your new personality, Mr. Responsibility. Expecting Ashley to take you seriously might take time."

He knew that, especially after what he'd overheard about her ex. How he left her for a younger woman and made Ashley feel unattractive. Hell, she was dating guys without seeing their photos, which probably had more to do with not wanting people to see *her* photos. Absurd, considering how hot she was, but we all had hang-ups. Hearing Tara lay it out was sobering.

"But she might want some hot sex anyway?"

Tara smiled at him, seeing right through his effort to deflect. "Sure. And then you can reel her in with your charms. What's important is to treat her well, Dex. Treat her like the queen she is, and she might open up that armor by a sliver."

Snip. There went another chunk of hair along with some of his doubts.

Treat her like the queen she is.

He planned to do exactly that.

17

The Rebels have announced that Dex O'Malley is off injury reserve and will likely be on the roster for this evening's game against the LA Quake. This will be O'Malley's first game since his arrest for assaulting Kyle Hughes three weeks ago. Will that weigh on him or spur him to new heights? — @RebelsInsider

"MOM, where's my pink scarf? The one with the butterflies?"

Ashley looked in the mirror, pulled a face that made her look like a gargoyle, then applied a lipstick she hadn't worn since Vera had given it to her two years ago for Christmas. She was more of a Chapstick girl, yet here she was contemplating something that would dry out her lips because she worried she might not look attractive enough.

But he's already kissed you.

And there was no guarantee that would happen again. This was for Willa, who loved hockey and couldn't go to games because it was so expensive. Under no circumstances should Ashley be looking at this as a treat for herself.

"Mom!"

"Did you check the laundry hamper?"

Thumping around ensued, then "Nooooo!" and a second later, a resigned "I'll wear the purple one."

Crisis averted.

Vera walked in, looking like Elvira before she'd taken a bite from someone. "You're not wearing that, are you?"

Ashley dipped her gaze to her turtleneck and sleeveless puffy jacket. Her jeans were a little tight and gave her ass more love than it deserved, but otherwise she thought she looked good. Appropriate.

"What's wrong?"

"I know your vaj has dried up but it won't be getting any lubrication in that outfit."

"I'm a mom. And I'm dressing like one to escort my daughter to a hockey game where it will be cold."

Vera yanked open the closet and started ransacking the rails. "Here."

"I can't wear that." She'd worn that bustier for Halloween three years ago when she was on a Wonder Woman kick and thought accentuating her curves was a good thing. Pre-divorce. "This is a hockey game."

"And have you seen what some of those bunnies wear? They're letting it all hang out in a bid to get a hockey player husband."

"Not looking for a hockey player husband."

Vera pulled out a silk pink blouse that Ashley had forgotten about. "Okay, so this is more your speed. A little low-cut, let the girls get some air, and remind people that you are not quite dead below the waist."

"That's off the shoulder, I'll be freezing in that. And I'm not going to even see Dex. He's working, remember?"

Though he had promised a locker room visit, which was awfully sweet of him. Willa was going to love that. And

Ashley would not be showing up with her tits—or shoulders—flapping in the wind.

She pulled out a dark red peplum top with a looser drape to it, which should cover her stomach nicely. Not that anyone would be looking, but better not to worry about it.

"So how's this?"

Vera looked at her fondly. "Cuter."

She couldn't even get a "sexy" from her sister? Oh, well.

She checked her phone. It was just past six. "We'd better get going."

"Oh, you've plenty of time." Vera's phone pinged. "Or not."

"What does that mean?"

"Mom!" Willa's voice carried loudly from downstairs. "Come quick!"

"What now?" Ashley walked past her sister out to the top of the stairs. "Where's the fire?"

"Soon to be in your panties," her sister muttered behind her.

"Don't say that word. I hate that word."

"Mom, there's a limo outside."

Ashley headed down the steps quickly. "No, there's not. And if there is that couldn't be ..." She trailed off because Vera was smirking at her.

Maeve came out of the kitchen. "What's going on?"

"There's a limo to take us to the hockey game!" Willa was jumping up and down, all thoughts of her second-choice scarf forgotten.

"We don't know that's for us." She slid a glance at Vera who looked even more smug than usual. "Vera?"

Her sister held up her phone, displaying a text thread. "I have it on good authority that it's your ride."

"Did Dex do this? And he told you?" Absurdly, Ashley

did not like that idea at all. Not the limo—she loved the limo (oh my God, a limo!)—but the notion that Dex was texting her sister did not sit well.

Vera was, to put it mildly, a woman of action. Unlike Ashley, who was a mom with clay feet.

"He wanted you to have a beer and enjoy yourself."

She could have gotten an Uber or a taxi. A limo seemed so over the top.

But that was Dex. He was an OTT kind of guy. She considered her sister. Maybe she and Dex were better suited for each other.

Just thinking it made her ill. What was wrong with her? She had no claim over Dex O'Malley. He was just playing nice with her so he could get a good review for his court case.

Not exactly pleased with her muddled thought process, she checked her purse for her wallet—would she have to tip the driver?—as a knock sounded on the door. Despite knowing she was not supposed to answer, Willa did just that and said, "Hi!" to the man on the other side of the threshold. Heavy-set and gray-haired, he was dressed in a suit and a cap.

"Ms. Willa Adams?"

"That's me!" Willa looked so pleased at the manner of address that Ashley's dark thoughts faded away in an instant.

The driver smiled warmly. "Well, young lady, your carriage awaits."

Ashley couldn't be annoyed at that. Dex had given her daughter a fairy tale start to the evening.

"Got everything, Willa?" Ashley grabbed her jacket and put it on. She turned to her sisters. "We won't be out too late."

"Sure," Vera said with a wink. "Maybe send our niece home and stay out for a time afterward."

"That won't be happening. It's the game and that's it."

"We have to go to the locker room. Dex is expecting us!"

The locker room. Would it be filled with half-naked guys, or more specifically Dex in a towel, answering questions from some floozy sports journo?

She needed to not think of Dex in a towel or the man flirting with reporters. This was her daughter's night.

"Okay, let's go." She caught Maeve's eye and shriveled a touch at her sister's somber expression. "It's just a game."

"It is to him," her sister murmured.

"THIS VIEW IS AMAZING!" Willa stood before her seat in the Rebels arena, about four rows back from the bench, and took it all in. It might be amazing, but as far as Ashley was concerned, the music was loud, the people around them were rambunctious, and the entire experience was just a touch overwhelming.

Starting with the limo ride. The driver had told them to help themselves to the snacks in the car, so they munched on Pringles, Skittles, and ginger ale, even though they'd both had dinner. It just seemed a shame not to take advantage.

Once at the arena, they were met by someone called Mindy, who escorted them to their seats as Mr. O'Malley's special guests. Ashley wondered if this section was reserved for associates of the players.

Associate. Good word. Excellent description of her relationship with one of the Chicago Rebels star forwards.

Doing her best not to stare at the people seated around

her, she tried to gauge who might be related to a player. She didn't follow the gossip rags or even the sports media, but she was pretty sure that one of them was—

"Oh my God, that's Mia Wallace!" Willa waved at the dark-haired hockey star and Olympic gold medalist sitting kitty-corner behind them. "Hi!"

"Hey there," the woman said. "You excited for the game?"

"Big time. Dex O'Malley invited us," her daughter said proudly.

Ashley turned around and smiled an apology for her daughter's effusiveness. "Hello. I'm Ashley and this is Willa."

"I'm Mia. This is Sadie and Casey." She gestured at the two women to her left, who nodded and smiled warmly. "Friends of Dex, huh?"

Mia was married to one of the players, Cal Foreman, and was also sister to the captain, Vadim Petrov. While she probably had the inside track, Ashley wasn't sure how much people knew about Dex's volunteer gig, so all she could do was murmur, "Yep. Friends."

"He's volunteering at my mom's animal shelter so he doesn't get sent to jail."

"Willa! That's ..." She grimaced in the ladies' direction, only to find them grinning broadly. "Private," she added quietly.

"Nice to see people in these seats at last," Casey said cryptically.

"You're married to Erik Jorgenson!" Willa turned back to Ashley. "He's the goalie, Mom. From Sweden."

Casey chuckled. "I am." Seeming to realize that Ashley might not be aware of all the connections, she gestured to the strawberry-blonde beside her. "And this is Sadie Yates—"

"She's married to Gunnar Bond, Mom!"

Sadie smiled. "I am. Wow, you know your Rebels, young lady."

"I've heard of Sadie," Ashley said. "I love your dresses." Sadie Yates was famous for designing gorgeous dresses for full-figured women. Today she was wearing something with Outlander-meets-Malibu vibes.

"Thanks so much. And I love that top you're wearing. It's so cute."

"Oh, thanks." Before Ashley could speak further, she was distracted by all the people to her right exiting the row to allow the entrance of a glamorous blonde sporting very high heels.

"Thank you, thank you, thanks soooo much!" She sat down beside Ashley and let out a deep breath. "Wow, those steps are steeper than I expected. I'd better text the General and let him know I made it." With nimble fingers, she whipped off a quick text that was more emoji than alphabet, then turned to Ashley with an outstretched hand.

"Hi, I'm Tara! You must be Ashley."

Tara Fitzpatrick, wife of the general manager and Dex's former fiancée. Ashley took her hand and shook firmly.

"I am. Nice to meet you."

Tara looked past her to Willa, who was busy chatting with the women behind them. "Your daughter's adorable. I have that same Taylor Swift crossbody—love it. So are you looking forward to the game?"

"Definitely, though I'm not much of a hockey fan. I like the atmosphere, though, and Willa loves all things hockey."

"Oh, I'm with you there. I barely knew a thing about it when I started watching but I learned fast. How's Dex doing at the shelter? Any more accidents?"

Ashley swallowed, feeling a touch protective of Dex's time there.

"Great! He's a natural with the animals, really sweet with them."

Tara leaned in, sending a waft of expensive perfume up Ashley's nose. "Yeah, I don't think people see just how sweet Dex is. Have the Rebels PR people been out to take photos?"

Ashley wasn't sure how to respond to that. She thought Dex was very sweet, but also incredibly sexy, a combination that was rather hazardous to her mental well-being.

"Not yet. But I've taken a few."

Tara's eyes went as round as pucks. "Show me!"

"Um, okay." She took out her phone and backed up to the relevant photos.

"May I?" Tara took the phone before Ashley could voice her assent. "These are so good. Aw, look at him with the kitten."

Mittens was quite the scene-stealer, but then so was Dex.

"Would you mind sending me a few?"

"Sure."

"I'll pop my number in here and ... there we go!" She looked at the photos adoringly, so much so that Ashley wondered if she might still have a thing for Dex.

The text message came through on Tara's phone, where the screensaver was a picture of Tara with her husband and a baby.

"Speaking of photos ... could I see your little one?"

"Oh, you've done it now. My favorite subject." Out came the albums, but Ashley didn't mind. Tara's daughter, Esme, was absolutely adorable.

"I never want her to grow up. I want to dress her in cute outfits and put ribbons in her hair forever."

"It's nice when you can talk to them, though. You're

going to have some great conversations when she starts getting chatty."

"We already do!" Tara chuckled. "Well, Hale, my husband, understands her completely, no matter what she says. Oh, there's one of Dex holding her. He came over one afternoon, and I expected he'd be terrified, but no, he took to the baby-holding like a Rebel to an all-you-can-eat buffet."

Ashley had to admit Dex holding Tara's infant daughter was a powerful image. A natural protector, he gazed soulfully into the baby's eyes.

Tara appeared to be watching her closely. "So, our Dexter. Good with animals and babies ... he's going to make someone an excellent hockey husband."

A couple of cute photos of Dex with helpless creatures couldn't quite convince Ashley of his responsibility bona fides.

"He's kind of young to be settling down."

Tara shrugged. "I think he wants nothing more than to enjoy some stability. Oh, here they are!"

The arrival of the players cut the conversation short and left Ashley thinking about what Tara might mean. Had Dex enlisted Tara's help in winning her over?

Not that he needed help. Ashley was this close to falling before him and begging to take him up on his offer. Cute animal and baby pics had nothing to do with it—if anything they just made it more complicated. She'd much rather see Dex as the man who was good for one thing, and one thing only.

Everyone cheered as the players skated out and when Dex emerged from the tunnel, Willa, Ashley, and Tara all jumped to their feet and screamed their approval so loud that people turned to look at them.

Including Dex. His gaze seemed to land on them—on Ashley—with an unexpected weight. They were close enough to see his expression and it was one of surprise, even though he knew they were coming. Maybe it was because Tara was here. Or maybe it was how hard they had cheered for him.

Why not? He worked as diligently as anyone out there. He deserved to be celebrated because he was doing something amazing out there. Given his unsettling beginnings, it was wonderful to see where he'd ended up.

Every time he jumped over that wall, they hooted and hollered and screamed his name, as if Dex O'Malley was the star of the night. And soon the entire section—the players' section—were doing the same. Sure, they'd cheer when the players nearest and dearest to them came on, but they were extra loud when Dex cleared the gate and skated into the fray.

During the rare moments in the first period when he was resting on the bench, he would occasionally turn and look toward their section. The first time, Willa waved and he waved back.

The second time, during one of the play reviews, Willa was too focused on the special delivery of a hot dog—they didn't even have to go to the concession stand to order it. (Tara commented that this was not standard operating procedure for guests and that Willa must have done something right in a previous life.) Dex had given a thumbs up to the hot dog delivery.

By the time Dex turned around again, most everyone was distracted by Theo Kershaw's granny group dancing so hard it was a wonder they didn't each break a hip. (Apparently there was a raging rivalry between Theo's Tarts, led by his grandmother, and Reid's Rebelles, led by Kennedy's.)

That time, Ashley was studying Dex's broad shoulders and wondering how they would feel under her hands, when she found herself in an eye-lock with the man himself.

She felt his smile to her toes. How had she thought the arena would be cold? With Dex's heated gaze it was positively steaming in here. Feeling foolish, she gave him a small wave.

That made him smile bigger.

And then he was off again, chasing down the puck until with just a minute to go in the first period, he zipped past the LA defender and planted one right in the net.

The whole section, primed by Dex's newly-formed fan club to love him regardless, jumped to their feet and roared their approval. Dex accepted the pats and compliments from his teammates before sending a quick-flashed smile toward his guests.

Or one guest. At least that's how Ashley felt. Like she and Dex were connected through the plexi, and that goal was for her.

"Isn't Dex awesome, Mom?"

"Yes, he is." She turned and caught Tara's enigmatic smile. "What?"

"Oh, nothing."

18

DEX WASN'T USED to being the hero. But then he wasn't used to scoring a hat trick in a single game, either.

"Where the fuck has that guy been?" Kershaw stood before him, hands on hips.

"What guy?"

"The one we just saw on the ice, O'Malley. Finally, you decided to quit dicking around and show us how it's done."

Vadim Petrov, the Rebels captain, sent a slit-eyed gaze his way. "I heard you had a guest at the game."

"Three guests," Kershaw said as he pulled his sweatshirt over his head. "His ex, his new girl, and the new girl's kid. You don't half make it complicated for yourself, but whatever it takes to make you play better, Mr. Fuckin' Drama."

Dex hadn't expected to see Tara, but he shouldn't have been surprised. After her advice about how he needed to treat Ashley like a queen, which had resulted in a mad scramble to get the whole experience organized—tickets, limo, hot dogs—he suspected Tara would be nosy enough to get involved. There she was, hopefully talking him up and not reminding Ashley too much of Dex 1.0, the guy who needed a fake relationship and a volunteer gig at the puppy shelter to get him out of hot water.

Having Ashley in his corner had a positive impact on his game. He felt like he was skating for something other than points or glory or the cheers of the crowd. Sure, he craved all that, but having someone special in the stands made a difference.

It reminded him of when Anton would come see his games when Dex played at the University of Minnesota. Everyone had parents, family, tons of friends who took those seats and tickets for granted. Dex didn't have that, but when Anton showed his face, he wasn't so alone.

It had been a while since he'd even wanted to invite anyone.

Seeing Ashley and Willa—and okay, Tara—had cracked open something inside his chest. It felt gooey in there, as sticky as molten lava cake. He liked having Ashley up there. He liked scoring goals. And he liked the admiration of his teammates, even if they wanted to make up some weird correlation between his guests and his play.

"Something clicked tonight. That's all. For once, Durand Senior's passes were quality."

Reid scowled, ever the grump. "There's nothing wrong with my passes. Finally, you were in the right place when I sent one your way. Not sure why it took having a woman in your life to make you play better."

"That's not it, dammit—I play just fine, with or without a woman in my life."

Foreman chuckled. "It's okay, O'Malley. We all do better with a good woman—or man—warming our beds. Happy dick, happy stick."

"Not sure that's how it goes," Gunnar said. "But the sentiment isn't off. Your life is stable, you play better." He took a hard look at Dex. "Let's hope this isn't a one-off and that your woman remains a good influence on you."

"She's not my woman. She's just a ... friend."

That set them off.

"A friend?"

"Poor O'Malley, already in the friend zone!"

"This friend's benefits better be you playing like you're supposed to ..."

And so on.

He shook his head, half-annoyed by their assumption that his troublemaking ways led to a lack of focus. Perhaps there was a smidge of truth to that, but just because he liked seeing those lovely green eyes shining back at him from four rows back didn't mean he was suddenly ... fuck ... *reliable*.

And then Ashley walked in and every argument he had for her not being his woman fell apart in the face of her smile.

"Dex, you were amazing!" Willa threw her arms around him, crushing on the hip bruise he'd acquired during a particularly vigorous check in the last period, then peered up. "I loved that move you did with the—" Instead of verbalizing it, she made a few mad cuts in the air with an imaginary hockey stick. "So cool."

"Hey, thanks, Sparkle. I'm so glad you guys made it."

"And the limo? They had Skittles in there. Like tons of them."

He raised his eyes to meet the smiling gaze of Ashley. "I think they do that for all their customers."

"Really?" Willa sounded skeptical. "Mom said you knew I liked them."

"Did she? She's such a gossip."

That made Ashley laugh, and Tara—who was also present, because she was a meddler—gave a saucy wink.

"You alright?" he asked his stylist and friend.

"Never better. Good game, Dexter. Glad to see you earning the millions the team pays you."

Ignoring her, he finally gave Ashley his full attention. It was hard to do it without looking like a simpering idiot, but he wanted to drink her in without the entire world knowing his business.

"Did you have a good time?"

She blushed, which was weird because she'd never seemed shy with him in the past. Maybe she thought a guys' locker room wasn't such a good place to meet, even though this wasn't the real locker room. This was the meet n' greet one, used for press and visitors.

"Yeah, it was great. You shouldn't have gone to so much trouble, though."

"It wasn't any trouble." He turned to her daughter. "Hey, Willa, what's the word for the day?"

"Pernicious. It means having a harmful effect, in a gradual way."

"Like O'Malley's lack of focus until this point in time. Hi, Ashley," Kershaw said, inserting his bone-headed self into the conversation. "Great to see you again."

"Hey there, Theo. How's Bacon?"

"As naughty as ever, but he's so good with Hatch." Hatch was Kershaw's two-year-old kid. He and his wife Elle had just had another one, a little girl named Adeline. "You nailed it there. Excellent choice."

"Well, I love matchmaking for animals and their fur-parents. I knew Bacon would be a great fit with your family."

"Speaking of great fits, how's our boy doing?" Kershaw put his arm around Dex's neck and gave him a squeeze. "Keeping his nose clean? Whatever you're doing with him is definitely making him play better. Keep it up."

Ashley dragged her teeth along her lower lip in a way that made Dex's groin tighten. "That's all Dex, nothing to do with me. He's his own man."

That's what he would have thought before. No one had the capacity to influence his game or inspire him to a higher level. He had inner resources he could call on to ramp things up when needed ... except that he rarely called on those resources. Maybe because he liked the idea they were in his back pocket, for when he needed them most.

Or maybe they were illusory, just a smokescreen so he could justify why he didn't need anyone. But tonight he felt something different.

Pride in his play.

Pride that someone he cared about was there to witness it, and not just his teammates. Of course he wanted to make them proud, but they all seemed to have different motivations for their own stellar game. People they loved, families they adored, legacies to build.

And now he realized that he cared about Ashley. He liked her more than was good for him and he'd fucked it up by coming on strong. She thought he was only interested in sex or getting a good grade before his court case, and nothing else.

"Aren't you going to introduce us to your friends, O'Malley?" Foreman cut into his negative musings.

"We just met your wife," Willa said to Foreman, so damn excited about everything. Dex loved her enthusiasm, especially when he was on the receiving end. "She's amazing!"

Foreman's face went soft. "Yeah, she is. Not sure what she's doing with a lug like me, but as Petrov is fond of saying, we never deserve the women who've graced us with their favor."

Petrov was such a fucking drama queen. Dex glared at

his teammate, not needing that vibe in the room. "Anyway. This is Willa and Ashley. You've met Tara."

Tara and Cal had once dated, but Dex didn't hold that against him. In fact, right this minute he didn't care if Tara had dated the entire team and everyone else in the visitors' locker room. She was happy and he was happy for her, and he had something else in the hopper.

Someone else.

Only he had no idea how to approach this. How to win Ashley.

And he realized in the moment that he wanted that more than he'd ever wanted anything before.

"THANKS for the game tickets and the limo and the Skittles." Willa leaned in and kissed him on the cheek from her seat in the back of his Escalade.

Ashley turned to her daughter. "Honey, could you go inside so I can chat with Dex for a second?"

"Okay." Willa opened the car door. The blast of cold air from outside should have dampened his senses, but it seemed nothing could do that these days. "Bye, Dex! See you soon!"

"Bye, Sparkle," he said as she shut the door.

They both watched as the front door opened with Maeve pulling her in for a hug. Another wave from Willa, a look that could sour milk from Maeve, and then the door was shut.

He turned back to Ashley. "I think she had a good time."

"She did. You really didn't need to drive us home."

"You'd have preferred the limo?"

"It had Skittles."

He chuckled and rubbed his mouth. "I'm glad you came. It was nice seeing people in my seats."

"Someone said you don't usually have guests."

Of course people had noticed. "Tara?"

"No, someone else. Casey, I think. Though I thought Tara was your friend." The unspoken "and more ..." at the end of that sentence was loud in the quiet of the car.

No way would he be sharing the fakery of his original relationship with Tara. Another one of his screw-ups that just made him look immature and completely unworthy of this woman.

"When we were together, she usually attended the games in the owner's box. That's more her style. And now—well, she doesn't need to sit in the players' section when she has a comfy seat beside her husband. She took up one of my seats tonight because she's nosy."

Ashley held his gaze. "But you haven't offered them to other people? Isn't this your second season with the Rebels?"

"The people I know are mostly on the team and anyone else is kind of temporary. I haven't wanted to invite anyone before now." He ran a hand through his hair, feeling more and more like an idiot with each passing second. "I liked looking over my shoulder and seeing you there."

Was it his imagination or did Ashley move incrementally closer?

"I liked when you looked over your shoulder at me."

His pulse went bananas. "You did?" The words were rusty, barely formed.

"I need you to kiss me now, Dex."

"You do?" She did! *So kiss her, idiot.*

He closed the gap. Lips mere millimeters from each

other, and the anticipation was so, so sweet. He'd never been so nervous about his kissing technique.

He'd never used the words "kissing" and "technique" in the same sentence.

Their lips met. The kiss exploded, caught fire, and burned through his soul.

This is why I fucked up. So I could meet Ashley.

He pulled back an inch, met her heavy-lidded gaze. "I need to touch you."

She nodded, a hot puff of air escaping her lips as her hand palmed his chest.

Every voice in his head, his dick, and his balls urged him to go straight for her tits. He was a boob man, always had been, and Ashley was possessed of an amazing pair. But he also wanted to be respectful. They were parked outside her house, in her neighborhood, with her family nearby.

Instead his hand curved around her hip, which should have been a poor substitute, but even that was enough to make his cock thick in his sweats.

"This okay?"

"Mm-hmm."

He went back in for more of her sweet taste, claimed those lips and deepened the kiss, all while his palm mapped the exquisite curve of her hip. He coasted a hand down to her ass. She felt amazing in his palm, the perfect fit.

"Dex. More." She moved his hand to under her top, like he needed directions. He was Dex Fucking O'Malley! He could find a nipple in a freakin' snowstorm.

Her skin felt so hot, so soft and silky. He moved up over warm, supple flesh until he reached her tit. Still the barrier of her bra but feeling that gorgeous mound beneath his fingertips had him hard enough to slam a puck into the net with his dick.

Add that move to practice next time he was on the ice.

He coasted a thumb above the bra's edge, expertly moved the strap aside, and popped that baby out. Better. Perfect.

Her moan told him just how much. It reverberated in his mouth, sending a thrill of sensation through him.

Then she cupped his cock and he almost exploded in his seat.

"Fuck!"

"No?" She pulled back, eyes wide with concern.

"Fuck, yes. I mean, I love it but ..."

"But?"

"I-I think we need to slow down."

She blinked those apple-green beauties at him. "Oh." He felt her pull away, and not just physically.

Fumble recovery needed, ASAP. "Ashley, I want this. I want you."

She pushed her top down and sat back a couple more inches. "I had—we had a nice time tonight. Willa will be talking about it forever." She placed a trembling hand on the car door handle.

"Ashley." Her name came out sharper than he intended. "Do not move one more inch."

Another wide-eyed blink, and Ashley froze in place.

"I could make you come in seconds, you know that? Just pull down the zipper of your jeans, slide my hand in, and slip my fingers through your hot, wet pussy. A few strokes and you'd be gone."

Her eyes flashed in anger. "Well, thanks for telling me what I'm missing."

"That's not what I mean. What I'm trying to tell you in my ass-backwards way is that you deserve better. Better than a quick fumble-and-finger-job in the front seat of my car. You deserve a warm bed with a million-thread-count sheets and my attention for hours while I bring you to the edge over and over. This is killing me to say this because I'm hard as fuck for you—"

"You are?" She looked close to tears.

He cupped her jaw and drew her close, brushing his mouth over her lips. So damn sweet. "Baby, I am. I don't want to treat you like a forgettable quickie. Because nothing about you is forgettable and nothing about this should be quick. You're a special woman and I plan to show you just how much I want you."

Her phone went off. She ignored it.

"Do you mind if I check something?" she asked.

"Go ahead."

She cupped his cock again and gave it a gentle squeeze that drew his groan.

"I just had to be sure." She leaned in closer, searching his eyes. "So, this is really happening?"

It really was, and he'd never wanted anything more. And then they were kissing again while the phone rang and his cock throbbed and his pulse soared, every heartbeat affirming this new, strange feeling.

Happiness.

He pulled away because Ashley's kisses were the kind of drug that was going to make him forget his resolutions to be a better man. Less fuckboy, more respectful adult.

"Ashley ..."

"Hmm?"

"Why is your sister shooting a death ray in our direction?"

She looked over her shoulder at Maeve waiting at the open door with a shawl around her shoulders. She looked

like a witch about to cast a spell; in fact, he could've sworn
he saw her lips moving, reciting an incantation.

"Oh dear."

"I'm guessing she hates me."

"It's not personal. She doesn't want to see me hurt."

"I never would."

Her phone rang again and this time, she answered,
"What?!"

He couldn't hear exactly what was being said but he
didn't need to. Big Sis was exercising her authority as head
of household and insisting Baby Sis get out of the clutches
of that bad man.

Ashley slid a look toward him. "I'm on my way. Yes. Bye."

End call. Deep breath.

"I—"

"Have to go. I understand."

She let her gaze fall down his body, landing right on
where he ached the most. "I wish I could ... help with that."

"Don't worry, you will. I'll be thinking of you later when
I jerk off."

Color tagged her cheeks, and he leaned in to kiss her.
"Better not keep your mistress waiting."

"She worries about me."

With Dex in the picture, that was understandable. He
wasn't very good at making people happy.

But he could make people feel good. His lips met hers,
which was a mistake because now he wanted nothing more
than to bundle her up and take her back to his place. She
cupped his face and held on, and he let himself believe that
she wanted that as well.

The car felt like a steam bath of longing and sex, but she
had responsibilities, so he nuzzled her nose and did the
right thing.

He pulled away.

"Thanks for tonight," she whispered. "For everything."

And then she was gone.

He watched her head into the house and raised a hand when she turned to wave at him. Once she was safely inside, he sat still for a moment, letting the lingering comfort of her wash over him. Holding onto it for a little longer before the chill of the air and distance from her house would take it away.

19

Dex

Likes: Ashley Adams
Dislikes: Smirking hockey-playing assholes

DEX WAS ON CLOUD NINE.

Everyone was still hailing him as the hometown hero. Last night, for the first time in his life, he'd acted like an adult around a woman he wanted. Then he went home and jerked off like a randy teen because there was only so much adulting he could manage in one day.

"What's that grin for, O'Malley?" Killer Callaghan nudged him as they walked down the main street in Riverbrook after a vigorous morning skate.

"He's got a girlfriend," Kershaw said. "But she's the kind of gal who takes pity on waifs and strays, so there's that."

"The shelter lady?" Grey grinned. "I thought I saw her last night. Doesn't she have a kid?"

"She does," Dex said. "I invited her and Willa to the game. And she's not my girlfriend."

"Yeah, she friend-zoned him, remember?" Foreman's contribution.

"Plus she has a kid," Grey said, even more annoying than before.

"Why do you keep saying that?"

"Because that's a lot of responsibility to take on." Grey had that worried look he seemed to have a lock on. He was the most anxious player on the team. "Is that what you want?"

"You're marrying him off already?" Kershaw laughed. "Give him a chance to actually score with her."

Already have. So he hadn't made it past second base, but it felt like he'd won big.

Only he didn't enjoy Grey's assumption that he wasn't capable of handling a relationship with a woman with a kid. Better to downplay it. Keep expectations all around to a minimum.

"We're just friends right now. I'm not dating her." Even though he wanted to. Because as soon as he said the negative, he started thinking that was what he wanted. Needed. He didn't care that she had a kid, but maybe he should? Maybe that was a huge consideration when a guy wanted to be part of a woman's life. Because he wasn't just dating Ashley, he was dating her family.

Her kid.

Her sisters.

One of whom was not a fan.

Just as those rain-heavy clouds descended he realized something else. They'd reached their post-morning-skate eating destination and it wasn't the Italian deli.

"Thought we were going to Barzini's."

"Nah, I want the omelet they named after me." Kershaw signaled to the hostess that they had five.

"You mean the one you insisted they name after you?" Callaghan observed wryly.

"To-maytoes, to-mahtoes. Of which there are plenty in the Theo, along with chives, ham, and feta."

"Sounds like Greek to me," Foreman opined.

Dex's pulse had picked up. She might not be here. It was close to noon, so past the breakfast rush, and the place didn't look that busy. He took a quick glance around. No sign of her. Maybe it was her day off or she'd already been fired, which wouldn't have surprised him because she was an ex-con.

Things were going well for him, and he wasn't going to let Ruby O'Malley ruin it.

As they sat down, he took another look around and— shit, there she was at the counter, talking to the hostess. Arguing with her, perhaps? She looked over, frowned, and said something to her colleague.

She didn't want this table.

Perfect, he didn't want to deal with her, either.

Apparently, she lost the fight because she trudged over with a stuck-on smile.

"Hey, guys, can I start you off with coffee?"

"Yeah, I'll have a latte macchiato," Callaghan said.

Kershaw rolled his eyes. "They don't do that here, dummy. Ruby, I'll have regular coffee. I'm guessing it's the same for everyone."

They all nodded except Dex who was trying to get his head around the fact Theo Kershaw was on a first name basis with his ex-con mother. Maybe during all the times in the last few weeks he'd cried off the diner run post-practice, Ruby had been insinuating her way into his life in another way.

Through his teammates.

"How about you, hun?" she asked Dex directly.

"Yeah, coffee," he muttered without looking at her. She poured while Dex tried to get a grip on his emotions. This wasn't right. She shouldn't be here in his space. In his life.

One of the guys asked Ruby if she'd seen the game last night.

"Of course I did. Quite the barnstormer."

"Yeah, we have this guy to thank." Foreman nudged Dex. "He's playing like a dream."

He couldn't bear to look at her. Would she look proud, or would she keep a vapid blankness so as to ensure he wouldn't blow up in her face?

I made it, he wanted to yell at her. *No thanks to you.*

He kept his head down, even when he put in his order for a Denver omelet, even when she set it before him, like some twisted parody of his childhood when she'd serve up Sloppy Joes and a glass of milk.

Eat up, Dexy. You should be in bed before Kane comes over.

Already tipsy, alcohol fumes wafting off her, she'd sit and watch him eat and as soon as that last morsel passed his lips, it was, "Okay, Dexy. Go do your homework now." Banished to his room with Loki, he'd put on his headphones and try to analyze math problems that meant nothing to him and stuff that had happened to other people and seemed so far away from his life.

He'd hoped they'd get to stay in this apartment longer than the last one. Ruby had a habit of losing her jobs, usually because she was too hungover to make it in on time. But this last one, a receptionist at a tire repair shop on Chicago's North Side where Kane was her boss, seemed to be sticking.

Or maybe it was because Kane was sticking it to his mom.

Dex didn't like the guy and the feeling was clearly mutual. But if his mom was happy and somehow managed to remain employed, what did he care? This way, they could pay the rent and stay longer. And all he had to do was put up with a few sharp comments and the occasional slap across the mouth, the last one coming the week before when Mom had gone to the bathroom and Kane thought Dex was backtalking. Just because Dex wouldn't get him a beer from the fridge.

Better not to tell her that Kane got physical. Because there was a delicate balance to be maintained. Keep Mom happy. Keep Kane happy. Keep his mother in a job, even one where the boss might overlook her tardiness and vodka-perfumed breath. Keep them in this apartment, this one place they could call home, because Dex was sick of moving. Sick of change. Sick of being the new kid everywhere he went.

But it didn't matter in the end because the balance was too precarious. All Dex had to do was stay out of Kane's way, but even then, self-sabotage was his bag. He would see how far he could push, then push a little more. Until someone got hurt and the blood started to flow ...

Back in the present, he looked up, realizing that someone was talking to him. Not her, but one of the guys.

He forced a smile as if he knew what the hell they were yammering on about. She was gone, thank God. Hadn't even stuck around to congratulate him, which was fine. He didn't need her praise.

After lunch, Dex told the guys to go on ahead because he needed to use the bathroom. He headed back to the table where Ruby was clearing.

"What's going on?"

Silently, she continued stacking the plates, her focus on the task at hand.

"Laughing and joking with the guys? Is this your way of getting to me?"

She sighed. "I'm just doing my job. The guys are friendly and my job is to be friendly back. We work for tips, y'know."

"Well, here's a tip: stay away from my friends." Something else occurred to him. "Have you told anyone that you're my—" He hesitated, unable to say it aloud.

"Your mother, Dex." The words came drenched in acid, but then the next ones were softer, regretful. "Have I told anyone that we're related or that I'm sorry for everything I put you through or that I wish more than anything we could—"

"Nah ah, not doing this. You shouldn't be here. I'm building a life and I sure as hell do not need you here screwing it up again."

She looked like he'd struck her.

He felt like he had. His entire body was in some sort of meltdown, and all he had to do was say sorry and give her a kind word. That might fix how he was feeling, or it might make it worse. He didn't know, so going for the knife—ha, the irony—was the best way to escape this onslaught of emotion.

"Dex, I need to talk to you. To tell you things."

"And I need you to stay away. I won't come in here again until I know you don't work here anymore. I'm not saying you have to quit. Everyone needs to pay the bills, but as long as you're here, I won't be."

And then he turned and left before he could absorb the latest expression of pain wracking her face. The one thing, the *only* thing, they had in common.

20

Ollie
Boston Terrier mix
Likes: Chasing cars
Dislikes: Catching cars

ASHLEY SHOULD NOT BE FEELING SO light.

She should not be enjoying that feeling when you're in the start of a new relationship—whether it's with a TV show, a friend, a cupcake shop, or a guy.

Most of those she could relate to. The guy—well, it had been a while. She couldn't recall feeling like this with Greg. It had all happened so fast. One drunken night, not even sure they'd see each other again, and then boom, *we're having a baby*. The fluttery feeling of being with someone new had quickly morphed into shards of panic, then grief for the life she'd known quickly receding, soon to be over-taken with new experiences: dropping out of college, morning sickness, a baby.

She had to reach back to her teenage years to recall anything so fun.

That's what being with Dex felt like. Fun.

Of course there were a million reasons why she shouldn't be messing about with someone like him, most of which Maeve had enumerated this morning over breakfast when Willa had left the kitchen to get dressed for school.

"A guy like that is only after one thing."

"Good," Ashley had quipped. "Because that's all he's getting from me."

And he actually wants to give it to me in a bed! Not the back seat of a car like her first time with Greg. Dex's respectfulness had floored her.

"Messing about with him gives your daughter the wrong impression."

That one had given Ashley pause. She didn't want her daughter thinking Dex was the kind of guy who could be counted on. This hockey himbo was a distraction for Ashley, but he could never be anything more for Willa.

"He's just a temporary visitor to her life. She knows that." And if she didn't, Ashley would make sure of it.

Maeve had pinched her lips even tighter. "He'll break your heart."

"No, he won't. Because I won't allow him in."

Her sister's expression had been nothing but pity, as if the heartbreaking was inevitable. As if this was the job of a man and the lot of a woman. But Ashley would never take Dex seriously enough to put her heart in play. She knew what his game was: make nice with the woman who held his future in her hands. Get that reference, escape with a light tap on the wrist, and be on his way.

Not that she thought he was playing her. How could she be played if she knew the rules *and* the outcome of the game? Eyes open, heart closed, no one could get hurt.

With her resolve set, she opened the door to the shelter's

reception area just before one in the afternoon, ready to start her shift. Toby was on the phone and raised his eyebrows when he saw her.

"She's here now. You should tell her yourself."

Frowning, Ashley watched as Toby mouthed, "It's Death," and accepted the phone.

"Hello?"

"Hey, Ashley." Not Death, but Dex.

Her pulse skittered and she cursed Maeve for possibly being right. She might like this guy more than was sensible.

"Hi, is everything okay?"

"I was just calling to let you know I can't make it this afternoon." He sounded very subdued, not like the man who'd wowed her with words and kisses last night.

"What's going on?"

"Just a stomach bug. I'm sure it'll pass but I don't want to get anyone sick."

She agreed, but there was something about his tone that didn't ring true. Turning her back on Toby, who was watching avidly, she asked, "Is there anything I can do?"

"No, nothing. I'm sorry I can't come in. I know we were supposed to do some of the social media shots today. I've already told Sophie to postpone."

"Right. That's not a big deal."

"Listen, I have to go. I'm just not good company right now."

Something had happened, something that sent him into a spiral.

"Okay. Feel better."

"Ashley?"

"Yes?"

"I had a nice time last night. I'm not trying to avoid you or anything like that, if that's what you're worried about."

"I'm not worried," she lied. "I had a nice time, too. Willa's talked of nothing else." Best not to talk about the other, the promise of intimacy about which she'd gone to bed dreaming. "Just take care of yourself."

"Okay. Thanks, Ash."

He clicked off and she turned to find Toby looking at her with a supercilious grin. "What did you do?"

"What? Nothing! Dex got tickets for me and Willa for last night's game, that's all."

He narrowed his eyes. "Something else is going on here. Why are you being all whispery and secretive?"

"I'm not. Now catch me up with what else is going on."

She half-listened while Toby filled her in on the latest additions to their menagerie and the applications for foster care and adoption. Her mind kept straying back to the phone call. Dex had sounded so down and even she knew she wasn't the reason for that. So what was? How could she help?

An hour later, she made up her mind. After a quick pitstop, she checked the volunteer files for Dex's address, then headed to his building, praying that he was home as he said and wasn't (a) with someone female or (b) out and about after pretending he was too ill to leave his apartment.

The doorman smiled at her.

"Hi, I'm here to see Dex O'Malley. He should be expecting me."

"Your name?"

"Ashley Adams."

"Okay, let me call up." He picked up the phone. "Mr. O'Malley? A Ms. Ashley Adams is here to see you."

A moment passed in which Ashley questioned all her life choices, and then the doorman nodded her through. "Fourth floor, elevator is on the left."

"Oh, thanks so much!" *Don't sound so surprised to be admitted.* On exiting the elevator, she saw Dex standing outside a door about halfway down the corridor.

With a woman.

Oh, what a dummy she was. Tempted to turn on her heel, she decided that no, she was much more mature than that. She took a step forward and now noticed more details. Dex's arms were crossed, and he was in a full-on scowl that did not suit him. He met her gaze with a stormy one of his own.

"What's going on? Is Willa okay?"

"She's fine."

The woman with Dex was dressed to the nines, like she was either going to a gala or coming home from one. The Barbie-pink ballgown—because that was the only way to describe it—looked rather incongruous in the building's dimly-lit corridor.

She turned, sending her platinum blonde hair in a gentle flyaway over her shoulder. It was like something a model or one of Willa's fairies would do.

"Hi, there," she said cheerfully.

"Hello."

The woman held up a cute clutch in one hand. "Just got in and ran into Dex. Shooting the breeze and all that." She thrust her hand forward. "I'm Georgia, Dex's next-door neighbor."

"Ashley." She took the woman's fine-boned hand and gave it a shake.

"Ash, what are you doing here?" Dex cut in, sounding a touch testy. He was wearing a T-shirt that said "Adulting" with one of five stars filled in, and the words, "Would not recommend."

Georgia gave him a sharp look, then raised a conspiratorial eyebrow at Ashley. "Someone's a little cranky."

"Any chance you might *not* be throwing a wall-banging party tonight, Georgia?"

She giggled in a very pretty, but also kind of evil way. "You never know how I'll feel after I take my nap. Oh my gosh, is that a kitten?" Her mouth dropped along with her gaze to the cat carrier in Ashley's hands.

"It is, and I really should get him inside. Georgia, it was lovely to meet you but right now I need to have a chat with Dex."

Go, Ash, bringing the mom energy.

"Got it!" Georgia sounded like she approved immensely. "Later, Dex." Lifting her voluminous gown like a Disney princess, she took the few steps to her apartment's door and was inside before Mittens had started meowing.

"Ash—"

"Hold on, can you take this?" She handed off the shopping bag, which he took, albeit reluctantly. "I brought soup and cupcakes. I know you said you had a bug, but I figured one of those will hit the spot. When I'm feeling out of sorts, soup or cupcakes always make me feel better."

"Okay." He sounded—and looked—confused.

"It's a cheer-up visit, Dex. On the phone, it sounded like you'd had really bad news. You don't have to talk about it, but I just wanted you to know that Mittens and I are thinking of you."

His eyes went shiny, and he took a quick breath. She'd made the right call: he needed someone right now.

"I can't believe you brought Mittens and left Bandit behind."

"Bandit's not ready for field trips. Can we come in?"

"You don't play fair, Ashley Adams."

She shrugged. "Mittens needs out."

He stood back and let her in, placing the shopping bag on the floor. She followed that with the cat carrier, which she opened. Mittens came flying out like a mad thing and immediately went for the shopping bag.

"We probably should pick that—"

She didn't get a chance to finish because she was suddenly wrapped in the strong, steely arms of a gorgeous hockey player.

"I can't believe you're here," he whispered against her hair.

"Why?"

"Because I don't deserve it." Before she could respond, he said, "I am sick, y'know."

"Oh?" She tried to draw back because if he truly was, she didn't want to catch anything.

"But it's not contagious," he murmured against her temple. "At least not in the way you think. I'm down and I can't really go into it because I'm not going to drag you into my messed-up life."

She drew back and looked up at him.

"You can tell me anything." It sounded dramatic and premature, but as soon as the words slipped past her lips, she realized she meant it.

He shook his head, rather vehemently. "That's not what you signed on for."

"I haven't signed on for any—"

He cut her off with a kiss, deep and hot and wet. Her knees turned to limp noodles but she held on, drawing strength from him. When he let her up for air, they were both panting.

"Sorry, I should have asked," he said, sounding so serious.

"I loved it. You make me feel so ... desired."

"It's not hard. Well, it is." He raised a cheeky eyebrow. "If you know what I mean."

"I think I do." A giggle escaped her, and that made him smile.

The smile vanished quickly. "But I meant what I said last night about respecting you. Taking it slow. I don't want to be that guy."

"What guy?"

"The one who's always looking to get his rocks off. A user. You're a special person and I don't want you thinking I'm only after one thing."

He had a rather poor opinion of himself, and she suspected some of it related to what he'd overheard her saying about him. How he got around.

"Dex, can I be honest with you?"

"Always."

"So we got off to a rocky start but it didn't take long before I started looking at you differently. Noticing how sweet you are, how kind you are to the animals, how nice you treated my daughter. And I also noticed other things. How attractive you are, how I can't seem to think straight around you, how one look from you is enough to set me on fire. I'm not used to feeling like this, so—well, horny all the time."

His lips curved because male pride will always cheer a guy up.

She gave him a light thump against his incredibly hard pecs. "Yes, that's all you, and the idea that you'd withhold what I so clearly need is frustrating beyond belief! I'm dying with lust over here and you're apparently fine with fanning the flames and hiding the fire extinguisher!"

Add to the knowing smile a husky chuckle. So. Infuriating.

"Dex!"

"Sorry, I'm being a jerk." He cupped her jaw and drew her mouth close to his. "Dying, huh?"

"Oh my God, what does it take to get some around here?"

And then they both laughed before the kissing again superseded all, hot and deep, more urgent than before. The floodgates had opened and any thought of slowing down had thankfully vanished into the ether.

21

"You'll tell me if I'm going too fast?"

Immediately followed by more kisses that barely gave her time to think. Fast was good, fast was sexy.

"I'll tell you. Assume it's all good," she whispered.

"We'll see. I've never wanted anyone this much, Ash."

She didn't believe him, but she'd take his pretty words and work with them. She hadn't heard anything so appealing in years, and while it might be fake, it was a fakery she could get down with. She needed to be wooed, and if she had to kickstart the seduction to get there, so be it.

She gripped the hem of his tee and pulled it up a couple of inches.

"Can I?"

He nodded, so she continued to push up, up, revealing inch after inch of smooth, golden muscle. His six-pack was brimming with vitality and heat, and it was all she could do not to fall to her knees and start licking. Instead, she kept it classy and let her hands wander over his hot skin. His sharp intake of breath told her he approved.

With his help, she pulled his shirt up over his head.

"You're so beautiful," she murmured to his chest. She couldn't believe she was here, that this was happening. After last night, when he'd called a halt, she wondered if they'd get here. Because nothing in life was certain.

He slipped off her jacket and started undoing the buttons on her blouse.

His expression turned uncertain. "You sure, Ashley? Don't do this because you feel sorry for me."

She felt a lot of things right now; pity wasn't even close to the top of the list.

"I want you, Dex. I hope you want me, too."

His expelled breath was both relief and invitation. "Fuck, yes. Never doubt it."

He cupped her beneath her butt and lifted her against his body, leaving her no choice but to wrap her legs around his hips.

"I've been wanting to do that for a long time."

"What? Risk putting your back out?"

"Take you somewhere no one can find you and have you all to myself." He frowned. "Not in a creepy abduction way. Just a 'let me inside you and make you feel special' way."

"I got it," she whispered, not sure why that sounded so sweet to her ears. Something about Dex made her feel oddly cared for. She wasn't used to it, given that she spent so much of her time focused on the needs of other people. It was so wonderful to be the center of his attention.

Carrying her forward, he kept his gaze locked on hers, like he was worried she might disappear before his eyes. She could tell him she was here for however long he needed her, but she didn't want to make any promises. Eventually she'd have to return to the real world.

Gently he placed her on the bed and pushed her on her back. Now for the reckoning.

It was complete daylight.

She was about to get naked in front of an Adonis.

She was sincerely out of practice.

And definitely not wearing her nicest underwear.

He ran a hand over the front of her jeans, the same ones she'd worn last night. The zipper scrape was so loud she almost jumped.

"Okay?"

"Yeah, just yank them off."

He rolled them down an inch, while she tried not to let the released-into-the-wild muffin top bother her. Her underwear—plain black boy shorts—stayed on, so at least he had that to distract him.

Her blouse was already open, so he finished the job and slipped it off her shoulders. Kneeling between her legs, he moved his gaze over her with a focus that made her go stiff.

His gaze locked onto hers. "What's wrong?"

"It's been a while for me, Dex. I don't want to say how long because it would embarrass us both. And I'm not like the women you're used to. I've got a mom bod and I wasn't really prepared for this." It wasn't a complete jungle down there, never mind the jiggle when she moved, but neither was it ready for prime time with a man like Dex O'Malley.

Feeling self-conscious, she clamped her thighs together as if that could make this conversation any easier.

"Ashley, you are so beautiful. Do you not see that?"

Tears threatened. She hadn't heard that in a while. Or ever.

He ran his palm over the curve of her belly, then pressed the heel of it between her thighs. "I want this pussy pretty badly."

She inhaled sharply, both the touch and the words working to infuse a sensuous warmth through her veins. A pulse started up between her legs, a throb of need that could only be sated by this man.

"Really?"

"Absolutely." He leaned over and kissed her, slipping his tongue past her lips and twining it with hers. Within seconds, he'd skillfully removed her bra and panties, leaving her completely exposed to him.

Cupping one heavy breast, he rubbed a thumb over her nipple and watched as it rolled to a stiff peak.

"This okay? I really want to feast on these beauties."

He waited, ever patient, so different than her previous experience. One not-so-careful owner. With Greg, it was usually over before she knew it, which she'd never minded so much because she was happy to get back to a good book on her e-reader.

She wasn't thinking about books right now. Her mind was a haze of desire, every part of her taut with exquisitely painful need.

"Anything. You can do anything," she whispered.

Bending his head, he fed her breast into his mouth, suckling away like he couldn't get enough of her taste. Ahhh! It felt so good that a tear escaped, a solitary requiem for what she had missed. Such care. Such lovely care.

He moved his hand down until his fingers delved between her thighs and—

"Ohhh!"

He looked up, slight alarm in his eyes, and left off her breast. "We okay?"

She nodded, swallowed, rolled her hips, craving the sweet invasion. He slipped his fingers out, then ran one between her sensitive folds, testing her response.

A wriggle, a moan, none of it seemed to get what she needed.

"Dex."

"Hmm?" His gaze remained fixed to his hand, which flattened and rubbed gently over her mound. "Open wide for me."

If this was the only way to get what she so sorely needed ...

She did.

"Good girl."

Her next moan was embarrassing, the combination of his praise and his hand, reapplied with a firmer press between her widening thighs. She bucked, seeking that perfect friction as wetness seeped from her.

"There it is. Perfect." With two fingers, he rubbed either side of her clit, never touching it, driving her crazy with desire.

"Oh God, please. Harder. More. Don't stop."

He gave her what she needed, rubbing, stroking, yielding pleasure drop by drop while she arched into his hand. Desperately she grasped the sheets, anything to keep her earthbound when her entire body threatened to take off and fly to the heavens.

Finally, he touched that sensitive bundle of nerves, and she levitated for a few seconds while her body juddered, clamping around the rough male fingers inside her, greedily holding onto the sensation.

When she looked up, she found him watching her, his eyes dark and focused.

"You're amazing," he whispered, his voice filled with awe.

"I think that was all you."

Still he watched her, like he couldn't believe she was here. He moved up and over her, his hand still between her thighs, almost possessively. "I just want this to be special for you."

She leaned up on her elbows, her lips close to his. "Why does it matter so much?"

"Because it's not usually all that special for me. Don't get me wrong, it always feels good but more like a biological function and not something more ... significant." A flash of panic lit his eyes. "I know you're not looking for anything major here, that's not what I'm trying to say—"

She touched a finger to his lips. "It's okay to want a connection, Dex. Just trust that this feels good. I'd tell you if it didn't." Though she'd never shared that with her ex. This already felt so much more honest.

She moved her hand down over the tantalizing bulge straining his sweatpants. He shut his eyes, and she watched as his mouth twitched. When he opened them again, he looked less troubled. Like her words had made an impact.

She couldn't promise him anything more because they were in such different places in their lives. It didn't have to mean the world but neither did it have to be meaningless.

"Let me see you," she whispered.

Quickly, he pushed down his sweats, freeing his cock. *Oh, mama.* Long *and* wide, its head was already bathed in pre-come, and the shaft's veins pulsed with vitality. She wrapped her hand around him and gave a long, lusty stroke.

"Aw, Ash." His murmur was so heartfelt, like he couldn't believe she was touching him like this.

"Tell me how you like it."

"This. Everything you're doing. God, I can't wait to be inside you." He shook his head. "Sorry, I'm having a hard time focusing. I want your hands on me. And I want my hands on you. And I need to be wrapped tight in your—oh,

Christ!" His eyes rolled back as she stroked again. It was kind of fun having this much control over him.

"Do you have condoms?"

A dazed nod, and he reached over to the nightstand. Adeptly, he rolled it on while she lay back, her body aching to be filled. In this moment, she didn't care about her voluptuous body or imperfect grooming. She didn't care that she was a thirty-year-old woman who sometimes felt like forty with a few extra pounds on her too-short lunch break. She didn't even care about that nagging whisper in her ear that Dex only wanted to butter her up for his court case.

None of these things mattered because she was about to be fucked well and good at 2:30 on a Wednesday afternoon.

He cupped her butt and pulled her close as he nudged, notched, and sank inside slowly. Every part of her tingled as that glorious fullness overrode her senses. Pleasure trickled through her, igniting cells, creating new pockets of need. She grasped his ass and urged him deeper.

His moan was primal, his name on her lips a shock because she couldn't recall it ever spoken with that level of feeling.

"Ashley—you feel so fucking good."

He withdrew, pumped again, seemed to miraculously find another inch of exquisite depth. His chest met hers, the friction wonderful as her nipples stiffened. He kept his stroke to a slow rhythm, and when she looked up and found him staring at her, she stayed locked in, loving how his intensity seemed to heighten with every pump inside her. Loving being in this moment with him.

Before today, she would have expected him to be a good lover, a man with moves. She never would have suspected this singular focus nor the sheer pleasure of being the object of his single-minded attention. He was wringing something out of her that went beyond sexual.

He seemed to understand how much she needed this, not because she hadn't been laid in forever, but because she needed something for her own. And right now, that was this joy.

This moment.

Just ... this.

Realizing that brought out an incredible tenderness for him. He might not think he had much to offer other than his body and skills in the bedroom, but she saw a different man to the one he presented to the world. She saw his generosity.

So when she cupped his face and pressed her lips to his, it was done to acknowledge Dex the human being instead of Dex the sex machine.

It yielded another moan from him, from somewhere deep. He kissed her with fervor and passion, and thrust harder, hard enough to rub her clit with the return and unexpectedly, he was giving her more, squeezing more pleasure out of this than she would have thought possible.

That buzz in her belly started up again, lower, deeper, and within seconds she felt it everywhere. All extremities, a fire in her core, even her toes got in on the action.

"Dex!" she screamed as the orgasm hit her, making her muscles tighten and squeeze his cock. He didn't last long after that—how could he? He had nothing left to give but an animalistic groan and a collapse as he spent himself inside her.

A few seconds passed in lovely quiet, perfectly still. She stroked his hair and let herself enjoy the pleasurable weight of him. That fond feeling overcame her once more, manifested by a soft kiss to his cheek, a nuzzle of her nose so she could enjoy that rasp of stubble.

Up on his elbows, still embedded within her body, he faced her, his mouth stretched wide.

"That was incredible. And don't say it wasn't because it could not have been anything less than amazing. I knew we'd be good together, but hell, that was something else." He cocked an eyebrow, daring her to disagree.

"Hmm, it was something alright."

"Ashley!"

"Okay, okay, it was incredible."

He grinned. "Good girl."

And her body went to jelly.

"You like that, don't you?"

Embarrassed, she acted oblivious. "What?"

"When I tell you what a good girl you are. It happened in the coffee shop. You flushed and started fidgeting, like you needed to rub your thighs together."

He was still inside her and this conversation was doing weird things to her. Her pussy fluttered and re-activated, all because of his praise.

He felt it, too. His eyes smoked over, his cock thickened, and he cupped her rear and gave it a nice, long squeeze. "This ass does things to me, Ashley. I'm mad for this body. I love talking to you. But damn, when your eyes turn that flash of apple-green, when that sexy blush warms your cheeks, and you get all squirrely because I've told you you're a good girl, that makes me as hard as a rock. It's okay to admit you like it. I love it."

She opened her mouth to deny, but what was the point?

"I've never had any kind of praise kink before, or at least I didn't know I had. But when you said it before and now anytime you go there, it turns me on."

"Good. Be honest with me about what's good for you. I want to give you exactly what you need."

"That goes both ways, Dex."

It sounded like they were agreeing this was more than a one-shot deal. She wasn't entirely sure what he needed. When she arrived, he was obviously in some sort of emotional slump. Sex would cheer him for a while, but it wouldn't solve his problems.

With a nod of acknowledgment of her offer, he slowly pulled out. "Let me take care of this. Don't move."

Boneless and spent, she wasn't about to go anywhere, but she did pull the coverlet up over her exposed body.

A moment later he was back, naked as a babe, and holding Mittens. "Look who needs attention."

Stretching out on the bed, he let the kitten run over his expansive chest and faced her with a grin. "You hungry?"

"Always."

"Can you stay and eat with me?"

"I'd love that."

22

Dex didn't do sweet, but having Ashley in his bed had been about both the sexiest and sweetest experience ever. The way she'd clung to him, the way her body reacted when he praised her, hell, just having her here in his apartment was like a dream come true.

Now the sweetness was on overload because Mittens was glued to his neck and not showing any sign of detaching while Ashley heated up soup.

He couldn't stop looking at her. Unfortunately, she'd dressed—with firm intentions of leaving to return to work, she'd said—but that was okay because her ass looked great in those jeans and her breasts looked amazing in that blouse. But mostly she looked right in his home. Like she belonged here, with the kitten and the soup and cupcakes.

Better not skate before you can walk, boy.

"You don't have to do that," he said, thoroughly enjoying that she was doing it all the same. He was strangely digging the domesticity of it all.

"It's almost ready." She smiled. "Will sex for soup."

"Hmm, I like that word on your lips."

"Sex?"

"Soup."

She giggled, and he loved hearing that sound even if it was because of some nonsense out of his mouth. Ashley was kind of on the serious side, which made her his complete opposite. He didn't like to think of all the ways they were different, so he put that aside. With Mittens still latched on like a furry barnacle, he stood and helped Ashley bring the soup to the table.

"Did you make this?"

"No, I bought it at the Sunny Side Up Diner. They have this amazing chicken noodle, but they were out today so I went with the potato and leek." She must have noticed his reaction because her face fell. "Sorry, do you hate this kind of soup?"

"No, not at all." He fought for his composure. Here was his mother again, turning every nice thing into a problem. It really felt like this town wasn't big enough for both of them. "Do you go there a lot? The diner?"

"Not that much. Willa loves the French toast but it's more of a treat kind of place."

Her family must be financially strapped if French toast in a neighborhood diner was a treat. He tried the soup. It was good. Really good. He doubted his mother had any part in preparing it, so he sucked it up and smiled.

"It's great. Sorry, I'm just distracted. Big game in a couple of days in New York."

The look she sent his way said she didn't believe him, but she didn't push. One thing he'd noticed about Ashley was her quiet patience, which was incredibly calming. He didn't want to lie to her, so he came up with a version of the truth.

"Someone I don't get along with works at the diner and I

get weirded out whenever I hear its name. It's childish, I know."

"You can't help having a visceral reaction to the mention of it. I get it, honestly. When I hear 'Hey Ya' by Outkast, I feel like throwing up."

"You do?"

"It was playing at the coffee shop where I saw my ex kissing our babysitter. So now that song is ruined and is forever related to this thing that happened."

"That sucks." The more Dex heard about this ex, the more he hated the guy.

"Agreed. But to be honest, it was over long before then. We would have been better off co-parenting without the pressure of making a marriage work. I wanted to be married. And Greg didn't. He's not husband material. He's barely father material."

"Willa seemed hurt the other day when he didn't show. But kind of accepting, too. Like it's a regular occurrence."

"She's used to his neglect. I try to make it up to her—we all do. But then my sisters like to talk about what a jerk he is, and it just perpetuates this cycle. I try not to bad-mouth him. It's not fair on Willa. And I don't like to carry that kind of negativity around. It just eats away."

He knew *all* about that. "So you never get mad at him?"

"Sure I do. But I try to do it so Willa doesn't hear or know."

Willa knew. Ashley might think she was keeping that under wraps, but kids always knew.

His phone buzzed on the counter and he checked it quickly.

KERSHAW

Cards at Hunt's place at 7 p.m. Bring beer.
Nothing cheap.

"Everything okay?"

"Yeah, just an invite to a poker game at one of my team-mate's tonight."

"Oh, that's fun."

It should be yet the doubts about their motives niggled. "Maybe I won't go. They're all pretty tight and it sucks being the new guy." Even after a year and a half on the team.

Mittens chose that moment to give a plaintive meow, which from his spot on Dex's shoulder was more like a roar in his ears. Dex pulled him down into his lap.

"You know what it's like being the new guy, don't you, little one?"

He looked up to find Ashley watching him closely. "Sorry, there I go with my woe-is-me again."

"It's tough being new, forced to move around, especially when the team decides you're more useful as a trade. I'm betting you never get used to that."

"I should be. I've been on the constant move since I was ten."

She reached for his hand and curled her small one inside his. "Being used to it doesn't make it any easier. I'm guessing that holding part of yourself back is one way to make an exit hurt less."

He gripped her hand back, loving the warmth and understanding that flowed from her. "I might get kicked off the team if I'm convicted. Or they might decide to put me on waivers or boot me down to the AHL anyway."

"So no point in making an effort with the guys? Because

you could be gone any minute?" She said it gently, her hand still wrapped in his.

"I suppose that's been on my mind. Keeping things at a surface level just seems ..." *Safer.* "Easier."

Mittens climbed up his chest, digging his tiny claws into Dex's tee. He was so needy and Dex loved it.

"Yeah, I get it," Ashley went on, "and of course your teammates are tight. They've had time to build a community. Doesn't mean they don't have room for one more. But you need to show them you're interested, earn their trust."

"I had a good game last night, so I've made it into the inner sanctum." They'd thought he was a waste of space until he started playing better. Just further confirmation that his value lay in his performance, and he needed to focus on that.

She studied him for a moment. "Give them a chance to see you. The real you."

Not the party-loving fuckboy who was a magnet for trouble.

"That guy's kind of boring."

"Eats his vegetables"—she pointed at the empty soup bowl—"is kind to old ladies"—she shot both thumbs at her face—"and doesn't get into trouble with the law? That kind of boring?"

"Well, when you put it like that. Especially the kind to old ladies part." He studied her. "You're not that much older than me, though. Only five years."

Her nose twitched, but she didn't answer. Or rather that nose twitch said it all. Five years might not seem much, but her life experience was completely different from his. This woman had a kid, an ex-husband with co-parenting drama, a life where hockey games and diner visits were special occasions. Not just five years, it was a whole other lifetime.

Dismissing the (small) age difference was one way to let her know they weren't so far apart. He could give her pleasure, treat her like a queen, and make things better for her. The selfish part of him said that doing these things would make things better for him.

She picked up her soup bowl and took it to the sink. He followed with his and placed it on the counter.

"Can you stay the afternoon?"

She looked alarmed. "I know you're virile but surely, you're not ready to go again?"

He chuckled. "Actually, where you're concerned, I'm always ready to go. But I was thinking more along the lines of eating cupcakes, playing with a kitten, and relaxing. We could watch Netflix and chill, the original meaning. When's the last time you played hooky?"

"I can't remember. I'm too much of a—"

"Good girl?" He grinned and pulled her into his arms.

"You're not playing fair."

He kissed the top of her head. "I'm not asking you to stay for a marathon sex session, not that it's off the table. I just thought that maybe you could take it easy. Aren't there people you can rely on at the shelter?"

She peered up at him. "You're a bad influence, Dex O'Malley."

"So everyone tells me. For once, I'd like my bad influencing to result in something nice for a change. As in nice for someone else."

She bit her lip, which was so damn adorable he had to kiss her. Sinking into the kiss, she gave a small moan that set him on fire.

"Should we talk about this?" she murmured.

"Enough talking."

"I mean ..." She raised an eyebrow. "You should know I have no expectations."

You should, though. You should expect the sun and the moon.

"Okay."

"And we should keep it under wraps because I'm supposed to give you that reference. It wouldn't look good if it came out that we were, y'know."

"Whatever you want." And because he didn't like the implication of that—unserious, immature, fun-time Dexter —he kissed her again.

"I thought this was supposed to be relaxing." Her eyes were glassy.

"I can make it relaxing." He picked her up and brought her to the couch. "I can relax you so much you'll never want to leave."

23

DEX WAS NERVOUS, which was completely absurd.

These were his guys, his bros, his team. But it was the first time he'd been invited to Levi Hunt's place for poker night, and he wanted to make a good impression. When you spent most of your time making a bad one, this seemed especially important.

The door was opened by Jordan Hunt, Levi's wife, who was also a reporter with the Chicago Sports Network. Her red hair was in a ponytail, and judging by her outfit, it looked like she'd just come back from the gym.

"Hey, Dex!"

"Hey, Jordan. How's it going?"

"Good. Come on in." She gestured for him to enter. "I wondered when you might show up to one of these."

"Been waiting on the invite."

"Well, when Banks takes you for all your worth, you might regret that. Guy's a total shark, or so I hear." She took his jacket and hung it on a hook. "Listen, I was hoping for a word. I know you have your court case coming up and I'm guessing you were advised not to talk to the press."

"Ordered, more like."

Her smile was sympathetic. "Got it. But if you want to do an interview afterward, tell your side of the story, I'd love to be the one who gets that."

He'd always found Jordan to be a straight shooter, surprising considering she was a member of the sports media. But the last time he sat down for her hockey podcast, he shot his mouth off in a way that got him iced out by his teammates.

"I'm not sure I should talk about it. I'm trying to be more discreet these days, stay out of the headlines."

Not just to keep his spot on the team. Keeping his private life private would improve his chances with Ashley. He wanted to protect her and this growing connection between them.

"Okay, if you change your mind."

"O'Malley!" Levi Hunt emerged from what must have been the kitchen. "Finally." As if Dex had been holding out when he didn't even know this weekly meet-up existed.

"I brought beer." He held up a six-pack, then mentally kicked himself for not bringing a case.

"Sure, tote that bad boy in here." Levi smiled at his wife and pulled her in for a kiss. It lasted a little too long, so Dex had to turn away. Fucking married people. "We've got him, J."

"Okay, be nice. I've got a podcast to edit."

He followed Hunt into the kitchen where he found a counter piled high with cans of beer.

"Looks like we're in good shape."

Hunt opened the fridge which was packed to capacity with even more bottles and cans. "Yes, we are. Just leave that there. You nervous?"

"Why would I be?"

"No reason. You just seem a bit on edge."

He wanted to be liked. After eighteen months on this team, he wanted the guys to see more than just the party guy. *Let them see the real you.*

"I'm not that good at cards."

Hunt smirked. "Now that's your first mistake."

AN HOUR later Dex was six hundred bucks in the hole, but not too sad about it. The nerves had vanished, leaving in their place a feeling of contentment. Kind of how he felt with Ashley, minus the sexy.

"We need to handicap Banks," Reid said. "It's like the World Championships of Poker and he's the only person playing."

Banks looked smug. "You fuckers need to focus on your game instead of gabbing about your WAGs and your kids. Less domestic drama, more card counting."

"Knew he was cheating." Erik Jorgenson put his hand down. "Isn't it time to eat?"

"You just had half a veggie pizza, dude. And three slices of the shrimp one that no one eats because fucking shrimp." Kershaw gestured for two cards and eyed them hopefully. "Pity there's no lasagna."

"Lasagna?" Hunt looked up from his hand. "Where's that coming from?"

"Haven't you heard?" Sly side-eye sent toward Dex. "Dex's girl makes a mean Italian casserole. Or lasagna to the uninitiated."

"Turkey and fennel, I heard," Erik said. "Not the best combination." Jorgenson was a major foodie, but no amount of food snobbery would get him a pass on casting aspersions on Ashley's culinary prowess.

"That's where you're wrong." Dex had two queens, a king, and two cards under eight. Could he turn this into something decent? "It was amazing. She's a great cook."

And even better in bed. Just thinking of her gorgeous body, creamy skin, all that hair … Probably not the best time, given the cock-stirring situation down south.

Besides, she'd made it clear what they were doing. *You should know I have no expectations.* Was that because she wasn't interested in more or because she doubted his sincerity? Women were so hard to figure out.

"Don't bash a man's woman's cooking, Fish." Foreman picked up a card, then put it down again. "Especially when you haven't tried it."

Kershaw chuckled. "Yeah, he might give you a Hughes special."

That went over like someone had dropped a turd in the game pot. On the whole, people had been incurious about what happened in the Empty Net that night after the Pittsburgh game, assuming it was just another example of Dex O'Malley's poor judgment. Now a door had been opened.

Hunt was first to kick off the proceedings. "How's that going, O'Malley? You going to get off with a tap on the wrist?"

"Remains to be seen."

A couple of quick exchanged glances followed that nothing-burger of a statement.

Just give them a chance to see you. The real you.

"Hughes and I go back to juniors. We've never really gotten along."

Foreman discarded another card, then winced at what

he got in return. "You played at Minnesota together, too, if I recall."

But Dex had always been better. Hughes had never appreciated that, nor did he like the fact Dex came up with nothing but was still a success—and quicker, too, going straight into the NHL unlike Hughes who had to play a couple of years in the minors.

"His family fostered me as a kid. I lived with them for a year when I was fifteen."

That Dex had been in care wasn't exactly a secret. Most players' paths through the juniors and college was public knowledge, and with that came details of players' personal lives. A couple of the gossip rags had picked up on his, crediting his current behavior to his tricky past. But he had never mentioned the F-word to anyone he played with. It drew too many questions, and he was done answering those in his teens.

He waited, his heart in his throat, for someone to dig deeper.

How did that happen?

Where are your parents?

No wonder you're so fucked up.

"Hughes took his time getting called up from the AHL." Hunt tilted his head, looking at his hand like it had insulted his wife. "That what he was chippy about?"

"Let's just say he and I have never been close. And he was rude to his girlfriend. Borderline abusive, in fact."

"Guy's always had a big mouth," Gunnar said. "Remember that time he got into it with Sorenson at the Chucks-Pitt game? So-So had to be restrained from whacking him into the stands."

"If anyone deserves to be thumped, it's Hughes, that's for

sure." Foreman lay down his hand, three tens. "Here we go, gentlemen. Beat that."

Of course Banks had the goods, which made everyone groan. The guy was a fucking poker-playing machine.

Kershaw took a swig of his beer. "One good thing came out of O'Malley's flirtation with the law, though."

Dex looked up and met the D-man's grin. "Enlighten me."

"You're playing like a dream. Which I'm putting down to either your sheer desperation not to get thrown off this team or the fact you want to impress a chick."

"She's his good luck charm." Foreman pointed at him. "Do not mess with that, Dexter."

He wasn't planning to. But it wouldn't hurt to get some advice.

"I like her." It was a tentative opening—or at least he'd thought so until he felt seven sets of eyes on him and the weird feeling that time had come to a standstill.

"Yeah, ya do," Kershaw said.

"So why so sad?" Jorgenson asked. "Because of the turkey-fennel lasagna?"

For fuck's sake. "I already said it was awesome. I'm just not used to hanging with someone so ... authentic. She's got this life that's very different from what I do. What we do."

"Worried she'll cramp your style at the club?" Reid gave him a dead-eyed glare which Dex was happy to return.

"No. I'm more concerned she'll think I'm not worth her time. That I'm not serious enough for her. After all, we just play hockey."

"Just play hockey?!" Kershaw exploded. "We are gods!" He beat his chest for good measure which drew chuckles at his absurdity.

She'd also made a semi-decent point about keeping it under the radar because of the court case. At least, that was her reasoning, but maybe she preferred no one knew because she was embarrassed. He probably shouldn't be talking about it to the guys, but he couldn't keep it to himself.

Foreman put his hand face down. "Sounds like you've got the old self-doubt monster knocking at your door. So you like this girl."

"Woman."

That yielded a smirk from the Mouthy Southie. "Gotcha."

"You do?"

"You think she's got all this life experience while you've been pissing about with your dick out on the dance floor. That you're not on the same page or even reading the same book. But all that's behind you, right?"

He nodded, because it seemed important that not only Ashley know that he had changed but the guys know, too.

Foreman held his gaze. "Then who cares what you were like a year ago? Or even a month ago."

Kershaw chuckled. "Knew you had it bad for her. And her kid. And her lasagna."

Banks cleared his throat loudly. "Are we playing cards or does O'Malley need anyone else to weigh in on his woman problems?"

"At least he has a woman," Reid said, which had everyone laughing except Banks who scowled, then proceeded to take them for another cool grand.

24

Vera
Likes: Her sisters, her niece, men who follow orders in bed
Dislikes: Her ex-husband and that bitch he's now remarried to.

"WHERE DID YOU GO, ASHLEY ADAMS?"

Ashley turned over her phone and placed it on the kitchen table. Not that there was anything untoward going on. Dex had just sent her a dog-going-nuts video he found amusing, that was all.

She returned to chopping carrots and smiled at Vera, who'd asked that pointed question. "Just toiling away doing the cooking no one wants to."

"You volunteered."

"If I didn't, we'd only eat takeout."

Vera smiled serenely. "Your point?"

Maeve came in and grabbed a wine glass. "Just heard from Jenny Gulliksen. Bob's been boning his PA."

Vera rolled her eyes at Ashley. "Made your day, has it?"

"No! It's merely another data point."

"It's a good thing I'm only using them for sex. Like Ashley."

Ashley froze, then carefully started chopping again. "Not sure what that means."

Maeve's phone rang so Vera's observation didn't penetrate. She stabbed at the screen and answered with a resounding "Yeah, I heard! That bastard." Out she went with a glass of wine in a swish of indignation.

"Hard to get laid with that attitude." Vera picked up a carrot piece and popped it in her mouth. "So how was lunch?"

"Lunch?"

"Yeah, I stopped by the shelter about two, but Toby said you had went out to run errands on your lunch hour, though your shift only started at one."

"Y'know. This and that."

She leaned in. "Let me rephrase. How was he?"

"Who?"

"You think I can't tell when my baby sister is getting wham-bammed, thank you, Mr. O'Malley?"

Ashley shook her head. She couldn't lie.

"It was just a one-off."

"No good?"

"Too good. Good enough. Not something I need to repeat because now I've ... cleared the pipes, as they say."

Vera hooted. "Are you telling me you wouldn't go in for seconds if he asked?" She narrowed her eyes. "You like him, don't you?"

"I wouldn't sleep with someone I didn't like."

"I would. Sometimes the sex is better that way. But Ashley, you and Dex O'Malley—"

"Shush! I don't need the whole world knowing."

"Why? I'd be shouting that one from the rooftops. The

guy is fit!" She grinned. "I'm very pleased for you. I hope it was all you wished for."

"He's very ... forthright."

"Oh yeah? Dirty talker?"

Yes, but more than that. An honest talker. At least, that's what it felt like. He was clear about how much he enjoyed her body. How much it turned him on.

How much he liked her.

Now she was wondering why. Any of the paparazzi photos she saw of him always showed him with slender, glamorous women. Ashley was not his usual type.

Why her? What did she offer?

"Don't do this, Ash."

"What?"

"Overthink it."

She couldn't help it. Ideally she would like a man to be attracted to her in a normal fashion, not because she had something he needed (a reference for a judge, a need to satisfy a big girl fetish, the accidental mother of his child). This smacked of a little too much fairy tale thinking.

Ashley was far too sensible for fairy tales.

Surreptitiously, Ashley watched Dex from the entrance to the dog yard. He was on his knees outside Bandit's cage, holding out a squeak toy to the pup who was studiously ignoring him.

Or was he?

Bandit sniffed at the ground but whenever Dex moved a few feet away or turned his back, the dog took a quick look, his eyes filled with such hunger! But then as soon as Dex paid him any mind, he found his inner moody teenager.

This went on for a good ten minutes. Ashley felt a movement at her side. Gillian, one of their volunteers, stood there, her kohl-rimmed eyes soft and shiny.

"That's pretty adorable."

"Yeah. I probably should photograph it, shouldn't I?"

Gillian nodded. "Evidence of his good deeds. Definitely."

Ashley snapped a few photos with her camera then filmed about fifteen seconds of video, just enough to catch Dex shaking his head in mock exasperation. He turned and caught her filming, and because he was obviously used to the attention, out came the kill-her-dead smile.

"Mama likey," Gillian murmured.

This mama agreed, but she couldn't say that aloud. She was supposed to be a mentor-type to Gillian, not that she'd ever asked for it. But aspiring-to-middle-aged frumps couldn't be seen drooling over younger himbo hunks.

She lowered the phone. "Have you had a chance to sweep out the cattery?"

Gillian raised a diamond-studded eyebrow. "On it, boss."

"I'm not the—" But Gillian had already sauntered off, leaving Ashley worried she might have offended her. It just seemed strange for them both to be standing there watching Dex, and for some reason, she couldn't be the one who walked away first.

Now, she had no excuse. She had work to do, invoices to file, schedules to create, an Empty the Shelters event to organize, and yet, here she was placing one foot in front of the other as she headed toward Dex.

"Hey there," she said softly.

He turned and grinned at her. "Hey, yourself. You look lovely."

She might have put a little more effort into her appearance this morning, but the compliment still threw her. Warmth toasted her cheeks; she managed to murmur "thanks," then, "How was the card game?"

"Good. Really good."

"And how's Bandit today?"

"A tease."

She chuckled. "Let's take him out." Dex had walked him a few times on a leash in the play area, but Ashley thought he might be ready for some more unstructured interaction.

With his cage open, Bandit still held back and had to be coaxed out to the open. Ashley attached his leash and handed it off to Dex. "Your move, hotshot."

Dex smiled, though he seemed a little nervous, like he wanted to get this right. "C'mon, fella." He walked Bandit out toward the dog run, though the little devil growled at a few of his neighbors on the way.

"So cranky," Dex said softly. "But y'know something, I like you just the way you are. You can be bad-tempered and act like you got out of your dog bed on the wrong side all you want. I won't care. I'll still think you're a good dog, the best one there is." All the way out to the dog run, Dex spoke in that soothing voice, telling Bandit it was okay to be emotional, it was okay to be different, because Dex loved him anyway.

Ashley's heart squeezed with every gentle word.

"Should I let him off the leash?"

"Sure."

Dex did, and Bandit ran to the other end of the small park area they had set up to exercise the dogs. There he stayed, sniffing around the bushes.

Sighing, Dex turned back to Ashley. "Tough crowd."

"Don't take it personally. He hears all your sweet talk and it's just a matter of time before he'll respond."

He moved in closer, his hand brushing her hip. "I've had better luck with you, I think."

Her heart rate picked up. "Oh, I'm much easier than Bandit."

"I loved hanging with you yesterday." He inclined his head and stole a quick kiss. "I loved eating soup and playing with Mittens and making you come."

Her breath caught. "I loved it, too."

"Would you like to do it again, sometime?"

She looked over his shoulder, checking to see if any of the volunteers were around. Gillian often came out for smoke breaks.

She swallowed. "I would."

He opened his mouth to say something, then his eyes went wide.

"Ashley," he whispered. "It's happening."

Yes, it is. It so is. And I'm completely on board with whatever this is.

"Tell me how to play it."

Oh. She realized now what was going on. Bandit had returned, probably wondering why no one was paying him any heed, and was currently nudging Dex's hand.

Dex looked down tentatively then back up at Ashley, his expression one of mild panic. "What should I do? Ignore him? Pet him? I don't want to scare him off."

Ashley lowered her voice and leaned in closer. "Just remain still and let him sniff you. If he starts to lick, you'll know—"

Dex's jaw fell. "He's licking my fingers! I really want to hug him but what if that's too much?"

Oh God, Ashley's heart exploded. Dex had so much love to give, and how adorable was his reaction to Bandit's affection?

"Let him get used to you then hunker down to his level, slowly."

"Okay. Okay." He inhaled deeply, then after a moment, lowered himself to a squat while still letting Bandit stay close. Running a hand over Bandit's head, he went eye to eye with him. "You're such a good dog, Bandit. Don't you know how much everyone loves you?"

Bandit did what Ashley wished she could have done: he licked Dex's face.

Dex looked up at her, his joy plain as day. "Did you see that?"

"I did. Looks like you've made a breakthrough."

In fact, both man *and* this man's best friend might have.

"Don't think I've forgotten what we were talking about." He continued to rub Bandit but his attention was fixed on her. "About a repeat performance of our Netflix and chill without the Netflix. Modern definition."

"I haven't forgotten either."

Dex grinned, charmer of dogs and moms alike. "Excellent."

25

Jasper
Part pug, part divo
Likes: Outside
Dislikes: When I don't get to go outside

DEX WASN'T LOOKING FORWARD to his shift at the shelter today. Not because he didn't want to be there with Ashley and Bandit and Mittens, but because it was about to be tainted.

Today was photoshoot day.

Sophie was bringing her PR team to gather evidence of his do-goodery. Now that he'd had a good game, and the heat was off, it was an appropriate time for him to go Insta-official on the volunteering gig.

"This sucks."

"It hasn't even started yet." Ashley rubbed his arm, and just having her near made him feel 1000% better. She looked especially hot today with those tight jeans he loved and a cute pink blouse that fell off her creamy shoulders. "It'll be a couple of nice photos and a little promo for you and the Empty the Shelters event. No biggie."

"You'll have to be careful. Don't look at me with lust or anything."

She rolled her eyes. "You think I can't resist you?"

"I know you can't." He checked behind him and pulled her in for a kiss. "But that's okay. I'll give you the cold shoulder and we should be good."

She scrunched up her nose. "I thought you were okay with this. The way we're handling it."

"I am." But he didn't sound like he was okay, and he didn't feel like he was okay, and the lie was no better than acid in his mouth. He was a little bit crazy about Ashley and he wanted other people to bear witness.

"Helloooo!" Tara's voice carried from the reception.

"Oh, I didn't know Tara was coming." Ashley sounded a little off there, maybe a touch jealous.

Shouldn't like that idea. No, I should not.

"Neither did I." His fake ex was sticking her nose in, looking for gossip. He headed out to find not just Tara but Fitz and Esme, too.

"Esme really wanted to visit with the kittens." Tara waved at Ashley. "Hello, great to see you again!"

Ashley was already zeroing in on Esme. "She's even more gorgeous in person!"

"We're pretty proud," Fitz said.

Dex wanted to begrudge the guy's smug expression but couldn't. After all, that wasn't what he wanted, was it? Dex's life was fine the way it was. He had a woman who was happy to treat him as fling material while he worked on playing a good boy for the press. That nagging feeling of discontent was probably indigestion.

Sophie breezed in with her minions carrying lighting

and photography equipment. Dex was a little hung up on watching Ashley as she held Esme to her warm, curvy body.

She looked like a mom when she was with Willa, but with Esme, it was like a bomb went off in Dex's head, one that said: *Me Want!*

But what exactly? Not a kid. He didn't want to be married or to be tied down. But seeing Ashley and Esme all cozy and cute had him hankering after something.

Community. Belonging. All that junk he'd pushed down deep since he'd become that transient kid with a transient life, who grew up to be a transient adult.

Ashley was making funny faces at Esme when the infant spotted Dex and reached out a chubby fist.

"Aw," Tara said. "Uncle Dex has entered stage left."

Which was his cue to let her curl a hand around his little finger and hold on for dear life.

"Hey, little vampire, did you miss me?"

"Dax!"

"Did she just say my name? Is that her first word?"

Tara grinned. "No, she's very advanced. She's been chatting up a storm in the last couple of weeks."

"But she knows my name!"

"Pretty sure she was calling for her daddy." Fitz shot him a dirty look, which Dex accepted cheerfully. He knew what he'd heard.

He leaned in, his head close to Ashley, and spoke in a low voice to Esme. "You did miss me, didn't you? Well, I missed you, too." It wasn't completely untrue.

His gaze slid to Ashley who was considering him in what he hoped was a new light. *See? I'm more than a party-loving playboy.*

"What can I say? All the girls love me."

"Now, that does *not* surprise me." But she was surprised,

if that soft expression was anything to go by.

Sophie cut in. "I'd take a lovely photo of this tableau if I didn't think our general manager wouldn't be on board."

"Yeah, no using my daughter in Rebels promo." Fitz gifted another look that would kill at Dex. The man clearly did not want to be here, but probably didn't like the idea of Tara and his kid in Dex's orbit without his gloomy presence. "Let's do the necessary so we can let everyone get back to business."

Tara smirked and took Esme back.

The next hour was spent posing with the animals in a combo of video and photo montages: Dex with kittens, Dex with more kittens, Dex cleaning out the litter boxes in the cattery (Fitz insisted on that one), and some shots of Dex playing fetch with the smaller, more friendly dogs.

While Fitz entertained his daughter, Tara would consult with Sophie and Ashley on shot setups. About an hour in, Ashley brought Bandit out from his cage, attached to a leash.

"We gave him a bath this morning and he looks so handsome in his Rebels collar."

"What a prince!" Dex hunkered down to pet his buddy. "You're going to be good today, right, Bandit?"

Sophie frowned. "Wait, is that the dog that bit you?"

"All has been forgiven."

Sophie shook her head. "We can't have a dangerous dog in this campaign. Besides, he's a bit rough around the edges."

Dex opened his mouth to speak but Ashley got there first.

"He might be rough around the edges, but this dog is a champion."

Sophie looked taken aback. "I merely mean that we can't

have an ugly dog in the shoot. We need one that's cuter. Like that one over there." She pointed at one of the cages where an admittedly handsome cocker spaniel was mugging, angling for his fifteen minutes.

Ashley wasn't having it. "Why is cute more deserving? Bandit might not be the prettiest dog, but he's come along in leaps and bounds and deserves a little love."

Sophie held up her hands. "Okay, okay! Sheesh, I'm just trying to do what's best here." She exchanged a look with Tara who merely shrugged. "But if he exhibits any threatening behavior, we cannot use him."

"Not a problem," Dex said with a grin at Ashley. She still looked a tad miffed on Bandit's behalf, and it was adorable.

"Got him?" She handed off the leash to Dex.

"Yeah, but you should stay in this shot. He's better when we're both here."

"I'd rather not be on camera."

He knew she was shy, had some hang-ups about her appearance, but this was all for a good cause. Or maybe it was that she didn't want to be seen on camera with someone like him.

"It's good PR for the shelter, playing with a troubled pup." He leaned in so only she could hear. "And the little dog, too."

She let out that laugh, the filthy one that went right to his balls. "You don't need my help here. I'm sure Sophie would prefer if it was just you."

Tara cut in. "I think both of you would be great. This campaign is all about bringing Dex back into the fold of normal, functioning society where people don't do unmentionable things in nightclubs or punch hockey assholes in bars." Extra disapproving look at him. *Et tu, Tara?* "Seeing Dex doing something fun with a normal member of that society will look good." She turned to Ashley. "Just a few minutes. If you don't feel comfortable or don't like the footage, we won't use it."

Ashley didn't look convinced.

"Could you give us a second?" Without waiting for permission, he cupped her elbow and brought her and Bandit a few feet away.

"What's the real issue here?"

"The real issue? I—it's what I said. I'm not a fan of how I look on camera."

"Even if I say you look hot as fuck and I know what the hell I'm talking about?"

"Dex ..."

"Remember you were telling Willa that looks don't matter and that what's inside counts? That she's beautiful in every possible way and screw the haters?" So her ex hadn't been kind about her curves. Fuck him. He placed a hand on a generous hip, part of this woman's body that he adored. "I want to touch you everywhere, your round ass, your plump breasts, those gorgeous thighs I want to live between. I think you're beautiful, your daughter thinks you're beautiful, and there's no one better to represent this organization than you. Unless it's that you don't want to be seen with me? Just pretend I'm a very naughty dog in your care and no one will know that I've been drilling you six ways from Sunday for the last couple of weeks."

Her mouth dropped open and color tagged her cheeks. "You're right. I shouldn't care what anyone thinks, and this is the example I want to set for my daughter. But you're wrong about one thing."

"Now, that doesn't surprise me."

She touched his chest, gently. "I'm not ashamed to be seen with you. I just don't want you to have to explain anything when I'm looking at you like I can't wait to get you off camera for a thorough licking."

Okay, then. He liked *this* Ashley. He liked her very much.

"How about we get this over with quickly then, so we can get started on the lick-fest sooner?"

Those apple-green eyes sparkled. "Okay."

"You guys ready?" Tara called out.

You bet we are.

"Let me introduce you guys to my favorite guest at Riverbrook Animal Shelter," Dex said, keeping his finger under his little friend's collar. "This is Bandit and he's a ... uh, what kind of dog is he, Ash?"

"Well, Dex, Bandit is a good dog."

His mouth twitched. "Right. He *is* a good dog. But do we have any specifics on his breed?"

"Oh, his breed?" She grinned and gave Bandit a furry fondle. "He's a terrier mix, probably some Yorkshire in there. We've been working on his coat which was in pretty bad shape when he arrived."

"I'm guessing it made him a bit cranky."

"That's for sure. We all get a bit irritable when people aren't so nice to us. That's what happened with Bandit. He wasn't treated so well, but we've been giving him lots of TLC. Actually, Dex has been. He spends a good chunk of his time here with Bandit, bringing him out of his shell. Both of them, such good boys." She gave a very hammy wink. "Did I get that right?"

Dex laughed. "Your check's in the mail."

"Cut, cut, cut!" Sophie threw up her hands. "You can't imply that this is a setup."

"I'm sorry," Ashley said, not sounding sorry at all. "I was being a smart-ass."

Sophie shook her head and glared at Dex like he was the bad influence here. That was all Ashley! "Let's go again, and fewer references to Dex's bad behavior or the reason why we're all here."

"Yes, Ashley," Dex said seriously. "You need to pretend I'm here doing good all by myself, not because I was mandated by my Rebels overlords. Plus we need to mention the Empty the Shelters event. Sell it!"

Another head shake from Sophie and then they tried again.

This time, Bandit got a little rambunctious and buried his nose in Ashley's crotch. "Lucky devil," Dex muttered.

"Cut, cut!"

When everyone but Sophie had stopped laughing (because she hadn't started in the first place), they took another shot at it. This time they managed a few minutes of footage, both with and without Ashley, that could be edited into something decent, according to one of Sophie's henchmen—sorry, photogs.

"Hmm, that went well," Dex said as Ashley grabbed Bandit's leash. "You're a natural."

"I had a good scene partner."

They were standing close and, even with the entire Rebels PR unit looking on, it felt like they were the only two people in the room.

"Thanks for doing this. And for standing up for Bandit." He tucked a strand of hair behind her ear, gratified when she shivered under his touch. Christ, he could spend all day enjoying that reaction.

He was completely in his Ashley Adams era.

"He needs someone to have his back." She peeked up at

him. "We all need that."

Too fucking right. "You make me feel good."

"I do?"

He might be seeing this all wrong, but her fighting for Bandit felt like she was fighting for *him*.

"Just glad you're here. That I know you. That this happened." He shuffled closer so no one could listen in. "Not because you're gorgeous, though you are. Not because I want to fuck you constantly, though I do. But because you're an awesome human being who makes me feel like a decent human being."

"Oh, Dex. You're an awesome human being, too. Don't let anyone tell you differently." Her sincerity floored him, but then everything about her always did.

He was crazy about this woman.

"Mom!"

They both turned to see Willa standing behind Sophie, waving away. With her was a man who Dex assumed was her dad. The asshole ex. Dex was supposed to be the adult here, so he wouldn't thump him even if he had once made this beautiful woman cry by telling her he wasn't attracted to her anymore.

But that was in the past, and this guy's loss was Dex's gain.

Dex waved at Willa while Ashley went to meet them. Approaching Sophie, Dex tried not to stare at the sight of this familial unit he didn't belong to.

"What do you think? Get what you needed?"

"Yes, I think so. Though ..." Sophie pulled him aside. "If we post that video of you and Ashley, people might get ideas."

He bristled. "Meaning?"

"That there's something going on between you." She

looked at him seriously. As much as he wanted to yell, "yes, we're together," he couldn't because (a) they weren't in an official way (b) Ashley didn't want anyone to know and (c) he was under strict orders not to let his dick get him into trouble again. Sophie would not approve, Fitz would go ballistic, and adios to his shot at a contract renewal.

"We're just friends and I'm a flirting machine, you know that."

Sophie looked relieved. "It's just that people can get mean and not everyone has the capacity to handle that. She didn't even want to be on camera, so any spotlight might hurt her."

This was true. He didn't want anyone saying mean things about Ashley, not after the ordeal she went through with her ex.

"You have some footage of me with the dog. Maybe just use that?"

"Okay."

"But send me the other stuff anyway. I'd like to have it. And Soph?"

"Yeah?"

"I'm sorry for making your life a misery these last eighteen months."

She smiled placidly. "It's my job, Dex."

"Sure, but it's not fair that you have to spend so much of your resources on me. I've been a total asshole and I apologize."

Her surprise was evident. "Thanks, I appreciate that. Let me talk to the photographer and make sure he has what he needs."

Next, he sought out Ashley, who appeared to be in a whisper-fight with her ex. About to stick his nose in, his path forward was halted by Fitz.

"O'Malley."

"El Jefe."

Fitz squinted at him. "I'm glad to see you digging deep. You're playing well, staying out of trouble, and this"—he looked around—"is a good fit for you."

"Sophie's idea. She's been a trouper."

"She has. But you've stepped up, on the ice and off it, and your effort hasn't gone unnoticed."

Dex tried his damnedest not to enjoy the warm glow in his chest. Best to dim it with reasonably minimum expectations. "Still have my court appearance to get through."

"Yes, about that. You do realize that Ms. Adams is supposed to supply a reference for you?"

He swallowed. "Yeah, I know that."

"I'm guessing you can't help yourself when it comes to the flirting, but maybe don't be so obvious."

"Obvious?" He wanted to scream in this guy's face that he was in love.

Damn. Was that what he was feeling? Because he liked it. He liked the man he was with Ashley, which translated to being a good teammate, and maybe even a better person.

"You need to stay focused, O'Malley. Your agent's been in touch, reminding me what a good boy you've been, how valuable you are to the team. I'm seeing that, too."

Was that a contract dangling over his head? The dream result. He just needed to keep his nose clean.

"But you're here at the shelter for a reason. Good PR, not to flirt with the manager and piss her off when she figures out your game. Because she will. Don't screw up now when you're so close to the finish line."

Dex could only nod as Fitz returned to the bosom of his perfect family.

26

Bodidley
Part sheepdog
Likes: How you smell
Dislikes: The works of Proust (too sad)

SOMETHING WAS UP WITH GREG. He usually went out of his way to avoid Ashley when he dropped off Willa, so his continued presence here was highly suspect.

Distracted by Esme, Willa moved off to say hi to Tara.

"What's going on?" she asked her ex-husband.

"Just curious about what's happening. If this Dex O'Malley character is inviting my daughter to hockey games, I'd like to meet him."

That was two weeks ago. Why the sudden interest, Ashley had no idea. Greg was looking more shifty than usual, avoiding eye contact as he scoped out the shelter's play area.

"Are Lottie and Emily okay?"

"They're fine, but I do have some news. The Bunking with Butterflies thing is off."

There it is. "What happened?"

"A bunch of the kids in Darren's daughter's friend group came down with an RSV infection so they had to cancel it." Greg had asked a work colleague to include Willa in an upcoming event at the Nature Museum. Though, knowing Greg, he might not have arranged for Willa's inclusion on the tour at all, and this was his way of weaseling out of it.

"How did she take it?" Because she looked fine ... *oh, no.* "You didn't tell her?"

"You're so much better at those conversations than I am."

"I've learned to be because I'm the only one willing to do it. You know, you can't leave Lottie to all the hard convos with your other daughter."

He shook his head, as if to say, *Poor Ashley, of course I can.*

Dex was just finishing up his chat with Sophie, who cast an assessing glance Ashley's way, then averted her gaze quickly. Talking about her, she supposed. The Rebels PR lady did not approve of Ashley, that was for sure.

"What's going on with you and the hockey player?"

Heat rose to her cheeks. "Why do you assume anything's going on?"

"I came in during the filming. You were flirting with him —I remember that much!" His laugh sounded pitying. "I know he's a manwhore but that's probably not a good idea. Assuming he'd go for it."

He's already gone for it, Greg. Over and over and over ...

Before she could respond, he added a rather cantankerous, "Inviting you to a hockey game is one thing, expecting anything else is quite another."

"He was just being nice. To Willa."

"And you had him over for dinner?" Greg shook his head, disbelief a negative energy field around him. "You're not throwing yourself at him, are you?"

"More like the other way around," came a sexy, graveled response. Dex's strong arm circled her waist and pulled her back to his chest. His other arm was outstretched toward Greg. "Craig, is it? I'm Dex."

"Greg," he said, taking Dex's hand and giving it a manly shake. "Ashley's husband."

"Ex-husband, right? You've come on a good day while we do some promo stuff for the shelter."

"Yeah, I see." Greg took another recce, noting the people fluttering about. "Is that Hale Fitzpatrick?"

"Yeah, he's overseeing things. Big fan of this place. We want to make sure the Empty the Shelters event is a huge success this year. You planning to help out there?"

"Uh, no. I have a new baby, so all my time is taken with that."

Dex rested his chin on Ashley's head, a curiously comfortable gesture. His arm tightened, giving her strength. Greg's dark gaze dipped to Dex's thick, muscle-corded forearm, so at home around the body he'd rejected.

"Hi, Dex!" Willa left off from admiring Esme and Dex left off from holding Ashley. But she easily forgave him because he raised his hand to high five her daughter, who happily obliged.

"Hey, Sparkle, what's the word today? Stump me."

"Okay. It's … peregrinate!"

"Right. I know that one."

Willa looked incredulous. "You do?"

"Yeah, it's a type of fruit. Heart healthy."

Willa shook her head. "Nope."

"Wait, I know. It's a baby penguin." He turned to Ashley and Greg with a cheeky wink. "Pretty sure I've got that right."

Willa shook her head, her lips stretched wide in a smile. "Wrong again."

"Darn. I was so sure I had it. Alright then, tell me."

"It means to travel or wander from place to place."

"Wow! So when I'm on the road for a hockey game, I'm peregrin—what is it?"

"Peregrinating! Exactly." Willa loved when the words had a real-world application, and Ashley loved when her daughter's smarts were engaged in a fun way.

Greg was intimidated by his daughter's intelligence and interest in science, as if it made him seem less smart, but Dex was wonderfully unbothered by it. He had no ego and didn't have to be the big man on campus. It made for such a nice change.

She loved that he treated her daughter so well.

That he treated her so well.

Greg was quietly seething. Ashley recognized that look, the one where he had nothing to say but was trying to think of a way to verbalize it. Usually it was some snide comment, and it didn't take long for him to come up with one.

"This is some PR thing, I suppose, because of your legal issues?" The sneer was added for free.

"It is, yeah," Dex said amiably. "At least it started that way." He shot a quick grin at Ashley that had her melting. "I'll probably be signing up for more shifts, though. Can't get enough."

The implication was clear—to the adults, anyway— what exactly Dex couldn't get enough of. He ran a hot palm over her back just in case it wasn't.

"Dex, could I have a moment please?" Sophie called out.

"Nice to meet you, Craig," then to Ashley, "Later, babe," before he swaggered off.

Later, babe?

She had never been "babe" to anyone, and she thought she might like it. Or maybe she just liked Greg's sourpuss expression.

Greg turned to Willa. "Honey, could you let me and your mom have a quiet word?"

Willa grimaced. "Uh oh."

"No uh oh," Ashley said. "We'll just be a second."

Willa wandered off to check on the kittens while Greg pulled her aside.

"Really, Ash? You're sleeping with him?"

She held up a hand and headed toward the back office, with him following.

"What if I am?"

"He's ..." Spluttering ensued. "A total slut! And far too young for you."

Trust Greg to pick at the older/younger scab.

"You don't know him."

"Sure I do. Everyone does because he's always in trouble. And why is he so friendly with my daughter? This man is reckless and shameless and not the kind of person I want in my daughter's life."

A red mist clouded Ashley's vision. "He's been nothing but kind to Willa and an absolute gentleman to me. We're just spending time together."

"And with my daughter!"

"She's met him a few times. She hasn't been corrupted nor will she be. You haven't been around much so she's just enjoying the attention of a friendly adult who actually likes talking to her."

His eyes went wide. "Are you saying I don't spend enough time with my daughter? Or enjoy talking to her? You know how much work there is with the baby."

Yes, Greg, I do. I remember it well.

"I'm saying that Willa is sensitive and she picks up on attitudes, especially yours. When you bail on spending time with her or barely listen to her when she's telling you about her day, then of course she's going to think that." Ashley lowered her voice. "And now this butterfly thing. You promised and you're not even able to come through because your attention is with your new family. I get it, Lottie's important. The baby is important. But you have other responsibilities."

"And you think this manwhore hockey player can do a better job? That's your problem, Ash. Always assuming the grass is greener. Nothing's ever good enough and now you've got the attention of this guy who sleeps with anything. Of course you're going to go gaga and put up with any crumbs he can offer." He moved to walk away then spun back for another assault. "Is this because I told you I wasn't attracted to you anymore? Your revenge is to let a scumbag like that into your bed?"

She pointed a finger in his face. "Don't you dare call him names. He's ten times the man you are, both in and out of the bedroom. And sure the orgasms are great but that's not why I like spending time with him. He makes me feel good. He makes me feel special. In fact, he makes me feel, period, something I haven't experienced in a very long time. Instead of wasting my time on someone with the emotional complexity of a boiled potato—that would be you—I'm actually enjoying myself. Because Dex does that for me. He's kind, generous, and intuitive."

"Everything alright here?"

Dex stood at the door, his brow lined with concern. Moving forward, he came alongside Ashley, taking up an almost protective stance.

Remembering the reason he was volunteering at the

shelter in the first place, Ashley quickly spoke to put him at ease. The last thing they needed was for Dex to employ the five-fingered solution.

"Fine. Greg was just leaving. I'll explain to our daughter that she can't attend the butterfly event, okay?"

Greg scowled. "I told you it was unavoidable. Besides, it's no different than a daytime visit. I can take her to see them anytime."

"I'll be sure to let her know."

Still in a dark mood, Greg sent one more dagger of a look Dex's way then turned on his heel and left.

Dex took her in his arms and pulled her close. "You okay?"

"Yeah, fine. There goes my ex. A stand-up guy."

"What's the butterfly thing?"

"It's an overnight event at the Nature Museum. Greg was supposed to get Willa a spot with a kids' group associated through his work, but now it's off apparently." Her daughter was going to be crushed. "Listen, I'm sorry you had to witness that drama. Definitely not what you signed on for."

"You kidding? I love the drama! You're looking at the biggest scenery-chewer in the history of hockey. Well, apart from Petrov." He pressed a gently kiss to her forehead. "Did you mean what you said? About me being kind and all that?"

"Yes, I did. How much did you hear?"

"Enough. So I make you feel good, and not just in the bedroom?"

Ashley sighed. "Have I told you that your tendency to eavesdrop is really annoying?"

"It's only annoying when I hear things that paint me in a poor light. For the first time, I actually heard good stuff about me. Ten times the man both in and out of the bedroom? Kind, generous, intuitive? And the best thing of all—how good I make you feel? Damn, those are *awesome* things to overhear. I should eavesdrop more often!"

Feeling slightly soothed, she peered up at him and all his impossible handsomeness. Greg's words, spiteful as they were, lingered like a burr under her saddle, but in Dex's arms, it didn't hurt as much.

"I don't care for his opinion." It was a lie but better to put it out there as a manifest wish.

"Well, I don't care for it either, especially the scumbag label or the idea that you might have jumped into bed with me as some sort of revenge plot. That's crazy, isn't it?"

The thread of doubt in his voice was unmistakable, and she was quick to do her best to banish it. "Yes, it is. I'll be the first to admit that seeing Greg's face when you put your arm around me was priceless, but I don't make dating decisions to show my ex what he's missing."

He grinned. "Dating, huh?"

"Oh, that's not what I meant. I know you're not looking for that."

A cloud scudded across his features for the barest of seconds.

"What if I was? Looking for that?"

She must have looked shocked because he rushed on.

"It's just you said that not only do I make you feel good, orgasms, and all that, but that I also make you feel. That you haven't felt that good in a long time. And the way you defended me there, it felt ... really good, too. Something *I* haven't felt in a long time. I'm not used to that because people think I'm a fuck-up. I get it if you were just saying it to piss off your ex or because you don't want your decisions second-guessed. But if there's a chance you meant it ... well,

I just think it's nice that we're able to be there for each other."

She hitched a quick breath. She knew exactly what he meant but it seemed so crazy that they could meet these needs for each other. Or was it? Maybe this amazing chemistry stretched to include something more ... real?

"I meant it. I think you're a fantastic guy, and I defended you because I will always have your back."

His eyes misted over, but before she could analyze that drift to emotion, he picked her up and kissed the breath out of her lungs. His hands cupped her ass and cleaved her close, and her only thought was that, *yes, he's right, we do something amazing for each other.*

And then there was no more thinking, only kissing.

27

Looks like the Rebels PR machine is in overdrive. Dex O'Malley is
spending his free time with puppies ahead of his court date.
Yeah, we don't believe it either.
— *@Coby "Big Dog" Dawson, ESPN*

AHEAD OF MORNING SKATE, Dex walked into the locker room
to the tune of whoops and whistles.

"A star is born!" Callaghan called out.

"You mean the dog, right?" Kaz answered. "Because
O'Malley and his dick are already mega stars."

"Ha ha," Dex deadpanned. Sophie had posted photos
and video of him doing his thing at the shelter. He was
disappointed that his video with Ashley hadn't made the
cut, but he understood Sophie's point. He'd hate for Ashley
to be a target of his more rabid fanbase.

He had, however, seen the recording of the two of them
with Bandit, and damn they were cute as hell together. His
infatuation was obvious, at least to him. He'd tried telling
her after she defended him against that Greg douche, but it
came out as him being all emo about no one having his

back, not that he and Ashley were a good fit. While he had no doubt some part of her thought of him as a boost to her self-esteem, what if that's all it was?

Dex O'Malley, ladies, a real tonic to your sex life!

He'd broached the idea of dating but she hadn't really responded. Or rather, they started making out because that was easier than talking about anything serious.

Which maybe said it all.

The two of them were acting like safe crackers, turning the dial by fractions and listening for a response that would either click it all into place or doom any chance they had of taking this all the way. Perhaps that was as it should be. What Fitz had said still weighed on him. He needed to focus, secure the contract, and not mess up this volunteer gig by messing around with the person who was on deck to say nice things about him to a judge.

"So, you've done your good deed, O'Malley." Petrov dropped his gym bag on the bench. "When's your court appearance?"

"Two weeks. Just before the playoffs start."

"We'll wave at you when the bus to the airport is going by Cook County Jail." Kershaw nudged him. "Do they show hockey in the Big House?"

"I'm not going to jail, dickhead."

"No, it's called prison," Callaghan said, which set everyone off.

They were only kidding around—at least, he hoped so—but he was still nervous. Petrov was looking at him, assessing him with those ice-blue Russian eyes.

"I'm going to be okay," he said, more for himself than any of these losers.

"Let us hope. We need you for the playoffs."

That was probably the nicest thing Petrov had ever said

to him, and it made him even more determined to clean up his act.

After practice where he managed to run circles around Banks and Foreman, he found he had a message from Anton. Once he'd changed, he headed to one of the exam rooms to call him in private.

"Hey, Anton."

"Dex, how are you?"

"I'm good. Better than good, actually. I'm great."

Anton chuckled. "Saw your animal shelter spot. You seemed in good form. Happier."

"I am. Things are going well. Kit said the bosses like what they saw." His agent had called this morning with an update on how pleased Sophie and Fitz were with the reaction to the campaign.

"Any update on the contract?"

"Not yet. I might not be Rebels material."

"It's okay to say you want it, son."

Dex rubbed a hand over his mouth. "Saying it out loud seems like tempting fate."

Anton must have been shocked at Dex's uncharacteristic display of vulnerability because he didn't speak for a long beat.

"They're probably waiting on the outcome of the court case. That's coming up soon, right?"

"Yeah. It's hard to know which way it's going to go."

Anton didn't tell him it would be okay, for which Dex was grateful.

"Listen, you're in New York in a couple of days, right? Any chance of a ticket for an old friend?"

Dex started. "You want to come to the game?"

"Hell, yeah. Maybe we could get together for lunch beforehand."

"You'd have time for that?" Anton always seemed so busy with his coaching gig, but maybe he'd thrown himself into work since losing his beloved wife a few years ago. Maybe he was as lonely as Dex.

The older man sighed. "I always have time for you, son. For the last couple of years, you've gone down a different road and you didn't need me nagging you to straighten yourself out. You had to figure that out for yourself."

Dex hadn't wanted to be a bother, but now he realized he might have been too closed off when it came to the people in his life. Anton had always been there for him, yet Dex had preferred to think of himself as a lone wolf with no connections.

"I'd love to meet up."

Anton sounded pleased. "It'll be good to see you, son."

Yes, it would.

ASHLEY VIEWED the video created by Rebels PR and let the voices in her head run their mouths off.

She'd assumed—wrongly, it seemed—that they'd use the one with her, Dex, and Bandit. She'd had fun. Possibly too much fun.

You were throwing yourself at him, Ash! Everyone could see it. It was just an embarrassment.

Someone had evidently decided it was too much, which was probably for the best. What Greg had said gnawed at her, and while Dex was lovely about it all in defending her, even going so far as to mention "dating," he was probably only doing that to stick one to her ex.

The video they did use had plenty of likes and re-posts, and the shelter had received several calls this morning about volunteering. Donations were up as well, so it looked like both organizations had benefitted.

Of course there was still the reference letter she was supposed to write to the judge. That would be easy. She would have no problem telling anyone who asked what a good guy he was.

Your honor, Dex O'Malley swaggered into my animal shelter, made friends with human and animals alike, charmed me and my daughter, then proceeded to seduce me in all the ways you can imagine (and ways you probably can't). I'm a little bit in love with him, but I expect it'll pass because that's how the universe works.

So ridiculous! She needed to get over herself because that would be the quickest way to get over Dex O'Malley.

Work. That was what she'd do, starting with the pile of mail she needed to sort. Elbow-deep in it, she looked up when the door to the shelter opened. A woman stepped inside, eyes darting around tentatively before she took a step toward the counter. Dressed in a dark blue shirt and plain black pants, she looked like she was trying to make herself smaller.

Ashley smiled to put her at ease. "Hi, there."

The woman swallowed. "I've come to ask about volunteering."

"Well, you're in the right place. Have you volunteered at an animal shelter before?"

The woman looked around again, over Ashley's shoulder toward the door that led to the animal care area.

"Um, no. I used to have a dog a few years ago, but where I live now, they don't allow them."

"Yeah, that's often the case." And was often a reason why people asked to volunteer. Lately there had been another reason.

Dex O'Malley.

They'd had an uptick in applications, mostly from young, giggling women, who were quickly weeded out when they answered questions with vapid statements like "I love working with animals" and "I can come in any time the Rebels are in town," with "any" underlined three times.

But this woman was older and appeared to have had a rough life. Her brow was lined, her cheeks spotted a rosacea red, her hair tied back in a tidy chignon. Attracting a super-star hockey player's attention did not seem to be on her agenda.

"We have an application form you can complete. You can do it online or fill it out by hand."

"By hand would be better. I don't have a computer."

"Of course." Ashley handed her a clipboard with the form and a pen and led her to a seat in reception. "You can sit here while you fill it out."

The woman nodded but hesitated. "I have a job in the mornings, so afternoons are better for me. Would that be okay?"

Concern threaded her voice. Ashley was used to entitled would-be volunteers who thought they were doing you a huge favor, but this lady didn't give off that vibe.

"We're looking for people to fill all time slots. If you can commit to a couple of shifts a week, we can usually work around your schedule."

She bit her lip, still appearing undecided. On cue a howl emerged from somewhere close, just to remind everyone that animals were on the premises.

"It's okay if you've changed your mind. Sometimes the reality of it hits you when you think you have it all worked out."

"You're telling me." She looked up from beneath dark lashes. "Is there any paid work going?"

"Not right now, I'm afraid. We have quite a few volunteers so luckily we can save costs that way."

"Oh, that's okay. Just thought I'd ask." More firm in purpose now, she took a seat and started reading the form on the clipboard.

"Are you a cat or a dog person?" Ashley called out, eager to know a little bit more about the sad-eyed woman.

"Oh, both. I'm hoping my landlord will let me get a cat, but for now this is my best option." She smiled, and wow, it transformed her.

A couple of minutes later, Ashley emerged from the back with a furry friend. Cleo was one of a litter of kittens abandoned at their door a few days ago. She couldn't have been more than a couple of weeks old, and one of her sisters had already died because of the cold. But Cleo was coming along by leaps and bounds.

"I thought maybe you'd like to meet one of our guests."

The woman's eyes lit up on spying Cleo, who made a lunge. Ashley restrained her until she could be sure the woman wanted to play.

"This is Cleo. Cleo, meet ..."

"Ruby." She spoke the name quietly, almost as if trying it on for size.

"Ruby. Nice to meet you, Ruby. Would you like to hold Cleo?"

"I could do that?"

"Of course. She loves to be held, and she's really too small to do any damage."

Ashley got the distinct impression this woman had not been around animals for a while. Sadness rolled off her, a cloud of despair. But the moment her fingers wrapped around Cleo's soft, furry body, Ruby's demeanor changed. The raincloud lifted and in its place was a big ball of sun.

"She's so soft."

"She is. And look at those eyes—she's gonna be a heart-breaker."

Ruby was suddenly lost in the joys of holding the kitten. Ashley had seen it before, how animals soothed and made a person's problems fade away, if only for a while. It couldn't heal all wounds, but it certainly made the harder moments better.

"Can you manage her while you fill out the application?" Ashley was curious to see if Ruby was a multitasker.

"I think so. Even if she is quite the attention hog."

"You know there's a cat café just off the main street where you could get your fix."

The woman nodded. "Because I can't volunteer here?"

"Oh no, not at all. Just giving you more options for cat interaction if you want."

Deciding to give the woman space, Ashley stood, just as the door opened and Dex walked in. She'd thought he might not show since his PR duties had received such a positive response, and relief on seeing him coursed through her. He still wanted to be here, maybe even continue to see her ...

"Hey there," she said to Dex, who smiled at her in a way that seemed oddly familiar.

She didn't have time to think about that because the smile vanished in an instant. Dex's gaze had switched to the woman playing with the kitten and shifted to a darkness she barely recognized.

"What the fuck are you doing here?"

Ashley blinked and moved her gaze to Ruby. The clipboard fell from her hand and she held the kitten over her chest like armor.

"I was hoping to see you," the woman said. "You haven't stopped by the diner—"

"There's a reason for that. You're supposed to have gotten the message."

"I saw that online post that said you were volunteering here. I thought maybe you might be open to talking."

"You thought wrong." He moved in closer, brushing by Ashley who may as well not be here. "You need to give back that kitten because no one is *less* qualified to look after it."

The woman looked like she'd been struck. Quickly she stood and held out the kitten for Dex to take it.

Which he did.

In that moment, Ashley despised him for it. Like he'd stolen something precious, this woman's brief connection with joy.

"Dex! You can't do that."

He turned, his mouth still twisted with fury. Not even the kitten in his hands could change it.

"What's she doing here?"

"Volunteering. At least, that's what she said ..."

The woman—Ruby—was moving toward the door. She caught Ashley's eye. "I'm sorry. I didn't mean to cause any trouble."

"No, it's ok—"

But she was already gone, leaving behind sadness.

Ashley turned to Dex. "What was that about?"

"You need to do a better job of vetting the volunteers."

"Don't you dare tell me how to do my job! That woman had barely sat down before you came barging in with your demands. I can't believe you took her kitten away."

She curled her hand around Cleo and did exactly what Dex had just done to Ruby. See how he liked it!

"*Her* kitten? Since when?"

She opened her mouth, closed it again. So it wasn't her kitten but they'd had a brief connection, and here was Dex stomping all over it.

"So, who is she?" Though she already knew. That crooked turn to her smile was all Dex.

Shaking his head, he walked behind the counter just as Toby came out.

"Toby, could you man the reception for a bit?"

"Sure. Everything okay?"

Dex had already blown past the entrance to the animal care area.

"Yeah, just need a minute." She followed him, knowing where he was heading. Bandit's cage. Sure enough, when she found him, he was already seated cross-legged in front of the little guy.

"No fingers," she said gently.

His shoulders lifted, fell. She sat beside him, Cleo still attached to her shoulder.

"I'm sorry. I shouldn't have shouted." She nudged his arm with hers.

"I shouldn't have raised my voice either. I was just surprised to see her."

"Was that your mom?"

"How'd you guess?"

"I have a daughter. Moms know when their kids are mad at them."

"I'm not mad at her. I just don't know why she thinks this is a good idea."

Because she's hurting and seeing you is a balm.

"You haven't seen her in a while?"

"She works at the Sunny Side Up Diner, and four weeks ago was the first time I'd seen her in fourteen years." He slid a look her way. "She's been in prison."

"Oh. Wow. That must have been a shock."

"She got out a year ago. I knew it was happening. Her lawyer sent me a letter about it. A different lawyer than last time, who was different than the time before that. But I didn't expect her to edge her way back into my life. I don't want to know her but lately, she's everywhere I turn."

How awful for him, but also awful for his mom. She'd seemed so woebegone when she walked in.

"Do you mind me asking what she was in prison for?"

"Drug offenses and assault." He pressed his hand against Bandit's cage. The pup unfurled his tongue and gave it a lick.

"Good boy," Dex murmured.

"When was the last time you really talked to her?"

He snorted. "Really? When I was ten, when she was arrested. I didn't see her after. They asked if I wanted to, but I didn't." He raised his gaze to her. "Makes me quite the dick, right?"

"You were a kid."

"But now I'm not. I need to grow up—is that what you're saying?"

"Not at all. You don't have to talk to anyone you don't want to."

He shook his head. "And here I was this morning, excited to come in to see you—"

"Already awkward enough."

"No." He turned to her, his expression grave. "Not at all. I thought the shoot went really well and I loved meeting Craig—"

"Greg."

"Right, Craig, and telling him what's what. I know that's sort of immature, but I never claimed to be an adult. Basically, things are looking up. I had a bounce in my step, Ashley, and that was because of you. And now she's here and she's ruined it."

Before he could spiral into even more upset, Ashley leaned in and kissed him. "It doesn't have to be ruined."

He softened as she pulled gently on his lips, encouraging him to open up to her. With a breathy sigh, he surrendered and went all in.

"I'm sorry," he murmured.

"For what?"

"Bringing more drama into your life. You're supposed to be the place I can turn to for a sliver of peace."

She was? Maybe he meant the shelter, but she suspected not. She could be the harbor he needed. "I can still be that for you. I've said it before, Dex. Anything you need."

"I don't know how I'm supposed to feel about this. About her. And I don't want to think about it, to be honest. It just makes me angry, and I don't like that feeling. Some guys can feed off that, but it doesn't work for my play or my life. The more stable things are, the better I play. The better I feel. I'm only starting to realize that lately. That maybe boring, regular guy Dexter is a more productive player. Or person." He ran a hand over her back. "That woman symbolizes chaos and the past. I buried it and I don't want to unbury it just because she says so."

Ashley nodded. "This is your boundary to cross, and I'm sorry you had to see her first thing. I thought I'd be spending these few weeks fighting off your fans with a stick, I had no idea long-lost relatives would be coming out of the woodwork." She kissed him lightly. "Nothing's ever simple with you, O'Malley."

That made him laugh, and just that sound made her blood bubble with joy.

"Thanks, Ash. Don't know what I'd do without you."

It was a throwaway line, but it settled in Ashley's chest. Because she had been thinking something very similar, contemplating what a future without Dex in it looked like, and not liking the conclusion one bit.

28

"IT'S ABOUT TO START, MOM!"

"Okay, okay, I'm here." Ashley brought the popcorn in and set it down on the coffee table. Her eyebrows rose at the sight of Maeve on the sofa. "You're watching hockey?"

"Sure." More like watching Ashley, looking for clues that she was too excited about Dex O'Malley.

A few weeks ago she'd played hooky for the first time in living memory and now she was in a secret relationship with a younger professional hockey player. Though relationship was probably too strong. A friends with benefits situation perhaps? They weren't co-workers and she wasn't his boss—not really. (She'd repeated this to herself *several* times.)

A couple of days ago, he'd shared about his mother, though she imagined there were more details. Ugly ones. For all Dex's honesty about his desire for her, he was remarkably close-mouthed about everything else, especially his past. From the age of ten he'd been shunted around from place to place, unable to settle, needing to belong. No wonder he was leery of establishing relationships with his teammates. The nature of the business, when you could be traded at any moment, definitely discouraged connections of the deeper variety.

As if she needed another reason not to fall for this man.

No. She would enjoy this moment, live in it, but not expect it to last any longer than one of Willa's butterflies.

"Oh, there's Dex, Mom! Look how fast he is."

She pressed a hand to her chest, anything to hold in the heart catching at the sight of him. The moment his blades connected with the ice, he was off, scrambling for the puck and making things happen. Twice he made an assist that almost resulted in a goal, once he almost lit the lamp himself only to be foiled by the New York tender. And that was just in his first two shifts. Her man was on fire tonight.

Her man? Oh, that would not do.

By the end of the first period, the Rebels were up by two goals, one from Levi Hunt, the other from Cal Foreman, both of them with assists from Dex.

That all changed in the second period. Dex was on a breakaway, seemingly in the clear, when the New York goalie came out to cut the angle of approach. But Dex didn't stop, and the two of them crashed into each other.

The goaltender was up in a second. Dex, on the other hand, remained flat on the ice without his helmet. Somehow, it had come off in the clash and Dex was out cold.

Ashley's heart shot into her throat. *Get up. Please get up.*

"He's going to be okay, Mom, isn't he?"

"I'm sure he will be, honey."

"O'Malley appears to be unconscious. The medics are on hand ... and there he is. Awake and moving."

Ashley's heart was still clattering wildly. "See? He's fine." But she wasn't. Dex was being helped back to the bench— no, taken out of the game altogether, which meant they needed to attend to him outside of the glare of thousands of people and the press.

"He's not playing anymore?" Willa sounded distressed.

"After a hit like that, they need to run some tests. Remember when you got a baseball in the head last summer? We had to bring you into the ER to get you checked out."

"Okay ..." Willa still sounded worried. "Can I text him?"

"Maybe later? Let's give him a chance to recover."

She caught Maeve's eye, expecting the usual disapproval, but she got something else instead: empathy.

"I'm sure he's fine, Ash."

The game restarted, but it was impossible to focus. Midway through the second period, the broadcasters announced that Dex was okay, but was being assessed using the league's concussion protocol and would not be returning to the game.

"Hear that? He's fine. I'll send him a text with your well wishes."

"Tell him I saw a Red Monarch."

"Isn't it kind of early in the season for that?"

"It was on TV."

Ah. There was optimism for you. She shot off a text to Dex.

> You're supposed to stop when you get that close to the tender.

Almost immediately, she got a response.

> Right? Brakes failed.

ASHLEY

> You okay?

DEX

> Fine. Just a flesh wound.

Ten seconds later, her phone rang.

"Hello?"

"Is that Dex?" Willa yelled.

"You're watching the game, huh?"

"Of course I am!" Ashley hated, absolutely hated, the way her heart was galloping outside her chest. "I happen to know one of the idiots who's putting himself in harm's way while chasing a plastic disc."

"It's vulcanized rubber, actually, and I'm okay. Blacked out for a couple of seconds so they won't let me go back in, but it's just a growing goose egg and a killer headache."

It still sounded awful. "Will someone watch over you?"

"I feel like someone already is." His voice was low and husky. "I'm sorry if I worried you. I was surprised to see your text."

"Why? Lots of people are going to be worried about you. I bet Tara texted." Whyever did she say that?

"She did, but yours came in first. You win, good girl."

There she went again, lapping up his praise. "It's not a contest for your affections."

"You'd win every time, Ash."

She struggled to return her breathing to normal. Finally she said, "Could you say a word to Willa? She's hovering like a mad ghost here."

"Sure. Put my favorite lepidopterist on. That's a big word I learned a couple of days ago and I've been dying to use it."

Chuckling, she passed the phone to her daughter.

"Dex? That New Yawk idiot should have got a major penalty for that!"

Dex's laugh echoed across the miles. Ashley couldn't

help her smile as she watched her daughter chatting away to Dex, who was probably dying to end the call because headache and all.

Her sister murmured, "He makes you happy."

"What? No, nothing so dramatic. He's just a nice guy and he's kind to Willa, which is a big deal to me. That's it."

"Sure it is." She pressed her hand over Ashley's. "I don't want to see either of you hurt. It's not because I hate love or anything."

"I know." Since her divorce, Maeve had major trust issues but Ashley still saw her as the amazing older sister who was there for her after their parents died. Who took her and Willa in following the Greg debacle.

To her daughter, she said, "Hey, let Dex go. He needs his rest."

"Okay. Bye, Dex! See you when you come back to Chicago."

Ashley took the phone again and stepped outside the room.

"How's the head?"

"Not too bad. Seems better when I'm talking to you and Willa. That reminds me—are you guys free on Friday night?"

"For a hockey game?"

"Actually, no. It would be a surprise, and it would be an overnight thing for both of you. But close by."

"Hmm. Building blanket forts in your apartment?" Now, *that* sounded awfully appealing.

"Not completely off base. It's more of a surprise for Willa. I think she'd really like it."

"But you don't want to tell me? I'm sorry, Dex, but I need to know because it's my kid."

"Okay. Remember you said that Willa's butterfly event

was canceled because the kids were sick? Well, one of the guys is organizing something similar for his kid and he invited other team members' kids to join in. Not that Willa's my kid or anything but it's this Friday and I wondered—"

"Oh my God, yes! Are you kidding?"

"You thought I was going to take her to a club or something, didn't you?"

"No!" *Maybe?* "I just needed the details. Sorry to be such a mom about it."

"I love that you're a mom about it. That's important. Not enough parents think about those kinds of things."

The still-living ghost of Dex's mother made an appearance.

"This isn't something tentative, is it? I don't want to get her hopes up only to have them dashed."

"It's happening. But maybe don't tell her and we can surprise her? Well, I'll leave that to you to decide."

Willa was going to love it. "I think surprising her would be awesome. And this is a group thing? Who else will be there?"

"Bren St. James's daughter Franky—she's a fan of slugs, which I didn't know was a thing with its own fandom until yesterday. Remy and Harper's twins, Giselle and Amelie. They're seven, I think. Maybe a few others? It'll be small. We'll have the whole place to ourselves, get pizza in, the works."

Was he serious? "You'd stay overnight with the kids?"

"If that's okay."

"Of course it is! Just didn't think sleeping bags and pizza parties were your thing."

He chuckled. "Neither did I, but I'm guessing everyone has the capacity to embrace new things."

God, that was so sweet. "Thanks, Dex. She's going to be over the moon."

"Good. Whatever it takes to get in with her mom."

She giggled. That's what he did to her, turned her into a giggler. "You're already in. No need to use my kid, but I think it's sweet that you're thinking of her."

"She's a good kid. And I know she was disappointed about the trip."

And her dad being so neglectful. But Ashley had to be careful about relying on Dex as a replacement. This was fun for him—now. It wasn't real life.

"You should rest. But don't fall asleep." Yet again, she was hung up on who was going to take care of him. She hated that she was a thousand miles away.

But it wasn't her job to look after him. He was a valuable asset to the team. They'd be all over it, though it wasn't the same as having the personal touch of a friend. Or more.

"I'll be back in Chicago early tomorrow morning. Think you might want to check in on the patient?"

"If he needs a nurse."

"Oh, he will."

From the other room, her daughter yelled, "Mom! Those New York jerks scored!"

"You hear that? She wants to fight dragons in your honor."

His chuckle was soft. "Such a sweetheart. Listen, the doc's here for another checkup. I'd better go, but I'll text tomorrow, okay?"

"Okay," she said, not quite believing her life right now. "But text anytime, if you need to stay awake or just want someone to talk to."

"Okay. Night, Ash."

"Night, Dex."

29

Oreo
Half-Siamese, half-jerk
Likes: Fish treats (deal with it!)
Dislikes: The birds in that tree that must be destroyed

"Go on up, Ms. Adams." The doorman waved her through with a smile.

Dex was probably in pretty bad shape, so she told herself this would be just a nursing visit. No hanky panky, a situation that was assured when the door was opened by Tara Fitzpatrick.

The young mom was her usual glamorous self in high-heeled boots and a lovely teal wraparound dress that accentuated every curve. Beautifully highlighted blonde hair fell in gorgeous waves over her shoulders. Her makeup was perfectly on point.

Meanwhile Ashley, despite making an effort to look somewhat presentable (mostly with pretty underwear, which she couldn't exactly whip out in the presence of her imaginary rival), looked like something one of her dogs had thrown up.

"Hi!" Tara grinned. "So that's why he's been trying to get rid of us." She called over her shoulder. "Dexter, you should have said."

"Let her through," came the reply. "Then see yourself out."

Tara pulled Ashley into a hug. "So glad you're here. I knew you two had something special going on."

"I'm just here to check on him. A friendly visit."

"Okay!" Tara moved past Ashley across the threshold. "Come on, Georgia!"

The neighbor was here, too? The perfectly-put together socialite emerged from the living room in a tight-fitting strapless red cocktail dress and sparkly heels.

At ten o'clock in the morning.

"Hi, Ashley! Thank God you're here. Rather you than me, he's being a total bear."

"Are you going or coming?" Too late, Ashley realized she sounded rude—and possibly territorial. "Sorry, you look amazing."

"Oh, thanks. Who knew bankers were such party animals? Hold up a second, Tara."

Tara smirked. "Nice to see that chemistry paying dividends. You two are adorable together."

What was the point in denying it?

Georgia was Tara's smirk-twin. "You know something? Dex is always complaining about the noise from *my* parties, to which everyone has an invite, by the way, but I had no idea how thin the walls were until your visit a couple of weeks ago."

Ashley's cheeks heated to furnace levels. "I'm sorry. We were ... playing with the kitten."

"Right. Sometimes I call mine that, too." She called out, "Bye, Dex. We're really leaving now," then in a lower register to Ashley, "Have fun playing doctor and nurse."

"Okay, thanks."

Ashley closed the door and leaned against it.

"Are they gone?" Dex called out.

"Yeah." Ashley walked through to the living room and was greeted with the sight of Dex in the pose of a decadent prince, lying across the sofa in an erotically-thin pair of sweatpants—and that was it. All that was missing was a servant with a fan and another to dispense grapes right into his sensual mouth. His chest was exposed, a large darkening bruise on his torso above his hip.

Putting aside the fact this was how he was dressed while both Tara *and* Georgia were here—jealousy did not suit her! —she dropped her shopping bags and moved forward quickly.

"Are you okay? I thought it was a head injury."

"It was. This was from practice a couple of days ago."

She knelt before him, her fingers dancing over his pecs, while doubts danced a tango in her stomach. "Looks like you've been taken care of."

Trapping her hand against his chest, he lifted an eyebrow. "I didn't ask either of them to come over. I think Tara was hoping to catch us in the act."

"Really?"

"Yeah, she was checking out the bedroom and the bathroom, as if I was hiding you away."

His hand felt warm over hers, his heartbeat an unsteady thud under her fingertips. She pulled it away all the same. Being this close to him made it hard for her to think, and right now, she needed her common sense more than anything.

"And Georgia? Just on her way home from another party?"

"I think she's lonely."

"Have you and she ever ...?"

He shook his head. "No. She's definitely not my type."

If she wasn't, what the hell did that make Ashley?

"I made some food for you. Baked ziti." Standing, she returned to the bag and lifted it onto the kitchen counter. "It's easy to heat up. Just set the oven for 350 degrees for twenty minutes." She removed it from the bag and set it down.

Wincing, Dex stood and closed the gap. "What's wrong?"

"Nothing. I should go." She moved past him, but he snaked an arm around her waist and stopped her still. The temptation to relax into him, forget why she was irritated, was so strong.

"Ash, tell me. Is it about Tara? Or Georgia?"

"You have plenty of people looking out for you. The team, your ex-fiancée, your neighbor. You have more people who care about you than you think." Turning to face him, she finished her thought. "You don't need me here."

"That's where you're wrong." His tone was fierce, his intensity palpable. "You're the *only* person I need here."

When she didn't respond, when she couldn't, he went on.

"Ask me anything you want about Tara."

She peered up. "Tara?"

"I know you don't care about Georgia, but it bothers you that Tara's here. So ask me anything you want."

Anything? Jealousy felt like an ugly mass in her chest, but it was obvious she had issues. After being replaced by someone so much more attractive ... "You guys were engaged once, but people said it was a PR stunt because of what happened at that club. Your sex tape. So was it real?"

Is this real? Because Dex—or his PR people—was using her shelter in a similar fashion. To scrub his reputation clean and make him look like a saint. Ashley had understood the arrangement, but now that she was in this man's bed, she no longer liked the terms.

Dex raked a hand through his hair. "The engagement was real, but the relationship was fake. It was a setup but I'd also heard that Tara wanted to marry a hockey player. And she wasn't fussy. So for a while there I thought I had all the power. The leverage to string her along and make her do my bidding, which makes me sound like a jerk, I know. Then she started falling for Fitz and by then, I'd started to like her, but I think I liked being connected to something bigger than myself more. One of the guys who'd made it, part of this community. Being engaged to her was a success indicator, a sign I'd achieved some sort of status. But in the end it wasn't what she wanted. And I'm not sure it was what I wanted. Not really."

"And now?"

"Definitely not what I want. We weren't compatible at all. But no one likes to be rejected, even if it's for something you weren't super into anyway. We're just good friends now."

She believed him, and the relief at knowing this was immense. "Friends with your ex? There's a novelty."

"Well, she wasn't really my girlfriend or fiancée, not officially, so it's not awkward. We never slept together. Now she cuts my hair and listens to my problems."

"Sounds like a good friend. And she's so ... well, gorgeous."

He smiled. "She is gorgeous. And so are you."

"I wasn't fishing for compliments. I know I don't compare to Tara."

"No, you don't. You blow her out of the water. When I was attracted to Tara before, it was all surface. She was shiny and paid me attention and we needed each other for a very superficial reason."

"Like you and me now?"

He frowned. "Sure, I need you to say nice things about me and you need the Rebels to support the shelter. But if you think I'd go so far as to sleep with you to keep you sweet, then maybe you don't see me the way I see you." His arm fell away, and he took a step back. "Once, I thought I could use Tara like that, but I've learned my lesson. If you think I'm still a user, then I'm not sure I can change your mind."

His expression was harsh, but also tempered by hurt. She hated to be the cause of that.

"This is more my problem, Dex. My self-esteem. You're just so handsome and the minute I see your gorgeous friend, who looks like she had no trouble losing the baby weight, I wonder what you're doing with me." She took a breath, ready to be more honest than she'd been in a long time. "After the PR shoot, I expected the video you posted would include me. When it didn't, I wondered if maybe you didn't want people to see us together. Of course, we've been saying we'd keep quiet about it for all sorts of reasons, and it really wouldn't look good ahead of your court case to see us get flirty on camera, so I have no good reason to expect—"

Immediately he was on her, his hands cupping her face. "I wanted to use the video of us together with Bandit, but Sophie said the fans would go negative. Not because of you specifically. They'd go after anyone. I shouldn't have listened to her, but I was worried they might be assholes and you'd get hurt. And then I figured maybe you didn't want it out there anyway because everyone would see how into you I am, and you'd be embarrassed."

Into me? "I wouldn't be embarrassed." She hated the secrecy, but only because she worried she would feel foolish when it was over.

He continued. "I would have loved nothing more than to have that video be the one that tells the story. You should see it. It was awesome."

He dropped his hands and pulled his phone from his sweatpants. Within seconds, they were watching the video footage of the two of them playing with Bandit while they had a fun back-and-forth about the shelter and the work they did.

Maybe she wanted to believe, but what Dex said appeared to be true: in this footage, he was smitten. The fact that he even *had* the footage on his phone was a story in itself. When Ashley spoke on camera, he listened avidly, his expression curious and focused. It was a shock to see him so taken with her, hanging on every word.

And evidently, she had no problem returning the favor. She wasn't shy about gazing at him while he spoke or played with Bandit. Who was this woman?

"That's a great advertisement for the shelter."

"For the shelter? That's a great advertisement for *us*." He placed the phone down and pulled her close. "I'm not in this for a nice letter to the judge, Ashley. I'm in this for you."

His kiss took her by surprise, its sheer intensity and depth of feeling. But she shouldn't be surprised. Dex might have started out as lazy and unwilling at the shelter, but he'd more than made up for it. When Dex cared, he went all in. That was what she was witnessing here: a very engaged man.

Learning this was a revelation.

Ashley looped her arms around his neck and kissed him hard, twining her tongue with his. His "hmm" of pleasure reverberated through her, made her greedy for more. She pressed her body closer and yielded from him a quick intake of breath.

"Oh, your bruise. And we haven't even talked about your head injury yet."

"I'm okay." And to prove it, he lifted her up and walked her to the sofa. "Need you, Ash. Need you badly."

She was still wearing far more clothes than him, but he fixed that problem in an instant until she was left in only her new lingerie. Pushing his sweats down, he kicked them off and sat back, his erection standing proud.

His eyes went wide on seeing what she wore underneath. "Is this new?"

She nodded.

"Turn around."

She did, peeking over her shoulder after a few seconds of excruciating quiet. His hand was wrapped around his erection, and he was stroking slowly.

"You like?"

"Your ass looks amazing in that—what do you call it?"

"A hipster." She ran a hand over the lilac satin, edged with lace. "It's from Addison Williams's lingerie line." Addison was married to Ford Callaghan, one of his teammates.

"Did you buy that for me?"

"For me." She angled her head. "And for you."

His little moan of pleasure told her that pleased him. He patted his lap. "Over here, like a good girl."

Ashley's entire body fizzled, but she was hesitant. "I don't want to hurt you."

"I'll let you know if it's a problem."

She straddled him, first nudging against his thick, upright cock, then trapping it between their bodies. His hand curved around her ass, touching the bare cheek peeking from the lilac hipster. His other hand took the weight of one heavy and aching breast, his thumb rubbing over the lace edge of the bra and over her swollen nipple.

He pushed the bra strap off her shoulder, slipped a thumb under the edge of her panties and pushed into the cleft between her legs.

"This color is perfect against your skin. Your tits are so damn pretty, you know that?"

She didn't, but she was starting to believe.

He squeezed her ass cheek as his thumb sought liquid depths. She squirmed, inviting that thick digit inside, angling to draw it deeper. Leaning in, she touched her lips to the bump on his head.

"Does it hurt?"

He shook his head. "You make everything better."

The words were so sincere, matched by his intense gaze. Still watching her, he lifted her up and peeled off her hipster.

"It's pretty but I don't want to rip it. Which I will if you keep it on for much longer."

Good, because it was expensive. She pushed back up against his length, angling her body so that the friction worked for her. Without her underwear, he took advantage using his long, strong fingers to explore from behind. The palm of his hand rubbed between her legs from the front, resulting in a full-scale assault on her senses.

"Dex," she moaned.

"Take off the bra."

She unhooked it, freeing her breasts, now close to his

lips. His tongue darted out, a fast lick of her nipple then a long pull inside his mouth. Between his hands, his tongue, and the friction of his cock, she knew it wouldn't take long to reach the peak of pleasure.

"You're so wet."

"Now, *that's* for you."

"That's my girl. That's my beautiful, most excellent girl." He kissed her, tracing her lips with his tongue. He parted her folds and stroked his thumb through, once, twice.

"Ah!" She shuddered as the orgasm wracked her. He continued to rub, eeking out more waves of earth-shocking sensation.

Reaching over to his sweatpants he extracted a foil packet.

"Suit me up, Ash."

With shaking hands, she did it while he lifted her up and then spread her wide with his thumbs. Sinking down, she took him fully inside her, the instinct as natural as any she'd ever felt.

It's never been like this.

Which was a sorry state of affairs for a woman her age. But she'd never felt comfortable enough with her body to let go. With Dex, there was no need to hide. The honesty between them was as sexy as it was scary.

He liked her body. The way he reacted to her new lingerie and how it cupped and caressed every curve said he *loved* her body.

Turned out she was one of those pathetic women with limited wells of self-belief, who needed a guy to appreciate them because they couldn't appreciate themselves. A stupid tear escaped and was caught by Dex's thumb.

"Hey now, why so sad?"

"Just being weird."

He held her gaze. "Good thing I like weird. I like you."

But the words felt more intense than their meaning. They felt like salvation.

She was conscious of needing to avoid his bruise. She leaned back, which had the effect of making her breasts jut out. His gaze was inexorably drawn there, and now his hands wandered up her sides, one thumb rubbing her nipple, then adding a scrape of his nail that created new, exquisite sensations.

"Don't stop, baby. Keep going."

The rhythm caught fire, as she moved up and down. Enjoying this man and how he enjoyed her.

"Stay with me, Ash. Fuck, yes, you feel so good."

And then the words became moans, each one bringing them closer to release, and to each other. Each one, a word, a chapter, in the story of them.

30

A NIGHT out with his teammates at the Empty Net should have been a dream come true. Here Dex was, in the fold at last, surrounded by his ice brothers. Hell, he'd even made it onto the text chain. Yet all he could think of was what was missing.

Ashley.

Several of his teammates had brought their partners, and Dex wished he had *his* gorgeous woman on his arm. The sooner this court case was over, the better. Then he and Ashley could date for real—assuming she was interested in something more.

Banks nudged him at the bar. "Who pissed in your cornflakes?"

"Just missing someone."

"Your doggie daycare chick?"

"She manages an animal shelter. For rescues."

Banks looked skeptical. "Still haven't convinced her to climb aboard the O'Malley train?"

Sharing was definitely not caring. "We're taking it slow. I still have my court case to get through."

"Right. No chick wants to be shackled to a guy about to be incarcerated." Banks looked around, taking in the Rebels couples: Foreman and his wife Mia, Reid and the very pregnant Kennedy. Jorgenson had just arrived with Casey, and Bast and Pepper, Coach Calhoun's daughter, weren't far behind.

Banks's lips curved. "Ah, *you're* the one who wants to be shackled."

"These guys seem really happy."

He scoffed. "For now."

"You don't think there's a special someone out there for you?"

Special someone? Since when had Dex started talking like the heroine's bestie in a Hallmark movie?

His teammate's expression was pure disdain. "Fuck, no. Any chick would have to be insane to get involved with me."

Kind of a strange thing to say. Still, Dex would have liked to have his teammate's self-possession. Banks didn't give two fucks about anyone or anything and strode through life like it owed him a living.

"Want a drink?"

Dex shook his head. Banks shrugged and headed off to the corner where Foreman and Petrov were playing darts with their wives.

He shot off a text to Ashley, though it took him a few tries to get it right.

~~Thinking of you.~~

~~Can you come over to my place and wear that pink blouse with the white flowers, the one that does amazing things for your tits?~~

He settled on:

> How's Willa doing?

A text came in, but not from Ashley.

ANTON

How's the head?

He and Anton had met up for lunch in New York before the game. Dex had forgotten how much he enjoyed his former coach's company, his sharp insights, his generous praise. After spending a couple of years disappointing him, Dex had pulled away, and now it felt like they were in a better place.

Before he could respond, someone else slotted into the vacancy left by Banks, someone who smelled a good deal better.

"Hi, Dex."

Roxy, the last woman he'd been with before the fight with Hughes. Before he was told to clean up his act. Before Ashley made him forget every other chick. She'd texted a couple of times and he'd ignored her, which Dex 1.0 was fine with, and Dex 2.0 acknowledged was rude.

"Hey."

"Where've you been? Playing with the dogs at the shelter?"

"You saw that?"

"So. Cute." Moving in, she rubbed one of her tits against his arm. "I've missed you."

"Yeah, I'm sorry I didn't text you back. I'm seeing someone." Claiming Ashley felt so damn good. So she wasn't here and they weren't public, but just having her in his life was like ... fuck, something out of Hallmark.

"I don't mind that," Roxy said. "I'm seeing someone, too. Have been for months."

And she was fine with cheating? "I'm not on the market."

Her eyes sparked with a touch of anger. *Right there with*

you, sister. He turned away before he snapped at her. He needed to keep better company.

Hudson Grey had just arrived and was raising a hand to the bartender. "Drink?"

"No, think I'll head home."

Grey immediately picked up on Dex's mood. "You okay?"

"Just feeling kind of in limbo."

"How so?"

Hudson was the kind of guy who saw a therapist. With his sunny and open nature, he also seemed like confidant material. Better than Banks, anyway. "I want to be with someone but it's complicated."

"What's complicated about it?"

The court case, the need for discretion, the fact that Ashley had a very full life that might not have room for him.

"I'm not sure she wants to be part of my life. Of *this* life."

Grey nodded. "Then make an effort to be part of her life. Relationships are about compromise, figuring out how to fit the puzzle pieces together. Show her that you want to be there with her, for all of it and—" His words petered out as his attention was diverted elsewhere. "Hey, isn't that your neighbor?"

Sure enough, Georgia was at the bar's entrance, looking like she'd walked into the *Star Wars* cantina and was surprised to see aliens. As usual, she gave off big socialite energy, wearing another fancy dress, long and shimmery, the kind of thing angels might think appropriate for cocktail hour.

Spotting him, she waved and picked her way through the crowd, though in truth, they parted like the Red Sea because Georgia brought that kind of energy.

"Hey, Dex!"

"Georgia. What's up?"

"Oh, nothing." She cast an eye around imperiously. "So this is what this bar looks like. I've always wondered."

The Empty Net was not a Georgia type of place. Why she was living at Castle Apartments was a mystery. The building served as the temp stay for newer Rebels players, but was fairly down market for someone who clearly came from money.

"So most of your teammates drink here?"

"Sure, like Hudson. I think you might have met once."

Grey nodded at her. "Hello."

Georgia gave a wan smile, evidently distracted as her eye roved the bar. "Hi—oh, there you are!" Her face lit up with determination, as if she was readying herself for battle. Dex followed her gaze which was locked and loaded on ...

Banks.

"Georgia, you okay?"

"I will be." She remained still, hands on hips, psyching herself up.

"What's happening?" Grey murmured out of the side of his mouth.

"No idea, but I have a feeling we're about to find out."

Whatever vibe Georgia was giving off had an impact: Banks paused mid-throw of a dart, looked in their direction and froze, like he'd seen the Ghost of Socialites Past.

And then he moved their way, or rather, Georgia's way, his expression fierce and focused, not unlike his demeanor on the ice. Fucking scary, to be honest.

"Jesus," Grey muttered, which pretty much encapsulated Dex's thinking on the matter.

"Georgia," Banks said on arrival, like it pained him to speak those two syllables.

"Banks," came Georgia's reply, equally disdainful.

Then a stony silence.

Grey said under his breath, "What am I missing?"

Dex could either walk away or help the conversation along. The latter was a much more interesting prospect. "You guys know each other?"

Banks had moved his burning gaze from Georgia's face to her outfit, which seemed to offend him.

"I need to talk to you," Georgia finally said.

Without taking his eyes off her, Banks said, "O'Malley, how do you know Georgia?"

"She's my neighbor at Castle Apartments."

"Come down in the world, have you?"

"Nothing you need to worry about," Georgia bit out. "Could I have a moment of your time?"

Her voice sounded strained, like she was holding on by one of the sparkly threads in her dress.

"We have nothing to discuss."

"Ah, but we do."

Banks snorted. "No army of lawyers this time?"

Grey and Dex exchanged glances. "Lawyers?" Grey mouthed then turned back to the face-off, not wanting to miss a thing.

"This would be better done in private." Georgia's voice held a note of pleading.

"Don't think so, princess. Have a nice life."

He turned to leave, but before he could get far, Georgia said in a low voice, "We're still married."

"Fuck, no," Dex muttered at the same time as Grey.

Banks stopped, his body as tense as piano wire. Dex had earlier thought this guy was so self-possessed, with Rebels arena ice shavings in his veins, and that nothing could bother him. But this statement changed all that.

When he turned, his face was undiluted fury. "What did you say?"

"I think you heard me." She waved a hand, more casually now. Whereas before she'd been a ball of nervous energy, now she was back in control with Banks's reaction fueling her confidence.

She liked his discomposure.

"What the hell is this?" Banks's mouth was twisted in a sneer. "It was a done deal."

"There was a paperwork error. The divorce didn't go through." She examined her nails, which Dex could tell infuriated Banks. "So much for the army of lawyers."

If Banks could have glared Georgia below the peanut-shell covered floorboards, he probably would have stood there for eternity figuring out the right combination of expressions to do it.

As death-by-bad-mood wasn't yet possible, Banks instead turned to Dex and Grey. "You heard nothing."

Dex gave a zipped-lips gesture. Grey offered up a wide-eyed blink. Banks cupped Georgia under her elbow and dragged her to the other side of the bar.

During whatever-that-was, a text message had arrived from Ashley and Dex scanned it quickly.

Grey was still stunned. "Can you believe that?"

"Nope. But Banks has always been one sneaky fucker. Listen, I've got to go. Keep me posted on the hashtag-Borgia sitch."

Grey grinned. "Will do."

31

TWINKLING LIGHTS SPLATTERED like gold dust on the walls and ceilings of Willa's bedroom, but no amount of sparkle could fix the mood in the room. Ashley put her arm around her daughter's thin shoulders and gathered her close. Her baby was hurting.

"What about some hot chocolate?"

"It's just empty calories."

Ashley started. "Where did you hear about empty calories?"

"Lottie says I shouldn't eat or drink anything with no nutritional value."

The list was getting longer. Another person Ashley would be having words with before the night was through.

"They didn't believe me, Mom." Willa sounded so disillusioned. Today in school, she'd mentioned that Dex O'Malley had come to her house for dinner, invited her to a game, and that she'd met several members of the Chicago Rebels. When she showed the video advertising Dex's connection to the shelter, her "friends" had called her a liar.

"We'll have to get a picture of you with Dex and that'll show them."

"They said he wouldn't be friends with someone like me. I'm too ugly."

Ashley's mama bear instincts rose up. "You are not ugly. You are the most beautiful person I know and anyone who says different will have to deal with me."

She'd already been on the phone to that little miss Shana Connors's mom, telling her that her daughter was a menace. That went as well as expected. One less holiday card this year.

There was a knock on the door, and Vera put her head around.

"Hey, button, how ya feelin'?"

Willa shrugged, which broke Ashley's heart all over again.

Her sister made a face, beckoning for Ashley to come outside.

"Back in a sec, honey."

Out in the hallway, she got the surprise of her life.

Dex.

He leaned in, cupped her hip, and gave her a quick kiss. "How's Willa?"

"Willa?"

"I brought her flowers." He held up a bouquet, a mix of daisies and other flowers Ashley didn't recognize. "The florist was closed so I had to hit the gas station. Think she'll like them?"

"Yes, but—I thought you were out with your friends tonight."

"It was pretty boring except for one thing, which I'll spill the tea on later. When you texted that Willa wasn't feeling well, I thought I'd stop by, see how both my girls are doing."

Both my girls. Pushing past the lump of emotion in her throat, she tried to find the words. "She got into an argument with some of her friends at school."

Dex went on alert. "I thought you said she wasn't feeling well."

"I didn't want to go into it." Men didn't usually enjoy the details. "Some of her friends didn't believe that she'd met you."

He growled, and boy, was that hot. "Could I see her?"

Ashley sent a quick look Vera's way, got a nod of encouragement she didn't realize she needed, and stood aside.

Dex pushed open the door and immediately said, "Wow, look at this place!"

Willa set her iPad aside and sat up straighter. "Dex!"

"Hey, Sparkle." He stood just inside the threshold and looked around. "This is like a fairy palace. These lights are epic!"

"Are you here to see Mom?"

"Nope. I'm here to see you. I brought flowers." He moved forward with the bouquet and placed it on her lap.

"For me? No one's ever brought me flowers before."

Just hearing the joy in her voice made Ashley's heart sing.

"Yeah, they're mighty pulchritudinous, don't ya think?"

Willa's eyes went round. "What does that mean?"

Dex sat on the bed, but because he was so large, half his fine ass spilled over the edge. "Wait, have I found a word that the great and mighty Willa Adams doesn't know?"

"Did you make it up?" she asked, pity in her voice.

"I certainly did not! Pulchritudinous means attractive or radiant or beautiful."

Willa mouthed the word. "But it sounds like ... the opposite."

"I know, right? You're not the only one with the big vocab!" He leaned in and said in a stagey-whisper. "But this dumb jock had to look it up on the way over here."

Willa giggled. "You're not dumb. And we're not supposed to use that word. It's insensitive to people who can't speak."

"Oh, right. Always an education with you, Sparkle."

Ashley hated to interrupt but she had a mom duty to perform.

"Maybe we should put those flowers in water? Then we can set them in a vase on your vanity and they'll be the first thing you see when you wake up."

"Okay, Mom. And I can show Dex my art project." Bad day forgotten, she shifted over to make room for Dex. He took it, twisting around so that they sat side by side. On her way out Ashley caught his wink, which made her heart gallop all over again.

Heading downstairs, she found Maeve and Vera waiting in the kitchen.

"What's going on?" Maeve asked, sounding genuinely perplexed.

"He heard Willa was down and came by to cheer her up. He brought flowers." She pulled a vase from the cupboard and placed it under the tap while trying to calm her racing pulse. Getting overexcited about this wouldn't do.

"He also brought that." Vera pointed at a Trader Joe's shopping bag that Ashley hadn't noticed. "Wonder what's in it?"

Before Ashley could object, Vera and Maeve were unpacking the bag's contents. Chocolate-covered Laceys. Sea salt caramels. English breakfast tea. Massage oil.

Vera whooped, "what have we here?" and held up a pair of pink fur-lined handcuffs.

rt1

.rt
rteader

srt

"Ha, ha, very funny." Her sister had quite the collection and that was obviously a plant.

"Just giving you some ideas to keep it interesting."

Maeve looked like she had something to say.

"Okay, out with it."

Her sister winced. "I was going to say that I'm impressed."

"You are?"

Her oldest sister seemed surprised at her own reaction. "It's unexpected. And sweet."

"It is, isn't it?"

Barely stopping herself from bounding upstairs, Ashley returned with the vase and took a moment to spy through the door. Dex was stretched out on the bed, his sneakers off, one strong arm around Willa while she showed him her butterfly art. Just the sight of them made Ashley's heart feel far too big for her chest.

He'd brought tea. Cookies. Gas station flowers. (No handcuffs but she might keep them all the same.) But mostly he'd brought comfort to her daughter. If she wasn't half in love with him already, that just about tipped her over the edge.

32

Blu
Domestic short-haired cat
Likes: Playing with the toilet roll
Dislikes: The patriarchy

WORD about the Bunking with Butterflies event had spread. Dex had made sure to invite everyone on the Rebels roster with kids over the age of five, and while the recommended age range was 5-11, the Nature Museum was okay with older kids, too.

What Dex hadn't reckoned on was the "kid-at-heart" subset.

"Grey, what are you doing here? You don't have kids."

Hudson grinned while his usual blush lit up his cheeks. "Jude's on a shift at the firehouse tonight. Kershaw said everyone was invited."

Typical. "Yeah, it's fine. But at this rate we have more adults than kids."

Isobel was here with her nieces, Remy and Harper's seven-year-old twins and five-year-old, Maddie. (The parents had stayed home with their infant daughter, Josie.) Gunnar Bond had brought his sister-in-law Lauren, who, at fourteen, was a wicked hockey player, while Bren St. James, retired player and scorer of the goal that won the Cup seven years ago, had his daughter Franky in tow. She'd already made friends with Willa, bonding over pictures of her slug terrarium. Seven-year-old Max Callaghan, son of Ford and Addison, had thought that pretty "ew" but was looking forward to seeing the butterflies.

A guide named Matt met them in the lobby after the Nature Museum had closed.

"Hey, everyone, welcome to the Butterfly Garden!" He gestured to them to follow. "How about we drop off your sleeping bags and belongings? Then we can take a tour, check out the exhibits, and go over the agenda for your Night at the Museum."

"Night at the Museum," Kershaw said. "Sounds creepy."

His fourteen-year-old half-brother Jason grinned. "Sounds awesome."

"Well, duh."

Dex picked up Ashley's sleeping bag and hefted it over his shoulder.

"You don't have to do that." She tried to take it from him, but he swatted her away gently. She took a quick recce of the group, spotted Willa chatting with Franky and Matt the Butterfly Guy, and appeared to relax a touch.

"How much do we owe you for this?"

"You already paid in soup, cupcakes, and the other." He lowered his voice to a husky whisper. "Meaning orgasms."

"Hey, I know this isn't cheap. When we were set to do it before it was $100 a head, and that was before you factored in the pizza."

He couldn't bear to see Willa's disappointment at

missing out on this special time with the butterflies. A hundred dollars a head was a small price to pay to make a little girl happy. What was the point of all this money if you couldn't spend it on people you cared about?

Usually, they needed a group of fifty to make this worthwhile for the Nature Museum. They had about ten adults and ten children in this group and there was no way they were sharing with a bunch of strangers, so this was how it would go. He didn't mind paying a premium for the smaller group and the privacy.

"Dex!" Ashley shout-whispered, grasping his arm. "I thought you said one of your teammates organized it. Who should I talk to about paying our way?"

"It's sorted."

She stopped and stared at him. "*You* organized this!"

"Course I did. Just another brick in the wall of Dex O'Malley's rehabilitation. Not only does he pick up puppy poop and begs for charitable donations on Insta, he also plans slumber parties for kids at the Butterfly Garden. Wow, that guy must be a saint!"

She laughed. "You'll have to be to put up with this lot for a night."

"Ah, well, that's where you're wrong, Ashley Adams. Because you're going to be making it worth my while."

"I am?"

"Yep. Later you and I will be learning all about creating our own cozy cocoon. That's butterfly lingo, by the way. Foot rubs are included. Heard you're a fan."

She shook her head, but he didn't miss her smile at his cheeky charm. But there was more. The hollowness he carried with him was filling drop by drop with every moment he spent with Ashley and Willa. If someone had told him six weeks ago that he'd be doing everything in his power to win over a single mom and her kid, he'd have said they were high on their own supply.

AFTER THE 15-MINUTE ORIENTATION, they got a tour of the exhibits, the highlight of which was hanging in the Garden and using the supplied cheat sheet to identify as many butterfly species as they could. Willa insisted on being paired with Dex—"sorry, Mom, I can see you any day of the week!"—and they spent a fun half hour spotting all the different types of butterflies.

"Okay, Sparkle, how many are there?"

"There are twenty thousand species in existence, but this garden has about 40."

"What's that blue one called?" He took a snap so they could show their work later.

"That's a morpho. They're kind of common but they're also beautiful."

Agreed. "How about this one? This looks like one of these tiger deals." He referred to his cheat sheet.

"A tiger longwing. From South America."

"Long way to fly. Must be mighty tired."

Through her glasses, she shot him a look that told him he was being a doofus. He didn't mind. He kind of was.

"So how come you like butterflies so much?"

"People think I like them because they're pretty. And I'm not."

His heart clenched. "Who says you're not?"

She ignored that. "I like them for other reasons."

"Such as?" Still hung up on her matter-of-fact statement about not being pretty, he took another picture, this time of a green and black one with white markings polka-dotting its wings.

"They don't last long. Some of them only last for a few weeks, but in that short time, they bring so much joy to everyone. They make the whole world around them better. Kind of like you and hockey."

This kid. He had trouble getting the words out.

"Everyone has the capacity to do that." His special talent didn't make him better than anyone else. But he needed to appreciate it more. He was so lucky, and here he was squandering his privilege for what? Looking to fill the void left by his "woe-is-me" Mommy issues?

No, Ruby O'Malley was not invited to this party.

"You bring tons of joy to people, too, Sparkle."

"My mom." Said in a moms-have-no-choice tone.

"Sure. Your dad, too. And your aunts. Bandit likes to see you when you stop by."

"Bandit doesn't like anyone."

"Not true. So, he's one of those 'keeps it close' types of dog, but I can tell when he's a fan of someone. When I was a kid, I had this dog called Loki and he loved everybody. Which was fine and all, but Bandit's different. You have to earn his trust because he's been hurt."

She thought about that for a moment. "What happened to Loki?"

"I lost track of him after I went into care."

"You must have missed him."

He took a breath. "I did. But I lived with some families who had great dogs."

"But they weren't yours."

True, and whenever he left, he sometimes missed the dog more than the people.

"You're a pretty wise chick, kind of like your mom."

She giggled at the word "chick."

"So not only do you bring joy to your mom and aunts, you're also very cool and a bit of a sage. In fact, I would not be enjoying all these butterflies if you hadn't wanted to do it. None of us would, so that's on you. You're the reason all these people are having this great time. You're the Butterfly Queen."

A small, secretive smile curved her lips. "I am?"

"Absolutely."

"Dex?"

"Uh huh?"

"There's a Malachite on your head."

He hoped that was a butterfly. "Should we get an ussie? You can share it with your friends." *Take that, Shana Connors.*

By the time they took the photo, the butterfly had flitted away, but the memory was enshrined in his heart forever.

ASHLEY HAD to pinch herself every time she looked over to her daughter chatting with the big-shouldered lug of a hockey player. Just knowing that he was being kind—and she didn't need to hear the exact words he was using because Dex was always kind—made her heart skitter.

The way Willa looked up at him in admiration was so sweetly painful Ashley wondered if that same skittering heart might crack open any second. That Dex had gone to all this trouble to set it up still blew her mind.

"So what about this one? Cabbage white, I reckon."

She turned to her partner in butterfly spotting, Theo Kershaw, whose little brother preferred to hang with Lauren. Theo had volunteered to take Ashley under his wing (*butterfly wing? get it?*) but she suspected there were ulterior motives.

And his next words confirmed it.

"Be honest, hot mama, what are your intentions towards our Dexy?"

"My intentions?"

"Yeah. You're a woman of the world, probably on the lookout for a baby daddy for your kid. Lots of women in your position would be angling for a rich pro-athlete."

Her mouth dropped open. Was that what people really thought?

"Dex and I are just friends," she spluttered. "I don't have any intentions at all."

"Theo." Gunnar cut in. "Don't be so ... you."

"Listen, Dex is kind of a dummy when it comes to women," Theo went on. "You're obviously the smart one in this pairing. Kind of curious what you see in him."

"He's an awesome guy and there is no pairing. Like I said, we're just friends, which it sounds like he needs with teammates like you."

Theo laughed, then turned to Gunnar. "Hey, Double-O, what do you think of J-Dog and Lo? They make a cute couple, don't ya think?" He jerked his chin toward his brother and Lauren, who were standing close together, butterflies circling above them like something out of a cartoon.

"I think if he lays a finger on her he won't be playing hockey at camp this summer. What, with the broken legs and all."

Theo grinned at Ashley. "No one wants to give love a chance."

"They're kind of young."

"Yeah, but I like the idea. And G, it'll make us related."

"Christ," Gunnar muttered. "That's all I need."

Theo pointed. "You thought you'd retire and never see me again? Nope. We are family!" Cue a surprisingly tuneful rendition of the Sister Sledge classic, which sent a grumbling Gunnar wandering off to more closely chaperone the youngsters. Theo turned back to Ashley. "So you know I'm kidding about you being after O'Malley's money. You passed the test, Ash-Kicker. My way of seeing how serious you are about him because he's pretty serious about you."

Oh, look? A Monarch. Stifling the tremble in her hand, she marked her butterfly card with a check. "What makes you say that?"

Theo threw his hands up. "Look around you."

"He did this for Willa."

"Who's an extension of you. He had to talk to the Rebel Queen herself."

"The Rebel Queen?"

He shook his head at her ignorance. "Harper Chase, our fearless leader and CEO? She's on the board of the Nature Museum and this was kind of short notice, so she pulled some strings. Believe me, no one wants to talk to Harpoon because she gets all up in your personal life, trying to 'therapize' you. O'Malley had to pay a premium to get in here tonight."

Whoa. "That's so kind. I knew it was before, but to go to all that trouble."

"Sure, to impress you because he knows you're probably hard to impress. I'm imagining heartbreak in your past because of your divorce and all. And the way to your bruised heart is through your kid."

True. But that didn't mean Dex was right for Ashley or her family. Because when it came down to the wire, he was a young guy with not a whole lot of responsibility, and no evidence he wanted any more.

"He's just being nice. And my reference will do him some good for his court case."

Theo's brows drew together in a V. "His court case? He'd probably just seduce you if that was his game." At Ashley's blush, he chuckled. "Okay, so he's already scored a home run there. Awesome!" He raised his hand for a high-five that she refused to reciprocate. These boys. "Then he wouldn't be getting extra credit with your kid, would he? That would be mighty devious and O'Malley hasn't got a devious bone in his body."

She agreed, and that scared her even more. Because if Dex truly was interested in her for more than a good time and a few kind words to a stone-faced judge, then how was she supposed to deal with that?

Looking over to her giggling daughter, she wondered how either of them would ever recover.

MATT THE BUTTERFLY GUY, as Dex had labeled him, set the little kids up with a crafty activity, painting egg cartons so that they looked like caterpillars. The older kids worked on creating a butterfly feeder with Willa leading the way (she had very specific ideas about how it was supposed to go). It was fun to watch her be more outgoing and social, especially with more mature kids who could so easily give her a hard time. But Franky, Lauren, and Jason listened to her like every word out of her mouth was important.

Addison Callaghan, wife of Ford, mother of Max, and another gorgeous example of WAG-dom, sat down beside Ashley and offered her a gummy bear.

"They're not funny ones, are they?"

Addison laughed. "Not unless you think the sour faces my Max pulls when he eats them are funny. No, I wouldn't bring edibles to a kids' event."

"Sorry, I'm just never sure what people think is okay."

"Don't worry. I'm not offended." She smiled warmly. "So how are you enjoying dating a younger hunk?"

"I—well, we're just friends."

Addison held up her hands. "Oh, God, sorry! I thought you two ... Because he—never mind."

"He's volunteering at the animal shelter where I work and he heard that Willa missed out on an earlier tour, so he invited us to this one. It's really ..." She trailed off, realizing how absurd her protest sounded. After everything she'd learned about Dex's organization of this event, it was rather absurd to be sitting on the throne as Queen of the Nile.

"Nothing?" Addison mused with a quirked brow.

"I'm not fooling anyone, am I?" She spared a glance in Dex's direction. He was having a very deep conversation with Amelie, one of Remy and Harper's little girls. He looked so adorable, giving her all his attention. "What were you going to say? Why you thought we were together?"

"Oh, he asked for some recommendations for lingerie from my collection. He said you were a fan."

Dex was shopping for lingerie? "I am. It's so gorgeous and sexy. I feel like a different woman when I'm wearing it."

"That's the idea!" Addison stood suddenly. "Would you help me find the restroom?"

"Uh, sure."

Ashley followed her out and after a couple of corners, they found the ladies' room. Addison scanned the space, under the stall doors, then closed the door behind them.

"So, not to go all high school—"

"You just asked me to go to the restroom with you and locked the door."

That gorgeous smile reminded Ashley that Addison was still a highly-paid full-figured lingerie supermodel in between running her own business and raising a family.

"Dex likes you."

So everyone kept telling her. "I like him, too. But I have more than my needs to consider. He's younger than me, for a start, and I don't want to place a bet on him and have my hand go bust."

"Believe me, I get that. Ford's six years younger than me."

"I didn't know that." She'd never have guessed it, either.

"Yep, I just turned forty."

"Get out! You look much younger. Not that it matters what age you are—sorry, I'm making a mess of this." Ashley was ten years younger and would never look as good as this woman at thirty, never mind forty.

Addison rubbed Ashley's arm. "What I'm trying to say with my humblebrag is that age doesn't really matter when both of you are committed. Ford was ruthless in chasing me down. It was flattering but I had to wonder if I was just a challenge to him, and once conquered, he'd lose interest. Is that what you're worried about?"

Ashley sighed. "A little? Mostly I don't trust what I'm feeling. I spent a lot of time with a guy who wasn't there for me or my daughter when we needed it. Who didn't find me attractive, to be honest. This thing with Dex, it's that first flush of excitement but it's not real life. Eventually you have to come down to earth. He gets his charges dismissed and he's not obliged to volunteer anymore and—"

"His charges?" Addison frowned. "You think he's keeping you sweet for his court case?"

Ashley shrugged. "Not that I'm standing between him

and the pokey, but I'm supposed to give him a good reference. Once that's done, why would he stick around?"

The woman looked scandalized, as if Ashley would dare
say something so appalling about one of her husband's
teammates. She needed to remember who these people
were—friends of Dex.

"This butterfly thing is a lot of trouble for someone so
mercenary."

It was. Ashley felt awful for doubting Dex.

"That's not really it, or not all of it. He's young and just
finding his feet in the world. I've been around the block and
looking for a quiet life. Dex doesn't really equal a quiet life,
does he?"

"Maybe not. But if you talked to him about what his
intentions are, maybe it can help you figure out yours."

She wasn't wrong, but bringing it up made it seem like
they had a chance. What if she was jumping the gun, and
this was all fun and games for Dex?

Only she saw how he was with her daughter.

Felt how he was with her.

This was as real as it got, and that butterfly-like fluttering
in her chest was either excitement or terror—or a crazy
combination of both.

33

THE PIZZA PARTY WAS A HIT. Matt the Butterfly Guy had one more fun exercise for the attendees and then it was lights out by 10 p.m.

The kids wanted to sleep in the same room, an alcove set up near one of the butterfly exhibits, and Addison and Isobel said they'd sleep on the south end of the room with the younger ones. Theo, Gunnar, and Hudson set up camp on the other side with the older kids.

Ashley watched as her daughter rolled up her sleeping bag and gathered her belongings. "But don't you want to stay with me? I was going to let you read on your Kindle."

Willa rolled her eyes, suddenly appearing much older than nine. "Mom, I'm going to stay with my friends. And I would be reading on my Kindle anyway!"

"I know but—"

"See you tomorrow, Mom!" And then she was gone.

Addison smiled. "I'll keep an eye on her, I promise. Maybe enjoy this time for yourself."

"Lights out!" Matt was wandering around with a flashlight.

Dex arrived back from the bathroom with his toiletry bag. He wore flannel PJ bottoms and a gray Rebels tee, but not even his perfect musculature, woodsy scent, or devastating sex appeal could cheer her.

"Where's everyone?"

"Apparently they all want to sleep in the other room, closer to the exhibit."

"Willa too?"

"Yeah, she's making friends." Ashley hated that she sounded so glum about it.

"Sucks when they move on, huh?"

"She hasn't moved on." She worried her lip. "Has she?"

Dex grinned. "Flying the coop, baby. Had to happen sometime."

"She's nine!"

Laughing, he sat down on his sleeping bag, then leaned over to kiss her. "Don't worry, you can look after me tonight."

This reeked of a setup. "Did you organize this?"

"You know I did."

"I mean this private hideaway."

"Wish I'd thought of it," he said, but there was no missing the slight upward turn of his lips. God, he was such a delicious rogue.

"Okay, I'm going to the bathroom. Back soon."

A couple of minutes later she returned only to find the spot where she'd left her sleeping bag empty. A strong arm encircled her from behind. "Come on, I found us somewhere else to hide out."

"But Willa—"

"Is okay. Addie and Isobel will take care of her." He took her hand and led her to another place, hidden away under an arch with fun butterfly art above them. He had zipped their sleeping bags together. "This way we can have a little space for us."

For us. It sounded lovely. "Can I have a second?"

"Sure."

She headed back to the other room and through the entryway to the bunk-down spot.

"Willa?"

"Mom?"

Her daughter was snuggled up in her sleeping bag, Kindle in hand, with Addie on one side and Giselle, one of Harper Chase's daughters, on the other.

"Just checking you're okay."

"I'm fine." She sounded a little embarrassed. So soon? "Are *you* okay?"

No. "Perfect. I'll be next door. Well, the next room over, so let me know if you need anything, okay?" She smiled at Addison. "Thanks for taking care of her."

"Not a problem. Go get some rest." Ashley didn't imagine the implied snigger in her tone.

"Night, Mom!" Clearly anxious to get rid of her.

"I'm going," she grumbled.

She returned to where Dex had set up their sleeping bags. He was already inside the quilted pocket, and he looked up, his brow furrowed. "Everything okay?"

"Yeah, she clearly doesn't want me around."

"That's not true. She's just flexing her independence muscles in a safe space."

That sounded awfully wise. "Any room in there for a sad, unwanted mom type?"

"I think I can fit you in."

He pulled back the cover, inviting her into his web, and she snuggled in beside him as they adjusted their legs and found a way to puzzle-piece their bodies together. A little like what they were doing as a couple.

Because there was no doubt that's what they were becoming.

She faced him and drank him in, in all his handsome glory.

"You're exceptionally good-looking, you know that? Of course you know that. How could you look in the mirror and not know that?"

"Looks aren't everything, y'know. A wise woman told me that once."

Had she offended him? "I know there's more to you than this straight nose and perfect cheekbones and these lips." She ran her thumb over the bottom, fuller one. "I just wanted to acknowledge the pretty."

"Right back at ya, gorgeous." He pushed a strand of hair behind her ear. "Speaking of superficial attention to a person's appearance, I had an interesting chat with your daughter earlier. She thinks she's not pretty."

Alarm checked her heart. "She said that?"

"Yeah, we were talking about why she likes butterflies and she just said it. I'm not sure I handled it right."

"How did you handle it?"

"Well, after I picked my jaw up off the floor, I got kind of grouchy saying stuff like, who said you're not, etcetera, etcetera. And then we chatted about butterflies and the joy they bring people, and she said I do that with hockey, and I said she does that with being the Butterfly Queen. She's the reason everyone is here tonight, all because of her love of the butterflies. We pretty much bigged each other up."

"Oh." Ashley could feel tears welling and she willed them away.

"Shit, did I say the wrong thing? I really don't know how to deal with kids."

Yes, you do. What you said was perfect. You *are perfect.*

She touched his lips, staying his protests. "No, you said exactly the right thing. She's been down about her dad being so focused on his new family. She thinks she's not as pretty as the new baby."

"A baby? That's what she's comparing herself to?"

"Babies tend to be beautiful."

He scoffed. "Have you seen some of the Rebel babies? Not these grown ones, but there are some ugly ones with hockey player genes. For example, Esme was no oil painting when she first arrived, all crinkled like a potato and scowly like her father. We need to tell Willa that this baby can't hold a candle to her."

She giggled, loving his over-the-top reaction. "She likes you. You treat her like she's special."

"She is. I can't believe your ex is so hands off."

"He's never been one for multitasking. One family, one decision, is the most he can manage at any one time, and he's made his choice."

"Then we'll make sure she doesn't miss that attention. Shower her with everything she needs."

Was there anything sexier than a man who loved your kid unconditionally? How could she not love this guy?

How could she not be *in* love with this guy?

She was supposed to have this under control! A hot fling with a hockey himbo with pipe-cleaning and cobweb-clearing and enough orgasms to boost her self-esteem and get her back on track.

This wasn't supposed to happen. None of it.

Emotional as all fuck, she swiped at a tear. This was the kind of relationship she'd longed for with Greg, one with strong girders supporting her and her family. But to pin her hopes on a man like Dex …

"Hey, what's going on? I haven't even unveiled my dick yet."

"I love hearing you say those things about my daughter. I don't have any expectations about … this. But I do want good people in Willa's life and you're a good person."

He rubbed away a tear, caught another, and leaned in to kiss any more strays away.

"I'm not good, but I'm touched that you'd think I'm worthy to be in your daughter's life."

"You underestimate yourself," she said, eager to defend the man who wouldn't defend himself. "You're like Bandit. Your first instinct is to bite the hand that feeds you but once you know that someone cares, you get some confidence in yourself."

His eyebrow scooted northward. "You think I lack confidence?"

"Oh, you know you're hot and talented and charming, but you don't believe in yourself. Not the way you need to."

"It's a lot of work trying to boost my ego all by myself. I haven't always had that self-belief."

"But people must have believed in you as a kid. You had to start somewhere with hockey."

He gripped her waist and pulled her close. "People saw something in me, a talent on the ice. But they weren't really thinking of me, more of how it would benefit them. How much money they could make." His mouth twitched. "Why else would someone pick me out of nowhere and tell me I was worth something? Because I wasn't. At least not up until then. Once I figured out the hockey thing, I realized I had something to contribute. And as long as I have this to offer, then someone will always want me."

What a dummy. "You have more to offer than hockey, Dex."

"Tell it to the judge." He grimaced. "Sorry, just an expression. I don't really think you have to say that to anyone."

The quid pro quo hung between them. Deciding it was better not to think of it, she thought back to something else he'd said.

"Why did you think you weren't worth anything before someone discovered you could play hockey?"

"Because I was just some useless kid in foster care. No one could deal with me. I was like Bandit, snapping at every hand, making enemies before they could kick me, wearing people out. That's what I do. That's what I did and Ruby paid the price."

Ruby? She needed to tread carefully. "How did you wear people out?"

"Mad energy, playing the attention hog, the usual." He bit his lip, seemed to think a moment before going forward. "Like now. It's always about me."

But he was going to say something else. Something about his mother.

"You came to hockey pretty late?"

"Yeah, Clifford Chase—he used to own the Rebels, you met his daughter Isobel tonight—saw me on a rink when I was twelve and put me in touch with a coach, Anton. He let me live with his family for a while but then his wife got cancer and it was too much work to have an extra kid in the house. So I ended up back at the care home, then eventually billeted with another hockey family, the Hughes. That's when I came into my own."

There he went again, assuming that he only deserved

good treatment because of his talent. She wanted to shake him.

"Wait a second. Hughes. Is that something to do with Kyle Hughes?"

He scowled. "Yep. I lived with his family for a year and let's just say, Kyle and I did not get along. We came up around the same time, but I was the better player. There's always been friction."

"Is that why you guys got into that bar fight?"

"He slashed my wrists on the ice. It should have been an ejection but all he got was a major. By the time the game was over and we were in the Empty Net, it was a powder keg ready to blow. He was a prick to his girlfriend and I used that as an excuse to go nuts on him."

There was something else. Ashley could sense that wasn't the whole story.

"What did he say to provoke you?"

He paused before responding. "That I was a charity case and that was why Clifford Chase took pity on me."

Anger flared. "What an asshole. He's lucky he only ended up with a broken nose!"

Surprise at her response flashed in his eyes.

"I don't like bullies," she said quietly.

"Neither do I. I'm not proud of my reaction. It was immature and now I need to pay the piper."

"Sounds like you've grown up a lot in the last few weeks. The lessons of cat litter and dog poop."

He chuckled and nuzzled his nose against hers. "I've learned so much."

"What were some of the other foster families like?"

"Mixed. A lot of them are just interested in the monthly check, so they're letting you run riot. But if you're too wild they need to rein you in because they don't want to risk children's services getting involved."

"Rein you in how?"

"Locking the fridge, chores to keep you busy, the belt."

Ashley's heart just about gave out. How awful it must have been for him, feeling so abandoned and alone.

Seeing the welling in her eyes, he cupped her jaw. "Don't be sad for me, Ash. Some of it was miserable but hockey saved me. And I haven't really appreciated it as much as I should have. I have this amazing career doing something I love, and I've been acting like I don't give a fuck. Like it doesn't matter if I'm on this team or the third line or playing in the AH-fucking-L. But it does matter. Willa said the team relies on me and she's right. The fans expect more and that's right, too. I want to be a better man and sometimes that means having something—someone—worth fighting for. I've been letting all this shit with the past get in the way. No more."

Easier said than done, but she could see that Dex had come so far. Still, there was that last push to the get him home. "Sometimes you have to deal with the past before you can move on."

"I have. Or I will, once I get through this court case." He shook his head, almost vehemently. "I don't need her, Ash. I just need to focus on the here and now."

Her, meaning his mom. She was always there, hovering above the man Dex was trying to become.

She rubbed a thumb over his eyebrows, applied a kiss to his chin.

"Talking to her might help you get some closure."

He snorted. "I'm just one of her stops on the apology tour. Some twelve-step shit. That's her problem, not mine."

Ashley recognized Dex's resistance to the idea of any

kind of détente with Ruby, but she also understood that mothers will always feel something for their kids. She'd never forget the pain on the woman's face on seeing her son —and being rejected by him again. If Willa was to ever look like that in Ashley's presence, she'd die of a broken heart.

"I'm not going to tell you what to do."

"Oh, but you want to, don't you?" His tone was a mix of amused and chiding.

"Sorry, it's the mom in me. It sounds like she's cleaned up her act. Holding down a job, even volunteering. Kind of like someone else I know. You guys might have more in common than you think."

"She came into the shelter to get to me, not to actually volunteer."

"Perhaps? But I think she was interested. She was really into Cleo, one of the new kittens."

He sighed. "Ashley, you're a pushover, you know that?"

"I am not!"

He kissed her softly. "How else do you explain why you're here with me in my sleeping bag?" He pulled at the waistband of her PJs. "Only a soft-hearted woman would fall for what I'm peddling."

So endeth the serious conversation. That was okay. He'd opened up more than she expected, and she felt she knew him a little bit more than she did before.

It was thrilling.

But then so was being in love.

34

ASHLEY WAS WAITING for her English breakfast tea at the coffee shop bar when she felt eyes on her. Dex O'Malley's eyes—except they weren't in his face. That would have been easier.

These eyes belonged to his mother, who was staring at Ashley from her spot in the line. A nod didn't seem like enough, and Ashley had never known what was good for her, so she walked over.

"Hi," she said.

Ruby took a breath. "Hello."

"Listen, I'm sorry—"

"About what hap—"

They both stopped speaking, and Ashley smiled because the woman looked like her world was about to collapse.

"Can I buy you a coffee?" Those were the actual words out of Ashley's mouth.

She shouldn't interfere. She should leave well enough alone. But she could tell that Dex had mixed feelings about his mother. It wouldn't hurt to hear what she wanted, though Ashley could probably guess. It was what every mom wanted.

To make sure her child was safe.

Was that what Ruby O'Malley had craved all those years ago? A stable place to live, a job to pay their way, a man to take care of her?

Ashley knew about those wants. But she didn't need a man, at least not to take care of her.

"I can get my own but maybe we can talk?" Ruby's voice was thick with so much need it made Ashley's heart crack.

Ashley picked up her tea and took a seat in the same booth where she and Jerome had shared their first and only date. A couple of minutes later, Ruby came over with a small cup of her own. Fellow tea drinkers. Perhaps it was a sign.

"The tea at the diner isn't as good as this. They only have Lipton."

"Do you like working there?"

"I do. The boss isn't a jerk, the other waitresses are friendly. Nice customers, too, especially the boys from the hockey team."

Ashley hadn't thought about that. "They eat there regularly? What about Dex?"

"He came in with them a couple of times, but no more. Avoiding me." She swallowed and picked up the string of the tea bag to dunk it. "How is he?"

Ruby could see that he was healthy, strong, amazing at how he earned his living. But that wasn't what she was asking.

"He's trying his best to figure things out. It gave him a shock to see you and he doesn't know what to do with it. He's still carrying a lot of pain."

She nodded slowly, thinking her next words through,

like she needed to impress Ashley, the connection to the boy she'd lost. "I saw that he got hurt in that game. Is he okay?"

"Yeah, just a goose egg and a bruise. He's made of stern stuff." Ashley decided to jump in feet first. "You moved here to be close to him?"

"I'd been here a couple of months, trying to get up the courage to see him. He was in the news and I wanted to reach out, but he had so much going on in his life. Complicated stuff, and I didn't want to make it worse. I'd just started the job and a few weeks later, he walked into the diner with one of his teammates and sat at the counter. I was so nervous I threw up in the restroom, and then when I came out, there he was right in front of me. And his face, when he ..." Her eyes welled up. "Oh, he wasn't happy, not at all. But even though I was causing him pain, it was still the best feeling in the world. To finally be close to him again." She shook her head. "It's selfish of me, I know. You probably don't understand."

"I'm a mom as well."

She looked up, her expression hopeful. "You are?"

"A nine-year-old girl. She's amazing, the best of me and her father. We're divorced. So I understand how you're feeling. That joy and pain is unique to motherhood."

She frowned. "Except I don't deserve to feel the joy part. Not after everything I put him through."

Dex was there, too. There would always be a cloud, no matter how successful he was.

"Could you tell me a little bit about what's going on with you now?"

She hesitated.

"It would help to know what your life is like."

"You want to know if I'm clean? I am. Fourteen months. I wanted to be sober for a year before I came ... here."

Before she came for her boy.

She held Ashley's gaze, her intent a burning focus. "Are you two together?"

"Yes." It sounded so good to say it.

"And he told you? About me?"

"Well, he had to after what happened at the shelter." He didn't have to say a thing, but he shared that with her. And more, later.

So much more.

Inside he was hurting, trying to navigate this situation with his mom. Ashley could help, but the hard work would have to be done by the two of them.

"I can talk to him, but I can't make any promises."

35

JoJo
Part Irish Setter
Likes: Eye contact
Dislikes: That woman in the express checkout line with more than 10 items

"No, I completely understand. You really need to rest up."

Ashley clicked off her phone and turned to Willa. "That's two more down. Toby sprained his ankle skateboarding and Mabel has a cold."

"Kind of sus." Perry frowned beneath her colorful bangs. Today, they were pink, a la Frenchie from *Grease*. "Both of them out."

"Well, I can't make them come in. But now we're three short."

Willa looked up from her e-reader. "Aunt Maeve said she'd stop by. But Aunt Vera is on a date."

"On a Saturday morning?" Ashley shook her head. "Forget I said that. I don't want to know what your aunt gets up to at this time of the day."

"Like what?"

"Never mind."

Sometimes she forgot how young her daughter was, especially as she seemed to possess a world-weary wisdom in her lovely blue eyes. But not today.

Since the Bunking with Butterflies event last weekend, she seemed to have retrieved some of her old vivacity. Ashley loved seeing her daughter like this, and she had Dex to thank.

Willa snuck a look out the window. "The line's getting longer."

The perils of having a celebrity volunteer in their ranks. Ashley hoped that people were interested in the animals and not just the connections at the shelter. She'd already fielded a call from Cora this morning, who was back from her cruise and hanging in Florida, reminding Ashley of all the things already on her list.

Were the puppies bathed?

Did she have enough adoption applications?

Oh, and don't forget that the Rebels PR people will be by to take photos.

Ashley knew all these things, but knowing didn't make it any easier. And now she was three volunteers down.

Her phone buzzed again.

DEX

Can you let me in the back?

She headed to the back entrance and opened the door. "Hi!"

"Hey." He wrapped her up close and kissed her as if it was a perfectly natural thing to do. Like he was her boyfriend.

"I missed you," he murmured against her lips.

"I missed you, too." Dex had been on a road trip and this was the first time she'd seen him in five days. Then she recalled who she'd spoken to a couple of days ago and the promise she'd made.

"Your fans are rattling the gates."

"I'm sure most of those people are dying to pet a puppy." They wanted to pet something alright. "Is Willa here?"

"Yeah, she's out front. Dex, I need to tell you some—"

"Okay, in a sec. I got her something." He opened his hand to reveal a box with a hair clip shaped like a butterfly. It's blue and silver stripes sparkled, even in the dim light of the corridor.

"Oh, that's lovely. She's going to love that."

"I saw it in a little store in Dallas and immediately knew it had to come home with me. Not that I put it in my hair or anything." He waved a hand. "Okay, maybe once just to see what it looked like."

She giggled. He was such a goof. But she needed to talk to him, tell him about running into his mom.

Her phone buzzed. "No, no, no."

"What?"

"Another volunteer down! That's four people now."

"Why didn't you say?"

Because you're amazing and I didn't want to bring on the bad vibes before I actually have to.

"You kissed me, and it went clear out of my head. But now reality is back, and she's pissed."

"Maybe we could get a few friends in?"

"You mean hockey-playing friends?" She wasn't sure if that would help or hinder. More bodies were good, but what if there were bite-y accidents or they couldn't control the animals? That Rebels PR woman would have a fit.

He read her mind. "I'll be in charge of them. I promise we can make this work. Do you trust me?"

"Yes, I do."

He looked so pleased, so she left him to make some calls and prayed she'd made the right decision.

∾

"THIS IS JELLYBEAN. He's three months old and has a lot of personality."

On cue, the kitten raised its paw to Dex and gave a jaunty salute. What a showcat!

"I love him!" the little redheaded girl said. "Dad, can we bring him home?"

"I thought you wanted a dog, pumpkin." The man locked eyes with Dex over his daughter's head, wearing the put-upon expression of dads who know they'll be on the hook for fifteen years of pet care. "We can't have a dog *and* a cat."

"I'll look after them."

"Heard that one before," came the mutter back. He took another look at Dex. "You had an amazing game the other night in Dallas. That goal was out of this world."

Dex smiled. "Yeah, it was a good game. But everyone played well."

"Too right," Kershaw butted in. "The way the press is talking lately, you'd swear this team had *one* player only."

Petrov cleared his throat. "Perhaps if you worried more about your own play instead of others, the press might talk about you again, Theodore."

Dex caught the eye of the kitten dad, who was agog at this behind-the-scenes insight into Rebel team dynamics.

"There's a lot of jealousy amongst the players," he offered.

Theo laughed. "Uh, no. I think it's great you're finally playing up to your potential. Hey, who owns this kitten?" He picked up Jellybean and held him to the little girl's face. "I think he wants to go home with you. But if you don't want him, I can probably find someone ..."

"Dad!" the girl wailed. "We have to take him!"

"Okay, but no dog, Libby."

"We'll see," Libby said with determination now that step one of her evil plan had yielded fruit.

Dex put an "Adopted" tag on Jellybean's box, then watched with Vadim and Theo as his new family headed off to the kennels, "just to see."

"We are killing it," Theo said.

"Sure, threaten to take every kitten home," Petrov said. "That should work."

"Uh, yes, it will! Oh, look out, there's someone else who needs some encouragement." Off he bounded to work his sales magic on more unsuspecting victims.

Dex turned to Petrov. "Thanks for coming out today. Didn't expect it, to be honest."

"Why? Because I am the captain and above all things?"

"You said that, not me."

Petrov smiled. "I like to be involved. Not on the text chain, of course, let them have their bitching about me. But other things, it is good. And Isobel said I must be nice to you because you are practically family."

Dex couldn't have heard that right. "She said that?"

"Yes, because you were discovered by Clifford. The man was a dick but he had a great eye. He saw something in you and now you are on this team, where you are meant to be. It is Kismet. Also, I will be retiring soon."

Petrov had been retiring for the last five years. "Oh yeah?"

"Yes, you cheeky pup. It is important that the next generation is ready to take over."

Was the captain implying Dex O'Malley might have developed sufficient responsibility to be considered "ready to take over"?

He looked over at Ashley who was busy showing a pair of twins a couple of black and white kittens. Their eyes met and there it was again, the fireworks, the boom, the everything. His life had done a 180 in the last six weeks and it was all down to her.

Vadim's lips quirked. "She is special, your Ashley."

Dex swallowed. "Yeah, she is. I try to tell her all the time, but it never comes out right."

"Sometimes it is hard to find the right words. But your actions are speaking as loud as your heart is thumping. She can hear it. We can all hear it!"

The cap was so dramatic, but he was also right. Dex's heart went into overdrive whenever he even thought of Ashley. Willa, too. He loved them both and he needed Ash to know that.

"What should I do?"

"Tell her what's in here." Vadim beat a fist against his chest. "What do you have to lose?"

"Except your deep-seated fears and long-held insecurities," Theo said, stealth-moving into position.

"Jesus, where did you come from?"

"Over there." He thumbed behind him. "Where I got three families set up with a Fanta special, a New York cookie, and a Jean Luc Picard."

"A what the what?"

"A Tabby, a black and white, and a gray one. As in Earl

Grey hot." Kershaw's quick-firing brain needed Google fucking Translate. "So you're going to break the bad news to Ashley?"

"The bad news?" Dex slid a glance to Petrov who offered nothing.

"That you love her. And now she has to put up with your shenanigans for the rest of her life. Bad news for her, but if she's into it ..."

"Fucker."

"Yep. But I've got my personal life sorted. Which makes me awesome, at least in the eyes of my wife and kids."

Dex snuck another look at Ashley. Could he really just put it out there and say what he felt? What if she said ... well ... no? But he saw how she studied him, not just because he had a good body and a nice jaw. She got this soft look about her, though maybe it wasn't all that different from how she looked at some of the strays in her care. Dex O'Malley, sad little orphan, no better than a troublemaking, barely house-trained puppy.

Maybe after the court case. That way she wouldn't think he had any ulterior motive. But that didn't mean he couldn't spend time with her. After all, with her, he felt like the best version of himself.

"Later, dudes."

"He's goin' in," Kershaw said, adding a couple of bars of the *Indiana Jones* theme, which didn't seem relevant at all except maybe, Dex had a giant stone ball hurtling toward him. Or he was about to fall into a pit of writhing snakes.

"Hey," he said as he came alongside her. She looked wrecked. "You need a break."

"Oh, I'm fine."

"What time did you get up this morning?"

"Well, I didn't actually get to sleep—"

"Go take five. I've got this."

"But—"

He leaned in, his lips brushing the shell of her ear. "Do you want me to carry you out of here over my shoulder? Because I'll do it."

Those apple-green eyes flashed in alarm. "There are more forms under the counter, but don't promise anyone anything until I get back, okay?"

"Got it." He patted her on her curvy tush. "Now go."

FIVE MINUTES LATER, Toby limped in, wearing a big grin.

Dex looked up from where he was helping Daisy, a Riverbrook grandmother and Chicago Rebels fan, fill out an adoption application for JoJo, one of the shelter's dogs.

"Thought your ankle was sprained?"

"Just twisted. Is this the entire Rebels franchise?"

"Pretty much. Hey, do you think you could take over? I wanted to get some tea for Ash."

Toby's grin stretched wider. "Sure thing. Hey, wanted to ask you: have you any idea why the Boss Lady won't let Bandit be adopted?"

"She won't?"

"Yeah, since that video, we've had tons of offers but she tells everyone he's not available. Were you planning on taking him? Because you said your schedule wouldn't allow it."

No, he wasn't. But he also hated the idea of anyone else having him.

"I'll ask her."

A short while later, he found her in the office, feet up, eyes closed. She started awake on hearing him come in.

"What? Do you need me?"

"Toby just showed up. Apparently his ankle is feeling better. He jumped right in—well, on his good foot."

Her shoulders sagged in relief. "Okay."

He placed a cup of English breakfast tea and a cranberry-orange scone on her desk. "Just a little something."

Her smile spread sunshine in his chest. She stood and approached him.

"What's going on?" he asked.

Throwing her arms around him, she kissed him slow and deep and hard. This was the stuff. He couldn't get enough of her.

"You are. I can't believe how helpful you are today."

He chuckled. "Because that's not really me, is it?"

"No, that's not what I meant. Not because of you, but because I don't usually expect that kind of assistance."

She fostered an image of independence and can-do, but he saw right through it. He lay his forehead against hers. "You work so hard. I want to take some of that burden off you."

Usually she would toss off some quick denial about not working all that hard or how it's a mom's lot in life. Today, she accepted his observation. Leaned into the comfort he was giving her.

He wanted to be the one she came to in time of need. He was so crazy about her.

Screw the court case. Just tell her how you feel.

"Thank you. For being here and running with the ball. I so appreciate it." She looked up and sighed. "I need to talk to you about something. It's important."

Not as important as what I have to say. But he'd hear her out. "Okay."

She bit her lip. "Maybe have a seat?"

He sat in her boss's chair and pulled her down into his lap. She squirmed a little, not settling as much as he'd like, and with her next words, he understood why.

"I talked to your mom."

Fuck. He stiffened, blinked, expelled a small puff of air. "When?"

"A couple of days ago."

"She come back here?"

"No, I ran into her at the coffee shop. We talked for a little while."

"Why?" Why the hell would Ashley give this woman the time of day?

"She hurt you and I needed her to know that."

Okay, that sounded ... better. Like Ashley had his back. Still, he didn't want her cozying up to his mother. He didn't want Ruby in Ashley's life because that meant the inevitable thinking about Dex 1.0, the one with the junkie mom, the guy who was a hair's breadth from a prison sentence of his own.

Like mother, like son.

"You don't think it was clear already? I've been ignoring her. Why else would I be doing that if she hadn't hurt me?"

She stood and leaned against the desk. He hated that look on her face, the one that people got around him because he needed to be scolded or have something explained to him very slowly.

"I understand you're hurt. And I understand you don't want to see her. And you don't have to. But I talked to her, and I thought you might be curious."

He was, damn her. A part of him—the sad, lonely, lost little boy or maybe the increasingly responsible, compassionate man—wanted to know if his mom was okay.

What was prison like?

Did anyone hurt her inside?

And did she still blame Dex for what happened?

Because Dex did. Ruby had brought on so much of it herself, but Dex had a role in this cluster. One he'd been ignoring for years.

Ashley blew out a breath, evidently gearing up for another assault. "She's been clean for over a year."

Jesus, Ruby was clearly following the reformed ex-con playbook.

"Sure she has. But once a junkie, always one." He stood and scrubbed a hand through his hair. "I don't understand why you had to get involved. You can't fix this."

She placed her hands on his chest. "I know you're not ready, but I wanted to put it out there. It'll take a while for you to come around. I get that. And maybe you never will, which is okay as well. But this could be the first step."

His heart was beating wildly beneath her fingertips. The first step? To what? Ruby insinuating her way into this good life he was building. It was bad enough she was on a first name basis with his teammates. Now she wanted a piece of his woman?

He couldn't speak so Ashley continued, making the case for Ruby O'Malley's sins to be forgiven. How lucky his mother was to have an amazing woman like Ashley in her corner. Thing was, Dex was selfish. He didn't want to share.

"She wants to make amends. That's why she's back in your life."

"She wants to ruin everything. You don't know what she's capable of."

She rubbed his chest. "Dex, I can't make you do anything you don't want to, but she's here now so it might be a good idea to face it. Face the future."

The future, which had been ticking along just fine,

coming up on him at an easy trot as he dealt with each problem, one at a time. His legal issues, his career, his personal
relationships. Now it was an out-of-control truck, the brakes
cut, the driver slumped over the wheel after a heart attack.

He couldn't deal with this, and when Ashley knew the
truth—the whole truth—she wouldn't want to deal with it,
either.

"What about Willa?"

"What about her?"

He shook his head. "You want a woman like that around
your daughter?"

She looked taken aback. "She's sober and making
amends."

"Says she is."

Now she looked annoyed with him, like she couldn't
understand his recalcitrance. "She's paid her debt to
society."

God, ever the bleeding heart. But then she only knew
half the story. "She's a criminal, Ashley, and she shouldn't be
around your daughter."

I shouldn't be around your daughter.

"She's a recovering addict, Dex. I like to think I'd have
enough compassion for a woman trying to pick herself up
from the dirt."

"She's not just an addict. She's more than that." He took
a sharp inhale. "She almost killed someone."

36

Killed someone? There was an "almost" in there, but those were the words she heard clearer than any other.

"Still think she's worth your time? Because she's not. She's bad news."

Dex's eyes were wild, his arms crossed over his chest—in defense or protection.

"Tell me what happened."

"So you can justify it? Make up some excuse for her?" He walked to the window. "I come from a long line of trouble-makers, Ashley. I already told you not to put me on a pedestal."

"I want to know."

She leaned against the desk, giving him time to gather his thoughts. After a tense, drawn-out moment, he started speaking.

"Ruby drank a lot back then. Drugs, too. Mostly weed, but sometimes harder stuff. She had a tough life, barely making ends meet, and I didn't make it easy on her. Always hungry, too much energy. She'd managed to hold onto this one job for a while, mostly because she was sleeping with her boss. Kane was his name. Just that—I don't think I ever learned his full name. He'd come over and well, he didn't like me. Didn't like how I looked or maybe how I looked at him. A couple of times he cracked a palm across my face and I kept it to myself. Because I wanted to stay in the same apartment for once and keeping the peace seemed the easiest way to do that. I kept my mouth shut.

"But one day he cuffed my ear so hard I howled, and Ruby heard and she went nuts on him. She was already halfway to hammered, screaming and pushing, and he hit her. That's when she grabbed a knife and stabbed him in the arm."

She covered her mouth, the twist to the tale unexpected even when he'd told her it wouldn't be good.

He faced her, his eyes blazing like midnight-blue coals.

"He backhanded her again and then I was—shit." He swiped at his eyes. Ashley made a move toward him and he held up a hand.

"I got involved, in between them, and he hit me, and then she did it again. Stabbed his shoulder."

Her heart broke for him. What a terrible situation to be in. "She was defending you."

Fury came over him. "She was a drug addict and an alcoholic who attracted the worst people. She brought it all down on herself, and yeah, she was defending me. But it wouldn't have happened if she hadn't been such a screw-up."

Like me. The unspoken part was louder than a bomb. *He thinks he's like her.*

"The police were called and there were drugs on the kitchen table and before I knew it, I was in care and Ruby was doing a thirteen-year stretch for assault and possession.

She'd already been in trouble for drug stuff and it was her third strike so they threw the book at her."

He met her gaze, his own still on fire.

"You want someone like that in your life? In your daughter's life? Because that's what's happening when you play do-gooder, Ashley. When you try to make everything better."

In his words she heard his guilt.

I didn't make it easy on her.

Too much energy.

She was defending me.

He blamed his mother, but he also blamed himself.

"I'm sorry, I didn't know."

"Well, now you do. And we both know that having someone like that in Willa's life is a terrible idea. Shit, I'm not much better."

And there it is. "You're putting yourself in the same category as your mom?"

He snorted. "Are you kidding? Did you not see what I did to Kyle Hughes's face? I'm a menace, Ashley. I might be good with puppies, but I'm not good with people. With real life."

She approached him, not tentatively, not gently, but in the knowledge that he needed the woman who loved him unconditionally. That was her truth, blazing in her chest.

On tiptoes, she reached up and cupped his face.

"You *are* a good person, Dex. Something awful happened to you as a child. None of it was your fault. Your mom made some decisions that had a lasting effect on you but look at your life now."

He shook his head, determined to resist any justification. Any recognition of the good-hearted, kind man he'd become.

"Yes, look at it," she urged. "It's a good life, an amazing

life, especially considering how far you've come. You're responsible for that. You built it. Sure you've screwed up because that's what people do sometimes. But you're trying to change. To be a better man."

Placing his hands over hers he dragged them away from his face. His eyes burned with pain.

"I'm bad news." He squeezed her hands and held them against his chest. "Always have been."

"No, you're not. I couldn't fall in love with someone who was bad news."

It just came out, and she didn't regret a word. At least, not until she saw his expression.

It might have been disbelief, or disgust, or more likely embarrassment that he'd let it get this far.

His body language changed. Shuttered completely. "You hardly know me."

"I know enough." Desperately, she plowed on in the knowledge that she might get just one shot to make her case. She had to scoot through before he closed the door on this chance for them. "You're such a great guy, Dex. A kind, generous, decent human being. You think your past makes you unworthy of great love. People have left you, shunted you around, made you think that your only value is this talent you have on the ice. It's more than that. You're more than that."

He wanted to believe. She could see the hope simmering in his eyes. All he had to do was let her in, let that hope take root.

"I'm not, Ash." He sounded so melancholy, like she'd given him the worst possible news. "You shouldn't have talked to her. Now it's all messed up."

It? Did he mean them? It didn't have to be. But she heard

the whine in that voice in her head. It was a little too familiar, a reminder of those final months with Greg.

We can make this work. Do what's best for Willa.

Only she hadn't been thinking of Willa, not entirely. Ashley had held onto her marriage long past its expiration date because the thought of being alone scared her. Since then, she'd figured out that riding solo was better than letting her happiness be dependent on a man. And no matter how kind that man treated her daughter, she wouldn't compromise like she had before.

Putting this lovely thing out there, her love for this man, should have filled her with joy, so why did she feel like the bottom of her world had fallen out?

Because she'd misjudged. Reached too far. Singed her butterfly wings.

She wouldn't beg. If he couldn't respond positively to her profession of love—which seemed like hours ago—then she had to recognize defeat.

She withdrew her hands from his and took a step back.

"You're not ready. Maybe you'll never be." About his mom, about them.

His eyes turned to hard, flat discs. "You don't approve of my stance here."

"This is your choice. Your decision on how to handle it. But problems don't just go away because you ignore them."

He shook his head. "You should have left it alone."

Perhaps, but she hadn't come this far without facing her own problems head-on. She'd already spent a decade of her life with a man-child, who left her to do all the hard things. The feedings, the school pick-ups, any difficult conversation with their daughter. She needed a man to ride shotgun with her, not one who was afraid to step up and do what was difficult.

Or recoiled at the mention of the L-word.

She was a problem-solver, always had been, so she assumed Dex's relationship with his mom could be tackled the same way.

That telling him she loved him would make him feel safe.

But apparently not.

Watching him leave, she realized that some people preferred the safety of the status quo—and that, in the coming days, she might wish she'd chosen that path for herself.

37

Belated congratulations to Georgia Goodwin, who was recently revealed to have married in a Las Vegas wedding ceremony in January. Ms. Goodwin is the daughter of Penny and Marcus Goodwin, owners of the AmeriTrust Corporation and noted Chicago area philanthropists. Ms. Goodwin's new husband, Dylan Bankowski, plays hockey.
— Chicago Tattler

FOREMAN THREW his stick to the floor of the locker room where it promptly cracked.

"What the fuck was that, guys?"

Dex looked down at his skates, wishing he could shrink inside them. They'd probably smell funky but at least they'd be dark and dingy, the perfect spot for him to hide out.

"So we had a bad game." Grey blushed, unused to speaking up first and drawing attention to himself. "It happens."

"Sure. It happens." Foreman pointed at Kershaw. "Zip it."

"Didn't say a word."

"But you were going to. Some inane Kershaw Super-glutes bullshit that's supposed to make us all laugh and forget we just played like slugs."

"Slugs." Kershaw grinned, then turned to Dex. "But I think we all know why that game was a disasterpiece. *O'Malley.*"

He jerked his head up to find the entire locker room laser-focused on him. Sure, he'd not been as in the zone as he'd have liked. A couple of missed passes on his dance card, but he wasn't the only one who sucked eggs during the game.

Kershaw was shaking his head. "You broke up with Ashley, didn't you?"

"We were never together."

Kaz threw up his hands. "That's it! O'Malley's been playing like a demon and now he screws it up because of his love life. Perfect!"

"She was supposed to be your good luck charm." Fore-man's tone was threaded with disgust. "Did I not say what would happen if you mess with that shit? Break up in the off-season."

"We're not a couple. We weren't." So he'd played like a donkey rather than a slug, and his argument with Ashley was definitely foremost on his mind, but he wasn't the only player out there.

"Maybe it's Banks's fault," Jorgenson said as he pulled off his pads. "He didn't invite anyone to his wedding. That has to be unlucky."

All eyes turned to Banks, who was busy taping his stick *after* the game, for some fucked up reason.

"Those All-Star games are always trouble," Reid said, referring to the magical weekend when Banks tied the knot.

Everyone was salivating for the details, which the man refused to share.

The recent groom raised his gaze to Dex and tried to fry his brain with an X-ray stare. Dex had already explained that he wasn't the one who'd spilled the beans. Not Grey either. Someone else had overheard them in the Empty Net and tipped off the press.

"Let us know when you set up the registry," Kershaw said. "Make sure you put 'sense of humor' on it along with a tuxedo for all those fancy galas you have to attend with your socialite wife."

Banks looked like he was considering which of Kershaw's orifices would be most receptive to the stick in his hand when Coach came in and began a post-game blast of each of them for their ice-crimes. As Coach was going in alphabetical order, Dex got his about halfway through the litany.

"O'Malley, when I put you in, I expect you to move into position ASAP, not dawdle about posing for photos."

"Coach, I didn't—"

But Coach had already moved on, for which Dex was supremely grateful. Could have been much worse.

"Petrov, you keep threatening to retire and maybe one of these days you'll do us a favor and pull the trigger. Your modeling career will thank you. Hell, the entire coaching staff will thank you."

"Yes, Coach," Petrov said with a crooked turn to his mouth that said he'd heard every insult there was and nothing could bother him at this stage.

An hour later, they were in the Empty Net, stashed away in a private room that the owner, Tina, sometimes set aside for them, especially on nights when they couldn't bear to talk to the fans. Dex would have thought no one would want to hang, but this team preferred to hash out their problems as a unit. Knowing there were a group of brothers who had a similar mindset was comforting, especially when you felt like your world had ended.

Kershaw and Bond came through with drinks on a couple of trays and set them down. "First round's on Foreman," Kershaw said.

"How do you work that out?"

"You were mean to me earlier, so now you're on the hook for my drink, and the rest. Calling us slugs. Blaming Oh-Em-Gee because he has woman troubles."

The man from Boston shook his head. "*You* brought O'Malley up! Sure, we're all to blame, we win as a team, we lose as a team. But we also know that you don't make big relationship changes right before the playoffs. It's bad enough we might lose O'Malley to prison—"

"Not going to prison."

Foreman shot him a glare, unappreciative of the interruption or facts.

"But he has to compound it by dumping his girl."

Kershaw nodded sagely. "Nah, she dumped him."

Dex exploded. "No one dumped anyone! We weren't dating."

Kershaw was on a roll. "He came out of her office at the shelter looking like Banks had taken all his cash at the poker game. She definitely gave him the heave-ho."

Kaz sniffed. "Probably figured out he'll be in the Big House by the playoffs."

"I'm not—"

"More likely she realized he's not the settling down type." Burnett raised a glass. "Here's to O'Malley and his return to the clubs. The VIP lounges have missed you."

"If you must know, I ended it, because she and her kid deserve better. Okay?"

She had said she'd fallen in love with him. Or rather that she wouldn't fall in love with someone who was bad news.

Those glorious words had exited her gorgeous mouth, and what did Dex do? Told her she had it wrong. Invalidated those feelings.

He'd gone into that office, intending to tell her how *he* felt, but then she dropped the Ruby bombshell and all he could feel was shame. He wished she'd never talked to his mother because then he wouldn't have had to explain how toxic she was, and how, underneath it all, Dex wasn't much different.

The crew stared at him.

"Seriously?" Foreman asked. "That was your reason?"

"It's as good a reason as any. She's perfect and fucking hell, I am not."

Petrov eyed him. "No man is good enough for his woman. Or, for some of us, his man."

The entire room groaned.

"Not this shit," Reid muttered.

Dex arced a gaze over the group. "What now?"

"You've opened up a can of Petrov-scented turds of wisdom," Foreman said with a sigh. "My Russian bestie has opinions. Strong opinions."

"Young Dexter, listen and listen well," Petrov said after a withering look at Foreman and the rest of the crew. "Women are not meant to be our equals. They sit above us in clouds of spun gold, occasionally showering us with rays of sun. If we catch a sliver of their attention, we are blessed. This woman, for some strange reason beyond your comprehension and most certainly ours, has smiled at you—I have seen it. She gazes at you with more affection than she does the puppies and kittens in her care."

Kershaw chuckled. "Yep, O'Malley, you're just above the dogs in her estimation."

Vadim waved a hand. "I know what I have seen. You make her happy. Will you ever be good enough for her?" He looked around the table, where everyone agreed with nods, grunts, and clear-cut body language that no, Dex would never achieve this exalted status. "Then you have to accept that unless she has told you to fuck yourself, then she thinks you are worthy of her attention."

"She did say I needed to meet my problems head-on."

Foreman squinted. "And she said this because?"

Because like a dog, he had buried his bone in the yard and was happy to leave it there where it couldn't bother him.

Couldn't she see the favor he was doing her? It was better to get out before any more shit hit the fan. His mother. The court case. Whatever disaster was lined up on the center line waiting for a stick to strike it.

"Because I don't want to deal with my shit."

The big Russian stared at him without blinking. "Then that is your problem, not hers."

AN HOUR LATER, he visited the men's room where he ran into Petrov again.

"Listen, thanks for the pep talk earlier."

"You don't believe what I say, though, do you?"

"I believe you think that's the way the world works. The way relationships work."

Petrov nodded. "Is this about your mother?"

Dex's heart thudded to the dirty tile. "My mother?"

The captain leaned against the restroom door and threaded his tattooed arms over his chest. "You know we have an intelligence-gathering apparatus for the team. Background checks, that kind of thing."

Sounded very Cold War era. All Dex could do was nod.

"Your mother got out of prison and now works at the Sunny Side Up Diner. I saw you talking to her a couple of weeks ago. Neither of you looked happy."

Shit. "Does anyone else know?"

"Harper, Isobel, and Fitz. We like to keep a finger on the pulse, in case it affects the players' psychology. Is this where you get your inferiority complex?"

Petrov was weirdly direct, and Dex appreciated it.

"When she went to prison, my life upended. I grew up in foster care. It wasn't the best, but it is what it is."

He held his breath, waiting for a sharp comment.

Petrov responded with, "Mothers are difficult, especially when they are not wanted. I too have a mother who insisted on turning up when I had decided I was better off without her."

That sounded familiar, something about his mother leaving him in Russia and raising his sister, Mia, in the States. They'd been estranged for years.

"You and your mom are good now?"

"Yes, but it took time. My Bella helped me realize that I was letting it reframe my thinking in a negative way. I could not embrace a good life with my woman, with my sister, even with my game, until I fixed the situation with the woman who gave birth to me."

The guys were right. Petrov was a total drama queen, but there was sense embedded in the scenery-chewing.

"Well, there's nothing wrong with my game. Fixing

things with my mom isn't going to suddenly make me a better player. I'm already a great player."

"Yes, you are. But you are inconsistent. Sometimes your head is elsewhere, such as tonight, yes?"

His head had been with Ashley, thinking about how he'd thrown away this amazing thing because he couldn't trust it to stay good. Assumed he would mess it up like he messed up everything.

"I wasn't so focused," he admitted.

Petrov nodded. "You are not the reason we lost tonight, but you are an important cog in this machine. We need you well-oiled, working perfectly, and when you are distracted or sad or depressed, the machine suffers. We can get to the playoffs without you. Probably. But our chances of going further improve if you're with us and on an even keel. Some players feed off the drama in their lives, but you were not a better player when you were getting into trouble. Nightclub blow jobs, drag-racing, fighting—all of these things made you a second- or third-line player. This last month?" He shrugged. "You have become a first-line guy. Because you are happy."

He *was* happy. Even with his mother's return to his life weighing on him, he found solace in his time with Ashley, in the curves of her body and the peace of her mind. Their moments together had kept him sane and given him hope that maybe he wasn't the fuck-up everyone thought he was. This amazing woman had seen something in him, something worthwhile. He missed her and Willa, and it had only been two days!

He covered his face with his hands. "I screwed up."

"You are young." Petrov gripped his shoulder. "You will screw up again. But it is important that you do not screw up in the same way. You must learn from each mistake. Now what do you want?"

He moved his hands away. "Want?"

"If you could have anything, what would it be?"

Hearing the question phrased in such simple terms made it easy to focus, distill his muddled thoughts to the essence of needs.

"Ashley. A multi-year contract with this team." He swallowed. "A family."

Petrov paused for an extra-charged beat. "Not the Cup?"

"Don't want to be greedy."

That yielded a smile. "Putting these things out into the universe is the way to make them happen. Keeping them inside, buried deep, does not give your hopes the air they need to breathe."

Not sure he bought that, but he did feel oddly lighter, not unlike after he'd discussed his career goals with Anton when they met up in New York. Talking about shit felt good. Who knew?

Dex hauled in a breath. "Could I ask a favor?"

"All this wisdom I give for free is not enough?"

"It's a big one."

He gestured for Dex to go on.

"I have my court case in a week and my lawyer thinks my good deeds are going to go in my favor but ..."

"But what?"

"Ashley was going to say something nice about me, and I've messed that up."

"You would like me to tell the judge what a harmless young idiot you are?"

"Something like that."

Curt nod. "You can count on me."

38

ANOTHER WEEK, another book club.

Ashley had actually read the book this time, a World War II epic with a nice romance subplot, not that it made a difference. All anyone wanted to talk about was Dex.

Since his volunteer gig at the shelter was made public, she'd received plenty of texts from people she knew, most of them asking if he was as charming in real life as he seemed on camera.

More. So much more.

Now the Book Club Divorcees wanted details.

"Is he the worst flirt?" Eva asked. "I bet he is."

"I bet he hit on every volunteer there," Mallory said. "Extra with Ashley."

Vera bristled. "Why'd you say that?"

Mallory smiled. "Because he needs her to say nice things about him."

Eva leaned in. "C'mon, Ashley, spill the tea."

She smiled wanly. "There's nothing to spill. He put in a few shifts at the shelter, we did some promo that benefited us both, and now he's on his way."

She'd written the letter he needed and sent it to Sophie in Rebels PR. There was no reason to hope Dex would come by and ask for it himself. That was why he had people.

And she was just one of those people. Someone he met along the way, a fleeting presence in his drama-soaked life. Except she knew he was hurting, and she suspected he hurt less when he held her in his arms.

Had she done the right thing, telling him to fix things with his mother, with himself? Who was she to have such high expectations?

Mallory giggled. "Well, he definitely did a good job sucking up to Ashley. I saw he posted that picture with Willa at the butterfly garden."

"A bunch of the players were there." Eva tilted her head at Ashley. "Hanging with hockey royalty for a while. Must be nice."

"It was," Ashley said. "And he wasn't sucking up to me. He's just a considerate guy."

"When he wants something." Lainey scrolled on her phone. "I bet he's a total tease. He's probably praying for a lady judge so he can work his magic for his court case."

Ashley opened her mouth, but Vera got there first. "He gets an unfairly bad rap. When we had him over for dinner, he was the nicest guy. Really humble."

"*Dinner?*"

"*He was here?*"

Vera shared a smug look with Ashley. "Yeah, if you must know—"

"Vera," Ashley warned.

"What? So you guys didn't work out but hell, if you're giving him the time of day, Ash, then he's got to be worth the effort."

Maeve pointed at Vera. "Stop gossiping."

Eva's mouth gaped. "You and Dex O'Malley ... had a thing?"

"No. As I said before, we were just friends. Are."

Mallory nodded in sympathy with a look that said: *got what he wanted, did he?*

Ashley's cheeks flushed hot. "Could we talk about something else? What did we think of the mime character in the book?"

Vera wasn't finished. "You think my sister can't attract a guy that gorgeous?"

Lainey weighed in. "Of course she can. That's not what we meant." She continued, "But he's not here now and there's a reason for that. It's not real life, is it? It's not being there when you need him or picking up the kids from school or doing laundry. Guys like that are a nice distraction, but they're not for keeps."

"What guys are?" Ashley had finally found her voice.

"Excuse me?" Mallory asked.

"What guys are for keeps? Because listening to everyone here, none of them are. Not a single one can be trusted. Everyone cheats and lies and runs off with the nanny or the personal assistant or the babysitter. I don't want to spend my life expecting to be hurt and I don't want to raise my daughter with those levels of distrust. So Dex O'Malley might not be right for me but he was sweet and kind, generous and passionate. One day, he'll make someone very happy."

Just not her.

She stood and grabbed her half-full glass of wine. "Even in the midst of war, people found a way to love each other. I don't know why you guys bother with these books when you've already given up on everything."

Leaving them with mouths agape, she headed into the kitchen.

A few seconds later, Maeve appeared behind her. "You okay?"

"Fine! Absolutely perfect."

"You haven't said what happened. With Dex."

She turned to her sister. "What you said would happen. What *they* said would happen." She gestured at the living room. "He's not ready for something real. He's not ready to trust anyone with his heart and I've realized that I'm not there, either."

This was more than his situation with his mother. Dex had gone much of his life thinking he wasn't worthy of love, that his value was tied up in being a hockey player. She had tried to imbue in him a sense of self-love and the recognition that he had so much more to give, the values she believed in and taught to her daughter.

When he told her she'd messed up in talking to his mom, she knew it was his hurt heart talking. But she also saw him reaching for the easy out, a way to exit this fling because he wasn't ready for the commitment she needed.

And she'd offered it to him, hadn't she? She told him she loved him, that he needed to face his fears. Implied that only when he stepped up, would he become worthy of her. She didn't truly believe he'd stick around, and when pushed out the door, he'd taken the chance to leave and proven her right.

Her sister looked concerned, to which Ashley scoffed. "I'm taking a leaf out of your book."

Vera came into the kitchen. "Cat amongst the pigeons, Ash. Now they're talking about the good things their exes do. It's a short conversation." She frowned. "What's wrong? Other than the obvious?"

KATE MEADER

Maeve pointed at Ashley. "It's finally happened. We broke her."

Vera cocked her head. "That's probably what needed to happen. Rock bottom."

"I've already been there when Greg left."

Vera laughed. "Oh no. As humiliating as it was to be dumped in favor of the babysitter, you have to admit to a certain relief that it happened. It should have happened years ago. You didn't love Greg."

Ashley couldn't disagree with that. She'd been wasting her life on a man she'd never loved, out of a sense of duty as a mother and fear of being alone.

"But when he left, it really hurt."

"Of course it did," Vera said. "But how are you feeling now?"

She leaned on the counter, for the first time acknowledging the pain that practically had her doubled over. "Crushed. I-I don't know why I feel like this."

Vera shared a glance with Maeve. "Because you guys really connected. I saw it that first night."

"I told him I loved him," she whispered as if a lower volume could disguise the horror.

"Oh, Ash." Maeve covered her mouth.

Vera looked concerned. "And what did he say?"

"That he wasn't good enough for me. We had a fight about something else and—it doesn't matter. I shouldn't have let my heart get involved. You were right about that." She addressed that last statement to Maeve.

"Maybe it's for the—"

"Best?" Vera snapped. "Is that what you're going to say? Because what I see is you so down on men that she's never going to trust again."

"And you," Maeve said, pointing at Vera, "just see men as

vessels to be used. Sex machines with nothing else to recommend them."

"That wasn't the case here, was it? Maybe at first, but Dex was the perfect boost to her self-esteem. Until he wasn't." Vera put an arm around Ashley's shoulders. "I'm sorry, Ash. I shouldn't have invited him over to dinner."

"You meant well, Ms. Meddler. You wanted me to get back out there. Now, I can move on, get back on the apps."

No more lookers, though. No more ocean-blue eyes and wavy hair and strong arms that felt perfect around her body. No more giggling in sleeping bags or wistful sighs at the sight of a man showing kindness to her daughter.

Vera looked stricken, and Maeve, who would usually have an opinion, wasn't much better.

"You guys should get back to the club. Make sure no one is drunk dialing their ex or planning a murder."

While Ashley would get back to her boring black-and-white life before it received a Technicolor boost from one Dex O'Malley.

A SUN-KISSED CORA looked up from the pile of paperwork on her desk and grinned at Ashley.

"These numbers are amazing! Almost three-quarters of the cats adopted or fostered, and half the dogs. And I've heard from the Rebels people—cha-ching! The donation is in. It should keep us going for another year." She sat back in her chair. "And all you had to do was put up with an oversexed, immature hockey player. I hope it wasn't too awful."

Ashley screwed her smile on tight. "A rocky start, but we made it in the end. Everyone's a winner."

Cora glanced at the numbers again. "Don't know what I'd do without you. Didn't your shift end ten minutes ago?"

"Yep, just waiting for Greg to drop off Willa."

A couple of minutes later, she headed into the kennels and found her daughter, sitting in front of Bandit's cage.

"Hey, Mom!"

"Hey, honey, I didn't know you were here. How were things with your dad?"

Willa smiled. "Emily spat up all over him and he freaked out. It was kind of funny."

"I bet. You ready to go? We could hit DQ on the way home."

"Could we walk Bandit first?"

"Toby already took him out earlier." Tomorrow she would sort through the multiple applications to adopt him. She'd held back on placing him, hoping that Dex might come up with a solution. But it wasn't fair on Bandit. He needed a happy home.

Willa pointed above his cage. "But his sign says he likes walks. Plural."

His sign? Ashley peered at the label, which was different than the one she'd placed a few weeks ago.

Bandit
Likes: Walks
Dislikes: How his heart hurts like a mother

"Did you make that?"

Willa gave her a look. "Mom, I don't have time to make signs. I'm very busy."

"Yeah, I suppose you are. Grab a leash from the hook. Let's take this little guy for a spin."

After hooking Bandit up, they headed toward the play

area but on the way, Ashley was distracted by the signs she had definitely not made above some of the cages.

Peanut

Likes: Belly rubs

Dislikes: That feeling you get when you know you've been a jerk but you're not sure how to fix it.

Ashley's pulse went *tat-a-tat-tat*.

Over Jenny the bulldog's cage was another new one.

Likes: Dog biscuits shaped like bones.

Dislikes: The fact time travel has yet to be invented because it would sure come in handy right about now.

Bandit pulled on his leash. "Okay, okay, I'm coming."

Out in the play area, Ashley released the dog and watched as he scooted off toward a bush to investigate.

Willa adjusted her glasses. "Do you think we're going to see Dex again?"

Blinking back the emotion that question raised, Ashley faced her daughter. "Probably not. He was just hanging out for a short stint as a volunteer. Sometimes people pass through our lives and don't become permanent fixtures."

Willa considered that for a second, then touched the butterfly hair clip Dex had given her. "But he loved you, Mom."

She laughed, though it emerged as more of a bark and made Bandit lift his head. "Where did you get that idea?"

"The way he looked at you. We were supposed to be spotting butterflies, but he was spotting *you*. Because you're prettier than any butterfly."

"That's sweet of you to say. You're such a lovely, kind

person." She put her arm around Willa's shoulders. It was the best way to stop from trembling. "I hope we see him again, but we can always watch his games."

"Is it okay if I text him?"

She couldn't bear it if her daughter's messages went into the ether, only to be ignored.

"He's probably very busy."

Willa rolled in her lips. "I already told him about my art project, how I wanted to do dragon fairies. He thinks it's one of my best ideas." She pulled her iPad from her Dragon Ball Z backpack, and sure enough there was a text thread with Dex, the most recent message dated this morning. "I didn't want to hide it from you."

He was still here, giving her daughter comfort. Despite the pain he was in, he had time for her little girl.

Had she expected too much from him, too soon? Throwing that mom-bomb into the mix, exploding things between them, probably looked like a test. One she had set for him to see if he would respond maturely. Or at the very least, the way Ashley felt he should.

That wasn't fair on him. And now she longed for a do-over.

A few minutes later, Bandit was back in his cage and Ashley went to find Willa in the cattery. She was helping Perry with the food bowls, placing them carefully in the cardboard boxes. Most of the cats had left them during the Empty the Shelters event, but the boxes were already filling up with new arrivals.

Mittens was still with them, and above his box was a new sign:

Likes: Lying in the sun
Dislikes: Idiot hockey players

"Where did that come from?" she asked Perry.

"Dex stopped by yesterday to see Bandit and Mittens. He took a few minutes to do some updates."

He'd chosen a time he knew she wasn't here. Sparing her the pain, she supposed.

Yet these signs seemed ... hopeful. She loved that he was communicating through the animals they both loved, though she'd prefer he spoke to her directly.

Idiot hockey players?

Idiot shelter managers, too.

39

HE HAD to be sure none of the guys would be on site because the last thing he needed was an audience. Kershaw, Foreman, and Grey left first, and then he waited another ten minutes in case one of the guys was still in there stinking up the can. Satisfied there would be no Rebels on hand to witness what came next, he headed across the street just as Ruby came out. She wore a jacket over her uniform and carried a big purse over her shoulder.

Her eyes, the same deep blue as his, went round on seeing him.

"I'm just leaving," she said quickly.

"Right."

"So, you can go in there and not worry about me souring the whipped cream on your waffles."

"I'm here to talk."

Her eyebrows rose and she took what looked like a juddering breath. For a moment, he expected her to argue, but then he realized she wouldn't dare. After all, he had all the power, didn't he? She wanted access and he controlled the gateway to the thing she craved.

A way back to her son.

Ashley and her old lady wisdom. He almost laughed.

"There's a coffee shop over there." He thumbed behind him.

"My co-workers might see. I know another place."

She was worried people would see them together? That was supposed to be his concern.

She took off, her stride quick. "Tough game last night. You okay?"

"I'm fine. Why wouldn't I be?"

"You used to get so disappointed when you lost at anything."

That was another lifetime. He'd like to think he'd matured somewhat and could take the lows in his stride but given how he was dealing with this Ashley business, achievement definitively not unlocked.

He didn't respond to her observation. She didn't have a right to make it, to call up something from the past, like she knew him better than anyone else.

Until Ashley. That woman knew him, the guy inside struggling to get out. She saw a different version of Dex, one who didn't need clubs or women or fans to tell him he was good enough. He just needed to graduate from this course in manning the fuck up.

A couple of minutes later they arrived at their destination. "A cat café?"

"You don't like cats?"

"I love cats. And they love me. You should see them go nuts for me at the shelter."

Except she couldn't because he'd thrown a fit when he saw her with Cleo.

"They're great for de-stressing," she said, as if this was

new information to him. He volunteered at the local animal shelter!

She headed inside and he followed, taking in the surroundings. The cats seemed to have free rein here, much different than his usual gig.

"What would you like?" he asked her.

"English breakfast tea, please," she said to the girl behind the counter.

Like Ashley. Freaking universe doing its freaking thing.

When he asked for a coffee and tried to pay for the entire order, Ruby shook her head. "I'll pay for my own."

"Okay."

Petrov's advice had resonated, meshing perfectly with Ashley's words about facing his problems: he needed to get back on an even keel, not let his emotions rule on the ice, which meant fixing things off the ice. But he had no clue how to do this without getting all emo about it. The ground underfoot was shaky and unsure.

Ruby took her cup of tea and headed to a table in the corner. A cat was sitting on the other seat and she picked him up, a cute tabby, and placed it in her lap. Dex was allowed to sit, apparently.

He aimed for a neutral icebreaker. "How was work?"

"Fine. It keeps me busy."

He nodded, wishing he could fast forward to a finished conversation and a clue what came next.

"Dex, what did you want to talk about?"

"Nothing. Everything. I don't know how to begin." He took a sip of his coffee, which was still too hot, not unlike this explosive-loaded conversation.

"Tell me how you've been."

"How I've been? Fantastic. I got into trouble and there's a court case. And there was a whole lot of stuff last year. You probably saw." Shame stole over him at the idea his mother had read about his exploits. Or worse, witnessed them on YouTube.

"I did."

"But then I met someone."

"Ashley."

Just hearing her name was a comfort. "Yeah. She doesn't take my shit and I guess I'm not used to that. I've relied on hockey for so long to carve me an out. People gave me a pass, excused my shenanigans, but she didn't. She challenged me to be better, to grow up."

She petted the cat, who purred under her touch. "Challenged? Not anymore?"

"We're no longer ... friends. Well, we might be friends but nothing else. I bring a lot of drama and I don't want to inflict that on her."

She frowned. "Am I the reason you're not with her anymore?"

No, I am. "She didn't know the details about you, the whole story. I didn't tell her until recently and it's not fair to expect her to deal with that on top of everything else. She has a kid, a great kid, and I need to keep her safe." He shook his head. "We didn't break up because we weren't officially together."

Liar, liar, dumpster fire.

"I'm sorry that I'm still affecting your relationships, even now."

He shot her a sharp look. "What did you expect would happen when you came back into my life? That we just become friends and it doesn't have any impact on me and the people I care about? That I was going to be all calm and reasonable about it?"

Color flagged her cheeks. "I didn't know what else to do. I

waited until I was sober for a year. I wanted you to see that I'd changed, but maybe you won't ever be able to understand that."

He was here, wasn't he? He was trying to initiate the first tentative steps in a truce, but it was so freakin' hard.

"I can't just wipe the slate clean and pretend nothing happened. You weren't around. I fucked up and you left and—"

She put her hand out over his. The touch, so unexpected and soft, electrified him.

"What do you mean you fucked up?"

He'd meant to say she did, but it came out wrong. The Freudian whatsit.

"I talked back to him. I started it. Made trouble and … that's why we're here."

"Oh, Dex, that's not why it happened. I was not in a good place. Self-medicating, accepting crap because it was easier than trying."

He snorted. "Know what that's like."

"Well, maybe we're not so different. But where we are miles apart is on the subject of culpability."

"That's a Willa word." At her querying expression, he explained. "Ashley's daughter. She learns a new word every day. I think she'd like that one."

But he didn't. Despite being a total dumbass, he understood perfectly its meaning.

"You're not to blame for what happened to Kane. I did that. I hurt him."

"Defending me."

She shook her head. "Yes, but he started that fight. My reaction was all on me. I didn't have to spend my life high as a kite, neglecting you, moving us from place to place because I couldn't keep things steady. That was no way to live and no way to raise a child. What happened with Kane was my fault, but it was better that you were taken away from me. I wasn't fit to be your mom."

He shook his head. For so long, he'd carried this weight. He'd started it, the first of many acts of self-sabotage. Dex the troublemaker, Dex the fuckboy, Dex the sad little orphan.

"You think foster care was better?"

"You survived, didn't you? You found hockey." She squeezed his hand, and he found himself squeezing back. "Did you think that would have happened if I was around? Sports cost money and I would have rather spent it on drink and weed than my own boy. That's a fact."

Probably. But no one should have to grow up without his mom.

"I know it was a shitty situation, Dex. No matter which way you looked at it. Damned if you do, damned if you don't. But something had to change. I needed a wake-up call and prison was it for me. I'd be dead now if it hadn't happened. Instead of thinking that you started this sequence of events, think that maybe you saved my life. Me jumping in to defend you from him brought us here. One of us trying to get back on track, the other sitting on top of the world because he's so beautiful and talented and amazing." She brushed away a tear from her cheek. "I'm so proud of you and everything you've done. So proud of the man you've become. My wonderful son."

He didn't deserve her pride, not when he felt so unworthy.

"It would have been better if you were there." His actions put his mom in prison and a ten-year-old boy in care, and he needed to deal with that.

She sighed, but it was a patient one, the kind a mother doled out to a son.

"Maybe. But that's not what happened. I know it's mixed up. You're taking this on, while also laying the past at my door. We can play the blame game until the cows come home, but it won't give either of us any peace. My actions still hurt you, made you think you weren't worthy of a home, of a family, of good things, and for that I'm so sorry."

She was right, of course. Holding onto this jagged-edged weapon of self-destruction and blame would only keep him in the dark. He wanted a path to the light, a way back to Ashley. He wanted to be free of it.

"I don't know where to go from here," he said.

"A cup of tea, a mug of coffee, and a kitten." She smiled as she petted the tabby. "That's where."

40

FOR THE FIFTH time in as many minutes, Dex looked over his shoulder at the entrance to the courtroom.

"You know we don't need her," Mr. Grady, the lawyer, said. "The statement she sent will suffice."

He'd already cut a deal with the prosecutor. Apologize to Hughes, make a donation to the asshole's favorite charity, and express adequate contrition. Then Dex O'Malley would ride again.

It was up to the judge to sign off on the deal. His lawyer had said that some judges liked to flex their independent thought muscles and ask a lot of questions, looking for evidence that the defendant was truly sorry for his actions.

Like this one.

"Well, Mr. O'Malley, you seem to have done the minimum necessary to satisfy the requirements of the prosecutor. This letter detailing your volunteer work is to the point without being overly effusive as are the character references from your team captain, Mr. Petrov, and former coach, Mr. Ballard."

Dex slid a quick look at Anton who had made a surprise

appearance in court today. He'd asked him for a reference but hadn't expected the man would come in person, and just knowing he was prepared to speak on his behalf sutured some of the wounds. Anton nodded and waved for him to pay attention to the judge.

"I hear you've apologized to Mr. Hughes, yet I have to wonder at your sincerity. If maybe you're checking the boxes to get you out of trouble. Would you like to tell us more about your path to the courtroom today?"

His lawyer touched his elbow, encouraging him to stand.

Dex pulled himself upright. "Your honor, I've made a mess of things. I get that."

There was a commotion behind him. The judge frowned again and held up a hand for Dex to halt speaking.

He turned and spotted Tara, who gave him a wave. None of the guys could show to give their support in person because the team had already left this morning for the away game in Dallas, but seeing Tara was nice.

Ah, not just Tara.

Behind her was Fitz. Kind of strange, but Tara had her husband wrapped around her little finger. Still, the boss was not going to like having to delay his travel.

Only it didn't stop at Fitz. Next came Kershaw in his game day suit and his hand raised in a cheery salute. On his heels was the clown car of hockey franchises as what looked like every one of his teammates shuffled in and took seats in the back of the room. When those seats were filled, the remaining players stood at the back, leaning against the wall and eyeing the surroundings suspiciously.

Foreman caught his eye and nodded. Petrov lifted an aristocratic eyebrow. Gunnar Bond gave a chin jerk while Reid Durand looked like he was hating every minute along with everyone around him. Seeing everyone here ... Dex would not have expected that at all.

The arrival of the Chicago Rebels roster had a predictable effect. The murmurs were increasing in volume when the judge held up his hand again.

"This courtroom will not tolerate any interruptions. Mr. O'Malley, you were speaking."

"Yes, your honor. I was talking about how I've made a mess of things. I should have acted more maturely and for that, I apologize. To the court, Mr. Hughes, the team, and the fans."

"Go, O'Malley!" That sounded like Kazminski.

The judge cleared his throat and glared over Dex's shoulder. "Am I right in assuming these new arrivals in my courtroom are your teammates?"

"Yes, sir. I mean, your honor. They should be on a plane right now, so I'm surprised to see them."

"Can we say a few words in O'Malley's defense, your holiness?" Kershaw piped up.

The judge pursed his lips. "No, you cannot. Mr. O'Malley has all the legal assistance he requires."

Dex hid his smile. He took another quick look and got a thumbs up from Hudson Grey and a big grin from Tara. This had to be her doing.

But, as heartwarming as it was to see them, he'd have traded every single one of them for a glimpse of Ashley.

"Well, Mr. O'Malley," the judge said. "Continue."

"Over the last two months I've learned a lot about myself. I'm in a position of great privilege. I have an amazing team of people in my corner. I like cats and dogs equally."

"Not possible," someone muttered, only to be shushed by the team.

"Mostly, I've learned that I need to face up to my prob-

...

lems like an adult. My response to Mr. Hughes was disproportionate and I hope we can put this incident behind us."

The judge held them all in suspense for a good five seconds longer than was truly necessary.

"Mr. O'Malley, it looks like you've met the requirements of the prosecutor's office. The plea deal you've worked out shall remain in place, but please be aware that not everyone gets as many chances as you do. You have health, wealth, talent, and good fortune. I hope you'll remember that the next time you're tempted to let your temper override your common sense."

Outside the courtroom, he was mobbed by the team.

"I can't believe the judge didn't let me speak!" Kershaw was outraged at the slight. "But luckily you didn't need it."

"I think he saw you all there and was worried there'd be a riot if he didn't sign off on the deal. Shouldn't you guys be on a plane?"

"Like we could leave you alone at your time of need." Foreman winked. "Petrov told Fitz no one was flying until we'd put in an appearance. There was talk of slipping you a file and breaking you out, if it came to that."

"Need you in Dallas, man," Kaz said. "Even Coach was grumbling about it. Said the justice system has ridiculous timing!"

Dex wouldn't quite put it that way. He'd let his emotions rule and that was on him.

Anton came over and shook his hand. "Congrats, son."

"Yeah, thanks so much for making the trip. I never would have expected it."

His old coach shook his head in disbelief. "Maybe you need to expect it."

The man was right. He had a team on his side, but he'd never take it for granted. Even the brotherhood of ice took work.

Fitz approached, Tara by his side. "Looks like you can make this trip after all, O'Malley. Glad to see this episode is behind you."

Tara hugged him. "You're free and clear, friend! Ashley's going to be thrilled."

"Ashley?" Just hearing her name sent him into a tizzy.

"She was here a moment ago."

"Here?" He looked around. "But she wasn't in the courtroom."

"She was sitting outside with—" She lowered her voice. "Your mom. They didn't want to upset you. Oh, there's Ruby."

Ruby? Tara was on a first name basis with his mother? Of course she was.

He looked over to the end of the corridor. Ruby was standing at some distance, smiling tentatively. They'd met one more time at the cat café. She was right: it was a great de-stressor.

Still no sign of Ashley.

But seeing his mom gave his heart a lift. It would take time, but they were on the right road.

A couple of the Rebels front office staff were trying to corral the team and guide them to the exit and a waiting bus. Dex watched as Ruby turned away and headed for the entrance to the street. He took a step toward her, just as Kershaw spoke.

"Isn't that Ruby from Sunny Side Up? Hey, favorite server, what are you doing here?"

Pivoting to face them, she looked uncomfortable while she searched for an excuse that wouldn't embarrass Dex.

"Guys, Ruby's my mom."

"Right, your mom," Kaz said, mocking, but then his jaw fell open as Dex closed the gap between them on the courthouse steps. "Hi, there."

"Hello," she said quietly. "I didn't mean to stick around so long. Tara texted to say everything worked out for you and I just wanted a glimpse for myself."

"It's okay. The guys know."

"They do?" She looked over his shoulder at the team, who were busy staring at the mother-son duo and probably wondering why Dex had blanked this woman whenever he ordered eggs bennies. Put like that, he was rightly ashamed of his behavior.

"I didn't expect you here." He hadn't expected anyone, and now that everyone was showing up for him, he had no idea what to with so much of a good thing.

"It's okay. Ashley told me because apparently you were incapable of telling me yourself. Or maybe you felt I would embarrass you?"

"No, not at all. I just didn't want our first official public outing to be you waving at your son in a courtroom."

"Tabloids would've loved it," she said with a smirk that made him laugh.

"I'm glad you're here. Honestly." He took a breath. "Where's Ash?"

"She didn't want to be in the way." At his open mouth, she added, "Her words, not mine. She basically held my hand until Tara came out."

Of course she did. That was his woman, compassionate to her core.

"O'Malley, we need to head out," Foreman said as he walked by, with a nod at Ruby.

"Yeah, I can't go."

Foreman exploded. "What the fu—Petrov! This ingrate says he can't go."

Now the entire team, formerly crowded around the bus entrance, turned back.

Reid sent slitty eyes of death his way. "You make it very difficult to pull for you, O'Malley."

Petrov spoke next. "Explain."

"I need to talk to Ashley and—"

The captain held up a hand. "We will stop there on the way to the airport."

"It's fourteen miles out of the way," Reid said, ever Mr. Fucking Logical.

"The plane cannot take off without us and we cannot leave without O'Malley." He turned to him. "You will bring your mother on the bus, and we will visit your woman so you can apologize for being an idiot."

Ah, hell. "You guys just want to watch me grovel."

Foreman grinned. "Can't fucking wait."

41

WALKING INTO THE SHELTER RECEPTION, Toby pulled his bike helmet off and set it on the counter.

"There's a big bus outside."

Ashley peered around his shoulder to confirm that, yes, there was indeed a big bus outside. The door opened and in walked Dex, followed by Theo Kershaw, Vadim Petrov, and Cal Foreman, all in gorgeous suits that made them look like European supermodels.

"Dex!"

"I missed you at the courthouse." No preamble, just barely-veiled urgency.

"I had to get back to work. Congrats on the good resolution."

"Your letter helped."

"Not sure about that. You had a lot of support. Much more than you realize."

He leaned in, while she gripped the counter to stay upright. It was so good to see him again.

"Could we talk?"

She looked at his teammates, who had hung back. Now

Vadim Petrov stepped forward. "Hello again, Ashley. We'd appreciate if you heard O'Malley out so we can get back on the bus to the airport. There is a time element, and we need to be in Dallas ahead of the game tomorrow."

"Okay, let's talk in the back." She turned to Toby. "Could you—?"

"Oh yeah, I've got this." Her assistant had planted himself at the counter, his gaze glued to the eye candy in the reception.

Heart thumping, she walked toward the kennels area. When she turned, Dex was behind her, looking so handsome in his suit she could cry.

He opened his mouth—and out came barks. Not from Dex, but from a nearby cage.

"Is that my Bandit?"

My Bandit. The boisterous pup had recognized Dex and was going a little crazy.

Dex looked baffled. "I thought he would have been adopted by now."

"He is to be. By me."

"Really?"

"You know me. A total pushover. I thought he'd do best with someone he's familiar with."

"Yeah, he would." Dex took her by the hand and led her further into the kennels away from Bandit. *He's holding my hand.* "And I could come visit him. If that's okay."

"Of course it is."

"Or we could share custody or ... Jesus, I'm really bad at this. Ashley, I fucked up. You know that. Of course you do. It's all I ever do, and this time I let it crowd in on me. Make me push you away."

She squeezed his hand. "You had a lot going on. I get it."

"Of course you get it. Because you're the most understanding, sweet, patient person I've ever met. But you shouldn't have to put up with it. I can be better, I can—"

"Dex." She placed her hands on his broad chest. "Breathe."

"Hard to do when you're so close to me."

Tell her about it. Her lungs were having a tough time, too.

"I can put up with the odd meltdown because that's what people who love each other do. They take the bad with the good and as long as the amazing outweighs the not-so-amazing, they consider that a win."

He searched her face. "People who love each other? Like … friends?"

"Friends, lovers, hockey fans." Now wasn't the time to undercut with humor but she couldn't help herself. She'd put her heart on the line before, and it had boomeranged back with a slap in the face.

His expression was as fierce as she'd ever seen it. "Don't joke about this, Ash. I love you and that's no fucking joke. I love you so much that I'm going out of my mind with it. I couldn't bear the thought of you thinking badly of me after everything I told you. About Ruby and what I did. Striking first before you could dump me seemed like the safest bet. Tara says I have great instincts for self-preservation."

She nodded, the threat of tears burning her throat.

"I told you what happened with my mom, that it made me bad news. A threat to you and Willa. And I did believe that for a while, and when you said you couldn't fall in love with someone who was bad news, I couldn't bring myself to believe it. That I've a right to love from a woman as amazing as you. And when you said I needed to face up to my problems, I let that confirm everything I thought about us. That's the part I heard. I'm not good enough or adult enough. I can't make you happy. Because I can't make myself happy."

She spread her hands over his chest. "This isn't all on you, Dex. Expecting you to jump right in and fix things with your mom when I just dropped that news about meeting her? That wasn't cool. I was setting you up to fail. Because I was terrified, too."

A slight curve of his lips told her he understood. They were both excellent at this self-sabotage thing.

"I needed to sort stuff out. With the team. My mom. This court case. I wanted to come back to you without all that baggage, but I'm starting to realize that I'll always have it, something that makes me less than perfect."

"We all do. It's how we work through it that matters, and that's something we should be able to do together. I'm sorry I wasn't there for you."

He shook his head. "I wasn't ready to listen, even when you said you'd fallen in love with me. I didn't imagine that, did I?"

She shook her head, fighting the tears that insisted on coming. "No, you didn't imagine it."

"Good, because I definitely screwed up there. I panicked, which is ridiculous because I headed into that office to tell you that I loved you."

Oh God. "And then I blindsided you with the mom-bomb."

He nodded. "It was a lot. But I took what you said inside of me, let it settle in my heart. Then I talked to some people —Petrov, the guys, Petrov again. That guy has a shit-ton of opinions about women and love. I mean, he could write a book. And Ruby brought me to a cat café."

"Lula's? I love that place."

"Yep, super cute, and I can't believe you didn't tell me

about it! Willa would have a blast there. Well, we talked, me
and my mom, and it was good to just ... let it out, I suppose.
It opened up a valve or something, and now all I want to do
is talk. Mostly I want to talk to you. About the future and
whether we have one and Willa and how her art project
went—"

Keeping the smile off her face was an impossible task, so
why try? "It went well. She got an A-minus."

"Minus? Whose head do I need to crack?"

How she loved that protective streak. She loved everything about this man. "She's fine. She misses you."

"I miss her. And I've missed you." Someone coughed
significantly on the other side of the door.

Dex growled. "I need to go. I didn't think I'd be playing
but the boys are expecting it and—"

"It's okay. We can talk tonight on the phone."

He cupped her face with both hands and ran a thumb
over her lips, his focus fierce and hungry.

"Or not?" she whispered while her heart beat an insis-
tent tattoo.

Dex. Dex. Dex.

"I don't expect that everything's solved because I showed
up in a very dramatic and romantic fashion and swept you
off your feet."

"It helps," she said with a smile because it might seem
like a fanciful gesture, but Dex's heart and soul was behind
it. The sensible part of her, the woman with years of experience, knew this was just the beginning. "And we're going to
figure it out. As a team."

His eyes shuttered, then opened again, brighter and
bluer than ever.

"Before I go," he said, his voice graveled with emotion, "I
just want to spend a moment memorizing this face I love.

I've known this was it for me since the moment I turned around and saw you in my seats. In my corner. We hadn't spent much time together, except for a bad date with another guy, an out-of-this-world kiss, and a dinner you didn't invite me to. But something clicked for me at that game. It was the beginning of something special."

She nodded, unable to speak but agreeing all the same. She couldn't believe how sure she was, how deeply she trusted this man to have a care for her heart and the heart of her daughter.

Someone knocked on the door and she finally managed to find her voice.

"You'd better go," she said, though neither of them made a move.

"I'm going to miss you so much. I can't stand the idea of being apart from you for a minute." He kissed her, a deep, soulful, forever melding of lips. "I love you, Ash."

The words were simple, unlike the complicated path they'd taken to get here.

"I love you, too. So much."

Bandit barked, wanting in on the action, which made them both laugh.

Stretching up, Ashley pressed her lips to Dex's and murmured, "We'll be watching the game tomorrow. Just look at the camera and think about us, in your seats. In your corner. We'll always be there."

On a jagged breath, his eyes grew shiny. All that emotion that needed an outlet over the years was finally finding a safe place to express it.

How could she not love that? How could she not love *him*?

She kissed him again, savoring this moment. There would be more to come but this one she wanted to cherish.

Together, hearts beating as one, souls connected, when all seemed right with the world.

"Look after my family for me, Ash."

He didn't need to explain. Willa, Ashley, and Ruby would be waiting for him. On cue, Bandit barked to remind everyone he was part of the Dex crew as well.

"I'll keep everyone safe. Until you come back to us."

EPILOGUE

Five months later

ON A PERFECT DAY IN SEPTEMBER, under a cloudless sky, with an expanse of lawn laid out like an emerald carpet before him, Dex O'Malley finally understood the meaning of that phrase, *be careful what you wish for.*

"Kershaw, if I have to tell you to keep your mitts off those burgers one more time, I am sending you home."

Theo raised the flipper an inch off what had to be at least the fifth burger he'd pressed on the grill. Dex's grill, Dex's burgers, Dex's damn backyard! Not that it made a difference to Kershaw, or Jorgenson for that matter, who'd already weighed in about how he'd do things differently if he was on grill duty. *(Those patties are too small, O'Malley.)*

Kershaw pointed with the flipper. "As I only live three doors down, then it's not exactly a hardship, Oh-Em-Gee. It'll give me a chance to check in on Bacon and make sure he hasn't destroyed any more furniture in the den." He squinted at the burger. "Think this one is done."

Dex snatched the flipper away from him and held it aloft in a threatening manner. "This cookout was a mistake."

"Your burger game is a mistake," Foreman interjected from twenty feet away, only to be thumped on the arm by his wife, Mia, who added, "You're doing great, Dex. This guac is awesome."

Somewhat mollified, Dex transferred a couple of—okay, *slightly* well-done—burgers to a platter. So it was his first time hosting the team for a cookout, and while he'd had plenty of practice cooking for Ashley, Willa, and the Wicked Not-Stepsisters, as well as his mom, it was different with this crowd of know-it-alls. Every asshole had an opinion.

"Can't believe I moved into a house so close to you," he muttered to Kershaw. "Should have gone for the ranch-style place ten blocks north."

"And miss out on my gardening wisdom? Those mums are coming in nicely."

Dex chuckled. Yeah, he'd hate to have missed out on *that*. Willa was the gardening expert, though. After manga and butterflies and Taylor Swift and Mittens the kitten, she'd found a new thing to love, growing flowers in the yard of their new house. Once the team had exited the playoffs after a sudden death finish against Nashville in the second round, Dex had made it his mission to buy a home. Before long, he'd found a modern Tudor in Riverbrook, not too far from the lake and Rebels HQ, with plenty of room for Willa and Ashley. Bandit, too, who needed space to run and chase the birds. He hadn't expected that Ashley would be okay with moving in so soon, but she jumped at the chance when he asked, then jumped his bones on his sofa. (New houses were aphrodisiacs, apparently.)

"Okay, I have to check on the burger buns." Willa liked the sesame seed ones, and right now only sourdough options were on the checkered-cloth-covered table. "Can I trust you to not squeeze all the juice out of the meat?"

Kershaw opened his mouth.

"Don't answer that. There are kids present."

"I'll keep an eye on him," a soft voice cut in.

"Ruby Tuesday!" Kershaw hugged his mom, forever known as "his favorite server," and looked her over. "New do?"

His mom blushed and touched her hair, which was shoulder-length and in dark, loose waves. "Tara did it. She thinks it takes years off me."

"You look good, Mom." She did, less careworn, more at peace. He kissed her on the cheek. "How's my little sister?"

"Getting into trouble, as always."

That would be Cleo. His mom had adopted the kitten, which gave her oodles of pleasure. Seeing how calm and content time with Cleo made her, Dex encouraged her to seek those pleasures out in the rest of her life. At first, Ruby insisted on keeping her job at the diner, but Ash set her up with an interview at the cat café, and now she was moving on up over there as well as putting in a volunteer shift at the shelter, usually at the same time as Dex. The place had become a family affair.

Mom and son had work to do. He'd suggested therapy (Bond and Grey swore by it) but she preferred when they just met for tea and chatted while petting kittens.

It wasn't a bad way to get to know a person.

To get to know himself.

"Talk later?"

With a nod, she hugged him, adding an extra-long squeeze, and turned her attention to the grill and Kershaw, who was already rambling on about Theo Burger Theory.

Dex headed toward the kitchen, not just on a burger bun

mission, but also eager to see Ash. During the off-season, he had more time on his hands, and he got antsy when he couldn't spend it all with his woman. She'd been working long days at the shelter, and with Willa in a nature-focused summer camp, there were only so many hours he could fill at the gym, taking Bandit on long walks in the forest preserve, and learning to bake croissants (with mixed results. His lamination needed work).

On the way, he checked in with his guests, mostly his teammates sitting on assorted patio furniture, drinking him out of house and home.

House and home. He'd never get sick of that.

He even took a moment to offer up some babble to Miles, Reid and Kennedy's new little. Stroking a gentle thumb along the baby boy's soft cheek, he was unreasonably thrilled to earn a happy warble in return.

"How's my favorite Rebel?"

"Pretty good," Reid said in a rare moment of levity.

Kennedy chuckled. "He's enjoying meeting all his uncles, aren't you?" She smiled at Dex. "Maybe it's time you graduated from fur-parenthood to the real thing."

She had his number. Just seeing the tiny, swaddled bundle had him hankering after one of his own.

"It's been less than six months, Ken."

She shrugged and exchanged a knowing glance with her husband. "When you know, you know."

He agreed, but as Ashley would have to carry most of the burden, he needed her to be sure. There'd be no repeat of the dynamic with her ex.

In the kitchen, yet another obstacle impeded his progress. This band of brothers-slash-hosting business was a double-edged sword. Tara grabbed him by the arms in her usual dramatic fashion. "Dexter! Nice apron."

Across his chest were the words: *Dogs and hockey make me happy. Humans make my head hurt.*

And getting truer by the second!

"Gift from my beautiful girlfriend."

"Well, your beautiful girlfriend won't let me take her to see my personal shopper. She thinks I'll make her wear something that emphasizes *her amazing curves.*" That last bit was spoken at a higher volume and with a touch of annoyance that Ashley wasn't bowing to Tara's iron will.

Ashley called out, "I have enough clothes."

Tara rolled her eyes. "Can you talk to her? It would be so much fun."

"Sure, T."

"Oh, I meant to ask sooner. Have you heard anything from Banks?"

He shook his head. "Georgia?"

Tara winced. "Complete radio silence. I hope it's a sign that they're working things out."

Dex had his doubts. The drama of the playoffs had nothing on the saga of Banks and Georgia.

With Tara off to check on her daughter and husband, Dex finally made it home. He snaked his arms around Ashley, resting his chin on her shoulder. "She just wants to be your friend."

"I know. I'd rather drink margaritas than go shopping." She turned from salsa-making duties and faced him, blowing a strand of caramel-blonde hair out of her eyes. "How's it going out there?"

"One of these days, I'm gonna kill Kershaw. For now, he makes a half-decent wingman on the grill, so I can slip away and ravish my girl."

She shook her head, laughing. "No ravishing! Not when we have guests."

"That's what makes it more exciting." He brushed his lips over the delicate shell of her ear and relished her shiver. "Just a few minutes upstairs." Another kiss preceded a light suckle of her earlobe. "Though at this rate I might only make it to the downstairs bathroom."

"Dex," she moaned. All those soft curves felt like a dream in his arms, and he prayed he'd never wake up.

"Okay, the hallway closet. My final offer."

The urgent pad of doggy feet interrupted them, followed by a little yelp of disapproval, though Bandit had seen worse. (Much worse.) He pushed his nose against Dex's calf, which was usually his signal that he wanted to be taken for a walk.

"Not now, little guy. I have a woman to woo."

"Again?" Willa walked in, making a big deal of covering her eyes. "You're so uxorious."

"Am not!"

Ashley grinned. "Do you even know what that means?"

"Not a clue, but I don't like the sound of it." He put an arm around the shoulder of his stepdaughter, who in the last five months seemed to have aged another ten years. "Okay, educate me, Sparkle."

She leaned into him, which he loved. "It means, when a man is too fond of his wife."

Dex raised his eyebrows at "his wife" and grinned. So they weren't officially his wife or stepdaughter—yet—but that day would come. "Okay, I *do* like the sound of it, though I'm not sure I can ever be *too* fond of my woman. Now where's that closet?"

Ashley firmed her lips against a smile while Willa moved on to more pressing problems. "Do we have sesame seed buns?"

"On the counter, honey," Ashley said.

"I'll save you a burger, Mom! Come on, Bandit, let's go eat." Out she bounded in her Rebels sneakers with a bag of buns in her hand and an enthusiastic pup on her heels.

"No saving burgers for me, I guess."

Ashley's eyes misted over at the sight of her daughter so happy. "She loves it here. So do I."

"I know," he said softly, while his heartbeat echoed the sentiment.

She cupped his hips and pulled him close. "Last blowout of the off-season, O'Malley. How do you think it's going, apart from wanting to unalive Theo and ravish me in a bathroom?"

"Or closet." He grinned. "Kind of surprised the guys took me up on it, to be honest. Usually, the last shindig of the summer is held at Chase Manor. Which reminds me, Harper and Remy just texted to say they're on their way with the brood. Are we ready for Rebels royalty to descend amongst the commoners?"

"Better practice my curtsey." She kissed him softly. "You shouldn't be surprised, though. They want to support you, to welcome you as one of their own."

Training camp began in a week, which meant the official start of his three-year contract with the Rebels.

His three-year, fifteen-million-dollar contract.

It wasn't about the money, but it sure was nice, especially for someone who'd grown up with barely two cents to rub together. The contract signaled security for him and his family, a confirmation that he had found a good place to hang his skates at last.

His family. That phrase still had the capacity to turn him to mush. Six months ago, the idea that he'd be enjoying hosting duties for the team but looking even more forward to when they left so he could chill and watch a Disney flick with his girls would have sounded like Dullsville. But boring, regular-guy Dex had apparently been struggling to get out all this time.

"Penny for 'em," Ashley whispered.

He took her by the hand and led her out of the kitchen, away from the chirps and murmurs outside, his destination a private bubble for two.

"Come with me, good girl, and I'll tell you all about it."

ACKNOWLEDGMENTS

Thank you to my editor, Kristi Yanta - as usual, you hit the nail on the head with everything! Thanks also to proofreader Julia Griffis for your amazing attention to detail.

To my classic cover designer Michele Catalano Creative, thanks for another great Rebels cover, and to the team at Qamber Designs, my gratitude knows no bounds for the beautiful illustrated covers you've created for this series.

To my agent, Nicole Resciniti, thanks for another great year.

Thanks to my family and friends, who came to visit us in far-flung places and put us up when we came to visit them. We can't wait to see you in another fun location.

And finally, to Jimmie — thanks for all your support this last year as we adjusted to life as nomads. I can't imagine doing this with anyone else.

ABOUT THE AUTHOR

Originally from Ireland, *USA Today* bestselling author Kate Meader cut her romance reader teeth on Maeve Binchy and Jilly Cooper novels, with some Harlequins thrown in for variety. Give her tales about brooding mill owners, over-sexed equestrians, and men who can rock an apron, a fire hose, or a hockey stick, and she's there. Now based on the road, she writes sexy contemporary featuring strong heroes and amazing women and men who can match their guys quip for quip.

ALSO BY KATE MEADER

Rookie Rebels

GOOD GUY

INSTACRUSH

MAN DOWN

FOREPLAYER

DEAR ROOMIE

REBEL YULE

JOCK WANTED

SUPERSTAR

WILD RIDE

HOCKEY WIFE

Chicago Rebels

IN SKATES TROUBLE

IRRESISTIBLE YOU

SO OVER YOU

UNDONE BY YOU

HOOKED ON YOU

WRAPPED UP IN YOU

Hot in Chicago Rookies

UP IN SMOKE

DOWN IN FLAMES

HOT TO THE TOUCH

For updates, giveaways, and new release information,
sign up for Kate's newsletter at katemeader.com.

Made in United States
Orlando, FL
18 April 2024

45950668R00232